Enid Blyton's

THE MYSTERY

OF THE PANTOMIME CAT

Enid Blyton's

THE MYSTERY
OF THE PANTOMIME CAT

MAMMOTH

First published in Great Britain 1949
by Methuen & Co. Ltd
This edition first published 1990 by Dean
an imprint of the Hamlyn Publishing Group
Published 1996 by Mammoth
an imprint of Reed International Books Limited,
Michelin House, 81 Fulham Road, London SW3 6RB

Reprinted 1996, 1997,1998

ISBN 0 7497 1973 7

A CIP catalogue record for this book
is available at the British Library

CONTENTS

1 AT THE RAILWAY STATION

LARRY and Daisy were waiting for Fatty to come and call for them with Buster and Scottie. They swung on the gate and kept looking down the road.

'Nice to be home for the hols. again,' said Daisy. 'I wish Fatty would buck up. We shan't be in time to meet Pip and Bets' train if he doesn't buck up. I'm longing to see them again. It seems ages since the Christmas hols.'

'There he is!' said Larry, and jumped off the gate. 'And there's Buster. Hallo, Fatty! We'll have to hurry or we won't be in time to meet Bets and Pip.'

'Plenty of time,' said Fatty, who never seemed in a hurry. 'I say, it'll be fun to be all together again, won't it—the Five Find-Outers, ready to tackle the next super-colossal mystery!'

'Woof,' said Buster, feeling a bit left out. Fatty corrected himself. 'The Five Find-Outers *and Dog*. Sorry, Buster.'

'Come on,' said Daisy. 'The train will be in. Fancy, we've had almost a week's holiday and haven't seen Bets and Pip. I bet they didn't like staying with their Aunt Sophie—she's frightfully strict and proper. They'll be full of pleases and thank-yous and good manners for a few days!'

'It'll wear off,' said Fatty. 'Any one seen old Clear-Orf these hols?'

Clear-Orf was the name the children gave to Mr. Goon, the village policeman. He couldn't bear the five children, and he hated Buster, who loved to dance round the fat policeman's ankles in a most aggravating way. The children had solved a good many mysteries which Mr. Goon had tried to puzzle out himself, and he was very jealous of them.

'He'll say "Clear-orf!" as soon as ever he spots one of us anywhere,' said Larry, with a grin. 'It's sort of automatic with him. I say—I wonder if there'll be any more mysteries these hols. I feel I could just use my brains nicely on a good juicy mystery!'

The others laughed. 'Don't let Daddy hear you say that,' said Daisy. 'You had such a bad report that he'll wonder why you don't use your brains for Latin and Maths., instead of Mysteries!'

'I suppose he had "Could use his brains better," or "Does not make the best use of his brains," on his report,' said Fatty. 'I know the sort of thing.'

'You couldn't *ever* have had those remarks put on *your* report, Fatty,' said Daisy, who had a great admiration for Fatty's brains.

'Well,' said Fatty, modestly, 'I *usually* have "A brilliant term's work," or "Far surpasses the average for his form" or . . .'

Larry gave him a punch. 'Still the same modest but conceited old Fatty! It's marvellous how you manage to boast in such a modest tone of voice, Fatty. I . . .'

'Stop arguing; there's the train's whistle,' said Daisy, beginning to run. 'We simply *must* be on the platform to meet Pip and Bets. Oh, poor Buster—he's getting left behind on his short legs. Come on, Buster!'

The three children and Buster burst through the door

on to the platform. Buster gave a delighted bark, and sniffed at the bottom of a pair of stout dark-blue trousers, whose owner was standing by the book-stall.

There was an exasperated snort. 'Clear-orf!' said a familiar voice. 'Put that dog on a lead!'

'Oh—*hallo*, Mr. Goon!' chorused Fatty, Larry, and Daisy, as if Mr. Goon was their dearest friend.

'Fancy seeing *you*!' said Fatty. 'I hope you are quite well, Mr. Goon—not feeling depressed at this weather, or . . .'

Mr. Goon was getting ready to be very snappish when the train came in with a thunderous roar that made it impossible to talk.

'There's Pip!' yelled Larry, and waved so violently that he almost knocked off Mr. Goon's helmet. Buster retired under a platform seat and sat there looking very dignified. He didn't like trains. Mr. Goon stood not far off, looking for whoever it was he had come to meet.

Bets and Pip tumbled out of the train in excitement. Bets ran to Fatty and hugged him. 'Fatty! I hoped you'd come and meet us! Hallo, Larry, hallo Daisy!'

'Hallo, young Bets,' said Fatty. He was very fond of Bets. He smacked Pip on the back. 'Hallo, Pip! You've just come back in time to help in a super-colossal mystery!'

This was said in a very loud voice, which was meant to reach Mr. Goon's ears. But unfortunately he didn't hear. He was shaking hands with another policeman, a young, pink-faced, smiling fellow.

'Look!' said Larry. 'Another policeman! Are we going to have two in Peterswood now, then?'

'I don't know,' said Fatty, looking hard at the second policeman. 'I rather like the look of Goon's friend—he looks a jolly sort of chap.'

'I like the way his ears stick out,' said Bets.

'Idiot,' said Pip. 'Where's old Buster, Fatty?'

'Here, Buster—come out from under that seat,' said Fatty. 'Shame on you for being such a coward!'

Buster crawled out, trying to wag his tail whilst it was still down, in a most apologetic way. But as the train then began to draw out of the station again with a terrific series of chuffs, Buster retired hurriedly under the seat once more.

'Poor Buster! I'm sure if I was a dog I'd hide under a seat too,' said Bets, comfortingly.

'It's not so long ago since you always stood behind me when the train came in,' said Pip. 'And I remember you trying to . . .'

'Come on,' said Fatty, seeing Bets beginning to go red. 'Let's go. BUSTER! Come on out and don't be an idiot. The train is now a mile away.'

Buster came out, saw *two* pairs of dark-blue legs walking towards him, and ran at them joyfully. Mr. Goon kicked out.

'That there dog!' he said, balefully. He turned to his companion. 'You want to look out for this here dog,' he told him, in a loud voice. 'He wants reporting. He's not under proper control, see? You keep your eyes open for him, Pippin, and don't you stand no nonsense.'

'Oh, Mr. Goon, don't say there's going to be *two* of you chasing poor Buster,' began Fatty, always ready for an argument with Mr. Goon.

AT THE RAILWAY STATION

'There's *not* going to be two of us,' said Mr. Goon. 'I'm off on a holiday—about time too—and this here's my colleague, P.C. Pippin, who's coming to take over when I'm away. And I'm very glad we've seen you, because now I can point you all out to him, and tell him to Keep his Eye on You. *And* that dog too.' He turned to his companion, who was looking a little startled.

'See these five kids? They think themselves very clever—think they can solve all the mysteries in the district! The trouble they've put me to—you wouldn't believe it! Keep your Eye on them, Pippin—and if there's any mystery about, keep it to yourself. If you don't you'll have these kids poking their noses into what concerns the Law, and making themselves Regular Nuisances.'

'Thanks for the introduction, Mr. Goon,' said Fatty, with a grin. He smiled at the other policeman. 'Pleased to welcome you to Peterswood, Mr. Pippin. I hope you'll be happy here. And—er—if at any time we can help you, just let us know.'

'There you are! What did I tell you?' said Mr. Goon, going red in the face. 'Can't stop interfering! You clear-orf, all of you and take that pestiferous dog with you. And mind you, I shall warn P.C. Pippin of all your little tricks and you'll find he won't stand any nonsense. See?'

Mr. Goon stalked off with his friend Pippin, who looked round at the children rather apologetically as he went. Fatty gave him a large wink. Pippin winked back.

'I like him,' said Bets. 'He's got a nice face. And his ears . . .'

'Stick out. Yes, you told us that before,' said Pip. 'I say, Fatty, I bet old Goon is going to have a wonderful time telling P.C. Pippin all about us. He'll make us out to be a band of young gangsters or something.'

'I bet he will!' said Fatty. 'I'd just love to hear what he says about us. I guess our ears will burn.'

They did burn! Mr. Goon was really enjoying himself warning P.C. Pippin about the Five Find- Outers—and Dog!

'You keep a firm hand on them,' said Mr. Goon. 'And don't you stand any nonsense from that fat boy—regular toad he is.'

'I thought he looked quite a good sort,' said P.C. Pippin, surprised.

Mr. Goon did one of his best snorts. 'That's all part of his artfulness. The times that boy's played his tricks on me—messed me up properly—given me all kinds of false clues, and spoilt some of my best cases! He's a half-wit, that's what he is—always dressing himself up and acting the fool.'

'But isn't he the boy that Inspector Jenks has got such a high opinion of?' said P.C. Pippin, frowning in perplexity. 'I seem to remember him saying that . . .'

This was quite the wrong remark to make to Mr. Goon. He went purple in the face and glared at Pippin, who looked back at him in alarm.

'That boy Sucks Up to Inspector Jenks,' said Mr. Goon. 'See? He's a regular sucker-up, that boy is. Don't you believe a word that the Inspector says about him. And just you look out for mysterious red-headed boys dashing about all over the place, see?'

P.C. Pippin's eyes almost popped out of his head. 'Er—red-headed boys?' he said, in an astonished voice.

AT THE RAILWAY STATION

'I don't understand.'

'Use your brains, Pippin,' said Mr. Goon in a lofty voice. 'That boy, Fatty—he's got no end of disguises, and one of his favourite ones is a red wig. The times I've seen red-headed boys! And it's been Fatty dressed up just to trick me. You be careful, Pippin. He'll try the same trick on you, you mark my words. He's a Bad Lot. All of those children are pests—interfering pests. No respect for the Law at all.'

P.C. Pippin listened in surprise, but most respectfully. Mr. Goon was twice his age and must have had a lot of experience. P.C. Pippin was very new and very keen. He felt proud to take Mr. Goon's place whilst he was away on holiday.

'I don't expect anything difficult will turn up when I'm away,' said Mr. Goon, as they turned into the gate of his little front garden. 'But *if* something turns up, keep it to yourself, Pippin—don't let those kids get their noses into it, whatever you do—and just you send for me if they do, see? And try and get that dog run in for something. It's a dangerous dog, and I'd like to get it out of the way. You see what you can do.'

P.C. Pippin felt rather dazed. He had liked the children and the dog. It was surprising to find that Mr. Goon had such different ideas. Still—he ought to know! P.C. Pippin determined to Do His Very Best for Mr. Goon. His Very, Very Best!

2 A NICE LITTLE PLAN FOR PIPPIN

THE Find-Outers were very pleased to be together again. The Easter holidays were not so long as the summer ones, and almost a week had gone by before Pip and Bets had arrived home from their stay with their aunt, so there didn't seem to be much time left.

'Not quite three weeks,' groaned Larry. 'I do hope the weather's decent. We can go for some bike-rides and picnics then.'

'And there's a good little show on down at the Little Theatre,' said Daisy. 'It's a kind of skit on Dick Whittington—awfully funny. I've seen it already, but we might all go again."

'Oh—is that little company still going?' said Fatty, with interest. 'I remember seeing some of its plays in the Christmas hols. Some of the acting was pretty poor. I wondered if they'd like to try *me* out in a few parts. You know, last term at school . . ."

'Fatty! *Don't* tell us you took the leading part in the School play *again*,' begged Larry. 'Doesn't any one else *ever* take the leading part at your school but you?'

'Fatty's very, very good at acting—aren't you, Fatty?' said Bets, loyally. 'Look how he can disguise himself and take even *us* in! Fatty, are you going to disguise yourself these hols? Do! Do you remember when you dressed up as that old balloon-woman, and sold balloons?'

'And old Clear-Orf came along and wanted to see

your licence,' chuckled Daisy. 'But you had so many petticoats on that you pretended you couldn't find it.'

'And Bets spotted it was you because she suddenly saw you had clean finger-nails and filthy, dirty hands,' said Larry, remembering. 'And that made her suspicious. I always thought that was smart of Bets.'

'You're making me feel I must disguise myself at once!' said Fatty, with a grin. 'What about playing a little joke on P.C. Pippin? What a lovely name!'

'Yes—and it suits him,' said Bets. 'He's got a sort of apple-cheeked face—a nice round ripe pippin.'

Every one roared. 'You tell him that,' said Pip. 'Go up to him and say "Dear nice round ripe pippin." He'll be *so* surprised.'

'Don't be silly,' said Bets. 'As if I would! I quite liked him.'

'I wish something would turn up whilst Goon is away,' said Fatty. 'Wouldn't he be wild to miss a mystery! And I bet we could help Pippin beautifully. He'd *like* our help, I expect. He doesn't look awfully clever—actually he might not be so good at snooping about as Goon, because Goon's had a lot of experience, and he's older—Pippin looks rather young. I bet we could tackle a mystery better than he could. We've solved a lot now. Six, in fact!'

'We can't possibly expect a mystery *every* hols.' said Larry.

'Let's make up one for P.C. Pippin,' said Bets, suddenly. 'Just a teeny-weeny one! With clues and things. He'd get awfully excited about it.'

The others stared at her. Fatty gave a sudden grin. 'I say! That's rather an idea of Bets, isn't it? Larry's right when he says we can't possibly expect a mystery every hols. and somehow I don't feel one will turn up in the next three weeks. So we'll concoct one—for that nice round ripe Pippin to solve!'

Every one began to feel excited. It was something to plan and look forward to.

'I bet he'll make a whole lot of notes, and be proud to show them to Goon,' said Larry. 'And I bet Goon will smell a rat and know it's us. What a swizz for them!'

'Now this is really very interesting,' said Fatty, pleased. 'It will be a nice little job for Pippin to use his brains on, it'll be some fun for us, and it will be *most* annoying for Goon when he comes back—because I bet he's warned Pippin about us. And all he'll find is that Pippin has wasted his time on a Pretend mystery!'

'What mystery shall we make up?' said Bets, pleased that her idea was so popular with the others. 'Let's think of a really good one—that Fatty can use disguises for. I love it when Fatty disguises himself'

'Let's all think hard,' said Fatty. 'We want to Rouse Suspicions, first of all—do something that will make P.C. Pippin think there's something up, you know—so that he will nose about—and find a few little Clues . . .'

'That we put ready for him,' said Bets, with a squeal of laughter. 'Oh *yes*! Oh, I *know* I shan't think of anything. Hurry up, every one, and think hard.'

There was silence for a few minutes. As Bets said, she could think of no idea at all.

'Well—any one thought of anything?' asked Fatty. 'Daisy?'

'I *have* thought of something—but it's a bit feeble'

said Daisy. 'What about sending Pippin a mysterious letter through the post?'

'No good,' said Fatty. 'He'd suspect us at once. Larry, have *you* thought of anything?'

'Well, what about mysterious noises in Pippin's back-garden at night?' said Larry. 'Very feeble, I know.'

'It is a bit,' said Fatty. 'Doesn't lead to anything. We want to do something that will really get Pippin worked up, make him think he's on to something big.'

'I can only think of something feeble too,' said Pip. 'You know—hiding in a garden at night till Pippin comes by—and then letting him hear us whisper—and then rushing off in the dark so that he suspects we've been up to mischief.'

'Now, there's something in *that*,' said Fatty, thinking over it. 'That really could lead on to something else. Let's see now. I'll work it out.'

Every one was respectfully silent. They looked at Fatty as he pursed up his mouth and frowned. The Great Brains were working!

'I think I've got it,' said Fatty, at last. 'We'll do this—I'll disguise myself as a ruffian of some kind—and I'll lend Larry a disguise too. We'll find out what Pippin's beat is at night—where he goes and what time—and Larry and I will hide in the garden of some empty house till he comes by.'

He paused to think, and then nodded his head, 'Yes—and as soon as we hear Pippin coming we'll begin to whisper loudly so that he'll hear us and challenge us. Then we'll make a run for it as if we were scared of him and didn't want to be seen.'

'But where does all this lead to?' said Larry.

'You wait a bit and see,' said Fatty, enjoying himself. 'Now, we'll escape all right—and what will Pippin do? He'll go into the garden, of course, and shine his torch round—and he'll find a torn-up note!'

'Oooh, yes,' said Bets, thrilled. 'What's in the note?'

'The note will contain the name of some place for a further meeting,' said Fatty. 'We'll think of somewhere good. And when our nice round ripe Pippin arrives at the next meeting-place he'll find some lovely Clues!'

'Which we'll have put there!' said Pip, grinning. 'Oh yes, Fatty—that's fine. We'll lead Pippin properly up the garden path.'

'The clues will lead somewhere else,' said Fatty, beaming. 'In fact it will be a nice wild-goose-chase for Pippin. He'll love it. And won't Goon's face be a picture when he hears about it all—he'll know it's us all right.'

'When can we do it? Oh, Fatty, let's begin it soon,' begged Bets. 'Can't you and Larry begin to-night?'

'No. We have to find out what Pippin's beat is first,' said Fatty. 'And we've got to spot an empty house on his beat. We'd better stalk him to-night, Larry, and find out where he goes. Goon always used to set off about half-past seven. Can you manage to come to my house by that time?'

'Yes, I think so,' said Larry. 'We have supper at seven. I can gobble it down and be with you all right.'

So it was decided that Larry and Fatty should stalk P.C. Pippin that night and see exactly what his beat was, so that the next night they could prepare their little surprise for him. Bets was thrilled. She loved an adventure like this—it hadn't got the frightened excitement of a real mystery, it was under their control, and nothing horrid could come out of it except perhaps a scolding from Goon.

Larry was down at Fatty's house at twenty-five past seven that night. It was almost dark. They were not disguised, as there was no time to dress Larry up. The two boys slipped out of Fatty's house and made their way to the street in which Mr. Goon's house was. P.C. Pippin had it now, of course.

The boys could hear the telephone trilling in Pippin's front room, and could hear him answering it. Then the receiver was put down, and the light in the room went out.

'He's coming!' whispered Fatty. 'Squash up more into the bushes, Larry.'

P.C. Pippin walked down to his front gate. He had rubbers on the soles of his boots and he did not make much noise. The boys could just see him as he turned up the street, away from them.

'Come on,' whispered Fatty. 'He's beginning his beat. We'll see exactly where he goes.'

They followed cautiously behind P.C. Pippin. The policeman went down the High Street, and was very conscientious indeed about trying doors and looking to see if the windows of the shops were fastened. The boys got rather bored with so much fumbling and examining. Each time P.C. Pippin stopped they had to stop too and hide somewhere.

After about an hour, P.C. Pippin moved off again, having decided that no burglar could possibly enter any

They followed cautiously behind P.C. Pippin

shop in the High Street that night, anyway. He shut off his torch and turned into a side-street. The boys padded after him.

Pippin went down the street softly, and then went to examine a lock-up garage there. 'Why doesn't he get on with his beat?' groaned Larry, softly. 'All this stopping and staring!'

Pippin went on again. He appeared to have quite a systematic method—going up one side of the road and down the other, and then into the next road and so on. If he did this every night, it would be easy to lie in wait for him somewhere!

'It's nine o'clock,' said Fatty, in a low voice, as he heard the church clock strike loudly. 'And we're in Willow Road. There's an empty house over the other side, Larry. We could hide in the garden there to-morrow night, just before nine. Then we could startle Pippin when he gets along there. Look—he's shining his torch on the gate now. Yes, that's what we'll do—hide in the garden there.'

'Good,' said Larry, with relief. 'I'm just about tired of dodging round like this, and the wind's jolly cold too. Come on—let's go home. Meet to-morrow morning at Pip's to tell the others what we've decided, and make our plans.'

'Right,' said Fatty, who was also very glad that the shadowing of P.C. Pippin was at an end. 'See you tomorrow. Sssst! Here comes Pippin again.'

They squeezed themselves into the hedge and were relieved when the policeman's footsteps passed them. 'Gosh—I nearly sneezed then,' whispered Larry. 'Come on—I'm frozen.'

THE MYSTERY OF THE PANTOMIME CAT

They went quietly home, Larry to tell Daisy, his sister, that they had found a good place to hide the next night, and Fatty to plan their disguises. He pulled out some old clothes and looked at them. Aha, P.C. Pippin, he thought, there's a nice little surprise being planned for you!

3 TWO RUFFIANS—AND P.C. PIPPIN

THE five children discussed their plan with great interest the next day. Buster sat near them, ears cocked up, listening.

'Sorry, old thing, but I'm afraid you're not in this,' said Fatty, patting the little Scottie. 'You'll have to be tied up at home. Can't have you careering after me, yapping at Pippin, when he comes by our hiding-place.'

'Woof,' said Buster, mournfully, and lay down as if he had no further interest in the subject.

'Poor Buster,' said Bets, rubbing the sole of her shoe along his back. 'You hate to be left out, don't you? But this isn't a *real* mystery, Buster. It's only a pretend one.'

The children decided that Larry and Fatty had better get into their disguises at Larry's house, as it was near to the garden where they were to hide. Then they could sprint back to Larry's without much bother.

'I'll bring the clothes along in a suitcase after tea,' said Fatty. 'Any chance of hiding the case anywhere in your garden, Larry? In a shed or something. Grown-ups are always so suspicious of things like that. If I arrive at your house complete with suitcase your mother's quite likely to want to know what's in it.'

'Yes. Well, there's the little shed halfway down the garden,' said Larry. 'The one the gardener uses. I'll join you there whatever time you say—and we might as well change into our disguises there, Fatty. We'd be safe there.

What are we going to wear?'

'Oh, *can* we come and see you getting into your disguises?' said Bets, who didn't want to miss anything if she could help it. 'Do let's. Pip and I could slip out when we are supposed to be reading after supper.'

'Mother is going to the Little Theatre to see the show there to-night,' said Pip, remembering. 'We'll be quite safe to come and see you disguising yourselves.'

So, at eight o'clock that night, Fatty, Larry, Daisy, Pip, and Bets were all shut up in the little shed together. Fatty pinned a sack tightly across the tiny window so that no light would show. Then he and Larry began to disguise themselves.

'We'd better make ourselves pretty awful-looking,' said Fatty. 'I bet Pippin will shine that torch of his on to us, and we'll let him get a good look at our ruffianly faces. Here, Larry—you wear this frightful moustache. And look, there's that red wig of mine—wear that too, under an old cap. You'll look horrible.'

Bets watched the two boys, fascinated. Fatty was extremely clever at dressing up. He had many books on the art of disguising oneself, and there wasn't much he didn't know about it! Also he had a wonderful collection of false eyebrows, moustaches, beards, and even sets of celluloid teeth that fitted over his own teeth, and stuck out horribly.

He put on a ragged beard. He screwed up his face and applied black grease-paint to his wrinkles. He stuck on a pair of shaggy eyebrows, which immediately altered him beyond recognition. Bets gave a squeal.

'You're horrible, Fatty! I don't know you. I can't bear to look at you.'

'Well, don't then,' said Fatty, with a grin that showed black gaps in his front teeth. Bets stared in horror.

'Fatty! Where are your teeth? You've got two missing!'

'Just blacked them out, that's all,' said Fatty, with another dreadful grin. 'In this light it looks as if I've got some missing, doesn't it?'

He put on a wig of thinnish hair that straggled under his cap. He screwed up his face, and waggled his beard at Bets and Daisy.

'You look disgusting and very frightening,' said Daisy. 'I'm glad I'm not going to walk into you unexpectedly to-night. I'd be scared stiff. Oh, look at Larry, Bets—he's almost as bad as Fatty. Larry, *don't* squint like that.'

Larry was squinting realistically, and had screwed up his mouth so that his moustache was all on one side.

'Don't overdo it,' said Fatty. 'You look like an idiot now—not that that's much change for you.'

Larry hit him on the back. 'You mind what you say to me,' he growled, in a deep voice. 'I'm Loopy Leonard from Lincoln.'

'You look it,' said Daisy. 'You're both horrible. Pippin won't believe you're real when he sees you!'

Fatty looked at Daisy. 'Do you think he'll see through our disguises then?' he asked, anxiously. 'Have we overdone it?'

'No. Not really,' said Daisy. 'I mean, a policeman sees

lots of awful ruffians and scoundrels, I expect, and some of them must look as bad as you. Ugh, you do look revolting. I shall dream about you to-night.'

'I say—time's getting on,' said Pip. suddenly, looking at his watch. He had been silent and a little sulky because he was not going too. But, as Fatty pointed out, he was not tall enough to pass for a man, whereas he and Larry were. They were both well grown, and Fatty especially was quite burly now.

'Right. We'll go,' said Fatty, and Larry opened the door of the shed cautiously.

'We'll have to go past the kitchen door,' he said. 'But it's all right, no one will hear us.'

The two horrible-looking ruffians tiptoed up the path and round by the kitchen door. Just as they got there the door opened and a bright beam of light fell on the two of them. There was a loud scream and the door was banged shut.

'Golly! That was Janet, our cook,' whispered Daisy. 'She must have had the fright of her life when she saw you. Quick, get off before she tells Daddy!'

The two boys scurried away into the road. Bets went home with Pip. Daisy went in at the garden door and heard Janet telling her father in a most excited voice about the two frightful men she had seen. 'Great big fellows, sir,' she said, 'about six feet high, they were—and they glared at me out of piercing eyes, and growled like dogs.'

Daisy chuckled and slipped upstairs. She wasn't at all surprised at Janet's horror. Those two certainly had looked dreadful.

Fatty and Larry made their way cautiously to the empty house. They crossed over whenever they heard any one coming along the dark streets. Nobody saw them, which was a good thing, for most people would certainly have raised the alarm at the sight of two such extraordinary-looking rogues.

They came to the empty house. They slipped in at the front gate very quietly indeed. There was a side gate as well.

'When Pippin comes by, we'll start our whispering here, under this bush,' said Fatty. 'And then when he comes in at the front gate to investigate, we'll sprint out of the side gate. Let him shine his light on our faces, because he can't possibly tell who we are, in these frightful disguises.'

'Right,' said Larry. 'Got the torn-up note, Fatty?'

Fatty felt in his pocket. He drew out an envelope. In it was a dirty piece of paper, torn into six or eight pieces. On it Fatty had written a cryptic message.

'Behind Little Theatre. Ten p.m. Friday.'

He grinned as he took out the torn pieces and thought of the message on them. 'When Pippin turns up behind the Little Theatre on Friday we'll see that he finds a lovely lot of clues,' he said to Larry. He scattered the bits of paper on the ground below the bush they were hiding behind. They fell there and lay waiting for the unsuspicious Pippin to pick them up later on in the evening!

'Sh!!' said Larry, suddenly. 'He's coming. I know his funny little cough now, though I can't hear his footsteps.

Ah—now I can.'

The boys waited silently until P.C. Pippin was near the garden. Then Fatty said something in a sibilant whisper. Larry then rustled the bush. Fatty said 'Ssssst!' and P.C. Pippin switched on his torch at once.

'Now then! Who's there? You come on out and show yourselves!' said Pippin's voice, sounding very sharp indeed.

'Don't run yet,' whispered Fatty. 'Let him get a look at us.'

Larry rustled the bush again. Pippin turned his torch on to it at once, and was horrified to see two such villainous faces peering out at him. What ruffians! Up to no good, *he'd* be bound!

'Now for it!' said Fatty, as the policeman swung open the front gate.

The two boys at once sprinted out of the back gate, and raced off down the road, with P.C. Pippin a very bad third. 'Hey, stop there! Stop!' he shouted. This was more than the boys had bargained for! Suppose somebody *did* stop them! It would be very awkward indeed.

But fortunately no one stopped them or even tried to, though the village butcher, out for a walk with his wife in the fine spring night, did step out to catch hold of them. But when he saw Fatty's horrible-looking face in the light of a street-lamp he thought better of it, and the boys raced by in safety.

They turned in at Larry's gate thankfully. They went to the little shed and sank down, panting. Fatty grinned.

'Nice work, Larry! He'll go back there with his torch

and snoop round—and he'll find the torn bits of paper and turn up on time for his next clues on Friday. I enjoyed that. Did you?'

'Yes,' said Larry. 'I only wish I didn't have to take off this wizard disguise. Can't we go round the town a bit and show ourselves to a few more people?'

'Better not,' said Fatty. 'Come on—let's take our things off. My word—I wish it had been old Goon who came along and spotted us—what a thrill for him!'

Meanwhile P.C. Pippin had made his way back to the garden where the two ruffians had been hiding. He was excited. He had never hoped for anything to happen whilst he was taking Goon's place. And now he had surprised two horrible-looking villains hiding in the garden of an empty house, no doubt planning a burglary of some kind.

P.C. Pippin shone his torch on the ground under the bush where the two ruffians had stood. He hoped to see some footprints there. Aha, yes—there were plenty! And there was something else too—torn pieces of paper! Could those fellows have dropped them?

Mr. Pippin took his note-book from his pocket and placed the bits of paper carefully in the flap at the back. There were eight pieces—with writing on them! He would examine them carefully at home. Next he took out a folding ruler and carefully measured the footprints in the soft earth. Then he looked about for cigarette-ends or any other clue. But except for the bits of paper there was nothing.

P.C. Pippin was up till past midnight piecing together the bits of paper, making out the thrilling message, writing out a description of the two men, and trying to draw the footprints to measure. He felt very important and pleased. This was his first Case. He was going to handle it well. He would go to the Little Theatre on Friday night, long before ten—and see what he would find there! All this might be Very, Very Important.

4   PLENTY OF RED-HEADS—
    AND PLENTY OF CLUES!

THE five children chuckled over the trick they had played on the unsuspecting Pippin. Larry had met him the morning after, and stopped to have a few words with him.

Mr. Pippin, remembering Mr. Goon's words of warning about the five children, looked at him rather doubtfully. This wasn't the dangerous fat boy, though—it was one of the others.

'Good morning, Mr. Pippin,' said Larry, politely. 'Settled in all right?'

'Of course,' said Mr. Pippin. 'Nice place, Peterswood. I've always liked it. You at home for the Easter holidays?'

'Yes,' said Larry. 'Er—got on to any mystery yet, Mr. Pippin?'

'Shouldn't tell you if I had,' said Mr. Pippin, grinning at Larry. 'I've had a Warning about you, see?'

'Yes. We thought you probably would have,' said Larry. 'By the way, our cook had a fright last night. Said she saw two ruffians outside our back door.'

Mr. Pippin pricked up his ears at once. 'Did she? What were they like?'

'Well—she said one of them had red hair,' said Larry. 'But you'd better ask her if you want any particulars. Why? Have *you* seen them?'

'Perhaps I have and perhaps I haven't,' said Mr. Pippin, annoyingly.

He nodded to Larry and walked off. He was thinking

hard. So Larry's cook had also seen a red-haired ruffian. Must have been the same red-haired fellow that he too had seen that night then. What were they up to? He decided to interview Larry's cook, and did so. He came away with a very lurid account of two enormous villains, six feet high at least, growling and groaning, squinting and pulling faces.

One of them certainly had red hair. Mr. Pippin began to look out for people with red hair. When he met Mr. Kerry the cobbler, who had flaming red hair, he eyed him with such suspicion that Mr. Kerry felt really alarmed.

P.C. Pippin also came across the vicar's brother, a kind and harmless tricyclist who liked to ride three times round the village each morning for exercise. When Mr. Pippin had met him for the third time, and scrutinized him very very carefully, the vicar's brother began to think something must be wrong. Mr. Pippin was also surprised—how many more times was he going to see this red-haired tricyclist?

When Larry related to the others that he had met Pippin, and told him about the red-haired man seen by the cook, and when Fatty heard from Janet the cook that the policeman had actually been to interview her about him, he chuckled.

'I think a spot of disguising is indicated,' he said to the others. 'A few red-haired fellows might interest our nice round ripe Pippin.'

So at twelve o'clock a red-haired telegraph boy appeared on a bicycle, whistling piercingly. When he saw Mr. Pippin he stopped and asked him to direct him to an address he didn't know. The policeman looked at him.

Another red-haired fellow! There was no end to them in Peterswood, it seemed.

At half-past one another red-haired fellow appeared beside the surprised Pippin. This time he was a man with a basket. He had black eyebrows which looked rather odd with his red hair, and frightful teeth that stuck out in front. He talked badly because of these.

'Scuthe me,' lisped the red-haired fellow. "Pleathe, can you thay where the Potht Offith ith?'

At first P.C. Pippin thought the fellow was talking in a foreign language, but a last discovered that he was merely lisping. He looked at him closely. *Another* red-haired chap! Most peculiar. None of them really looked like the ruffian he had seen the night before, though.

At half-past two yet another red-haired fellow knocked at P.C. Pippin's door, and delivered a newspaper which he said must have been left at the wrong house. Pippin thought it was one that Goon had, and thanked him. He stared at him, frowning. All this red hair! Fatty stared back unwinkingly.

Feeling uncomfortable, though he didn't know why, P.C. Pippin shut the door and went back into the front room. He felt that if he saw one more red-haired man that day he would really go to the occulist and see if there was something wrong with his eyes!

And at half-past five, when he was setting out to go to the post, what did he see but an elderly looking man shuffling along with a stick—and with bright-red hair sticking out from under his cap!

'I'm seeing things,' thought poor Mr. Pippin to

himself. 'I've got red hair on the brain.'

Then a memory struck him. 'Well! What was it that Mr. Goon told me? He warned me against red-headed fellows dashing about all over the place, didn't he? What did he mean? What's all this red-haired business? Oh yes—Mr. Goon said it would be Fatty disguising himself! But that boy *couldn't* be as clever as all that!' Mr. Pippin began to review all the red-haired people he had seen that day. He thought with especial suspicion of the man he had seen three times on a tricycle.

'Ah! Wait till I meet the next red-head,' said Mr. Pippin darkly to himself. 'If there's tricks played on *me*, I can play a few too! I'll give the next red-head a Real Fright!'

It so happened that the next one he met was the vicar's brother on his tricycle again, hurrying along to catch the post at the post office. Mr. Pippin stepped out into the road in front of him.

The vicar's brother rang his bell violently but Mr. Pippin didn't get out of the way. So the rider put on his brakes suddenly, and came to such a sudden stop that he almost fell off.

'What is it, constable?' said the vicar's brother, astonished. 'I nearly ran you down.'

'What's your name and address, please?' asked Mr. Pippin, taking out his note-book.

'My name is Theodore Twit, and my address is the Vicarage,' said Mr. Twit, with much dignity.

'Ho *yes*,' said Mr. Pippin. ' "The Vicarage" I *don't* think! You can't put me off *that* way!'

Mr. Twit wondered if the policeman was mad. He looked at him anxiously. Mr. Pippin mistook his anxious look for fright. He suddenly clutched at Mr. Twit's abundant, red hair.

'Ow!' said Mr. Twit, and almost overbalanced from his tricycle. 'Constable! What does this mean?'

Mr. Pippin had been absolutely certain that the red hair would come off in his hand. When it didn't, he was horrified. He stared at Mr. Twit, his pink face going a deep red.

'Do you feel all right, constable?' asked Mr. Twit, rubbing his head where Mr. Pippin had snatched at his hair. 'I don't understand you. Oh—thank goodness, here is my sister. Muriel, do come here and tell this constable who I am. He doesn't seem to believe me.'

Mr. Pippin saw a large and very determined-looking lady coming towards him. 'What is it, Theodore?' said the lady, in a deep, barking kind of voice. Mr. Pippin took one look at Muriel, muttered a few words of shamed apology, and fled. He left behind him two very puzzled people.

'Mad,' said Muriel, in her barking voice. 'Goon was mad enough, goodness knows—but really when it comes to this man snatching at your hair, Theodore, the world must be coming to an end!'

It so happened that Miss Twit went to call on Fatty's mother that evening, and when Fatty heard her relate the story of how that extraordinary Mr. Pippin had tried to snatch at dear Theodore's red hair, he had such a fit of the giggles that his mother sent him out of the room in disgust at his manners. Fatty enjoyed his laugh all to himself, with Buster gazing at him in wonder.

'So old Pippin is up to that trick, is he?' thought Fatty.

'Right. It must be dropped. Hope he doesn't associate me with the red-haired ruffian he saw last night, though. He won't turn up at the Little Theatre and find his precious Clues if he thinks it's a trick.'

The five children had had a meeting that day, which was Thursday, to decide what clues they would spread for Pippin at the back of the Little Theatre. There was a kind of verandah there, under cover, where all kinds of clues might be put.

'Cigarette-ends, of course, to make Pippin think other meetings have taken place there,' said Fatty.

'Yes—and matches,' said Larry. 'And what about a hanky with an initial on it—always very helpful that, when you want clues!'

'Oh yes,' said Daisy. 'I've got an old torn hanky and I'll work an initial on it. What shall I put?'

'Z,' said Fatty, promptly. 'Might as well give him something to puzzle his brains over.'

'Z!' said Bets. 'But there aren't any names beginning with Z, surely.'

'Yes there are—Zebediah and Zacharias, to start with!' grinned Fatty. 'We'll have old Pippin hunting round for Zebediahs before he's very much older!'

'Well, I'll put a Z on then,' said Daisy. 'I'll get my needle and thread now. What other clues will you put down?'

'A page out of a book,' said Pip. 'Out of a time-table or something.'

'Yes. That's good,' said Fatty, approvingly. 'Any other ideas?'

'What else do people drop by accident?' wondered

Daisy. 'Oh, I know what we could do. If there's a nail or anything there, we could take along a bit of cloth and jab it on the nail! Then it would look as if whoever had been there for a meeting had caught his coat on the nail. That would be a very valuable clue, if it was a real one!'

'Yes, it would,' agreed Fatty. 'And we'll take a pencil and sharpen it there—leave bits of pencil-shavings all over the place. Gosh, what a wonderful lot of clues!'

'We must also leave something to make Pippin go on with the chase somewhere else,' said Larry.

'Yes. What about underlining a train in the time-table page that we're going to throw down?' said Pip. 'We're going to chuck one down, aren't we? Well, if we underline a certain train—say a Sunday train—old Pippin will turn up for that too!'

Every one giggled. 'And Fatty could dress up in some disguise, and slip a message into Pippin's hand to suggest the next place to go to,' said Daisy. 'We could send him half over the country at this rate!'

'Wait till Goon gets a report of all this,' said Fatty with a grin. 'He'll see through it at once—and won't he be wild!'

Soon all the clues were ready, even to the pencil-shavings, which were in an envelope.

'When shall we place the clues?' said Bets. 'Can I come too?'

'Yes. We'll all go,' said Fatty. 'I don't see why not. There's nothing suspicious about us all going out together. We can go on our bicycles and put them in the car-park at the back of the Little Theatre. Then we'll pretend to be looking at the posters there, and one of us can slip up to the verandah and park the clues. It won't take a minute.'

'When shall we go?' asked Bets again. She always wanted to do things at once.

'Not to-day,' said Fatty. 'There's a bit of a breeze. We don't want the clues blown right off the verandah. The wind may have died down by to-morrow. We'll cycle along after tea to-morrow, about six.'

So the next day, about ten to six, the five set off, with Buster as usual in Fatty's bicycle basket. They cycled round to the back of the Little Theatre and came to the car-park there. A good many children were there already, getting bicycles from the stand.

'Hallo!' said Fatty, surprised. 'Has there been a show here this afternoon?'

'Yes,' said a boy near by. 'Just a show for us children from Farleigh Homes. They let us in for nothing. It was jolly good. I liked the cat the best.'

'The cat? Oh, Dick Whittington's cat, you mean,' said Fatty, remembering that the show that week was supposed to be a skit on the Dick Whittington pantomime. 'It's not a real cat, is it?'

'Course not!' said the boy. Daisy, who had already seen the show, explained to Fatty.

'It's a man in a cat's skin, idiot. Must be rather a small man—or maybe it's a boy! He was very funny, I thought.'

'Look—there go the actors,' said a little girl, and she pointed to a side door. 'See, that's Dick Whittington, that pretty girl. Why do they always have a girl for the boy in a pantomime? And that's Margot, who is Dick's sweetheart in the play. And there's Dick's master—and his mother, look—she's a man, really, as you can see.

And there's the captain of Dick's ship—isn't he fine? And there's the chief of the islands that Dick visits—only in the play he's a black man, of course.'

The five children gazed at the actors as they left the side door of the Little Theatre. They all looked remarkably ordinary.

'Where's the cat?' asked Bets.

'He doesn't seem to have gone with them,' said the little girl. 'Anyway I wouldn't know what he was like, because he wore his cat-skin all the time. He was awfully good. I loved him.'

A teacher called loudly, 'Irene! Donald! What are you keeping us waiting for? Come along at once.'

The car-park emptied. Fatty looked round. 'Now,' he said, 'come on! The coast is clear. We'll all go and look at these posters here, and talk to one another—and then when we are sure no one is watching us, I'll slip up to the verandah and drop the clues.'

It was most annoying, however, because one or two people kept coming to the car-park, and for some reason or other walked across it. Fatty finally discovered that it was a short cut to a cigarette shop in the next street.

'Blow!' he said. 'We'll have to hang about till it shuts. It's sure to shut soon.'

It was boring having to wait so long, and talk endlessly about the posters. But at last the shop apparently did shut and nobody else took the short cut across the car-park. It was now getting dark. Fatty slipped up the three steps to the verandah.

He threw down the clues—cigarette-ends and matches—torn hanky with Z on—pencil-shavings—page torn from a time-table with one Sunday train underlined—and a bit of navy-blue cloth which he jabbed hard on a nail.

He turned to go—but before he went he took a look in at the window near by. And what a shock Fatty got!

5 P.C. PIPPIN ON THE JOB

A VERY large, furry animal was inside the window, looking mournfully up at him—or so it seemed. The eyes were big and glassy, and gave Fatty the creeps. He recoiled back from the window, and almost fell down the verandah steps.

'What's up?' asked Larry, surprised.

'There's something queer up there,' said Fatty. 'Horrible big animal, looking out of the window at me. I could just see it in the faint reflection cast by that street-lamp outside the car-park.'

Bets gave a little squeal. 'Don't! I'm frightened!'

'Idiot, Fatty! It must be the cat-skin of Dick Whittington's cat,' said Larry, after a moment. Every one felt most relieved.

'Well—I suppose it was,' said Fatty, feeling very foolish. 'I never thought of that. The thing looked so lifelike, though. I don't think it was just a *skin*. I think the actor who plays the cat must have still been inside it.'

'Gracious. Does he *live* in it, then?' said Daisy. 'Let's go and see if it's still there, looking out of the window.'

'I don't want to,' said Bets at once.

'I don't think I do either, really,' said Daisy.

'*We'll* go,' said Larry. 'Come on, Fatty, come on, Pip.'

The three boys stepped quietly up the verandah steps, and looked in at the window. That cat was no longer there, but as they stood watching, they saw it come in at the door of the room and run across on all fours to the fireplace. An electric fire was burning, and the boys could distinctly see the cat pretending to wash its face, rubbing its ears with its paws, in exactly the same way as a cat does.

'There it is!' said Fatty. 'It's seen us! That's why it's acting up like this. It thinks we're children who came to see the show, and it's still pretending to be Dick Whittington's Cat. Gracious—it gave me a start when I first saw it at the window.'

'Meeow,' said the cat, loudly, turning towards the window, and waving a paw.

'I somehow don't like it,' said Pip. 'I don't know why. But I just don't. I know it's only somebody inside the skin, but it looks a jolly sight too real for me. Let's go!'

They went back to the girls. It was now quite dark, and the church clock struck seven o'clock as they went to fetch their bicycles from the stands.

'Well—we've planted the clues,' said Fatty, feeling more cheerful as he undid Buster from where he had tied him to the stand. 'I say, Buster, old chap—good thing you didn't spot that cat. You'd have thought you were seeing things—a cat as big as that!'

'Woof,' said Buster, dolefully. He didn't like being left out of the fun, and and he knew something exciting had been happening. He was lifted into Fatty's basket, and then the five cycled slowly home.

'I wonder when Pippin will go along,' said Fatty, as he dismounted at his gate. 'He'll be sure to get there long before ten, so that he can hide before the meeting takes place—and there won't be a meeting after all! Only plenty of clues for him to find.'

'See you to-morrow, Fatty!' called Pip and Bets. 'Good-bye, Larry and Daisy. We'll have to hurry or we'll get into a row.'

They all rode away. Fatty went indoors, thinking of the way the cat had looked at him through the window. That really had given him a jolt! 'If I were Bets I'd dream about that!' he thought. 'I wonder if Pippin's going to hide himself on the verandah somewhere. If he gets a glimpse of that cat, he'll get the fright of his life.'

Pippin did not go to the verandah until about half-past eight. He meant to be there in good time for the meeting, whatever it was. He had been very thrilled indeed to find the message about the meeting at 10 p.m. behind the Little Theatre, when he had pieced together the torn bits of paper.

Goon would be pleased with him if he could unearth some mystery or plot, he was sure. Pippin meant to do his best. He had already snooped round the back of the Little Theatre the day before, to see where he could hide on the night. He had discovered a hole in the verandah roof through which he could climb, and then he could sit on the windowsill of the room above, and hear everything.

Pippin arrived at the verandah as the clock on the church chimed half-past eight, exactly an hour and a half after the children had left. He had his torch with him, but did not put it on until he had made sure that there was nobody about anywhere. There was a glow in the room behind the verandah. Pippin looked into the room. He saw that the glow came from an electric fire. In front of it, lying as if asleep, was what looked like a most enormous cat. Pippin jumped violently when he saw such a big creature.

He couldn't believe his eyes. *Was* it a cat? Yes—there were its ears—and there was its tail lying beside it on the hearth-rug.

Pippin gazed into the window at the great, furry creature outlined by the glow of the fire. It couldn't be a gorilla, could it? No, people wouldn't be allowed to keep a gorilla like that. Besides, it looked more like a cat than anything else.

Pippin was just about to give a loud exclamation when he stopped himself in time. Of course! It must be Dick Whittington's Cat—the one that acted in the skit in the pantomime. He hadn't seen it himself, but he had heard about it. Funny the cat keeping its skin on like that— because it was really somebody inside it. You'd think he'd want to take the hot skin off as soon as he could!

Pippin wondered if the meeting, whatever it was, would take place if there was that cat in the room near by. But perhaps the meeting would be in the car-park. In that case would it be much good him climbing up on the verandah roof? He wouldn't hear a thing.

Pippin debated with himself. He cautiously switched on his torch and flashed it round the verandah floor. And he saw the clues!

His eyes brightened as he saw the cigarette-ends, the matches, and the pencil-shavings. Somebody had been here before—quite often too, judging by the cigarette-ends. The verandah must certainly be the meeting-place. Perhaps the cat was in the plot too. That was certainly an idea!

Carefully Pippin picked up the cigarette-ends, the

matches, and even the pencil shavings. He put them all into envelopes. He then found the torn time-table page, blown against the side of the verandah, and was extremely interested in the underlined Sunday train.

He looked round and found the handkerchief with Z on it, and wondered if it could be the letter N sideways. Pippin could not for the life of him think of any name beginning with Z, not even the ones the children had thought of!

Then he spotted the bit of navy-blue cloth caught on a nail. Aha! Oho! *That* was the most valuable clue of all. Find somebody with a hole in a navy-blue coat and you were getting somewhere!

Pippin took another cautious look into the window of the room at the back of the verandah. The great cat was still lying in front of the electric fire. Very strange—especially if you considered that the cat wasn't really a cat but a human being inside a cat skin—or a furry skin of some sort. As he watched, Pippin saw the cat move a little, get more comfortable and apparently settle itself to sleep again.

'Funny creature,' thought Pippin, still puzzled, but very much relieved to see the cat move. 'I sort of feel if a mouse ran across the room, the cat would be after it—though I know it's not a real cat!'

He decided that it was quite time he climbed up through the hole in the verandah roof, and sat on the window-sill of the room above. The men might come at any moment now—one of them might be early—you never knew! It wouldn't do for him to be seen.

With all his clues safely in his pocket Pippin heaved

himself up through the hole in the roof. He felt his way to the window-sill and sat down on it. It was hard and cold, and much too narrow to be comfortable. Pippin resigned himself to a long and uneasy wait.

He had not been there more than a few moments when he heard a very queer sound. Pippin stiffened and listened. It sounded to him very like a groan. But where could it be coming from? The room behind him was in black darkness. There was nobody near him out of doors as far as he knew—and if it was the cat before the fire making a noise, how could he *possibly* hear that? He couldn't!

The noise came again, and Pippin felt most peculiar. There he was, sitting on a narrow window-sill in the dark, waiting for rogues to meet down below—and groans sounding all round him! He didn't like it at all.

He listened, holding his breath. The groan came again. It was *behind* him! Pippin suddenly felt sure of that. Well, then, it must be in the *room* behind him! Pippin felt round the window, meaning to open it. But it was shut and fastened from inside.

Pippin remembered his torch. He took it from his belt and switched it on, so that the light shone into the room behind. Its beam swung slowly round the room—and then came to rest on something very queer.

A man was sitting at a desk. He had fallen forward, his face on his out-stretched arms. Beside him was a cup, overturned in its saucer, the spoon nearby on the table. Pippin stared in horror.

Then the beam picked out something else. A big wall-mirror was standing on the floor, reflecting the light of the torch. A large hole showed in the wall near by, the place from which the mirror had been removed. A safe had been built in behind the mirror—but it was now empty, and the safe-door was swinging open.

'Thieves! A robbery!' said P.C Pippin, and rose to the occasion at once. He doubled his hand in folds of his big handkerchief and drove his first through the window! P.C. Pippin was on the job!

6   A MYSTERY BEGINS

THE five children knew nothing about P.C. Pippin's exciting night, of course. Pip and Bets were asleep in bed when he smashed the window at the back of the Little Theatre, and Larry and Daisy had been told they could listen to the nine o'clock news, and then go to bed. Fatty had been in his room trying out a wonderful new Aid to Disguise—little pads to put inside the cheeks and make them fat!

'I'll try these to-morrow,' thought Fatty, with a grin. 'I'll put them in before breakfast and see if any one notices.'

Fatty went to bed wondering if P.C Pippin had found the clues he had spread about the verandah, and how long he had waited for the mythical meeting. Poor old Pippin—he might have waited a long time!

If Fatty had only known what was happening he would never have gone off so peacefully to bed that night—he would have been snooping round the Little Theatre, looking for *real* Clues! But all he had done was to play a trick on P.C. Pippin that had placed that gentleman right on the Spot—the very Spot where a burglary had taken place not so long before. Lucky Pippin!

Next day at breakfast Fatty put in his new Aid to Disguise—the cheek-pads that forced out the soft part of his cheeks and made him look plumper than ever. His father, buried behind his paper, didn't seem to notice any difference. He always thought Fatty was too plump anyhow. But his mother was puzzled. Fatty looked different. What was it that made him look strange? It was his cheeks! They were quite blown out.

'Frederick—have you got toothache?' suddenly asked his mother. 'Your cheeks are very swollen.'

'Oh no, Mother,' said Fatty. 'My teeth are quite all right.'

'Well, you don't seem to be eating as much as usual, which is very queer, and certainly your cheeks look swollen,' persisted his mother. 'I shall ring up and make an appointment with the dentist.'

This was really very alarming. Fatty didn't want the dentist poking round his mouth and finding holes in his teeth. He felt quite certain that even if there wasn't a hole the dentist would make one with that nasty scrapey instrument of his.

'Mother—do believe me—not one of my teeth has holes in,' said Fatty, desperately. 'I ought to know.'

'Well, then, why are your cheeks so puffed out?' asked his mother, who never could leave a subject alone once she had really started on it. She turned to his father. 'Don't *you* think Frederick's cheeks are swollen?'

His father glanced up in an absent-minded manner. 'Always does look too fat,' he said. 'Eats too much.' Then to Fatty's relief he went on reading his newspaper.

'I'll ring up the dentist immediately after breakfast,' said Fatty's mother.

In desperation Fatty put his hands to his mouth and removed the two cheek-pads—but instead of being pleased that his cheeks were now no longer swollen, his mother cried out in disgust. 'Frederick! How *can* you behave like that! Removing food from your mouth with your fingers! What *is* the matter with you this morning? You'd better leave the table.'

Before Fatty could explain about the cheek-pads, his father gave an excamation. 'Well, well! Listen to this in the paper. "Last night it was disclosed that the manager of the Little Theatre, in Peterswood, Bucks., was found drugged in his office, and the safe in the wall behind him was open, the contents having been stolen. The police already have one suspect in their hands."'

Fatty was so astounded to hear this that he absent-mindedly put his cheek-pads into his mouth, thinking they were bits of bread, and began to chew them. He simply couldn't believe the news. Why, he and the others had actually been hanging round the Little Theatre half the evening, and they had seen nothing at all—except the Pantomime Cat!

'Could I see the piece, Dad?' asked Fatty, wondering why the bread in his mouth was so tough. He suddenly realized that it wasn't bread—ugh, how horrible, he had been chewing his cheek-pads! And now he didn't dare to remove them again in case his mother accused him of disgusting manners once more. It was very awkward.

'Don't talk with your mouth full, Frederick,' said his mother. 'And of course you can't have your father's paper. You can read it when he has finished with it.'

Very fortunately at that moment the telephone bell rang. The house-parlourmaid answered it and came to fetch Fatty's mother. So Fatty was able to remove the half-chewed cheek-pads and put them into his pocket. He decided never to wear them again at meal-times. He glanced longingly at his father's paper. Ah—he had folded it over again and the bit about the robbery was on the back, but upside down. Fatty managed to read it two or three times. He began to feel very excited.

Would it be a Mystery? Suppose they hadn't got the right Suspect? Then the Five Find-Outers could get on to it at once. Fatty felt that he couldn't possibly eat any more breakfast. He slid away quietly from the table before his mother came back. His father didn't notice him go.

Fatty flew off to Pip's at once. Larry and Daisy would be along soon, for they had planned a meeting there. Pip and Bets had a fine big playroom of their own, where they were not often disturbed, and it made a very good meeting-place.

Pip and Bets had heard nothing of the great news. Fatty told them, and they were amazed. 'What! A robbery committed last night at the Little Theatre! Did it happen whilst we were there?' cried Pip, in excitement. 'Here's Larry, with Daisy. I say, Larry, heard the news about the Little Theatre Robbery?'

Larry and Daisy had heard all about it. They knew even more than Fatty because Janet, their cook, knew the woman who cleaned the Little Theatre, and had got some news from her, which she had passed on to Larry and Daisy. Larry said Janet felt certain that the robbers were the two ruffians she had seen the other night in the beam of light from the kitchen door!

'To think we were all there last evening, mooching round, hanging about and everything!' groaned Fatty. 'And we never saw a thing. We were so busy preparing clues for old Pippin that we never saw anything of a real crime that must have been going on almost under our noses.'

'Janet says that Mrs. Trotter, the woman who cleans the Little Theatre, told her that last night the police found the manager stretched out across his office desk, his head on his arms, asleep from some drug—and behind him was his empty safe,' said Larry. 'It was one that was built in the wall, hidden by a big wall-mirror hanging in front of it. She said the police must have discovered the whole thing not very long after it was done.'

'The police! I suppose that means P.C. Pippin,' said Fatty. 'Gosh—to think we planted him there on that verandah, surrounded by a whole lot of false clues—and there he was right on the spot when a real robbery was committed! It's absolutely maddening. If only we'd snooped round a bit more, *we* might have hit on the mystery ourselves. As it is, we've presented it to the police—or rather to P.C. Pippin—and they will get in straight away, and solve the whole thing.'

There was a doleful silence. It did seem very hard luck.

'I suppose Pippin will think all those cigarette ends and hanky and so on are real clues now—clues to the real robbers, I mean,' said Bets, after a long pause.

'Gosh! So he will! He'll be right off on the wrong track,' said Fatty. 'That's awkward. Very awkward. I don't mind playing a silly trick on either Goon or Pippin—but I wouldn't want to do anything that would prevent them from catching the burglars. Those clues of ours will certainly fog them a bit.'

'You mean—they'll start looking for people whose

names begin with Z, and they'll go and watch that Sunday train?' said Daisy. 'Instead of going on the right trail.'

'Yes,' said Fatty. 'Well—I think I'd better go and see P.C. Pippin, and own up. I don't want to set him off on the wrong track—make him waste his time solving a pretend mystery when he's got a real one to see to. Blow! It will be very awkward, having to explain. And I bet he won't give me any information, either, because he'll be so annoyed with me for playing a trick on him. We could have worked in nicely with old Pippin. We never could work with Goon.'

Every one felt very glum. To think they had gone and spoilt a perfectly super *real* mystery by making up a stupid pretend one!

'I'll come with you to explain,' said Larry.

'No,' said Fatty. 'I take the responsibility for this. I'd like to keep the rest of you out of it—if Pippin takes it into his head to complain of us, my parents won't take a lot of notice—but yours will, Larry—and as for Pip's parents, they'll go right off the deep end.'

'They always do,' said Pip. His parents were very strict with him and Bets, and had been very much annoyed three of four times already when Mr. Goon had complained to them about the children. 'I don't want our parents to know a thing. Mother's already said she's glad Goon is away because now perhaps we won't get into any mischief these holidays, and make Goon come round and grumble about us.'

'I'll go and see Pippin now,' said Fatty, getting up. 'Nothing like getting a nasty thing done at once. I do hope Pippin won't mind too much. Actually I think he's rather nice. He'll be thrilled at getting a case like this when Goon is away.'

He went out, with Buster close at his heels. He whistled loudly to show that he didn't care about anything in the world. But actually Fatty did care quite a lot this morning. He felt guilty about all those false clues. He could have kicked himself for spoiling his chance of working in with P.C. Pippin. Pippin wasn't like Goon. He looked sensible, and Fatty felt sure he would have welcomed his, Fatty's, help.

He came to Goon's house, in which Pippin was now living whilst Goon was away. To his surprise the door was wide open. Fatty walked in to find Pippin.

There was a loud voice talking in the front room. Fatty stopped as if he had been shot. It was Goon's voice. *Goon!* Had he come back then? Was he going to take over the mystery? Blow!

Fatty stood there, wondering what to do. He wasn't going to confess to Pippin in front of Goon! That would be very, very foolish. Goon might even take it into his head to go and tell Inspector Jenks, the children's very great friend—and somehow Fatty felt that the Inspector would not approve of the little trick they had played on the unsuspecting Pippin.

Goon was evidently very angry. His voice was raised, and he was going for poor Pippin unmercifully. Fatty couldn't help hearing, as he stood in the passage, undecided whether to go in or out.

'Why didn't you send for me when you first saw those rogues under that bush in the garden? Why didn't you tell me about the torn-up note? Didn't I tell you to let me know if anything happened? Turnip-head! Dolt! Soon as I go away they put in a dud like you, who hasn't even got the sense to send for his superior when something happens!'

Fatty decided to go—but Buster decided differently. Aha! That was the voice of his old enemy, wasn't it? With a joyful bark Buster pushed open the door of the sitting-room with his black nose, and bounded in!

7 GOON—PIPPIN—AND FATTY

THERE was a loud exclamation from Goon. 'That dog! Where did it come from? Clear-orf, you! Ah, you'd nip me in the ankles, would you!'

Fatty rushed into the room at once, afraid that Goon would hurt Buster. Pippin was standing by the window, looking very crestfallen indeed. Goon was by the fireplace, kicking out at Buster, who was dancing happily round his feet.

Goon looked up and saw Fatty. 'Oh, you're here too, are you?' he said, 'Setting your dog on me again! What with having to deal with that turnip-head over there, and this dratted dog, and you, it's enough to make a man retire from the police force!'

To Fatty's horror he caught up the poker and hit Buster with it on the back. Buster gave a howl of pain. Fatty ran to Goon and twisted the poker out of his hand. The boy was white with fury.

'See?' said Goon, turning to Pippin, who was also looking rather white. 'See that? You're a witness, you are—that boy sets his dog on me, and when I protect myself, as I've a right to do, the boy comes and assaults me. You're a witness, Pippin. Write it all down. Go on. I've been after this pest of a boy and his dog for a long time—and now I've got him. You saw it all, didn't you, Pippin?'

Fatty now had Buster in his arms. He could not trust himself to speak. He knew Goon to be a stupid, ignorant man with a turn for cruelty, but Goon had never shown his real nature quite so openly before.

Pippin said nothing at all. He stood by the window, looking scared and very much taken-aback. He had been shouted at by Goon for half an hour, blamed for all kinds of things, called all kinds of names—and now he was supposed to take out his note-book and put down a lot of untruths about that nice dog and his master.

'Pippin! Will you please write down what I tell you?' stormed Goon. 'I'll have that dog destroyed. I'll have this boy up before the court. I'll . . ."

Buster growled so fiercely that Goon stopped. 'Look here,' said Fatty, 'if you're going to do all that, I think I'll put Buster down and let him have a real good go at you, Goon. He may as well be hanged for a sheep as for a lamb. He hasn't bitten you, as you very well know— but if you're going to say he has, well then, he jolly well *can*.'

And Fatty made as if he was going to put the barking, struggling Buster down on the floor!

Goon calmed down at once, and tried to get back control of himself. He turned in a dignified way to Pippin. 'I'll tell you what to put down. Come on now, stir yourself—standing there like a ninny!'

'I'm not going to put down anything but the truth,' said Pippin, most surprisingly. 'You hit that dog a nasty whack with the poker—might have injured him for life. I don't hold with behaviour of that sort, no, not even from a police officer. I like dogs—they never go for *me*. I wouldn't have that dog destroyed for anything. And all the boy did was to take the poker from you to stop you

Fatty twisted the poker out of his hands

hitting his dog again! A good thing he did too. You might have killed the dog with your next whack—and then where would you be? In a very awkward position, Mr. Goon, that's where!'

There was a dead silence after this unexpected and remarkable speech. Even Buster was quiet. Every one was most surprised to hear this speech from the quiet Pippin, and perhaps Pippin himself was most surprised of all. Goon couldn't believe his ears. He stared at Pippin with his mouth wide open, and his eyes bulged more than ever. Fatty was thrilled. Good old Pippin!

Goon found his tongue at last. His face was now a familiar purple. He advanced to Pippin and shook a fat and rather dirty finger under his nose.

'You'll hear more of this, see? I'm back again and I'm in charge of Peterswood now. *I'll* take charge of this new case—and you'll have nothing to do with it whatever. Nothing. If you thought you'd get a good mark for it from the Inspector you can think again. I'll make a bad report out on you and your behaviour—thinking you'd manage it by yourself and get all the praise—not letting me know anything. Gah!'

Pippin said nothing, but looked thoroughly miserable. Fatty was very sorry for him. Goon was enjoying ticking off Pippin in front of Fatty. It gave him a sense of power, and he loved that.

'You hand me over all them clues,' said Goon. 'Every one of them. Aha! Master Frederick Trotteville would very much like to know what they are—wouldn't you? But you won't know! You'll never know!'

Pippin handed over to Mr. Goon all the false clues

that Fatty had put on the verandah! They were in envelopes or paper so Fatty could not see them—but he knew very well what they were! In fact he could have given Goon quite a lot of information about them. He grinned to himself. Right! Let Goon have them and work on them. Much good would they do him! Served him right for being so beastly to Pippin.

'See what happens to people who work against me, instead of with me?' said Goon to Fatty, spitefully. 'I shan't let him have anything to do with this new case—and you kids won't neither! I'll manage it myself. Pippin, you can do my routine work the next two weeks, and keep your nose out of anything else. I don't want your help—not that a turnip-head like you could help a fellow like me. Don't you come mewling to me with any of your silly ideas—I just don't want to hear them.'

He put away all the clues in a box and locked it. 'Now I'm going along to interview the manager of the Little Theatre,' he said. 'Ho yes, I know *you've* interviewed him already, Mister Clever—but I don't care tuppence for what you've got out of him—it won't be anything worth while. Well, you get down to that writing I ticked you off about—and just remember this—I shan't forget your insubordination this morning over that there pestiferous dog. Yes, real, right-down insubordination—refusal to perform your rightful duties when commanded. Gah!'

Mr. Goon made a dignified and haughty departure, walking ponderously down the path to his front gate, and shutting it sharply. Fatty, Buster, and Pippin were left together in the little sitting-room. Fatty put Buster down.

He at once ran to Pippin and pawed eagerly at his legs, whining.

Pippin stooped down and patted him. He looked so miserable that Fatty wanted to comfort him.

'He's thanking you for sticking up for him,' he said. 'Thanks from me, too, Mr. Pippin. Awfully decent of you.'

'He's a nice dog,' said Pippin. 'I like dogs. I've got one of my own, back home. Goon wouldn't let me bring him here.'

'I bet you think just about the same of Goon as I do—as we all do,' said Fatty. 'He's a beast. Always has been. He'd no right to speak to you in that way, you know.'

'I thought I was on to such a good case,' said Pippin, sitting down and taking out his fountain pen to write. 'I was going to send for Goon this morning, of course—but he saw a notice in the paper and came tearing back, accusing me of not having told him anything. Now I've had to give him all my clues—and he'll use them instead of me.'

Fatty considered things carefully. Should he confess to Pippin now that they were not real clues? No—Goon had them—let him mess about with them! Fatty thought that possibly Pippin might feel he ought to tell Goon they were false clues, if he, Fatty, confessed to him that they were—and that would spoil everything. Goon would go and complain to their parents, they would be forbidden to try and solve this mystery, and Pippin would be called over the coals by Goon for being so stupid as to be taken in by false clues.

It would be very nice indeed if Goon would busy himself with those clues, and leave the way clear for Fatty and the other Find-Outers to go to work! Pippin might help them. That would be better still.

'Mr. Pippin, don't take any notice of what Mr. Goon says to you,' said Fatty, earnestly. 'I am sure that Inspector Jenks, who is a great friend of ours, wouldn't allow him to speak to you like that, if he knew.'

'The Inspector told me about you and the others,' said Pippin. 'He's got a very high opinion of you, I must say. Said you'd been no end of a help in solving all kinds of mysterious cases.'

Fatty saw his chance and took it. 'Yes—that's true—and, Pippin, I shall be on to this case too—and probably solve it! I should be very proud if you would help us—it would be nice to present the Inspector with another mystery correctly solved. He'd be thrilled.'

Pippin looked up at the earnest Fatty. Fatty was only a boy in his teens, but there was something about him that made people respect him and trust him. Brains? Yes. Character? Plenty! Cheek? Too much. Pluck? Any amount. Pippin saw all this as he looked at Fatty and sized him up. Well—if Inspector Jenks liked this boy and admired him, then he, Pippin, was quite prepared to do the same—very willing to, in fact, seeing that it looked as if Fatty was not going to work with Mr. Goon! Pippin couldn't help thinking it would be very nice indeed to help this boy to solve the mystery—what a sell for Mr. Goon that would be!

'Well,' he said, and paused. 'Well—I'd like to help you—but wouldn't I have to tell Mr. Goon anything we discovered?'

'But, Mr. Pippin, didn't you hear him tell you that he

didn't want your help?' said Fatty. 'Didn't you hear him say you weren't to go to him with any of your silly mewling ideas—whatever *they* are! You'd be disobeying his orders if you told him anything.'

This seemed a very sensible way out to Pippin. Yes—he certainly would be disobeying orders if he went and told Mr. Goon anything now. On the other hand, surely it was his duty to work on the case if he could. Wasn't he the one to discover the robbery?

'I'll help you,' he told Fatty, and the boy grinned with pleasure. 'I guess if the Inspector has let you meddle in other cases, he'd say you could meddle in this one too. Anyway—I'd like to pay Goon back for some of the beastly things he said to me.'

'Hear, hear—very human and natural of you,' said Fatty, agreeing heartily. 'Well now, Pippin, I'll lay my cards on the table—and you can lay yours there as well. I'll tell you all I know, and you can tell me all *you* know.'

'What do *you* know?' said Pippin, curiously.

'Well—I and the other four were round at the back of the Little Theatre from about half-past five last night till seven,' said Fatty. 'Just snooping about, you know—looking at the posters and things.

'Oh, you were, were you?' said Pippin, sitting up and taking notice. 'Did you see anything interesting?'

'I looked in at the window at the back of that verandah,' said Fatty. 'And I saw the Pantomime Cat there—at least, I feel sure that's what it must have been. It was like a huge furry cat. It came to the window and stared at me—gave me an awful scare. I saw it in the reflected light of the street lamp. Then when Larry and

THE MYSTERY OF THE PANTOMIME CAT

Pip and I looked in later we saw it sitting by the fire, pretending to wash itself like cats do. It waved its paw at us.'

Pippin was listening very earnestly indeed. 'This is most interesting,' he said. 'You know—there doesn't appear to have been any one at all in the Little Theatre when the robbery was committed—except the pantomime Cat! Goon wants to arrest him. He's sure he doped the manager and robbed the safe. Would you believe it—the Pantomime Cat!'

8 PIPPIN'S STORY—AND A MEETING

FATTY's brains began to work at top speed. 'Go on,' he said. 'Tell me all you know. What time were you there, Mr. Pippin—what did you see—how did you discover the robbery and everything? My goodness, how lucky you were to be on the spot!'

'Well, actually I was after two rogues I'd seen under a bush the other night,' said Pippin, and Fatty had the grace to blush, though Pippin didn't notice it. 'I thought they might be meeting at the back of the Little Theatre, and I was hiding there. I got there at half-past eight, and when I looked into the room at the back of the verandah—where you saw the Cat—I saw him too. He was lying fast asleep by the fire. Funny to wear a cat-skin so long, isn't it?'

'Yes. Must be a queer fellow,' said Fatty.

'Well—he *is* queer—queer in the head,' said Pippin. 'I saw him this morning, without his cat-skin. He's not very big, except for his head. He's about twenty-four, they say, but he's never grown up, really. Like a child the way he walks and acts. They call him Boysie.'

'I suppose he got dropped when he was a baby,' said Fatty, remembering stories he had heard. 'Babies like that don't develop properly, do they? Go on, Mr. Pippin. This is thrilling.'

'Well, I saw the Cat asleep by the fire as I said,' went on Pippin. 'Then, when the clock struck nine I reckoned I'd better hide myself. So I climbed up through a hole in the verandah roof and sat on the window-sill of the room above, waiting. And I heard groans.'

'Go on,' said Fatty, as Pippin paused, remembering. 'Gosh, weren't you lucky to be there!'

'Well, I shone my torch into the room and saw the manager lying stretched out on his desk, and the empty safe in the wall behind him,' said Pippin. 'And I smashed the window and got in. The manager was already coming round. He was doped with some drug. I reckon it had been put into his cup of tea. The safe was quite empty, of course. It's being examined for fingerprints—I got an expert on the job at once—and the cup is being examined for drugs—just a strong sleeping-draught, I expect.'

'Who brought the manager the cup of tea—did he say?' asked Fatty, with interest.

'Yes—the Pantomime Cat!' said Pippin. 'Seems pretty suspicious, doesn't it? But if you talk to Boysie—the Cat—you can't help thinking he'd got nothing to do with the whole thing—he's too silly—he wouldn't have the brains to put a sleeping-draught into a cup of tea, and he certainly wouldn't know where the safe was—or where to get the key—or how to find out the combination of letters that opens the safe door, once the key is in.'

'It's very interesting,' said Fatty. 'Who was in the Little Theatre at the time, besides Boysie?'

'Nobody,' said Pippin. 'Not a soul! All the cast—the actors and actresses, you know—had gone off after the free show they'd given to the children of the Farleigh Homes, and we can check their alibis—find out exactly where they were between the time of their leaving and eight o'clock. The deed was done between half-past five and eight—between the time the show was over and the time the manager had drunk his cup of tea, and fallen unconscious.'

'I see. And you've got to check the whereabouts of all the people who might have gone back and done the robbery,' and Fatty. 'Yes. But what's to prevent a stranger doing it—I mean, why should it be one of the actors?'

'Because whoever did it knew the best time to do it,' said Pippin. 'He knew where the safe was. He knew that the manager had put the takings there the day before and hadn't taken them to the bank that day as he usually did. He knew where the key was kept—in the manager's wallet, not on his key-ring—and he knew that the manager liked a cup of tea in the evening—and into it went the sleeping-draught!'

'Yes—you're right. No stranger would have known all those facts,' said Fatty, thoughtfully. 'It must be one of the cast—either an actor or an actress. It's queer that Boysie took in the tea, though, isn't it? Do you think he helped in the robbery?'

'I don't know! He says he doesn't remember a thing except feeling very sleepy last night and going to sleep in front of the fire,' said Pippin. 'That's certainly where *I* saw him when I looked into the room. He even says he didn't take in the cup of tea to the manager, but that's nonsense, of course—the manager says he certainly did, and he wouldn't be likely to be mistaken. I think Boysie is scared, and said he didn't take in the tea to try and clear himself—forgetting he is quite unmistakable as the Pantomime Cat!'

'Yes—it looks as if Boysie either did the whole thing or helped somebody else,' said Fatty. 'Well, thanks very much, Pippin. I'll let you know if we spot anything. And remember—don't you give away anything to Goon. He won't thank you for it!'

'I shan't open my mouth to him,' said Pippin. 'My goodness—here he is, back again—and I haven't even begun this report he wants! You'd better clear out the back way, Master Frederick.'

Goon loomed up at the front gate, looking most important. He was talking to the vicar, solemnly and ponderously.

Fatty tiptoed out into the hall and made for the kitchen, with Buster in his arms. He meant to go into the back garden, hop over the fence at the bottom and make his way to Pip's. What a lot he had to tell the others!

He heard Goon's loud voice. 'Do you know what the vicar tells me, Pippin? He tells me you were rude to his brother yesterday—snatched at his hat or something! Now, I really do think . . .'

But what Goon really did think Fatty didn't wait to hear. Poor Pippin! He was going to get into trouble over his curiosity about red-headed people now! Fatty couldn't help feeling very, very sorry!

'If we'd known Pippin was so decent we'd never have thought up all those tricks,' said Fatty to himself, as he made his way to Pip's, where he knew the others would be anxiously awaiting him. 'Still—I can make it up to him, perhaps by solving this peculiar mystery. The Mystery of the Pantomime Cat. Sounds good!'

Larry, Daisy, Pip, and Bets had got very impatient indeed, waiting ages for Fatty. He had been gone for an hour and a half! What in the world could he be doing?

'Here he is at last,' called Bets from the window. 'Rushing up the drive with Buster. He looks full of importance—bursting with it. He must have plenty of news!'

He had. He began to relate everything from the very beginning, and when he got to where Goon had actually struck poor Buster with a poker, Bets gave a scream, and flung herself down on the floor beside the surprised Scottie.

'Buster! Are you hurt? Oh, Buster, how *could* any one hit you like that! I hate Goon! I do, I do. I know it's wrong to hate people, but it's wronger *not* to hate cruel people like Goon. Buster, are you bruised?'

The whole tale was hung up for about ten minutes whilst Buster was carefully examined by all the Find-Outers. Fatty had been pretty certain that Buster was not really hurt, for he had an extremely thick coat of hair, but when he saw how concerned the others were, he began to wonder if poor old Buster *had* been badly bruised. The five children tenderly parted the thick hair along Buster's back and examined every speck of the remarkably pink body beneath. Buster was thrilled. He lay down on his tummy, wagging his plumy tail with pleasure at all this loving fuss. In fact he was so thrilled that he hung his red tongue out and began to pant with joy.

There was nothing to be seen at all except for a tiny mark in one place. 'That's where he was hit,' said Bets, triumphantly. 'I wish I could hit *Goon* with a poker— very, very hard.'

'How bloodthirsty you sound, Bets!' said Daisy in surprise. 'You know you'd run for miles if Goon so much as yelled at you!'

'I wouldn't be a bit surprised if Bets *did* take a poker to Goon if she thought he was going to hurt Buster,' said Fatty. 'She may be frightened of him herself—but she'd be all pluck and no fright if she thought he was going to hurt any one else! I know Bets!'

Bets was so pleased at this speech from Fatty. She went red and buried her face in Buster's neck. Fatty patted her on the back.

'I felt like banging Goon on the head myself when I twisted the poker out of his hand,' he said. 'Oh my goodness—you should have seen his face when he found that I had the poker and he hadn't!'

'Go on with the story now,' said Pip. 'It's getting more and more exciting. Gosh, I wish I'd been there.'

Fatty went on with his tale. The children squealed with laughter when they heard that Goon had demanded all the false clues, and had been solemnly handed them by Pippin.

'He'll meet that Sunday train, Fatty!' chuckled Pip. 'Can't we meet it too?'

'Oh *yes*,' begged Bets. 'Let's. Do let's. Goon would be awfully annoyed to see us all there. He'd think we knew the clue too.'

'Which we do,' said Larry. 'Seeing that we thought of it!'

'Yes—it's an idea,' said Fatty. 'Quite an idea. I've a good mind to disguise myself and arrive on that train—and arouse Goon's Suspicions and get him to follow me.'

'We could all follow too,' giggled Bets. We really

must do that. It's to-morrow, isn't it. Oh Fatty, wouldn't it be fun?'

'Go on with the tale,' said Daisy. 'Let's hear it to the end before we make any more plans. It'll be dinner-time before Fatty's finished.'

Fatty then told the rest of the tale to the end. The children were very glad to hear that Pippin had stuck up for Buster and Fatty. They all agreed that Pippin was very nice indeed. They were thrilled to hear about the Pantomime Cat, and the two girls wished they had been brave enough to peep into the verandah-room and see him the night before.

'Do you think he did it all?' asked Bets. 'If he took in the tea, he must have done it. He may be cleverer than we think.'

'He may be, Bets,' said Fatty. 'I shall have to interview him. In fact, I thought we all could—together, you know, just as if we were children interested in him. He may be on his guard with grown-ups. He wouldn't be with children.'

'Yes. That's a good idea,' said Larry. 'Gosh, what a thrill this is! To think we put our clues in the very place where all this was going to happen—and managed to put a policeman there too, so that he would discover the crime. It's extraordinary.'

'Well—we must set our wits to work,' said Fatty. 'We've only got just over two weeks to solve the mystery—and Goon is on the job too—hampered by a few false clues, of course! But we've got Pippin to help us. He may learn a few things that it's impossible for us to find out.'

How are we going to set to work?' asked Larry.

'We must make a Plan,' said Fatty. 'A properly set-out Plan. Like we usually do. List of Suspects, list of Clues, and so on.'

'Oooh *yes*,' said Bets. 'Let's begin now, Fatty. This very minute. Have you got a note-book?'

'Of course,' said Fatty, and took out a fat note-book and a very fine fountain-pen. He ruled a few lines very neatly. 'Now then—SUSPECTS.'

A bell sounded loudly from the hall. Bets groaned. 'Blow! Dinner-time already! Fatty, will you come this afternoon and do it?'

'Right,' said Fatty, 'Half-past two every one—and put your best thinking-caps on! This is the finest mystery we've had yet!'

9   PIPPIN IS A HELP

FATTY thought hard during his lunch. His mother found him very silent indeed, and began to wonder about his teeth again. She looked at him closely. His cheeks seemed to have subsided—they were not very swollen now—not more than usual, anyway!

'Frederick—how is your tooth?' she asked suddenly.

Fatty looked at his mother blankly. His tooth? What did she mean?

'My tooth?' he said. 'What tooth, Mother?'

'Now don't be silly, Frederick,' said his mother. 'You know how swollen your face was this morning. I meant to ring up the dentist but I forgot. I was just asking you how your tooth was—it must have been bad because you had such a swollen face. I think I'd better ring up the dentist, even though your face *has* gone down.'

'Mother,' said Fatty, desperately, 'that wasn't toothache—it was cheek-pads.'

Now it was his mother's turn to look at him blankly. 'Cheek-pads! What *do* you mean, Frederick?'

'Things you put in your cheeks to alter your appearance,' explained Fatty, wishing heartily that he had not tried them out on his mother. 'A—a sort of disguise, Mother.'

'How very disgusting,' said his mother. 'I do wish you wouldn't do things like that, Frederick. No wonder you looked so awful.'

'Sorry, Mother,' said Fatty, hoping she would talk

about something else. She did. She talked about the extraordinary behaviour of Mr. Pippin who had snatched at Mr. Twit's hair, or hat, she didn't know which. And she also told Fatty that the vicar had complained about it to Mr. Goon, now that he was back again to take charge of this new robbery case at the Little Theatre.

'And I do hope, Frederick,' said his mother,' I *do* hope you won't try and meddle in *this* case. Apparently Mr. Goon is well on the way to finding out everything, and has a most remarkable collection of clues. I do *not* like that man, but he certainly seems to have been very quick off the mark in this case—came straight back from his holiday, found all these clues, and is on the track of the robber at once!'

'Don't you believe it,' murmured Fatty, half under his breath.

'What did you say, Frederick? I wish you wouldn't mumble,' said his mother. 'Well, I don't suppose you know a thing about this case, so just keep out of it and don't annoy Mr. Goon.'

Fatty didn't answer. He knew a lot about the case, and he meant to meddle in it for all he was worth, and if he could annoy Mr. Goon he was certainly going to. But he couldn't possibly tell his mother all that! So he sank into silence once more and began to think hard about all the Suspects.

He would have to find out their names and who they were and where they lived. It was pretty obvious that only one of the theatre people could have committed the crime. One of them had come back that night, let himself in quietly, and done the deed. But which one?

PIPPIN IS A HELP

Fatty decided he must go to Mr. Pippin and get the list of names and addresses. He would do that immediately after his lunch. So, at a quarter to two, when he left the table, Fatty rushed off to see if Mr. Pippin was available. If Goon was at home, it was no good. He couldn't possibly ask Pippin anything in front of Goon.

He walked by the sitting-room window of the little cottage belonging to Goon. Pippin was there, facing the window. Goon was also there, his back to it, writing at the table. Fatty tiptoed to the window and tried to attract Pippin's attention. Pippin looked up, astonished to see Fatty winking and beckoning outside. He turned round cautiously to see what Mr. Goon was doing.

When he turned back again he saw, held up to the window, a piece of paper on which Fatty had written 'MEET ME IN HIGH STREET TEN MINUTES' TIME.'

Pippin grinned and nodded. Fatty disappeared. Goon heard the click of the gate and turned round.

'Who's that coming in?' said Goon.

'No one,' said Pippin, truthfully.

'Well, who was it going out, then?' said Goon.

'Can't see any one,' said Pippin.

'Gah! Call yourself a policeman and can't see who opens a gate in front of your nose,' said Goon, who had eaten too much lunch and was felling very bad-tempered. Pippin said nothing at all. He was getting used to Goon's remarks.

He finished what he was doing and then got up. 'Where are you going?' asked Goon.

'Out to the post office,' said Pippin. 'I'm off duty at the moment, Mr. Goon, as you very well know. If there's anything wants doing, I'll do it when I come back.'

And in spite of Goon's snort, Pippin walked out of the house and up to the post office. He posted his letter and then looked for Fatty. Ah, there he was, sitting on the wooden bench. Pippin went up to him. They grinned at one another and Buster rubbed against Pippin's trousers.

'Come into that shop over there and have a lemonade,' said Fatty. 'I don't want Goon to see us hob-nobbing together.'

They went into the little shop, sat down, and Fatty ordered lemonades. Then, in a low voice, Fatty told Pippin what he wanted.

'Do you know the names and addresses of the actors and actresses at the Little Theatre?' he asked.

'Yes,' said Pippin, at once. 'I got them all last night. Wait a bit—I think they're in my note-book. I don't believe I gave them to Mr. Goon. He's been out interviewing the whole lot, and I expect he got the names from the manager—same as I did.'

'Oh—he's interviewed them already, has he?' said Fatty. 'He can get going when he likes, can't he?'

'Yes,' said Pippin. 'He's found one of them has a name beginning with Z too—you know one of the clues was an old handkerchief with Z on it. Well, see here,' and he pointed to one of the names in the list he was now showing to Fatty, 'the name of Dick Whittington, the principal boy—who's acted by a girl—is Zoe Markham. Looks as if Zoe was out on that verandah for some reason or other—at a meeting of the crooks, perhaps.'

Fatty was horror-stricken. To think that there was

actually somebody with a name beginning with Z! Who would have thought it? He didn't know what to say. At all costs he would have to clear Zoe somehow. Fatty wished very heartily for the hundredth time that he and the others hadn't started Pippin on a false mystery complete with false clues.

'Has Zoe got an alibi—some one to swear that she was somewhere else between half-past five and eight o'clock?' asked Fatty, looking worried.

'Oh yes. They've all got alibis,' said Pippin. 'Every one of them. I interviewed them myself last night, the whole lot—and Mr. Goon gave them the once-over again this morning. Alibis all correct.'

'Queer, isn't it,' said Fatty, after a silence. 'I mean— it *must* be one of those theatre people, mustn't it? Nobody else had so much inside knowledge as to be able to give the manager a cup of tea, and then take down the mirror, find the key, work out the combination, and open the safe.'

'Don't forget it was the Pantomime Cat who took in the cup of tea,' said Pippin.

'Yes. That's queerer still,' said Fatty. 'Any one would think he'd done the job.'

'Goon thinks so,' said Pippin. 'He thinks all that business of the Cat saying he doesn't understand, and he doesn't remember, and bursting into tears is put on—good acting, you know.'

'What do *you* think?' asked Fatty. Pippin considered. 'I told you before. I think Boysie's a bit queer in the head—never grown up, poor fellow. You know, I've got a cousin like that—and he wouldn't hurt a fly. It's a fact, he wouldn't. I don't see how he could possibly have done all that. I'm sorry Mr. Goon's got it into his head that Boysie's done the job—he'll scare the poor chap into fits.'

'Well—it's quite possible that somebody hid in the kitchen somewhere when Boysie was making the tea, and popped something into the cup when Boysie wasn't looking,' said Fatty.

'Yes. There's something in that,' said Pippin. 'But we still come back to the fact that it can only have been done by one of the theatre folk—no one else knows enough to have done it—and they all have alibis—so there you are!'

'Can I have their names and addresses?' asked Fatty. 'I'll copy them down.' Pippin handed him over his notebook. Fatty looked through the pages with interest. 'I say—are these your notes about where they said they were between half-past five and eight o'clock last night?'

'That's right,' said Pippin. 'Take them along with you, if you like. Save you a lot of trouble! They've all been interviewed twice, so you can take my word for it they won't say anything different the third time—that's if you were thinking of interviewing them, Master Frederick.'

'We're making out a Plan,' said Fatty, stuffing the notes into his pocket. 'I don't quite know what it will be yet. I'll tell you when we know details. Thanks most awfully, Mr. Pippin.'

'If you ever see a villainous-looking tramp with red hair, let me know, will you?' said Pippin. 'I mean—you get about a lot on that bike of yours—and you might happen on the fellow—and his mate with him. The ones I saw under the bush that night in Willow Road, I mean.'

'Er—yes—I know the ones you mean,' said Fatty, feeling extremely guilty, at this mention of the red-haired villain. 'I'll certainly let you know if I see him again. But I don't think he had anything to do with this robbery job, you know.'

'Ah, you can't tell,' said Pippin, finishing his glass of lemonade and standing up. 'If ever I saw wickedness in any one's face it was in that red-haired fellow's. I wouldn't care to be seen in *his* company. I'll walk a little way with you, Master Frederick—it's a nice day. Your dog all right now?'

'Quite, thanks,' said Fatty. 'Takes a lot to bruise a Scottie with as thick a coat as Buster!'

'That properly turned me against Mr. Goon, that did,' said Pippin, as they walked down the High Street—and round the corner they bumped straight into Mr. Goon! He glared at them both, and Buster flew round him delightedly.

'Buster, come here,' ordered Fatty, in such a stern voice that Buster felt he had to obey. He put his tail down and crept behind Fatty, keeping up a continuous growl.

'You be careful of the company you keep, Pippin,' ordered Mr. Goon. 'I warned you against that boy, didn't I? Always interfering and meddling, he is! Anyway, he can't interfere in *this* Case much! Cast-iron, that's what it is! I'll be making an arrest any time now!'

Mr. Goon walked on, and Pippin and Fatty looked at one another with raised eyebrows.

'It's that Pantomime Cat he's going to arrest,' said Pippin. 'I saw it in his eyes! And before he's finished

Round the corner he bumped into Mr. Goon

with that poor Cat he'll make him confess to things he didn't do. He will!'

'Then I'll have to see that he doesn't,' said Fatty. 'I must set the old brains to work IMMEDIATELY!'

10   THE SUSPECTS AND THEIR ALIBIS

AT just after half-past two Fatty walked into Pip's drive for the second time that day, and was hailed by Bets from the open window.

'Hurry up, Fatty! We want to make our Plan!'

Fatty hurried, grinning at Bets' impatience. He went up the stairs two at a time, and found the other four waiting for him round the table.

'Ha! A Conference!' said Fatty. 'Well—I've got some information here which we'll study together. Then we'll really get going.'

He told the children quickly what Pippin had told him, and then got out the note-book with names, addresses and particulars of alibis in. The word 'alibi' was new to Bets, and had to be explained to her.

'Is it anything to do with lullaby?' she asked, and the others roared.

'No, Bets,' said Fatty. 'I'll tell you what an alibi is. Suppose somebody smashed this window, and your mother thought it was Pip—and Pip told her he was with me at the time, and I said yes, he certainly was—then I am Pip's *alibi*—he's got his alibi, because I can vouch for his being with me when the window was smashed.'

'I see,' said Bets. 'And if somebody said that at just this moment you had hit Goon on the head, and we said no, you couldn't have, because you were with us—we'd *all* be alibis for you.'

'Quite right, Bets—you've got the idea,' grinned

Fatty. 'Well—I've got a list of the alibis of all the Suspects here—which will be very, very useful. Listen, and I'll read out the names of the Suspects first, and then I'll tell you their alibis and what we know about them.'

He read from Pippin's notes.

SUSPECTS

No. 1. *Pantomime Cat,* otherwise Boysie Summers. Was in theatre at the time in question. Took Manager in a cup of tea before eight o'clock. Says he didn't, but admits he had a cup of tea himself. Says he went to sleep most of evening.

No. 2. *Zoe Markham,* who takes part of Dick Whittington. Says she left theatre with other members of the cast, and went to her sister's, where she played with the children and helped to put them to bed. Her sister is Mrs. Thomas, and lives at Green House, Hemal Road.

'I know her!' said Daisy. 'She's awfully nice. She's got two dear little children. One's having a birthday soon, I know.'

'I say,' said Larry, suddenly, 'Zoe Markham! I hope Goon doesn't connect up the Z for Zoe with the Z on that old hanky of Daisy's—the one we used for a false clue.'

'I rather think he has,' said Fatty. 'We'll have to do something about that, if so. Well—to continue . . ."

No. 3. *Lucy White,* who takes the part of Margot, Dick Whittington's sweetheart. Says she went to call on Miss Adams, an old-age pensioner who is ill, address 11 Mark Street. Sat with her till nine o'clock, and helped her with her knitting.

'Miss Adams is a friend of our cook's,' said Larry. 'She used to come and help with the sewing. Nice old thing she was.'

No. 4. *Peter Watting*, who takes the part of Dick's master,' went on Fatty. 'Elderly, and rather obstructive. Would not answer questions readily. Said he was out walking with Suspect No. 5 at the time.

Suspect No. 5. William Orr, who takes the part of the captain of Dick's ship. Young man, affable and helpful. Says he was out walking with Peter Watting at the time.

'Then those two are alibis for each other,' said Larry, with interest. 'What's to stop them from *both* going back to the theatre and doing the robbery, and then giving each other an alibi?'

'That's a good point, Larry,' said Fatty. 'Very good point. Pippin doesn't seem to have worked that out. Wait a bit—here's another note about it. "Suspects 4 and 5 (Peter Watting and William Orr) further said they had gone for a walk by the river, and had called at a tea-house called 'The Turret' for some sandwiches and coffee. They did not know the exact time".'

'Bit fishy, I think,'said Pip. 'Wants looking into.'

Suspect No. 6. *Alec Grant*, who takes the part of Dick's mother. Usually takes women's parts and is very good at them, a fine mimic and good actor. Says he was giving a show at Hetton Hall, Sheepridge, that evening, from six to ten—acting various women's parts to an audience of about one hundred.

'Well! That rules *him* out!' said Larry. 'He's got a hundred alibis, not one.'

'Yes. It certainly clears *him*,' said Fatty. 'Well, here's the last Suspect.'

Suspect No. 7. John James, who plays the part of the black king in the play. Says he went to the cinema and was there all the evening, seeing the film called 'You know How it is.'

'Not much of an alibi either,' said Pip. 'He could easily have popped in, and popped out again—and even popped back again after doing the robbery. Poor alibi, I call that.'

'Well now,' said Fatty. 'I imagine that Goon will check all these, if he hasn't already—but he's such a mutt that I expect he'll miss something important that *we* might spot. So I vote we all check up on the various alibis ourselves.'

There was a deep silence. Nobody felt capable of doing this. It was bad enough to interview people—it was much worse to check an alibi!

'I can't,' said Bets, at last. 'I know I'm a Find-Outer and I ought to do what you tell me, Fatty, but I really *can't* check an ali—alibi. I mean—it sounds too much like a *real* detective.'

'Well, we may be kids, but we're jolly good detectives all the same,' said Fatty. 'Look at all the mysteries we've solved already! This is a bit more *advanced*, perhaps.'

'It's frightfully advanced,' groaned Larry. 'I feel rather like Bets—out of my depth.'

'Don't give up before you've begun,' said Fatty. 'Now, I'll tell you what I propose we do.'

'What?' asked every one, and Buster thumped his tail

on the ground as if he too had a great interest in the question.

'There are three things we must do,' said Fatty. 'We must interview Boysie, and see what *we* think of him—and we'll interview him all together, as we suggested before.'

'Right,' said Larry. 'What next?'

'We'll see every other suspect too,' said Fatty.

There was a general groan.

'Oh *no*, Fatty—six people! And all grown-up! We can't possibly,' said Daisy. 'What excuse would we have for seeing them, even?'

'A very good excuse indeed,' said Fatty. 'All we've got to do is to find our autograph-books and go and ask for autographs—and we can easily say a few words to them then, can't we?'

'That's a *brilliant* idea,' said Pip. 'Really brilliant, Fatty. I must say you think of good ideas.'

'Oh well,' said Fatty, modestly, 'I've got a few brains, you know. As a matter of fact . . .'

'*Don't* start telling us about the wonderful things you did at school last term,' begged Pip. 'Go on with our Plan.'

'All right,' said Fatty, a little huffily. 'The third thing we must do, is, as I said, check up on the alibis—and if we think hard, it won't be so frightfully difficult. For instance, Daisy says she knows Zoe Markham's sister, who lives near her, and she also says one of the children is having a birthday soon. Well, Daisy, what's to stop you and Bets from taking the child a present, getting into conversation with the mother, and finding out if Zoe *was* there all that evening? Zoe's sister wouldn't be on her guard with two children who came with a present for her child.'

'Yes—all right, Fatty, I can do that,' said Daisy. 'You'll come too, won't you, Bets?'

'Yes,' said Bets. 'But you'll ask the questions, won't you, Daisy?'

'You've got to help,' said Daisy. 'I'm not doing it all!'

'Now the next Suspect is Lucy White who went to sit with Miss Adams, an old-age pensioner,' went on Fatty. 'Larry, you said she was a friend of your cook's, and used to come to help with the sewing. Can't you and Daisy concoct some sort of sewing job you want done, and take it round to her—and put a few questions about Lucy White?'

'Yes, we could,' said Daisy. 'I'll pretend I want to give Mother a surprise for Easter, and I'll take round a cushion-cover I want embroidering, or something. I've been there before, and Mary Adams knows me.'

'Splendid,' said Fatty. 'That's two alibis we can check very easily indeed. Now the next one—well, the next two, actually, because they are each other's alibis—Peter Watting and William Orr. Well, they apparently went to a place called The Turret and had coffee and sandwiches there. Pip, you and I will call there and also have coffee and sandwiches to-morrow morning.'

'But it's Sunday and I have to go to church,' objected Pip.

'Oh yes. I forgot it was Sunday,' said Fatty. 'Well, we'll do that on Monday or Tuesday morning. Now, Suspect No. 6 is Alec Grant, who was apparently giving a concert at Hetton Hall to about a hundred people. Seems hardly necessary to check that.'

'Well, don't let's,' said Larry.

'The thing is—a really good detective always checks *every*thing,' said Fatty. 'Even if he thinks it really isn't necessary. So I suppose we'd better check that too. Bets, you can come with me and check it. We'll find some one who attended the show, and ask them about it and see if Alec Grant really was there.'

'Right,' said Bets, who never minded what she did with Fatty. She always felt so safe with him, as safe as if she was with a grown-up.

'That only leaves one more,' said Fatty, looking at his list. 'And that's John James who says he went to the cinema all the evening.'

'Yes—and we thought it was a pretty poor alibi,' said Pip. 'Who's going to check that one up?'

'Oh—Larry and I could tackle that, I think, or you and Larry,' said Fatty.

'But how?' asked Larry.

'Have to think of something,' said Fatty. 'Well, there you are, Find-Outers—plenty for us to find out! We've got to see Boysie, got to get autographs from all the cast, and have a look at them—and got to check up all the alibis. Pretty stiff work.'

'*And*, Fatty, we've got to meet that train tomorrow and lead old Goon a dance,' Bets reminded him. 'Don't let's forget that!'

'Oh no—we really must do that,' grinned Fatty. 'I'll use my new cheek-pads for that.'

'Whatever are those?' said Bets in wonder, and

screamed with laughter when Fatty told her. 'Oh yes, do wear those. I hope I don't giggle when I see you.'

'You'd better not, young Bets,' said Fatty, getting hold of her nose and pulling it gently. 'Now what time's that train we underlined?'

'Half-past three to-morrow afternoon,' said Pip. 'We'll all be there, Fatty. What will *you* do—go to the next station, catch the train there, and arrive here at 3.30?'

'I will,' said Fatty. 'Look out for me. So long, every one. I've just remembered that my mother told me to be home an hour ago, to meet my great aunt. *What* a memory I've got!'

11   TREAT FOR MR. GOON

FATTY worked out the time-table for putting the Plan into action, that evening. They couldn't do much the next day, Sunday, that was certain. Daisy had better buy a present for Zoe's sister's child on Monday and take it in with Bets. The next day perhaps she and Larry could go and see Miss Adams and find out about Lucy White.

He and Larry would go to The Turret on Monday and have coffee and sandwiches and see if they could find out anything about Peter Watting and William Orr. They could leave Alec Grant till last, because it really did seem as if his alibi was unshakable, as it consisted of about a hundred people. He would not dare to give an alibi like that if it were not true.

'I can't think how to find out about the last fellow's alibi—what's his name—John James,' said Fatty to himself. 'Can't very well go and talk to a cinema and ask it questions! Still, I'll think of something.'

He paused and looked at himself in the mirror. He was thinking out his disguise for the next day—something perfectly reasonable, but peculiar, and with red hair so that it would attract Goon's attention. He would wear dark glasses and pretend to be short-sighted. That would make the children want to laugh.

'We'll go and see Boysie—what a name—on Monday morning,' thought Fatty, drawing a line round both his nostrils to see what effect it gave. 'Gracious! Don't I look bad-tempered! Grrrrr! Gah!'

He removed the lines and experimented with different eyebrows, thinking of his Plan all the time.

'We'll all go and ask for autographs after the afternoon performance at the Little Theatre on Monday,' thought Fatty. 'And dear me—why shouldn't we *go* to the performance and see every one in action. It mightn't tell us anything—but on the other hand, it might! That's a jolly good idea. Well—Monday's going to be pretty busy, I can see, what with interviewing and asking for autographs and checking up alibis. Now, what about that train to-morrow? Shall I speak to Goon when I see him or not? I'll ask him the way somewhere!'

He began to practise different voices. First, a deep-down rumble, modelled on a preacher who had come to his school to preach one Sunday, and who had been the admiration of every one because of his extremely bass voice.

He tried a high falsetto voice—no, not so good. He tried a foreign voice—ah, that was splendid.

'Please, Sair, to tell me ze way to Hoffle-Foffle Road!' began Fatty. 'What you say, Sair? I not unnerstand. I say, I weesh to know ze way to Hoffle-Foffle Road. HOFFLE-FOFFLE!'

There came a knock at his door. 'Frederick. Have you got Pip and the others in there with you? You know I don't like them here so late at night.'

Fatty opened his door in surprise. 'Oh no, Mother— of course they're not here. There's only me!'

His mother looked at him and made an exasperated

noise. 'Frederick! What have you done to your eyebrows, they are all crooked! And what's that round your eye?'

'Oh—only a wrinkle I drew there for an experiment,' said Fatty, rubbing it away hastily. 'And you needn't worry about my eyebrows, Mother. They're not really crooked. Look.'

He took off the eyebrows he was wearing, and showed his mother his own underneath. They were not at all crooked, of course!

'Well, what will you think of next, Frederick?' said his mother, half-crossly. 'I came to say that your father wants you to listen to the next bit on the wireless with him—it's about a part of China he knows very well. Are you *sure* you haven't got any one else with you here? I did hear quite a lot of voices when I was coming up the stairs.'

'Mother, look under the bed, behind the curtains and in the cupboard,' said Fatty, generously. But she wouldn't, of course, and proceeded downstairs—to stop in a hurry when she heard a falsetto voice say, 'Has she gone? Can I come out?'

She turned at once, annoyed to think there was some one in Fatty's room after all—but when she saw Fatty's grinning face, she laughed too.

'Oh—one of your Voices, I suppose,' she said. 'I might have guessed. I cannot think, Frederick how it is that you always have such good reports from school. I cannot believe you behave well there.'

'Well, Mother,' said Fatty, in his most modest voice, 'the fact is, brains *will* tell, you know. I can't help having good brains, can I? I mean . . .'

'Sh!' said his father, as they walked into the sitting-room. 'The talk's begun.'

So it had—and a very dull talk it proved to be, on a little-known part of China, which Fatty devoutly hoped he would never have to visit. He passed the dull half-hour by thinking out further plans. His father was really pleased to see such an intent look on Fatty's face.

The Find-Outers were finding the time very long, as they always did when something exciting was due to happen. Bets could hardly wait for the next afternoon to come. How would Fatty be disguised? What would he say? Would he wink at them?

At twenty-five past three Larry, Daisy, Pip, and Bets walked sedately on to the platform. A minute later Goon arrived, a little out of breath, because he had had an argument with P.C. Pippin, and had had to hurry. He saw the children at once and glared at them.

'What you here for?' he demanded.

'Same reason as you, I suppose,' said Pip. 'To meet some one.'

'We're meeting Fatty,' piped up Bets, and got a nudge from Larry.

'It's all right,' whispered Bets. 'I'm not giving anything away, really—he won't know it's Fatty when he sees him—you know he won't.'

The train came in with a clatter and stopped. Quite a lot of people got out. Mr. Goon eyed them all carefully. He was standing by the platform door, leading to the booking-office, and everyone had to pass him to give up their tickets. The four children stood near by, watching out for Fatty.

Bets nudged Pip. A voluminous old lady was proceeding down the platform, a veil spreading out behind her in the wind. Pip shook his head. No—good as Fatty was at disguises he could never look like that imperious old lady.

A man came by, hobbing along with a stick, his hat pulled down over his eyes, and a shapeless mackintosh flung across his shoulders. He had a straggling moustache and an absurd little beard. His hair was a little reddish, and Goon gave him a very sharp look indeed.

But Bets knew it wasn't Fatty. This man had a crooked nose, and Fatty surely couldn't mimic a thing like that.

It looked almost as if Goon was about to follow this man—and then he saw some one else—some one with *much* redder hair, some one *much* more suspicious.

This man was evidently a foreigner of some sort. He wore a peculiar hat on his red hair, which was neatly brushed. He had a foreign-looking cape round his shoulders, and brightly polished, pointed shoes.

For some peculiar reason he wore bicycle-clips round the bottoms of his trousers, and this made him even more foreign-looking, though Bets didn't quite know why it should. The man wore dark glasses on his nose, had a little red moustache, and his cheeks were very bulgy. He was very freckled indeed. Bets wondered admiringly how Fatty managed to produce freckles like that.

She knew it was Fatty, of course, and so did the others, though if they had not been actually looking for him, they would have been very doubtful indeed. But there was something about the jaunty way he walked and looked about that made them quite certain.

The foreigner brushed against Bets as he came to the exit. He dug his elbow into her, and she almost giggled.

'Your ticket, sir,' said the collector, as Fatty seemed to have forgotten all about this. Fatty began to feel in all his pockets, one after another, exclaiming in annoyance.

'This tick-ett! I had him, I know I had him! He was green.'

Mr. Goon watched him intently, quite ready to arrest him if he didn't produce his ticket! The foreigner suddenly swooped down by Goon's feet, and shoved one of them aside with his hand. Goon glared.

'Here. What are you doing?' he began.

'A million apologeeeze,' said the stranger, waving his ticket in Goon's face, and almost scraping the skin off the end of the policeman's big nose. 'I have him—he was on the ground, and you put your beeg foots on him. Aha!'

Fatty thrust the ticket at the astonished collector, and pushed past Goon. Then he stoppped so suddenly that Goon jumped.

'Ah, you are the pliss, are you not?' demanded Fatty, peering at Goon short-sightedly from his dark glasses. 'At first I think you are an engine-driver—but now I see you are the pliss.'

'Yes. I'm the police,'said Mr. Goon, gruffy, feeling more and more suspicious of this behaviour. 'Where do you want to go? I expect you're a stranger here.'

'Ah yes, alas! A strangair,' agreed Fatty. 'I need to know my way to a place. You will tell me zis place?'

'Certainly,' said Goon, only too pleased.

'It is—er—it is—Hoffle-Foffle House, in Willow Road,' said Fatty, making a great to-do with the Hoffle-Foffle bit. Goon looked blank.

'No such place as—er—what you said,' he answered.

'I say Hoffle-Foffle—you say you do not know it? How can zis be?' cried Fatty, and walked out into the road at top speed, with Goon at his heels. Fatty stopped abruptly and Goon bumped into him. Bets by this time was so convulsed with laughter that she had to stay behind.

'There *isn't* a house of that name,' said Goon, exasperated. 'Who do you want to see?'

'That ees my own beeziness—vairy, vairy secret beeziness,' said Fatty. 'Where is zis Willow Road? I will find Hoffle-Foffle by myself.'

Goon directed him. Fatty set off at top speed again, and Goon followed, panting. The four children followed too, trying to suppress their gigles. Hoffle-Foffle was, of course, not to be found.

'I will sairch the town till I see zis place,' Fatty told Mr. Goon, earnestly. 'Do not accompany me, Mr. Pliss— I am tired of you.'

Whereupon Fatty set off at a great pace again, and left Mr. Goon behind. He saw the four children still following, and frowned. Little pests! Couldn't he shadow any one without them coming too? 'Clear-orf!' he said to them, as they came up. 'Do you hear me? Clear-orf!'

'Can't we even go for a walk, Mr. Goon?' said Daisy, pathetically, and Mr. Goon snorted and hastened to follow 'that dratted foreigner,' who by now was almost out of sight.

Mr. Goon, in fact, almost lost him. Fatty was getting tired of this protracted walk, and wanted to throw Mr. Goon off, and go home and laugh with the others. But Mr. Goon valiantly pursued him. So Fatty made a pretence of examining the names of many houses, peering at them through his dark glasses. He was getting nearer and nearer to his own home by this time.

He managed to pop in at his front gate and scuttled down to the shed at the bottom of the garden, where he locked the door, and began to pull off his disguise as quickly as he could. He wiped his face free of paint, pulled off his false eyebrows and wig, took out his cheek-pads, straightened his tie, and ventured out into the garden.

He saw the four children looking anxiously over the fence. 'Goon's gone in to tell your mother,' whispered Larry. 'He thinks the suspicious foreigner is somewhere in the garden and he wants permission to search for him.'

'Let him,' grinned Fatty. 'Oh my, how I want to laugh! Sh! Here's Goon and Mother.'

Fatty strolled up to meet them. 'Why, Mr. Goon,' he began,' what a pleasant surprise!'

'I thought those friends of yours had gone to meet you at the station,' said Mr. Goon, suspiciously.

'Quite right,' said Fatty, politely. 'They did meet me. Here they are.'

The other four had gone in at the gate at the bottom of

the garden, and were now trooping demurely up the garden path behind Fatty. Goon stared at them in surprise.

'But—they've been following *me* about all the afternoon,' he began. 'And I certainly didn't see you at the station.'

'Oh but, Mr. Goon, he *was* there,' said Larry, earnestly. 'Perhaps you didn't recognize him. He does look different sometimes, you know.'

'Mr. Goon,' interrupted Mrs. Trotteville, impatiently, 'you wanted to look for some suspicious trespassers in my garden. It's Sunday afternoon and I want to go back to my husband. Never mind about these children.'

'Yes, but,' began Mr. Goon, trying to sort things out in his mind, and failing. How *could* these kids have met Fatty if he wasn't there? How dared they say they had met him, when he knew jolly well the four of them had been trailing him all that afternoon? There was something very peculiar here.

'Well, Mr. Goon, I'll leave you,' said Mrs.Trotteville. 'I've no doubt the children will help you to look for your suspicious loiterer.'

She went in. The children began to look everywhere with such terrific enthusiasm that Mr. Goon gave it up. He was sure he'd never find that red-haired foreigner again. *Could* it have been Fatty in one his disguises? No— not possibly! Nobody would have the sauce to lead him on a wild-goose-chase like that. And now he hadn't solved the mystery of who was coming by that 3.30 train! He snorted and went crossly out of the front gate.

The children flung themselves down on the damp

ground and laughed till they cried. They laughed so much that they didn't see a very puzzled Mr. Goon looking over the fence at them. *Now* what was the joke? Those dratted children! Slippery as eels they were—couldn't trust them an inch!

Mr. Goon went back home, tired and cross. 'Interfering with the Law!' he muttered, to P.C. Pippin's surprise. 'Always interfering with the Law! One of these days I'll catch them good and proper—and then they'll laugh the other side of their faces. Gah!'

12 ZOE, THE FIRST SUSPECT

THE next day, Monday, the Five Find-Outers really set to work. They all met at Pip's as usual. They were early, half-past nine—but, as Fatty pointed out, they had a lot to do.

'You and Bets must go and buy a birthday present for that child—Zoe Markaham's niece,' he said. 'Got any money?'

'I haven't any at all,' said Bets. 'I owed Pip three and threepence for a water-pistol, and it's all gone to pay for that.'

'I've got about a shilling, I think,' said Daisy.

Fatty put his hand into his pocket and pulled out some silver. He always seemed to have plenty of money. He had aunts and uncles who tipped him well, and he was just like a grown-up the way he always seemed to have enough to spend.

He picked out a two shilling piece and a sixpence. 'Here you are, Daisy. You can get a little something for half-a-crown. When's the child's birth-day?'

'To-morrow,' said Daisy, 'I met her little sister yesterday and asked her.'

'Good,' said Fatty. 'Couldn't be better! Now you go and buy something, you and Bets, and put a message on it, and deliver it to Mrs. Thomas, Zoe's sister. And mind you get into conversation with her and find out exactly when Zoe went there on Friday night, and what time she left.'

'How shall we get her talking, though?' said Daisy, beginning to feel nervous.

Fatty looked sternly at poor Daisy. 'Now I really can't plan every one's conversation! It's up to you to get this done, Daisy. Use your commonsense. Ask what the mother herself is giving the child—something like that—and I bet she'll take you in to see the present she's prepared.'

'Oh yes—that's a good idea,' said Daisy, cheering up. 'Come on, Bets—we'll go and do our bit of shopping.'

'I'm going to see Pippin for a few minutes, if I can,' said Fatty. 'I want to find out one or two things before I make further plans.'

'What do you want to know?' asked Larry, interested.

'Well—I want to know if there were any fingerprints on that wall-mirror which had to be lifted down to get the safe open, at the back of it,' said Fatty. 'And there might have been prints on the safe too. If there were, and the job was done by one of the actors or actresses, we might as well give up our detecting at once—because Goon has only got to take every one's fingerprints, compare them with the ones on mirror or safe—and there you are. He'd have the thief immediately!'

'Oh, I hope he won't!' said Bets, in dismay. 'I want to go on with this mystery. I want *us* to solve it, not Goon. I like this finding-out part.'

'Don't worry,' said Fatty, with a grin. 'The thief wouldn't leave prints behind, I'm sure! He was pretty cunning, whoever he was.'

'Do you think it *was* Boysie, the Pantomine Cat?' asked Daisy.

'No—not at present, anyway,' said Fatty. 'Wait and see what we think of him when we see him. Oh, and Larry, will you and Pip go along to the theatre this morning and get tickets for this afternoon's show? Here's the money.'

And out came the handful of silver again!

'It's a good thing you're so *rich*, Fatty,' said Bets. 'We wouldn't find detecting nearly so easy if you weren't!'

'Now, let's see,' said Fatty. 'We've all got jobs to do this morning, haven't we? Report back here at twelve, or as near that as possible. I'm off to see Pippin, if I can manage to get him alone. Come on, Buster. Wake up! Bicycle basket for you!'

Buster opened his eyes, got up from the hearth-rug, yawned and wagged his tail. He trotted sedately after Fatty. Bets went to put on her hat and coat, ready to do the bit of birthday shopping with Daisy. Pip and Larry went to get their bicycles, meaning to ride down to the Little Theatre to get the tickets.

Fatty was just wheeling his bicycle from Pip's shed. He called to the other two. 'Pip! Larry! Don't just buy the tickets—talk to as many people down there as you can! See if you can find out anything at all.'

'Right, Captain!' grinned Larry. 'We'll do our best.'

Off went all the Five Find-Outers—and Dog—to do a really good morning's work of Detection. Bets and Daisy walked, as Bets' bike had a puncture. They were soon down in the town, and went to the toy-shop there.

'Jane's only four,' said Daisy. 'She won't want anything too advanced. It's no good buying her a game or a jigsaw. We'll look at the soft toys.'

But there was no soft toy for half-a crown—they were all much too expensive. Then Bets pounced on a set of dolls' furniture, for a doll's house.

' Oh, look! Isn't it sweet! Let's get this, Daisy. Two tiny chairs, a table and a sofa—lovely! I'm sure Jane would love it.'

'How much is it?' said Daisy, looking at the price-label. 'Two shillings and ninepence ha'penny. Well, I've got Fatty's half-crown, and I'll put the other threepence ha' penny to it myself.'

'I'll give you the next penny I get,' said Bets. 'Oh, I do like these little chairs!'

Daisy bought the doll's furniture, and had it wrapped up nicely. 'Now we'll go home and write a message on a lable,and take it to Jane's mother,' said Daisy. So off they went,and wrote the label. 'Many happy returns to Jane, with love from Daisy and Bets.'

Then they set off once more to call on Mrs. Thomas, Zoe's sister. They came to the house, a small pretty one, set back from the road. They stopped at the gate.

Daisy was nervous. 'Now, whatever shall we do if Mrs. Thomas isn't in?'

'Say we'll come again,' said Bets, promptly. 'But she will be in. I can hear Jane and Dora playing in the garden.'

'What shall we say when the door is opened?' asked Daisy, still nervous.

'Just say we've got a present for little Jane, and then see what Mrs. Thomas says,' said Bets, surprised to see how nervous Daisy was. '*I'll* manage this if you can't, Daisy.'

That was quite enough to make Daisy forget all her nervousness! 'I can manage it all right, thank you,' she said, huffily. 'Come on!'

They went to the front door and rang the bell. Mrs. Thomas opened the door. 'Hallo, Daisy!' she said. 'And who is this—oh, little Elizabeth Hilton, isn't it?'

'Yes,' said Bets, whose name really was Elizabeth.

'Er—it's Jane's birthday to-morrow, isn't it.' began Daisy. 'We've brought her a little present, Mrs. Thomas.'

'How kind of you!' said Mrs. Thomas. 'What is it?'

Daisy gave it to her. 'It's just some dolls' furniture,' she said. 'Has she got a doll's house?'

'Well isn't that strange—her Daddy and I are giving Jane a doll's house to-morrow!' said Mrs. Thomas. 'This furniture will be *just* right!'

'Oh—*could* we see the doll's house, please?' asked Bets at once, seeing a wonderful chance of getting into the house and talking.

'Of course,' said Mrs. Thomas. 'Come in.'

So in they went and were soon being shown a lovely little doll's house in an upstairs room. Daisy led the talk round to the Little Theatre.

'Your sister Zoe Summers plays in the shows at the Little Theatre, doesn't she?' she said, innocently.

'Yes,' said Mrs. Thomas. 'Have you seen any of the shows?'

'We're going this afternoon,' said Bets . 'I do want to see that Pantomime Cat.'

'Poor Cat!' said Mrs. Thomas. 'Poor Boysie. He's in a dreadful state now—that awful policeman has been at him, you know—he thinks Boysie did that robbery. I expect you heard about it.'

Just as she said that a tall pretty young woman came into the room. 'Hallo!' she said. 'I thought I heard voices up here. Who are these friends of yours, Helen?'

'This is Daisy and this is Elizabeth, or Bets—that's what you are called, isn't it?' said Mrs. Thomas, turning to Bets. 'This is Zoe—my sister—the one who plays in the shows at the Little Theatre.

Well! *What* a bit of luck! Daisy and Bets stared earnestly at Zoe. How pretty she was—and what a smiley face. They liked her very much.

'Did I hear you talking about poor Boysie?' said Zoe, sitting down by the doll's house, and beginning to rearrange the furniture in it. 'It's a shame! As if he could have done that job on Friday evening! He hasn't got the brains—he'd never, never think of it, even to get back on the manager for his unkindness.'

'Why—is the manager unkind to Boysie?' asked Bets.

'Yes—awfully impatient with him. You see,' said Zoe. 'Boysie is slow, and he's only given silly parts like Dick Whittington's Cat or Mother Goose's Goose and things like that—and the manager shouts at him till poor old Boysie gets worse than ever. I couldn't bear it on Friday morning, when we had a rehearsal—I flared up and told the manager what I thought of him!'

'Did you really?' said Daisy. 'Was he angry?'

'Yes, very,' said Zoe. 'We had a real shouting match, and he told me I could leave at the end of this week.'

'Oh dear,' said Daisy. 'So you've lost your job, then?'

'Yes. But I don't mind. I'm tired and I want a rest,'

said Zoe. 'I'm coming to stay with my sister here for a bit. We shall both like that.'

'I expect you thought it served the manager right, when he was drugged and robbed that night,' said Daisy. 'Where were you when it happened?'

'I left at half-past five with the others,' said Zoe. 'And came here. I believe old Goon thinks I did the robbery, with Boysie to help me!'

'But how could he, if you were here all the evening?' said Bets at once. 'Didn't your sister tell Mr. Goon you were here?'

'Yes—but unfortunately I went out at a quarter to seven, after I'd put the children to bed, to go to the post office,' said Zoe. 'And my sister didn't hear me come back ten minutes later! I went up to my bedroom and stayed there till about a quarter to eight and then came down again. So, you see, according to Mr. Goon, I could have slipped down to the Little Theatre, put a sleeping-draught into the manager's cup of tea , taken down the mirror, opened the safe and stolen the money—all with poor Boysie's help! *And* 'Goon has actually found a handkerchief—it isn't mine, by the way—with Z on, on the verandah at the Theatre—and he says I dropped it when Boysie let me in that night. What do you think of *that*?'

13 LARRY AND PIP ON THE JOB

THE two girls were full of horror—especially at the mention of that unfortunate handkerchief. Daisy went scarlet when she remembered how she had sewn a Z on it in one corner, never, never thinking that there might be any one called Zoe.

They both stared at poor Zoe, and Bets was almost in tears. Daisy wanted to blurt out about the handkerchief and how she had put the Z on it—but she stopped herself in time. She must ask Fatty's permission first.

'Mr. Goon was most unpleasant,' said Mrs. Thomas. 'He cross- examined me about Zoe till I was tired! He wanted to see all the navy coats in the house too—goodness knows what for!'

The two girls knew quite well! Goon had got that bit of navy-blue cloth that Fatty had jabbed on a nail for a false clue—and he was looking for a coat with a hole in it to match the piece of cloth! Oh dear—this was worse and worse.

'He also wanted to know what kind of cigarettes we smoked,' said Zoe, 'And he seemed awfully pleased when we showed him a boxful—Player's!'

Daisy's heart sank even further, and so did Bets'. It was Player's cigarettes whose ends Fatty had scattered over the verandah. Whoever would have thought that their silly false clues would have fitted so well into this case—and alas, fitted poor Zoe so well!

Bets blinked back her tears. She was scared and

unhappy. She looked desperately at Daisy. Daisy caught the look and knew that Bets wanted to go. She wanted to go herself, as well. She too was scared and worried. Fatty must be told all this. He really must. He would know what to do!

So the two of them got up and said a hurried good-bye. 'We'll be seeing you this afternoon,' said Daisy to Zoe. 'We're coming to the show. Could we have your autograph, all of us, if we wait at the stage-door?'

'Of course,' said Zoe. 'How many of you? Five? Right—I'll tell the others, if you like, and they will all give you their autographs. Mind you clap me this afternoon!'

'Oh, we will, we really will,' said Bets, fervently. 'Please don't get arrested, will you?'

Zoe laughed. 'Of course not. I didn't do the robbery, and poor Boysie had nothing to do with it either. I'm quite sure of that. I'm not really afraid of that nasty Mr. Goon. Don't worry!'

But the two girls did worry dreadfully as they hurried away, longing for twelve o'clock to come, so that they could tell Fatty and the others all that they had found out.

'We did very well, actually,' said Daisy, when they got to Bets' playroom and sat down to talk things over. 'Only we found out things we didn't like at all. That *handkerchief*, Bets! I do feel so guilty. I'll never, never do a thing like that again in my life.'

Larry and Pip came along ten to twelve. They looked pleased with themselves.

'Hallo, girls! How did you get on?' said Pip. 'We did

very well!'

So they had. They had biked down to the Little Theatre, and gone to the booking-office to book the seats for the afternoon's show. But the office was closed. Blow!

'Let's snoop round a bit—because if any one sees us, we can always say we've come to buy tickets, and we were looking for some one to ask,' said Pip. So they left the front of the theatre and went round to the back, trying various doors on the way. They were all locked.

They came to the car-park at the back of the theatre. A man was there, cleaning a motor-bicycle. The boys had no idea who he was.

'That's a fine bike,' said Pip to Larry. The man heard their voices, and looked up. He was a middle-aged man, rather stout, with a thin-lipped mouth and bad-temper lines on his forehead.

'What are you doing here?' he said.

'Well, we actually came to buy tickets for this afternoon's show,' said Larry. 'But the booking-office is shut.'

'Of course it is. You can get the tickets when you came along this afternoon,' said the man, rubbing vigorously at the shining mud-guards of the motor-bicycle. 'We only open the booking-office on Saturday mornings, when we expect plenty of people. Anyway, clear off now. I don't like loiterers—after that robbery on Friday I'm not putting up with any one hanging around my theatre!'

'Oh—are you the manager, by any chance?' said Larry, at once.

'Yes. I am. The Man in the News! The man who was doped and robbed last Friday!' said the manager. 'If I

'What are you doing here?'

could only get my hands on the one who did that job!'

'Have you any idea who did it?' asked Pip.

'None at all,' said the manager. 'I don't really believe it was that idiot of a Boysie. He'd never have been able to do all that. Anyway, he's too scared of me to try on tricks of that sort—but he might have helped some one else to do it. Some one he let in that night, when the theatre was empty!'

The boys were thrilled to hear all this first-hand information. 'It said in the paper that Boysie—the Pantomime Cat—brought you in your cup of tea—the one that was drugged,' said Larry. 'Did he, sir?'

'He certainly brought me in the tea,' said the manager. 'I was very busy, and only just glanced up to take it—but it was Boysie all right. He was still in his cat-skin so I couldn't mistake him. Too lazy to take it off. That's Boysie all over. I've even known him go to bed in it. But he's queer in the head, you know. Like a child. He couldn't have done the job by himself, though he must have had something to do with it—he's so easily led.'

'Then—somebody might have come back that night— been let in by Boysie—your tea might have been drugged—and taken up by Boysie to you as usual, so that you wouldn't suspect anything,' said Larry. 'And , as soon as you were asleep, the one that Boysie let in must have crept up to your room, taken down the mirror, got the key from wherever you keep it, and opened the safe— and got away before you woke up.'

'That's about it,' said the manager, standing up to polish the handle-bars. 'And what's more, it must have been one of the cast, because no one knows so much about things as they do—why, whoever the thief was even knew that I didn't keep the safe key on my key-ring—I always keep it in a secret pocket of my wallet. And only the cast knew that for once in a way I hadn't put Thursday's takings into the Bank, because they saw me coming back in a temper with it, when I found the Bank was closed!'

The boys drank all this in. Some of it they already knew, but it sounded much more exciting and real to hear it from the lips of the manager himself. They didn't like him—he looked bad-tempered and mean. They could quite well imagine that he would have a lot of enemies who would like to pay him back for some spiteful thing he had said or done to them.

'I suppose the police are on the job all right,' said Pip, taking a duster and beginning to rub up the spokes of the wheels.

'Oh yes. That constable—what's his name—Goon— has been practically *living* here this week-end— interviewing every one. He's got poor Boysie so scared that I don't think he really knows what he's saying now. He shouts at him till Boysie bursts into tears.'

'Beast,' muttered Pip, and the manager looked at him in surprise.

'Oh, I don't know. If Boysie did it, he's got to get it out of him somehow. Anyway, it doesn't hurt him to be yelled at—only way to get things into his thick head sometimes!'

The bicycle was finished now, and shone brightly. The manager ran it into a shed. 'Well, that's done,' he said. 'Sorry I can't give you your tickets now. You'll get them easily enough this afternoon. There are never many people on Mondays.'

The boys went off, delighted at all they had learnt To get the whole story from the manager himself was simply marvellous. Now they knew as much as Goon did! It was certainly very, very mysterious. The Pantomime Cat *had* taken the drugged cup of tea to the manager—and if he hadn't put the sleeping- draught into it himself, he must have known who had done it—must even have let them in. He might even have watched whilst the thief took down the mirror and robbed the safe. Things looked very black for Boysie. Larry and Pip could quite well imagine how Goon must have shouted and yelled at him to try and make him tell the name of the robber.

'Come on—it's a quarter to twelve. Let's get back,' said Larry, who was bursting to tell his news. 'I wonder how the girls have got on. They had an easy job, really. And so had Fatty—just got to pump Pippin, and that's all.'

'I like this detecting business, don't you?' said Larry, as they cycled up the road. 'Of course it's more difficult for us than for Goon or Pipin—all they've got to do is to go to any one they like and ask questions, knowing that the people *must* answer the police—and they can go into any house they like and snoop round—but we can't.'

'No, we can't. But on the other hand, we can perhaps pick up little bits of news that people might not tell Goon,' said Pip. 'Look out—there's Goon!'

So it was—a frowning and majestic Goon, riding his bicycle, and looking very important. He called out to them as he came near.

'Where's that fat boy? You tell him if I see him again

this morning I'll goand complain to his parents. Poking his Nose where he's not wanted! Where is he?'

'I don't know,' said Pip and Larry together, and grinned. What could Fatty have been doing now?

'You don't know! Gah! I bet you know where he's hiding, ready to pick Pippin's brains again. Does he think he's on this Case, too? Well, he's not. *I'm* in charge of this. You tell him that!'

And with that Mr. Goon sailed off, leaving Larry and Pip full of curiosity to know what in the world Fatty had been doing now!

14   MORE NEWS—
AND A VERY FAT FACE

FATTY had had rather a hectic morning. He had biked down to the road where Goon lived, and had looked into the front room of the police cottage as he passed by. Only Pippin was there. Good.

Fatty leaned his bicycle against the little wall in front of the house, leaving Buster on guard. He then went down the front path, and knocked on the window of the room where Pippin was sitting, laboriously making out reports on this and that.

Pippin looked up and grinned. He opened the door to Fatty and took the boy into the front room.

'Any news?' said Fatty.

'Well,' said Pippin, 'there's a report on the safe and the mirror—about fingerprints. Not a single one to be found!'

'Then whoever did the job was wily,' said Fatty. 'Looks as if that rules out the Pantomine Cat!'

Pippin was about to speak again, when he heard Buster barking. They both looked out of the window. Goon was just dismounting from his bicycle, looking as black as thunder. Buster parked himself in the middle of the gateway, and barked deliriously, as if to say, ' Yah! Can't come in! Woof, woof! Can't come in! Yah!'

'You'd better go,' said Pippin, hurriedly. 'I've a bit more news for you but you must go now.'

As Buster now showed every sign of being about to attack Goon, Fatty hurriedly left the house and ran up to the front gate. He picked Buster up and put him in his bicycle basket.

'What you doing here?' blustered Goon. 'I've warned Pippin against you, Mr. Nosey Parker. You won't get anything out of *him*! He's not on this case. He doesn't know a thing—and he wouldn't tell you if he did. Clear-orf! I'm tired of that fat face of yours.'

'Don't be rude, Mr. Goon,' said Fatty, with dignity. He hated his face to be called fat.

'Rude! I'm not rude—just truthful,' said Mr. Goon, wheeling his bicycle in at the gate. 'I tell you, I don't want to see that fat face of yours any more to-day! I'm a busy man, with important things to do. I won't have you noseying around.'

He went in, pleased to think that Pippin had heard him treat that fat boy in the way he ought to be treated. Aha! He, Mr. Goon, was well on the way to solving a Very Diffcult Case. Got it all Pat, he had—and for once in a way Master Frederick Algernon Trotteville was going to have his nose put out of joint. Him and his fat face!

With these pleasant thoughts to keep him company Mr. Goon went in to fire off a few sharp remarks at Pippin. Fatty, anxious to have a few more words with Pippin, rode up the road a little way, and then leaned his bicycle against a tree, putting himself the other side of the trunk so that he might watch unseen for Goon to come out and ride off again. The policeman had left his bicycle against the wall of his cottage, as if he meant to come out again in a little while.

Fatty stood and brooded over Goon's rude remarks about the fatness of his face. Goon thought he had a fat face, did he? All right—he'd show him one! Fatty slipped his hand into his pocket and brought out two nice new plump cheek-pads. He slipped one into each cheek, between his teeth and the fleshy part of the cheek. At once he took on a most swollen, blown-out look.

Goon came out of his house in a few minutes, and mounted his bicycle. He rode slowly up the road. Fatty came out from behind his tree to show himself to Goon.

'You here again?' began Goon, wobbling in rage. 'You . . .'

And then he caught sight of Fatty's enormously blown-out cheeks. He blinked and looked again. Fatty grinned, and his cheeks almost burst.

Mr. Goon got off his bicycle, unable to believe his eyes, but Fatty jumped on his and sailed away. He waited in a side-road, riding up and down, till he thought Goon must have gone, and then cycled back to Pippin.

'It's all right,' said Pippin, from the window. 'He's gone to send a telegram off, and after that he's going to the Theatre car-park to snoop round again, and then he's got to go to Loo farm about a dog. He won't be back for some time.'

Fatty had now taken out his cheek-pads and looked quite normal again.

'I won't keep you more than a few minutes,' he told Pippin. 'I know you're busy. What other news have you?'

'Well, there *was* a sleeping-draught in that cup all right,' said Pippin. 'A harmless one, but strong. Traces of it were found in the cup. So that's proved all right.'

'Anything else?' enquired Fatty . 'Has the money been traced?'

'No. And it won't be either,' said Pippin ,' It was all in ten-shilling or pound notes, and silver.'

'Any idea yet who did the job?' asked Fatty.

'Well, I've seen Goon's notes, and if you want a *motive* for the robbery—some one with a spite against the manager—any of the company would do for the thief!' said Pippin. 'Mr. Goon wasn't going to tell me anything, as you know, but he's so proud of himself for finding out so much, that he gave me his notes to read. Said it would do me good to see how an expert got to work on a case like this!'

Fatty grinned. 'Yes—sort of thing he *would* say. But what do you mean—all the company had a spite against the manager?'

'Mr. Goon interviewed the manager, and got quite a lot out of him,' said Pippin. 'Now—take Miss Zoe Markham—she had a row with him that morning and got the sack. And now Lucy White—asked him to lend her some money because her mother was ill, and he raged at her and refused. And here's Peter Watting and William Orr—they want to do a series of decent straight plays here instead of this comic stuff, and the manager laughed at them —told them were only fit for third-rate comedy stuff. Said that third-rate people would have to be content with third-rate shows.'

'I bet they were angry,' said Fatty.

'Yes. They were furious, apparently,' said Pippin. 'Almost came to blows. Threatened to knock him down if he called them third-rate again. As a matter of fact they are quite good, especially William Orr.'

'Go on,' said Fatty. 'This is interesting. Who else has

a grudge against him?'

'John James wanted a rise in his salary,' said Pippin. 'Apparently the manager had promised him this after a six months' run. So he asked for it and was refused. The manager says he never promised him anything of the sort.'

'Nice amiable chap, this manager,' said Fatty with a grin. 'Always ready to help! My word, what a way to run a company! They must all hate him.'

'They do!' said Pippin. 'Even poor Boysie, the Pantomime Cat,detests him. Now let me see—is that the lot? No—here's Alec Grant. He wanted permission to go and act in another show on the days he's not on here—and the manager wouldn't let him. There was an awful row about that, apparently—so, you see, there are plenty of people who would very much like to pay the manager out for his spiteful treatment of them!'

'What about their alibis?' asked Fatty, after a pause to digest all this.

'All checked,' said Pippin. 'And all correct, except that there's a query about Zoe Markham, because she went out of her sister's house that evening, and nobody saw her come back; she says she went straight up to her room. So, what with that fact and the Z on the handkerchief found on the verandah, Goon's got her and Boysie down as Chief Suspects now!'

This wasn't very pleasant. Pippin bent over his paper. 'Well,' he said, 'that's all I can tell you for the present—and don't you let on I've told you, either! You'd better go now—and don't forget to let me know if *you've* got anything interesting up your sleeve.'

'I haven't at the moment,' said Fatty, soberly. 'Except

that I hope Mr. Goon was tired after his afternoon walk yesterday!'

Pippin looked up at once. 'What—trailing that red-headed foreigner! You don't mean to say he was *you*!'

'Well—I thought Mr. Goon might as well meet *somebody* off the three-thirty train!' said Fatty. 'You'd have thought he would have been a bit suspicious of red-heads by now, wouldn't you, Pippin?'

And with that Fatty went off whistling on his bicycle, thinking hard. A thought struck him. He put his cheek-pads in, and rode off to the post office. Goon might still be there.

He was. Fatty sidled into the near-by telephone kiosk as Goon came out of the post office. The policeman saw some one grinning at him from the kiosk, and stopped. He gazed in horror at Fatty, whose cheeks were now as enormous as when Goon had seen him a short time before.

Fatty nodded and grinned amiably. Goon walked off, puzzled. That boy! His face seemed fatter than ever. He couldn't be blowing it out with his breath, because he was grinning. He must have some disease!

Fatty shot off on his bicycle, taking a short cut to the car-park behind the theatre. He took his bike to the shed, and bent over it. In a moment or two Goon came sailing in on *his* bicycle, and dismounted to put it into the shed. He saw a boy there, but took no notice—till Fatty turned round and presented him yet another wonderful view of his great fat face.

Goon got a shock. He peered closely at Fatty. 'You got toothache?' he enquired. 'Talk about a fat face!'

He disappeared into the theatre, and Fatty rode off to Loo Farm. He waited there for ten minutes, sitting on his bicycle behind a wall. When he spotted Goon coming along, he rode out suddenly, and once again Mr. Goon got a fine view of a full-moon face shining out at him.

'Now you clear-orf!' yelled Mr. Goon. 'Following me about like this! You with your fat face and all. You go and see a dentist. Gah! Think yourself funny following me about with that face.'

'But Mr. Goon—it looks as if you're following *me* about,' protested Fatty. 'I go to the telephone,and you are there! I go to the car-park and you come there too. And I call at Loo Farm, and hey, presto, you come along here as well! What are you following ME for? Do you think *I* did the robbery at the Little Theatre?'

Mr. Goon looked in puzzled distaste at Fatty's fat face. He couldn't make it out. How could any one's face get as fat as that so suddenly? Was he seeing double?

He decided not to call at Loo Farm whilst that boy was hanging round with his full-moon face. Mr. Goon rode away down the road, defeated.

'Toad!' he murmured to himself. 'Regular toad, that boy. No doing anything with him. Well, he don't know how well I've got on with this Case. Give him a shock when he finds it's all cleared up, arrests been made, and sees the Inspector giving me a Pat on the Back! Him and his fat face!'

Fatty looked at his watch. It was getting on for twelve. He'd better go back and join the others. What news had they been able to get?

THE MYSTERY OF THE PANTOMIME CAT

He rode up to Pip's house. They were all there, waiting for him. Bets waved out of the window.

'Buck *up*, Fatty! We've all got plenty of news! We thought you were *never* coming!'

15   AT THE SHOW—AND AFTERWARDS

THE children sat down in Pip's big playroom, a bag of chocolates between them, supplied by Larry.

'Well—it looks as if we've all got something to report,' said Fatty. ' Girls first. How did you get on, Daisy and Bets?'

Taking it in turns to supply the news, Bets and Daisy told their story. 'Wasn't it *lucky* to see Zoe herself?' said Daisy. 'She's sweet, she really is. *She* couldn't possibly have done the job, Fatty.'

'But isn't it awful about the hanky with Z on?' said Bets. 'And oh, Fatty—she smokes the same kind of cigarettes as our cigarette - ends were made of—Player's!'

'Well, Goon will probably find that most of the others smoke them too, so we needn't worry so much about that,' said Fatty. 'I'm sorry about that hanky business, though. *Why* did we put Z on that silly hanky!'

'Don't you think we ought to tell Goon that—I mean, about us putting the hanky down for a false clue?' said Daisy, anxiously. 'I can't bear Goon going after poor Zoe with a false clue like that—it's awful for her.'

'It can't *prove* anything,' said Fatty, thinking hard. 'If it *had* been hers, she might have dropped it at any old time, not just that evening. I don't see that Goon can make it really *prove* anything.'

'Neither do I,' said Larry. 'We'll own up when the case is finished—but I don't see much point in us spoiling our own chances of solving the mystery by confessing to Goon.'

'All right,' said Daisy. 'Only I can't *help* feeling awful about it.'

'I must say you two girls did very well,' said Fatty. 'You got a lot of most interesting information. What about you, Larry and Pip?'

Then Larry and Pip told of their meeting with the manager, and related in great detail all he had said to them. Fatty listened eagerly. This was splendid!

'I say—that was fine,' he said when the two boys had finished. 'I feel there's absolutely no doubt at all now that it was Boysie who took in the doped tea. Well—if he *did* do the job—or helped somebody to do it—he certainly made it quite clear that he was in it, by taking the tea to the manager! I suppose he didn't realize that the remains of the tea would show the traces of the sleeping-draught. It's the sort of thing a mutt like Boysie would forget.'

'Well—we shall see him this afternoon,' said Daisy. 'I forgot to tell you, Fatty, that we arranged with Zoe to meet all the members of the show after it had finished this afternoon, for autographs. So we shall see Boysie as well.'

'Very good,' said Fatty, pleased. 'You all seem to have done marvellously. I consider I've trained you jolly well!'

He was well pummelled for that remark. When peace had been restored again, Larry asked him how he had got on—and he related all that Pippin had told him.

'It's funny that every single member of the show had a grudge against the manager, isn't it?' he said. 'He must be a beast. He did just the kind of things that would make people want to pay him back. Motives sticking out every where!'

'What are motives?' Bets wanted to know.

'Good reasons for doing something,' explained Fatty. 'Understand? The show-people all had good reasons for getting back at their manager—motives for paying him out for his beastliness.'

'It's a very interesting mystery, this,' said Larry. 'Seven people could have done the job—all of them have good motives for getting even with the manager—and all of them, expect Boysie, and perhaps Zoe, have good alibis. And we don't think either of those would have done the job! Zoe sounds much too nice.'

'I agree,' said Fatty. 'It's a super mystery. A proper Who-Dun-It.'

'What's *that*?' said Bets at once.

'Oh dear—Bets is an awful baby,' said Pip. 'Bets—a Who-Dun-It is a mystery with a crime in it that people have got to solve—to find out who did it.'

'Well, what's it called a Who-Dun-It for, then?' said Bets, sensibly. 'I shall call it a Who-Did-It.'

'You call it what you like,' said Fatty, grinning. 'So long as we find out who-dun-it or who-did-it, it doesn't matter what we call it. Now—what's the next step?'

'We'll all go to the show this afternoon, watch every one acting, and then go round and collect autographs, speak to all the members of the show, and take particular notice of Boysie,' said Larry, at once.

'Go up top,' said Fatty. 'And to-morrow we go after the rest of the alibis. Larry and Daisy will go to see Mary Adams, to find out if Lucy White's alibi is sound—and Pip and I will see if we can test Peter Watting's and

William Orr's. We shall have to find out how to check John James too—he went to the cinema all the evening—or so he said,'

'Yes—and Alec Grant's,' said Daisy. 'He went to Sheepridge and gave a show there on his own.'

'Silly to check that, really,' said Pip. 'So many people heard and saw him. Anyway, it will be jolly easy to check.'

'There's the dinner-bell,' said Pip. 'I must go and wash. What time do we meet this afternoon? And where? Down at the theatre?'

'Yes,' said Fatty. 'Be there at a quarter to three. The show starts at three. So long!'

They were all very hungry indeed for this meal. Detecting was hungry work, it seemed! Fatty spent a good time after his meal writing out all the things he knew about the mystery. It made very interesting reading indeed. Fatty read it over afterwards, and felt puzzled. So many Suspects, so many motives, so many alibis—how in the world would they ever unravel them all?

At a quarter to three all the Find-Outers were down at the Little Theatre. A grubby little boy was in the booking office, and gave them their tickets. They passed into the theatre and found their seats. They had taken them as far forward as they could, so as to be able to observe the actors very closely.

They were in the middle of the second row—very good places indeed. Some one was playing the piano softly. There was no band, of course, for the show was only a small one. The stage-curtain shook a little in the draughts that came in each time the door was opened.

The children gazed at it, admiring the marvellous sunset depicted on the great sheet.

The show began punctually. The curtain went up exactly at three o'clock, and the audience sat up in expectation.

There were two plays and a skit on Dick Whittington's Pantomime. In the first two plays, Boysie did not appear, but he came in at the last one, and the children shouted with delight as he shuffled in on all fours, dressed in the big furry skin that the boys had seen through the window on Friday night.

He was very funny. He waved to the children just as he had waved to the three boys when they had peered in to see him on the Friday night. He capered about, cuddled up to Zoe Marhkam (who was Dick Whittington and looked very fine indeed), and was altogether quite a success.

'Zoe looks lovely,' said Larry.

'Yes—but why do the Principal Boys' parts *always* have to be taken by girls,' said Daisy, in the interval of a change of scenery. 'Do you remember, in Aladdin, it was a girl who took Aladdin's part—and in Cinderella a girl took the part of the Prince.'

'Sh!' said Bets. 'The curtain is going up again. Oh, there's the Cat! And oh, look—his skin is splitting down by his tail!'

So it was. The Cat seemed to realise this and kept feeling the hole with his front paw. 'Meeow,' he said, 'meeow!' Almost as if he was a real cat, dismayed at the splitting of his coat!

'I hope he doesn't split it all the way down,' said Bets.

'I bet he'd get into a row with that awful manager, if he did. Oh, isn't he funny! He's pretending to go after a mouse. *Is* it a mouse?'

'Only a clockwork one,' said Daisy. 'Well, Boysie may be queer in his head and all that—but I think he's jolly clever in his acting. I do really.'

Fatty thought so too. He was wondering if any one quite so good at acting could be as silly as people said. Well—he would see if he could talk to Boysie afterwards—then he could make up his own mind about him.

The show came to an end. The curtain came down, went up once, and came down again. It stayed down. Every one clapped and then got up to go home. It was past five o'clock.

'Now let's rush to the stage-door,' said Fatty. 'Come on!'

So, autograph-books in hand, the five of them tore round to the stage-door, anxious to catch all the actors and actresses before they left.

They waited for five minutes. Then Zoe came to the door, still with some of the grease-paint on her pretty face. But she had changed into a suit now, and looked quite different.

'Come along in and meet the others inside,' she said. 'They won't be out for a few minutes and it's cold standing at the door.'

So, feeling a little nervous, the five children trooped in at the stage-door and followed Zoe to a big room, where one or two of the actors were gulping down cups of tea.

Peter Watting and William Orr were there, one elderly

and rather sour-looking, one young and rather miserable looking. They didn't look nearly so fine as they had done on the stage, when Peter had been Dick's master and Williams had been a very dashing captain, singing a loud, jolly song of the sea, the blue blue sea!

They nodded at the children. 'Hallo, kids! Autograph-hunting? Well, we're flattered, I'm sure! Hand over your books.'

The two men scribbled in each book. Then Zoe introduced them to Lucy White, a tall, gentle-looking girl who had been Dick Whittington's sweetheart in the play. She had looked really beautiful on the stage, with a great mass of flowing golden curls, which the children had admired very much. But the mass of curls now stood on a side-table—a grand wig—and Lucy was seen to be a quiet, brown haired girl with a rather worried face.

She signed the books too. Then John James came in, burly, dour, and heavy-footed, a big man, just right for the black king in the play. 'Hallo!' he said. 'You don't mean to say that somebody wants our autographs! Well, well! Here's fame for you!'

He signed the books too. Fatty began to get into conversation with William and Peter. Larry tried to talk to John James. Pip looked round. Surely there should be somebody else to ask to sign their books?

There was—and he came in at that moment, a small, dapper little man, who had played the part of Dick's mother on the stage. He had been very good as the mother—neat and nimble, using an amusing high voice, and even singing two or three songs in a woman's voice very cleverly indeed.

'Could we have your autograph, please?' said Fatty, going up to him. 'I say, I did like your performance. I could have sworn you were a woman! Even your voice!'

'Yes—Alec was in great form with his singing to-day,' said Zoe. 'Got his high notes beautifully! You should see him imitate me and Lucy—takes us off really well, so that you'd hardly know it wasn't us! We tell him he's lost in this little company. He ought to be on in the West End!'

'He thinks that himself, don't you, Alec?' said John James, in a slightly mocking voice. 'But the manager doesn't agree with him.'

'Don't talk to me about *him*,' said Alec. 'We all detest the fellow. Here you are kids—catch! And I hope you can read my signature!'

He threw them their books. Fatty opened his and saw a most illegible scrawl that he could just make out to be 'Alec Grant'—but only just.

Zoe laughed. 'He always writes like that. Nobody can ever read his writing. I tell him he might just as well write "Hot Potatoes" or "Peppermint Creams" and nobody would know the difference. I wonder your mother can ever read your letters, Alec.'

'She can't,' said Alec. 'She waits till I get home and then she gets me to read them to her. And I can't!'

Every one laughed. 'Well, so long,' said Alec, winding a yellow scarf round his neck. 'See you to-morrow. And, mind you none of you knock the manager on the head to-night!'

16   THE PANTOMINE CAT
HAS A TEA-PARTY.

THE children thought they ought to go too. Fatty felt as if they had stayed too long already. Then he remembered something.

'Oh—what about the Pantomine Cat? We haven't got *his* autograph. Where is he?'

'Clearing up the stage, I expect,' said Zoe, 'That's one of his jobs. But he won't sign your albums for you—poor old Boysie can't write.'

'Can't he, *really*?' said Bets, in amazement. 'But I thought he was grown up—isn't he?'

'Yes—he's twenty-four,' said Zoe. 'But he's like a kid of six. He can hardly read, either. But he's dear, he really is. I'll go and get him for you.'

But before she could go, the Pantomine Cat came in. He walked on his hind legs, and had thrown back the furry cat-skin head, so that it looked like a grotespue hood.

He had a big head, small eyes, set too close together, teeth that struck out in front like a rabbit's, and a very scared expression on his face.

He came up to Zoe and put his hand in hers like a child. 'Zoe,' he said. 'Zoe must help Boysie.'

'What is it, Bosyie?' said Zoe, speaking as if Bosyie was a child. 'Tell Zoe.'

'Look,' said Boysie, and turned himself round dolefully. Every one looked—and saw a big split in poor Bosyie's cat-skin, near the tail. It had got much bigger since Bets had noticed it.

'And look,' said Bosyie, pointing to a split down his tummy. 'Zoe can mend it for Bosyie?'

'Yes, Bosyie, of course,' said Zoe, kindly, and the cat slipped his hand in hers again, smiling up at her. He only reached to her shoulder. 'You're getting fat, Bosyie,' said Zoe. 'Eating too much, and splitting your skin!'

Boysie now saw the children for the first time and smiled at them with real pleasure. 'Children,' he said, pointing at them. 'Why are they here?'

'They came to talk to us, Bosyie,' said Zoe. (' He wouldn't understand what I mean if I said you wanted autographs,' she whispered to Fatty.)

Peter Watting and William Orr, tall and thin, now said good-bye and went. Lucy White followed, leaving her wig of golden curls behind. Boysie put it on and ran round the room, grinning, looking perfectly dreadful.

'See? He's just like a six-year old, isn't he?' said Zoe. 'But he's so simple and kind—does anything he can for any of us. He's very clever with his fingers—he can carve wood beautifully. Look—here are some of the things Boysie has done for me.'

She took down a row of small wooden animals, most beautifully carved. Boysie, still in his golden wig, came and stood by them, smiling with pleasure.

'Boysie! I think they're *beautiful*.' said Bets, overcome with admiration. 'How *do* you do such lovely carving? Oh, *look* at this little lamb—it's perfect.'

Boysie suddenly ran out of the room. He came back with another little lamb, rather like the one Bets admired. He pressed it into her hand, smiling foolishly, his small eyes full of tears.

'You have this,' he said. 'I like you.'

Bets turned and looked at him. She did not see the ugly face, the too-close eyes, the big-toothed mouth. She only saw the half-scared kindness that lay behind them all. She gave him a sudden hug, thinking of him as if he were a child much younger and smaller than herself.

'There! See how pleased the little girl is,' said Zoe. 'That's nice of you, Boysie.'

She turned to the others. 'He's always like that,' she said. 'He'd give away the shirt off his back if he could. You can't help liking him, can you?'

'No,' said every one, and it was true. Boysie was queer in the head and silly, he was ugly to look at—but he was kind and sincere and humble, he had a sense of fun—and you simply *couldn't* help liking him.

'I can't bear it when people are unkind to Boysie,' said Zoe. 'Sometimes the manager is, and I just see red then. I did last Friday, didn't I, Boysie?'

Boysie's face clouded over and he nodded. 'You mustn't go away,' he said to Zoe, and put his hand in hers. 'You mustn't leave Boysie.'

'He says that because the manager gave me notice on Friday,' said Zoe. 'He's afraid I'll go. But I shan't. The manager won't want to lose me really—though I'd like a bit of a rest. But he said this afternoon he didn't mean what he said last Friday. He's a funny one. Nobody likes him.'

'I say—I suppose we really ought to go,' said Fatty. 'Are you coming, Zoe—may we call you Zoe?'

'Of course,' said Zoe. 'Well, no, I won't go yet. I must

mend Boysie's cat-skin. I'll stay and have tea with him, I think. I say, Boysie—shall we ask all these nice children to stay to tea too?'

Boysie was thrilled. He stroked Zoe's arm, and then took Bets' hand. 'Boysie will make tea,' he said. 'You sit down.'

'Boysie, aren't you going to take off your cat-skin?' asked Zoe. 'You'll be so hot—and you might split it even more.'

Boysie paid no attention. He went off into a small cupboard-like place, and they heard him filling a kettle.

'We'd *love* to stay,' said Fatty, who thought Zoe was just about the nicest person he had ever seen. 'If we're no bother. Shall I pop out and buy some buns?'

'Yes. That would be a lovely idea,' said Zoe. ' Where's my purse. I'll give you the money.'

'I've plenty, thank you,' said Fatty, hastily. 'I won't be long! Coming, Larry?'

He and Larry disappeared. Boysie watched for the kettle to boil, which it soon did. Just as he turned off the gas Fatty and Larry came back with a collection of jammy buns, chocolate cakes and ginger biscuits.

'There's a plate in the cupboard where Boysie is,' said Zoe. 'My word—what a feast!'

Fatty went into the little cupboard. He watched Boysie with interest. The little fellow, still in his cat-skin, had warmed the brown teapot. He now tipped out the water from the pot and put in some tea.

'How may spoons of tea, Zoe?' he called.

'Oh, four will do,' said Zoe. 'Count them for him, will you—he can't count very well.'

'I can count four,' said Boysie, indignantly, but proceeded to put five in, instead. Then he poured boiling water into the pot and put on the lid.

'Do you make tea every evening?' asked Fatty, and Boysie nodded.

'Yes. He's good at making tea,' said Zoe, as Boysie carried the teapot in and set it down on the table. 'He usually makes it for us as soon as the show is over—and then he makes some for the manager much later. Don't you, Boysie?'

To the children's alarm Boysie suddenly burst into tears. 'I didn't take him his tea. I didn't,' he wept.

'He's remembering about last Friday,' said Zoe, patting Boysie comfortingly. 'That policeman keeps on and on at him, trying to make him say he took a cup of tea to the manager and Boysie keeps saying he didn't. Though the manager says he *did*. I expect Boysie has got muddled and has forgotten.'

'Tell us about it, Boysie,' said Fatty, rather thrilled at getting so much first-hand information. 'You don't need to worry about talking to *us*. We're your friends. We know you didn't have anything to do with what happened on Friday night.'

'I didn't, did I?' said Boysie, looking at Zoe. 'You all went, Zoe. You didn't stay with Boysie like to-day. I was in my cat-skin because it's hard to take off by myself. You know it is. And I went into the back room where there's a fire!'

'He means the room behind the verandah,' explained Zoe. 'There's an electric fire there that Boysie likes to sit by.'

'And I saw you—and you—and you,' said Boysie, surprisingly, poking his paw at Fatty, Larry, and Pip. 'Not you,' he added, poking Bets and Daisy.

'You never said that before,' said Zoe, in surprise. 'That's naughty, Boysie. You *didn't* see these children.'

'I did. They looked in the window,' said Boysie. 'I looked at them too. I frightened them! They looked again and I waved to them to tell them not to be frightened, because they are nice children.'

The five children looked at one another. *They* knew that Boysie was telling the truth. He *had* seen them that Friday night—he *had* waved to them.

'Did you tell the policeman this?' asked Fatty, suddenly.

Boysie shook his head. 'No. Boysie didn't remember then. Remembers now.'

'What did you do after the children had gone?' asked Fatty, gently.

'I made some tea,' said Boysie, screwing up his face to remember. 'Some for me and some for the manager.'

'Did you drink yours first?' asked Fatty. 'Or did you take *his* up first?'

'Mine was hot,' said Boysie. 'Very hot. Too hot. I played till it was cool, then I drank it.'

'*Then* did you pour out the manager's tea and take it to him?' asked Fatty. Boysie blinked his eyes and a hunted look came over his face.

'No,' he said. 'No, no, no! I didn't take it, I didn't, I didn't! I was tired. I lay down on the rug and I went to sleep. But I didn't take the tea upstairs. Don't make me say I did. I didn't, I didn't.'

There was a long pause. Every one was wondering

what to say. Fatty spoke first.

'Have a jammy bun, every one? Here, Boysie, there's an extra-jammy one for you—and don't you bother any more about that tea. Forget it!'

17   CHECKING UP THE ALIBIS

NO more was said about Friday evening after that. It was quite clear that talking about it upset Boysie terribly. Fatty was very puzzled indeed. Boysie *had* taken up the tea—the manager said so quite definitely, because, as now, he was still in his cat-skin and was quite unmistakable. Then what was the point of Boysie denying it? Was he trying to shield somebody, in his foolish way, by denying everything to do with the doped cup of tea?

If so—who was he trying to shield? Zoe? No! Nobody could possibly suspect Zoe of drugging any one's tea, or robbing a safe. Nobody—except Goon!

It was imperative to check up all the other alibis. If there was a single chink in any of them, that was probably the person Boysie was trying to shield. Fatty made up his mind that every other alibi must be gone into the next day without fail. If he couldn't find something definite, it looked as if the poor old Pantomime Cat would be arrested, and Zoe too! Because Goon would be sure that Zoe, whom Boysie obviously adored, was the person he was shielding.

It was a curious tea-party, but the children enjoyed it. Towards the end, a loud voice came down the stairs outside the room.

'What's all the row down there? Who's there? I can hear *your* voice, Zoe!'

Zoe went to the door. 'Yes, I'm here. I'm stopping behind to mend Boysie's cat-skin. It's all split. And there are a few children here, too, who came for our autographs.

They're having a cup of tea with me and Boysie.'

'You tell them to be careful Boysie doesn't put something in their tea, then!' shouted the manager, and went back to his room, banging the door loudly.

'Pleasant fellow, isn't he?' said Larry. 'We met him this morning. A very nasty bit of work.'

'I couldn't agree more,' said Zoe. 'Well, dears, you'd better go. Get out of your skin, Boysie, if you want me to mend it.'

The children said good-bye, shaking hands with both Zoe and Boysie. Boysie looked intensely pleased at all this ceremony. He bowed each time he shook hands.

'A pleasure,' he said to each of them. 'A pleasure!'

They all went to get their bikes, which they had left in the stand inside the shed. 'Well! Fancy getting asked inside, meeting every one, and having tea with Zoe and Boysie!' said Fatty, pleased.

'Yes. And hearing his own story,' said Larry, pushing his bike out into the yard. 'Do you believe him, Fatty?'

'Well, I know it's quite impossible that he shouldn't have taken in that cup of tea, but yet I feel Boysie's speaking the truth,' said Fatty. 'I've never been so puzzled in my life. One minute I think one thing and the next I think another.'

'Well, *Zoe* didn't do it,' said Bets, loyally. 'She's much, much, much too nice.'

'I agree with you,' said Fatty. 'She couldn't have done that robbery any more than *you* could, Bets. Well, we must look elsewhere that's all. We must check all the rest of the alibis to-morrow without fail.'

So the next morning the Find-Outers started off with

their checking. Larry and Daisy set off to Mary Adams' flat, to find out about the gentle Lucy White. Fatty and Pip went off by the river, to find The Turret and discover if William Orr and Peter Watting *had* been there on Friday night, as they said.

'Then we'll check up on John James and the cinema if we can this afternoon,' said Fatty, 'and on Alec Grant as well, if we've time. We'll have to look lively now, because it seems to me that Goon will move soon. If he sees that poor Boysie any more he'll send him *right* off his head!'

Daisy found a half-embroidered cushion-case which she had never finished. She took the silks that went with it and wrapped the whole lot up in a parcel. 'Come along,' she said to Larry. 'We'll soon find out about Lucy White—though, honestly, I think it's a waste of time checking *her* alibi. She doesn't look as if she could say boo to a goose!'

They arrived at Mary Adams' flat and went upstairs to her front door. They rang, and the old lady opened the door.

'Well, well, well—*what* a surprise,' she said, pleased. 'Miss Daisy *and* Master Larry. It's a long time since I've seen you—what enormous children you've grown. You come along in.'

She led the way into her tiny sitting-room. She took down a tin of chocolate biscuits from the mantelpiece and offered them one. She was a small, white-haired old lady, almost crippled with rheumatism now, but still able to sew and knit.

Daisy opened her parcel. 'Mary, do you think you

could possibly finish this cushion-case for me before Easter? I want to give it to mother, and I know I shan't have time to finish it myself, because I'm embroidering her some hankies too. How much would you charge for doing it for me?'

'Not a penny, Miss Daisy,' said Mary Adams, beaming. 'It would be a pleasure to do something for you, and especially something that's going to be given to your dear mother. Bless your dear heart, I'd love to finish it just for love and nothing else.'

'Thank you *awfully*, Mary,' said Daisy. 'It's very kind of you—and I'll bring you some of our daffodils as soon as they're properly out. They're awfully behind this year.'

'Have another biscuit?' said Mary, taking down the tin again. 'Well, it *is* nice to see you both. I've been ill, you know, and haven't been out much. So it's a real change to see a visitor or two.'

Here was just the opening they wanted!

'Do you know Lucy White?' said Larry. 'We got her autograph this afternoon. She's a friend of yours, isn't she?'

'Yes—dear Lucy! She came to see me every night last week, when I was bad,' said Mary. 'I had a lot of knitting to finish and that kind girl came in and helped me till it was all done.'

'Did she come on Friday too?' asked Daisy.

'Ah—you're like that Mr. Goon—he's been round here three times asking questions about Friday evening,' said Mary. 'Yes, Lucy came along about a quarter to six and we sat and knitted till half-past nine, when she went home. We heard the nine o'clock news, and she made us some cocoa, with some biscuits, and we had *such* a nice time together.'

Well, that seemed pretty definite.

'Didn't Lucy leave you at all, till half-past nine?'said Daisy.

'Not once. She didn't so much as go out of the room,' said Mary. 'There we sat in our chairs, knitting away for dear life—and the next day Lucy took all the knitting we'd done that week, and delivered it for me. She's a good kind girl.'

There came a ring at the door. 'I'll go for you,' said Daisy and got up. She opened the door—and there was Mr. Goon, red in the face from climbing the steps to Mary's flat! He glared suspiciously at Daisy.

'What are *you* doing here?' he demanded. 'Poking your noses in?'

'We came to ask Mary to do some sewing,' said Daisy, in a dignified voice.

'*Ho* yes!' said Mr. Goon, disbelievingly. 'Mary Adams in?'

'Yes I am,' called Mary Adams' voice, sounding rather cross.

'Is that you again, Mr. Goon? I've nothing more to say to you. Please go away. Wasting my time like this!'

'I just want to ask you a few more questions,' said Mr. Goon, walking into the little sitting-room.

'Theophilus Goon, since you were a nasty little boy *so* high, you've always been a one for asking snoopy questions,' said Mary Adams, and the two children heard Mr. Goon snort angrily. They called good-bye and fled away, laughing.

CHECKING UP THE ALIBIS

'I bet he *was* a nasty little boy too!' said Larry, as they went down the stairs. 'Well, that was easy, Daisy.'

'Very,' said Daisy. 'And quite definite too. It rules out Lucy White. I do wonder how the others are getting on.'

Bets was waiting at home with Buster. She had wanted to go with Pip and Fatty, but Fatty had said no, she had better stay with Buster. He and Pip had gone off down by the river, taking the road along which William Orr and Peter Watting had said they went.

They came to a tall and narrow house, with a little turret. On the gate was its name. 'The Turret. Coffee, sandwiches, snacks.'

'Well, here we are,' said Fatty. 'We'll try the coffee, sandwiches, snacks. I feel jolly hungry.'

So in they went and found a nice table looking out on a primrosey garden. A small girl came to serve them. She didn't look more than about twelve, though she must have been a good deal older.

'Coffee for two, please,' said Fatty. 'And sandwiches. And something snacky.'

The girl laughed. 'I'll bring you a tray of snacks,' she said. 'Then you can help yourselves.'

She brought them two cups of hot, steaming coffee, a plate of egg, potted meat, and cress sandwiches, and a tray of delicious looking snacks.

'Ha! *We've* chosen the right place to come and check up on alibis,' said Fatty, eyeing the tray with delight. 'Look at all this!'

The boys ate the sandwiches, and then chose a snack. It was delicious. 'Come on—let's carry on with the snacks,' said Fatty. 'We've had a long walk and I'm hungry. I don't care if I *do* spoil my dinner—it's a jolly good way to spoil it—most enjoyable.'

'But have you got enough money to pay, Fatty?' asked Larry, anxiously. 'I haven't got much on me.'

'Plenty,' said the wealthy Fatty, and rattled his pockets. 'We'll start on checking the alibi as soon as we've finished our meal. Hallo—LOOK who's here!'

It was Goon! He walked in as if he owned the place, and then he saw Fatty!

18 MORE CHECKING—
AND A FEW SNACKS

MR. GOON advanced on Fatty's table. 'Everywhere I go,' boomed Mr. Goon, 'I see some of you kids. Now, what are you doing *here*?'

'Snacking,' said Fatty, politely. 'Did you come in for a snack too, Mr. Goon? Not much left, unfortunately.'

'You hold your tongue,' said Mr. Goon.

'But you asked me a question,' objected Fatty. 'You said . . .'

'I know what I said,' said Mr. Goon. 'I'm Fed Up with you kids! I go to Mary Adams and I see some of you there. I come here and here you are again. And I bet when I go somewhere else you'll be there as well! Lot of pests you are.'

'It's funny how often we see *you* too, Mr. Goon,' said Fatty, in the pleasant, polite voice that always infuriated Mr. Goon. 'Quite a treat.'

Mr. Goon swelled up and his face went purple. Then the little girl came into the room, and he turned to her pompously. 'Is your mother in? I want a word with her.'

'No, she's not, sir,' said the little girl. 'I'm the only one here. Mother will be back soon, if you like to wait.'

'I can't wait,' said Mr. Goon, annoyed. 'Too much to do. I'll come to-morrow.'

He was just going when he turned to look at Fatty. He had suddenly remembered his fat cheeks. They didn't seem nearly so fat now.

'What you done to make your cheeks thin?' he said, suspiciously.

'Well—I *might* have had all my back teeth out,' said Fatty. 'Let me see—did I, Larry? Do you remember?'

'Gah!' said Mr. Goon, and went. The little girl laughed uproariously.

'Oh, you are funny!' she said. 'You really are. Isn't he horrid? He came and asked Mother and me ever so many questions about two men that came here last Friday night.'

'Oh yes,' said Fatty, at once. 'I know the men—actors, aren't they? I've got their autographs in my autograph album. Were they here on Friday, then? I bet they liked your snacks.'

'Yes, they came on Friday,' said the little girl. 'I know, because it was my birthday, and Peter Watting brought me a book. I'd just been listening to Radio Fun at half-past six, when they came in.'

'Half-past six,' said Fatty. 'Well, what did they do then? Eat all your snacks?'

'No! They only have coffee and sandwiches,' said the little girl. 'They gave me the book—it's a beauty, I'll show you—and then we listened to Radio Theatre at seven o'clock. And then something went wrong with the wireless and it stopped.'

'Oh,' said Fatty, disappointed, because he had been counting on the wireless for checking up on the time. 'What happened then?'

'Well, Peter Watting's very good with wirelesses,' said the little girl. 'So he said he'd try and mend it. Mother said, "Mend it in time for eight o'clock then, because I want to hear a concert then.'"

'And was it mended by then?' asked Fatty.

'No. Not till twenty past eight,' said the little girl. 'Mother was very disappointed. But we got it going by then, quite all right—twenty past eight, I mean—and then Peter and William had to go. They called the ferry and went across the river.'

This was all very interesting. It certainly proved beyond a doubt that William Orr and Peter Watting could not possibly have had anything to do with the robbery at the Little Theatre. That was certain. The little girl was quite obviously telling the truth.

'Well, thanks for a jolly good meal,' said Fatty. 'How much do we owe you?'

The little girl gave a squeal. 'Oh, I never counted your snacks. Do you know how many you had? I shan't half catch it from Mother if she knows I didn't count.'

'Well, you ought to count,' said Fatty. 'It's too much like hard work for us to count when we're eating. Larry, I make it six snacks each, the sandwiches and the coffee. Is that correct?'

It was. Fatty paid up, gave the little girl a shilling to buy herself something for the birthday she had had on Friday, and went off with Larry, feeling decidedly full.

'We've just got time to go to the cinema to see if we can pick up anything about John James' visit,' said Fatty. 'Oh dear—I wish I hadn't snacked quite so much. I don't feel very brainy at the moment.'

They went into the little lobby. There was a girl at a table, marking off piles of tickets.

'Good morning,' said Fatty. 'Er—could you tell us

anything about last week's programme?'

'Why? Are you thinking of going to it?' said the girl, with a giggle. 'You're a bit late.'

'My friend and I have been having a bit of an argument about it,' said Fatty, making this up on the spur of the moment, whilst Larry looked at him in surprise. 'You see, my friend thinks the programme was *The Yearling* and I said it was—er—er—*Henry V.*'

'No, no,' said the girl, graciously. 'It was *The Weakling,* not *The Yearling,* and *Henry the Fifteenth*, not *Henry V.*'

Fatty turned crossly and went out. He bumped into somebody coming up the steps.

He nearly fell, and clutched hold of the person he had collided with. A familiar voice grated on his ear.

'Take your hands off me! Wherever I go I find one of you kids! What you doing *here*, I'd like to know?'

'They wanted to take tickets for last week's programme,' called the girl from inside, and screamed with laughter. 'Cheek! I told them off all right.'

'That's right,' said Mr. Goon. 'They want telling off. Coming and bothering you with silly questions.' Then it suddenly struck him that Fatty was coming about the same thing as he was—to check up on an alibi. He swung round in a rage. 'Poking your N . . .' he began.

But Fatty had gone, and so had Larry. They were not going to stay and argue with Mr. Goon and That Girl.

'Cheek,' said Fatty, who was not easily out done in any conversation. 'I'm afraid Goon will get a lot more out of her than we shall.'

'Yes. We've rather fallen down on this alibi,' said

Larry—and then he stopped and gave Fatty a sudden punch. 'I say—I know! We can ask Kitty, Pip's cook. She goes to the pictures every single Friday. She told Bets so one day and I heard her. She said she'd never missed for nine years.'

'Well, I bet she missed last Friday, for the first time then,' said Fatty, gloomily. The cinema girl's cheek was still rankling. 'Anyway, we'll ask and see.'

'Well, thank goodness we're not likely to run into Goon in Pip's Kitchen,' said Larry.

They arrived at Pip's, and went into the kitchen. Kitty beamed at them, especially at Fatty, whom she thought very clever indeed.

'Kitty, could we possibly have a drink of water?' began Fatty.

'You shall have some home-made lemonade,' said Kitty. 'And would you like a snack to go with it?'

The very idea of a snack made Fatty turn pale. 'No, thanks awfully,' he said. 'I've just had a snack, Kitty.'

'Well, do have another,' said Kitty, and brought out some small and very tempting-looking sausage rolls. Fatty groaned and turned away.

'Sorry, Kitty—they look marvellous—but I'm too full of snacks to risk another.'

There was a pause whilst Kitty filled lemonade-glasses.

'Did you go to the pictures last week?' said Larry. 'You always do, don't you?'

'Never missed for nine years,' said Kitty proudly. 'Yes, I went on Friday, same as usual. Oooh, it was a *lovely* picture.'

'What was it?' asked Fatty.

'Well, I went in at six and the news was on,' said Kitty. 'Then a cartoon, you know. Made me laugh like anything. Then at half-past six till the end of the programme there was *He Loved Her So*. Oooh, it was *lovely*. Made me cry ever so.'

'A really happy evening,' said Fatty. 'See any one you know?'

Kitty considered. 'No, I don't know as I did. I always get kind of wrapped up in the picture, you know. It was a pity it broke down.'

Fatty pricked up his ears. 'What do you mean—broke down?'

'Well, you know what I mean, Master Frederick,' said Kitty. 'The picture sort of snaps—and stops—and there's only the screen, and no picture. I suppose the film breaks or something.'

'Did it do that a lot?' asked Fatty.

'Yes—four times,' said Kitty. 'All the way through, it seemed. Just at the wrong bits too—you know, the real exciting bits! Every one was grumbling about it.'

'Pity,' said Fatty, getting up. 'Well, Kitty, thanks awfully for the lemonade—and I hope you enjoy your picture *this* Friday.'

'Oooh I shall,' said Kitty. 'It's called *Three Broken Hearts*.'

'You'll weep like anything,' said Fatty. 'You *will* enjoy that, Kitty. It's a pity I'll be too busy to come and lend you my hanky.'

'Oh, you are a caution,' said Kitty, delighted.

'Come on, Larry,' said Fatty, and he pulled him out of

Kitty's kitchen. 'We've learnt something there! Now, if we only get hold of John James. and find out if *he* noticed the breaks in the picture—which he must have done if he was there—we shall be able to check *his* alibi all right!'

'So we shall,' said Larry. 'Jolly good work. But how can we get hold of John James? We can't just walk up to him and say, "Did you notice the breaks in the picture, Mr. James, when you were at the cinema on Friday?" '

'Of course we can't,' said Fatty. 'Gosh, it's almost dinner-time. We'll have to do that afterwards, Larry. Can you possibly eat any dinner? I can't.'

'No, I can't—and it's hot roast pork and apple sauce to-day,' said Larry with a groan. 'What a waste.'

'Don't even *mention* roast pork,' said Fatty with a shudder. 'Why did we eat so many snacks? Now my mother's going to worry because I can't eat a thing at dinner to-day—take my temperature or something!'

'What about John James?' said Larry. 'How are we going to tackle him? We don't even know where to find him. He won't be at the theatre because there's no show this afternoon.'

'I'll ring up Zoe when I get home and see if she knows where we can get hold of him,' said Fatty. 'We'd better take Bets too. She'll be feeling left out if we don't.'

'Right,' said Larry. 'See you this afternoon sometime.'

19 JOHN JAMES AND THE CINEMA

VERY fortunately for Fatty his mother was not in to lunch, so he was able to eat as little as he liked without any one noticing. He was only at the table about five minutes and then he went to ring up Zoe, hoping she was at her sister's as usual.

She was. 'Oh—hallo, Zoe,' said Fatty. 'I say, can you tell me something? I want to have a talk with John James, if I can. Do you know if he'll be anywhere about this afternoon?'

'Well—let me see,' said Zoe's clear voice over the telephone. 'I did hear him say something about going across the river in the ferry, and taking a picnic-tea up on the hill beyond. There's a marvellous view up there, you know.'

'Yes. I know,' said Fatty. 'Oh, good—I'll slip across and see if I can spot him there. Do you know what time he is going?'

Zoe didn't know. Then she told Fatty that Mr. Goon was going to see poor Boysie again that evening. 'And I heard him say that he's not going to stand any nonsense this time—Boysie's got to "come clean," the horrid fellow,' said Zoe, indignantly. 'As if he can make Boysie confess to something he doesn't know anything about!'

Fatty frowned as he hung up the receiver. He was afraid that Boysie *might* confess to the robbery, out of sheer terror and desperation. What a dreadful thing that would be—to have him confess to something he hadn't done—and have the real culprit go scot-free.

Fatty rang up Larry, and then Pip, telling them of John James' plans for the afternoon. 'We've got to go and check up on his alibi,' he said. 'And we can only do that by questioning *him*—to see if he really was at the cinema on Friday night. And as it's a smashing day, let's all take our tea and go for a picnic up on the hill across the river, and kill two birds with one stone—enjoy ourselves, and do a spot of detecting as well!'

The others thought this was a splendid idea. 'Fatty always thinks of such nice things,' said Bets, happily. 'It will be lovely up there on the hills.'

Fatty had told Pip to go and ask Kitty once more about the breaks in the picture on Friday night, just to make sure he had got it quite right. 'Ask if she remembers *exactly* how many breaks there were, when they came— and, if possible, the *time*,' said Fatty. 'Write it down, Pip, in case you forget the details. This may be important. It looks as if John James is our only hope now—I feel that we must count Alec Grant out, with his alibi of over a hundred people.'

The children met at the ferry at a quarter to three, laden with picnic-bags. Pip carried a mackintosh-rug. 'Mother made me,' he said, crossly. 'She said the grass is still damp. You're lucky to have a mother that doesn't fuss about things like that.'

'Mine fusses about other things,' said Fatty. 'And Larry's fusses about certain things too. Never mind, it's not much bother to sit down on a rug!'

'As a matter of fact,' said Bets, seriously, 'I've met one or two mothers who never never fussed about their children—but, you know, I'm sure it was because they didn't care tuppence about them. I think I'd rather have a fussy mother, really.'

'Here's the boat,' said Fatty, as the ferryman came rowing across. 'I'll pay for every one. It's only tuppence each.'

They got into the boat. 'Rowed any one across yet this afternoon?' asked Fatty. The boatman shook his head. 'No, not yet. Bit early.'

'Then John James hasn't gone across yet,' said Fatty to the others. 'Hey, Buster—don't take a header into the water, will you?'

They got across and made their way over a field and up a steep hill to the top. Fatty chose a place from where they could see the ferry.

'We'll watch and see when the ferryman goes out,' he said. 'I don't know if we could make out John James from here, but I expect we could. He's so burly.'

The spring sun was hot. The cowslips around nodded their yellow heads in the breeze. It was very pleasant up there on the hill. Larry yawned and lay down.

'You watch for J. J., you others,' he said. 'I'm going to have a nap!'

But he hadn't been asleep for more than ten minutes when Fatty prodded him in the middle. 'Wake up, Larry. Can you see if that's John James standing on the opposite side of the river, waiting for the ferry?'

Larry sat up. He had very keen eyes. He screwed them up and looked hard. 'Yes. I think it is,' he said. 'Let's hope he comes this way. I don't feel like walking miles after him.'

'Wake up, Larry, Can you see if that's John James?

Fortunately it *was* John James, and he *did* come that way. The children watched him get into the boat, land on their side of the river, and follow the same path as they had taken themselves.

'Now,' said Fatty, getting up, 'we'd better start wandering about till we see where he's going to sit. Then we'll settle somewhere near.'

'How are we going to start the checking up?' asked Pip.

'I'll start it,' said Fatty. 'And then you can all follow my lead, and ask innocent questions. Roll up your rug, Pip.'

The five children and Buster wandered about and picked cowslips, keeping a sharp eye on John James, who was coming very slowly up the hill. He found a sheltered place with a bush behind him, and lay down at full length, his arms behind his head so that he might look down the hill towards the river.

Fatty wandered near him. 'Here's a good place,' he called to the others. 'We'll have the rug here.' Then he turned politely to the man near by.

'I hope we shan't disturb you if we sit just here,' he said.

'Not if you don't yell and screech,' said John James. 'But I don't suppose you will. You look as if you'd all been well brought up!'

'I hope we have,' said Fatty, and beckoned to the others. Pip put down the rug. By this time the man was sitting up, and had put a cigarette in his mouth. He patted himself all over and frowned.

'I suppose,' he said to Fatty, 'I suppose you haven't

got matches on you, by any chance? I've left mine at home.'

Fatty always had every conceivable thing on him, on the principle that you simply never knew what you might want at any time. He presented John James with a full box of matches at once.

'Keep the whole box,' said Fatty. 'I'm not smoking till I'm twenty-one!'

'Good boy,' said John James. 'Very sensible. Thanks, old chap. I say—haven't I seen you before?'

'Yes,' said Fatty. 'We came into the back of the theatre yesterday—and you were good enough to sign our autograph albums.'

'Oh yes—now I remember you all,' said John James. 'Have you come up here for a picnic?'

'Yes. We're just about to begin,' said Fatty, though it was really much too early. But the effect of the snacks was beginning to wear off, and the lack of a midday meal was making itself felt! Fatty was more than ready for a picnic. 'Er—I suppose you wouldn't join us, sir—we've got plenty.'

'Yes, I will,' said John James. 'I've got some stuff here too. We'll pool it.'

It was a very nice picnic, with plenty to eat, and some of Kitty's home-made lemonade to drink. For a short while Fatty and the others talked about whatever came into their heads.

Then Fatty began his 'checking.' 'What's on at the cinema this week, Larry?' he asked.

Larry told him. 'Oh no,' said Fatty, 'that was last week!'

'You're wrong,' said John James at once. 'It was *Here Goes*, the first part of the week, and *He Loved Her So*, the second. Both absolutely frightful.'

'Really?' said Fatty. 'I heard that *He Loved Her So* was good. But I didn't see it. I suppose you did?'

'Yes. Saw it on Friday,' said John James. 'At least— I *would* have seen it, but it was so boring that I fell asleep nearly all the time!'

This remark disappointed all the Find-Outers very much indeed. If John James slept all the time, he wouldn't have noticed the breaks in the picture—and so they wouldn't be able to check his alibi.

'Hope you didn't snore!' said Fatty. 'But I suppose people would wake you up if you did.'

'I did keep waking up,' said John James. 'I kept on waking because of people talking and sounding annoyed. I don't quite know what happened—I think the picture must have broken unexpectedly—like they do sometimes, you know—and that made the audience fidgety and cross. But I soon went to sleep again.'

'Bad luck, to be woken up like that!' laughed Fatty. 'I hope you didn't get disturbed from your nap *too* many times!'

John James considered. 'Well, I should think that wretched picture must have gone wrong at least four times,' he said. 'I remember looking at the clock once or twice—once I got woken up at quarter to seven, and another time at ten past. I remember wondering where on earth I was when I woke up then. Thought I was in bed at home!'

'Bit of a boring evening for you,' said Fatty, watching

Pip take out his note-book and do a bit of checking up on times. He nodded reassuringly to Fatty. Yes, John James' alibi was safe all right. There was no doubt at all that he had been in the cinema that evening, and had been awakened each time the picture broke, by the noise of the impatient people around.

'Yes. It was boring,' said John James. 'But it was something to do. Help yourself to my cherry cake. Do. There's plenty.'

The talk turned to the robbery at the theatre.

'Who do *you* think did it?' asked Fatty.

'I haven't a notion,' said John James. 'Not a notion. Boysie didn't. I'm sure of that. He hasn't the brains or the pluck for a thing of that sort. He's a harmless sort of fellow. He just adores Zoe—and I'm not surprised. She's sweet to him.'

They talked for a little while longer and then Fatty got up and shook the crumbs off himself. 'Well, thanks for letting us picnic with you, Mr. James,' he said. 'We'll have to be going now. Are you coming too?'

'No. I'll sit here a bit longer,' said John James. 'There's going to be a grand sunset later on.'

The Find-Outers went down the hill, with Buster capering along on his short legs. 'Well,' said Fatty, when they were out of hearing, 'John James is out of our list of Suspects. His alibi is first-rate. He was in the cinema all right on Friday evening. Gosh, this mystery really is getting deeper and deeper. I'm stumped!'

'Oh *no*, Fatty!' said Bets, quite shocked to hear Fatty say this. 'You *can't* be stumped! Not with your wonderful brains!'

20 DEFEAT—AND A BRAINWAVE

FATTY racked his brains that night, but to no effect. However much he thought and thought, he could see no solution to the mystery at all. He was certain Boysie hadn't done the job. He was also quite certain that Zoe, whose alibi was a little shaky, had had nothing to do with it either. Every one else had unshakable alibis. It was true they hadn't checked Alec Grant's, but Fatty had looked up a local paper and had seen a report of the one-man concert that Alec had given on the Friday evening at Sheepridge.

'The report in the paper is a good enough alibi,' he said to the others. 'We needn't bother any more about Alec. But WHO is the culprit? Who did the job?'

In desperation he went down that evening to talk to P.C. Pippin. He was there, walking up and down Goon's little back garden, smoking a pipe. He was pleased to see Fatty.

'Any news?' said Fatty. 'I suppose Goon's out?'

'Yes, thank goodness,' said Pippin, feelingly. 'He's been at me all day long about something or other. Pops in and out on that bike of his, and doesn't give me any peace at all. He's gone down to see Boysie again now. I'm very much afraid he'll scare him into a false confession.'

'Yes. I'm afraid of that too,' said Fatty. 'What about

Zoe? Does Goon think she had anything to do with it?'

'I'm afraid he does,' said Pippin. 'He's got that handkerchief of hers with Z on, you know—that's one of his main pieces of evidence.'

'But that's nonsense!' said Fatty. 'The handkerchief might have been on that verandah for days! It doesn't prove she was there that night.'

'Goon thinks it does,' said Pippin. 'You see, he has found out that the cleaner swept that verandah clean on Friday afternoon at four o'clock! So the hanky must have been dropped after that.'

Fatty bit his lip and frowned. That was very bad indeed. He hadn't known that. Of *course* Goon thought Zoe had crept to that verandah that evening and been let in by Boysie, if he found a hanky there with Z on—a hanky which must have been dropped after four o'clock! That was a very nasty bit of evidence indeed.

'What annoys Goon is that Zoe keeps on denying it's her hanky,' said Pippin. 'Says she's never seen it before. It's a pity it's got Z on—such an unusual initial.'

'I know,' groaned poor Fatty, feeling very much inclined to make a clean breast of how he had planted the handkerchief and all the other 'clues' on the verandah himself. Well—if Goon did arrest Zoe and Boysie, he would certainly *have* to own up. He turned to Pippin.

'Telephone me, Pippin, if you hear any serious news— such as Goon getting a false confession from Boysie—or making an arrest,' he said.

Pippin nodded. 'I certainly will. What have *you* been

doing about the mystery? I bet you haven't been idle!'

Fatty told him how he had checked up all the alibis and found them unshakable—except for Zoe's. He was feeling very worried indeed. It would be awful if Goon solved the mystery the wrong way—and got the wrong persons! If only, only Fatty could see a bit of daylight. But he couldn't.

He went back home, quite depressed, which was very unusual for Fatty. Larry telephoned him that evening to find out if he had heard anything fresh from Pippin.

Fatty told him all he knew. Larry listened in silence.

'Well—what are we going to do next?' he asked.

For once Fatty was completely at a loss. There didn't seem anything to do at all. 'I don't see *what* we can do,' he said, miserably. 'I'm absolutely stuck. Fat lot of good we are at detecting! We'll have to break up the Find-Outers Band if we can't do better than this.'

'Come up at ten to-morrow and have a meeting,' said Larry. 'We'll think hard and talk and go over absolutely *every*thing. There's something we've missed, I'm sure—some idea we haven't thought of. There's no mystery without a solution, Fatty. Cheer up. We'll find it!'

But before ten o'clock the next day came, the telephone rang, and Pippin relayed some very bad news to Fatty.

'Are you there? I've only got a minute. Mr. Goon has got a confession from Boysie! And Zoe's in it too! Apparently Boysie said he and Zoe worked the thing together. He let Zoe in at the verandah door, they made the tea, Boysie took the cup up with the dope in to the manager—then when he fell asleep, Zoe went up and robbed the safe. She apparently knew where the key was and everything.'

Fatty listened in horror. 'But, Pippin! *Pippin*! Boysie couldn't have done it—nor could Zoe. Goon's *forced* that confession out of a poor fellow who's so queer in his head he doesn't really know what he's saying.'

There was a pause. 'Well, I'm inclined to agree with you,' said Pippin. 'In fact—well, I shouldn't tell you this, but I must—I think what Goon has let slip, he *did* force that false confession from Boysie, poor wretch. Now, see here, I'm helpless. I can't go against Goon. You're the only one that can do anything. Isn't Inspector Jenks a *great* friend of yours? Won't he believe what you say, if you tell him you think there's been a mistake?'

'But I haven't any *proof*,' wailed Fatty. 'Now, if I *knew* who the robber was, and could produce him, with real evidence, the Inspector would listen to me like a shot. I'll go and see the others, and see what they think. If we can't think of anything better, I'll cycle over to the next town and see the Inspector myself.'

'Well, you'd better make. . .' began Pippin, and then Fatty heard the receiver being put back with a click. He guessed that Goon had come in. He sat by the telephone and thought hard. This was frightful. Poor Zoe. Poor Boysie. What in the world could he do to help them?

He tore off to Pip's on his bicycle. The others were there already. They looked gloomy—and they looked gloomier still when Fatty told them what Pippin had said.

'It's serious,' said Larry. 'More serious than any other mystery we've tackled. What can we do, Fatty?'

'We'll go through all the Suspects and the Alibis, and run through all we know,' said Fatty, getting out his note-book. 'I've got everything down here. Listen whilst I read it—and think, think, think *hard* all the time. As Larry says—we've missed something—some clue, or some evidence that would help us. There's something very wrong, and probably the explanation is sticking out a mile—if we could only *see* it!'

He began to read through his notes—the list of Suspects. The alibis they had each given. The checking of all the alibis. Boysie's account of the evening of the crime. The manager's own account. The dislike that each member of the show felt for the manager, which would give each one of them a motive for paying him out. Everything in his note-book Fatty read out, clearly and slowly, and the Find-Outers listened intently, even Buster sitting still with ears cocked.

He finished. There was a long pause. Fatty looked up. 'Any suggestions?' he asked, not very hopefully.

The others shook their heads. Fatty shut his note-book with a snap. 'Defeated!' he said, bitterly. 'Beaten! All we know is that out of the seven people who are Suspects, the two who *could* have done it, didn't—Boysie and Zoe—we *know* they didn't. They're incapable of doing such a thing. And the others, who *might* have done it, all have first-class alibis. How *can* the Pantomime Cat have done the deed when it isn't in his nature to do it?'

'It almost makes you think, it must have been somebody else in Boysie's skin,' said Bets.

The others laughed scornfully, 'Silly!' said Pip, and Bets went red.

And then Fatty went suddenly and inexplicably mad. He stared at Bets with fixed and glassy eyes. Then he smacked her hard on the shoulder. Then he got up and did a solemn and ridiculous dance round the room, looking as if he was in the seventh heaven of delight.

'Bets!' he said, stopping at last. '*Bets*! Good, clever, brainy old Bets. She's got it! She's solved it! Bets, you deserve to be head of the Find-Outers! Oh my word, Bets, why, why, why didn't I think of it before?'

The others all stared at him as if he was out of his mind. 'Fatty, don't be an ass. Tell us what you mean,' said Pip. crossly. 'What's Bets been so clever about? For the life of me I don't know!'

'Nor do I,' said Larry. 'Sit down, Fatty, and explain.'

Fatty sat down, beaming all over his face. He put his arm round the astonished Bets and squeezed her. 'Dear old Bets—she's saved Boysie and Zoe. What brains!'

'*Fatty*! Shut up and tell us what you mean!' almost yelled Pip in exasperation.

'Right,' said Fatty. 'You heard what young Bets said, didn't you? She said, "It almost makes you think it must have been somebody else in Boysie's skin." Well? Well, I ask you? Can't you see that's the solution? Turnip-heads, you don't see it yet!'

'I'm beginning to see,' said Larry, slowly. 'But you see it *all*, Fatty, obviously. Tell us.'

'Now, look here,' said Fatty. 'Boysie says he did *not* take the tea in to the manager, doesn't he? But the manager swears he *did*. And why does he swear that? Because Boysie, he says, was wearing his cat-skin. All right. Whoever brought the tea was certainly the Pantomime Cat—but as the manager never saw who was *inside* the skin, how does he know it was Boysie?'

The others listened in amazement.

'And as it happens, it *wasn't* Boysie!' said Fatty, triumphantly. 'Let me tell you what I think happened that night, now that Bets has opened my eyes.'

'Yes, go on, tell us,' said Pip, getting excited as he too began to see what Fatty was getting at.

'Well—the theatre cast all departed, as we know, at half-past five, because we saw them go,' said Fatty. 'Only Boysie was left, because he lives there, and the manager was upstairs in his office.

'Now, there was a member of the cast who had a grudge against the manager, and wanted to pay him out. So that night, after *we* had gone home from our planting of false clues, this person came silently back—let himself in secretly, because Boysie didn't see him or he would have said so—and hid till he saw Boysie making the tea. He knew that Boysie always made tea and took a cup to the manager.

'Very well. Boysie made the tea, and poured himself out a cup. But he didn't drink it because it was too hot.

He waited till it was cooler. And the hidden person slipped out, and put a sleeping-draught into Boysie's cup.

'Boysie drank it, felt terribly sleepy, went into the verandah room and snored by the fire. The hidden person then made sure that Boysie was doped and wouldn't wake up—and he *stripped the skin off Boysie*. . .'

'And put it on himself!' cried all the others together. 'Oh, *Fatty*!'

'Yes—he put it on himself. And made a cup of tea for the manager, putting into it a sleeping-draught of course—and up the stairs he went! Well, how could the manager guess it was any one but Boysie in his Pantomime Cat-skin! Wouldn't *any* one think that?'

'Of course,' said Daisy. 'And then he waited till the manager had drunk his tea and fallen asleep—and did the robbery!'

'Exactly,' said Fatty. 'Took down the mirror, found the key in the manager's wallet, worked out the combination that would open the safe—and stole everything in it. Then he went down to the sleeping Boysie and pulled him into the skin again—and departed as secretly as he came, with the money!

'He knew that when the cup of tea was examined and traces of a sleeping-draught were found, the first question asked would be—*Who* brought up the cup of tea to the manager?' said Fatty. 'And the answer to that—quite untruly as it happens—was, of course, Boysie.'

'Oh, Fatty—it's wonderful,' said Bets, her face shining. 'We've solved the mystery!'

THE MYSTERY OF THE PANTOMIME CAT

'We haven't,' said Larry and Pip together.

'We *have*,' said Bets indignantly.

'Ah, wait a minute, Bets,' said Fatty. 'We know how the thing was done—but the *real* mystery now is—*who was inside the skin of the Pantomime Cat?*'

21 THE LAST ALIBI IS CHECKED

EVERY one felt tremendously excited. Larry smacked Bets proudly on the back. 'You just hit the nail on the head, Bets, when you made that brainy remark of yours,' he said.

Well—I didn't know it was brainy,' said Bets. 'I just said it without thinking, really.'

'I *told* you there was something sticking out a mile, right under our very noses,' said Fatty. 'And that was it. Come on, now—we've got to find out who was in the skin.'

They all thought. 'But what's the good of thinking it's this person or that person?' said Pip at last. 'If we say "John James," for instance, it can't be, because we've checked his alibi and it's perfect.'

'Let's not worry about alibis,' said Fatty. 'Once we decide who the person was, inside the cat-skin, we'll re-check the alibi—and what's more, we'll then find it's false! It must be. Come on, now—who was inside that cat-skin?'

'Not John James,' said Daisy. 'He was much too big— too fat.'

'Yes—it would have to be a small person,' said Fatty. 'Boysie is small, and only a person about his size could wear that skin.'

They all ran their minds over the members of the cast.

Larry thumped on the floor.

'Alec Grant! He's the smallest of the lot—very neat and dapper and slim—don't you remember?'

'Yes! The others are *all* too big—even the two girls, who are too tall to fit the skin,' said Fatty. 'Alec Grant is the only member who could possibly get into the skin.'

'*And* he split it! said Daisy, suddenly. 'Oh, don't you remember, Fatty, how Boysie came and asked Zoe to mend it for him—and she looked at the splitting seams and said he must be getting fat? Well, he wasn't! Somebody bigger than he was had used his skin and split it!'

'Gosh, yes,' said Fatty. 'Would you believe it—a Clue as big as that staring us in the face and we never noticed it! But I say—*Alec Grant*! He's got the best alibi of the whole lot.'

'He certainly has,' said Larry. 'It's going to be a hard alibi to break, too. Impossible, it seems to me.'

'No. Not impossible,' said Fatty. 'He couldn't be in two places at once. And so, if he was in the Pantomime Cat's skin at the Little Theatre on Friday evening, he was *not* giving a concert at Sheepridge! That's certain.'

'Fancy! The only alibi we didn't check,' said Larry

'Yes—and I *said* that a good detective always checks everything, whether he thinks it is necessary or not,' groaned Fatty. 'I must be going downhill rapidly. I consider I've done very badly over this!'

'You haven't, Fatty,' said Bets. 'Why, it was you who saw that my remark, which was really only a joke, was the real clue to the mystery! I didn't see that, and nor did the others.'

'How are we going to shake this alibi of Alec Grant's?' said Larry. 'Let's keep to the subject. We haven't much time, it seems to me, if Goon has got a false confession from poor Boysie. He'll be getting into touch with the Inspector any time now and making an arrest—two arrests, I suppose, if Zoe has to be in it too.'

'Any one got friends in Sheepridge?' asked Fatty, suddenly.

'I've got a cousin there—you know him, Freddie Wilson,' said Larry. 'Why?'

'Well, I suppose there's a chance he might have gone to Alec's concert,' said Fatty. 'Telephone him and see, Larry. We've got to find out something about this concert now.'

'*Freddie* won't have gone to a concert like that—to see a man impersonating women,' said Larry, scornfully.

'You go and phone him,' said Fatty. 'Ask him if he knows anything about it.'

Larry went, rather reluctantly. He was afraid that Freddie would jeer at his enquiry.

But Freddie was out and it was his eighteen year-old sister, Julia, who answered. And she provided an enormous bit of luck!

'No, Larry, Freddie didn't go,' she said. '*Can* you see him going to *any* kind of concert? I can't. But I went with Mother. Alec Grant was awfully good—honestly, you couldn't have told he was a man. I waited afterwards and got his autograph.'

'Hold on a minute,' said Larry, and went to report to Fatty. Fatty leapt up as if he had been shot. 'Got his *autograph*! Gosh—this is super. Don't you remember, idiot, *we've* all got his autograph too! I'd like to see the autograph *Julia* got! I'll eat my hat if it isn't quite different from the ones *we've* got!'

'But Fatty—Alec Grant was there, giving the concert,' began Larry. 'Julia says so.'

Fatty took absolutely no notice of him but rushed to the telephone, with Buster excitedly at his heels, feeling that there really must be Something Up!

'Julia! Frederick Trotteville here. I say, *could* I come over and see you by the next bus? Most important. Will you be in?'

Julia laughed at Fatty's urgent voice. 'Oh, Frederick— you sound as if you're in the middle of a mystery or something. Yes, of course. Come over. I'll be most interested to know what you want!'

Fatty clicked down the receiver and rushed back to the others. 'I'm off to Sheepridge,' he said. 'Coming, any one?'

'Of *course*,' said every one at once. What! Be left out just when things were getting so thrilling! No, every one was determined to be in at the death.

They arrived at Sheepridge an hour later, and went to find Julia. She was waiting for them, and was amused to see the whole five march in.

'Listen, Julia,' began Fatty. 'I can't explain everything

to you now—it would like too long—but we are very curious about Alec Grant. You say he really was there, performing at the concert? You actually recognized him, and have seen him before?'

'Yes. Of course I recognized him,' said Julia.

Fatty felt a little taken-aback. He had hoped Julia would say she dIdn't recognize him, and then he might be able to prove that somebody else had taken Alec's place.

'Have you your autograph-album with his signature in?' he asked. Julia went to get it. All the Find-Outers had brought theirs with them, and Fatty silently compared the five signatures in their books with the one in Julia's.

Julia's was utterly and entirely different!

'Look,' said Fatty, pointing. 'The autographs he did for us are illegible squiggles—the one he did for Julia is perfectly clear and readable. It *wasn't* Alec Grant who did that!'

'You'll be saying it was his twin-sister next,' said Julia with a laugh.

Fatty stared as if he couldn't believe his ears. 'What did you say?' he almost shouted. '*Twin-sister*! Julia—you don't really mean to say he's got a twin-sister?'

'Of course he has,' said Julia. 'What *is* all this mystery about? I've seen his sister—exactly like him, small and neat. She doesn't live here, she lives at Marlow.'

Fatty let out an enormous sigh. 'Why didn't I think of a twin?' he said. 'Of course! The *only* solution! He got his twin to come and do his show for him. Is she good too, Julia?'

'Well, they're both in shows,' said Julia. 'As a matter of fact, Alec is supposed to be much better than Nora, his sister. I thought he wasn't so good last Friday, really—he had such a terrible cold, for one thing, and kept stopping to cough.'

The others immediately looked at one another. Oho! A cough and a cold! Certainly Alec hadn't had one on Monday afternoon when they had all heard him sing. Nobody had seen any sign of a cold or cough then. Very, very suspicious!

'May we take this album away for a little while?' asked Fatty. 'I'll send it back. Thanks so much for seeing us. You've been a great help.'

'I don't know how,' said Julia. 'It seems very mysterious to me.'

'It *has* been very mysterious,' said Fatty, preparing to go. 'Very, very mysterious. But I see daylight now, though I very—nearly—didn't!'

The Five Find-Outers went off with Buster, excited and talkative. 'We've got it all straightened out now,' said Fatty, happily. 'Thanks to Bets. Honestly, Bets, we'd have been absolutely stumped if you hadn't made that sudden remark. It was a brainwave.'

They got back to Peterswood, having decided what to do. They would go and see Pippin first, and tell him all they knew. Fatty said they owed it to him to do that, and if he wanted to arrest Alec Grant, he could. What sucks for Goon!

THE LAST ALIBI IS CHECKED

But when they got to Goon's house, they had a shock. Pippin was there alone, looking very gloomy.

'Ah, Master Frederick,' he said, when he saw Fatty, 'I've been trying to telephone you for the last hour. Mr. Goon's arrested Boysie and Zoe, and they're both in an awful state! I'm afraid Boysie will go right off his head now.'

'Where are they?' asked Fatty, desperately.

'Goon's taken them over to the Inspector,' said Pippin. 'What's the matter with *you*? You look all of a dither.'

'I am,' said Fatty, sitting down suddenly. 'Pippin, listen hard to what I'm going to tell you. And then tell us what to do. Prepare for some shocks. Now—listen!'

22   A SURPRISE FOR THE INSPECTOR!

PIPPIN listened, his eyes almost falling out of his head. He heard about the false clues and frowned. He heard about the way the children had interviewed the Suspects by means of asking for autographs—he heard about the tea-party—the checking up of the alibis—and then he heard of Bet's bright remark that had suddenly set Fatty on the right track.

The autograph albums were produced and compared. The visit to Sheepridge related. The twin-sister came into the story, and P.C. Pippin rubbed his forehead in bewilderment as Fatty produced the many, many pieces of the jigsaw puzzle that, all fitted together, made up a clear solution of the mystery.

'Well! I don't know what to think,' said poor Pippin. 'This beats me! Goon's got the wrong ones, no doubt about that. And I think there's no doubt that Alec Grant is the culprit.'

'Can you arrest him then and take him to the Inspector?' cried Fatty.

'No. Of course not,' said Pippin. 'Not just on what you've told me. But I'll tell you what we *can* do—I can go and get him for questioning. I can take him over to the Inspector and face him with all you've said.'

'Oh *yes*—that's a fine idea,' said Fatty. 'Can we come too?'

'You'll have to,' said Pippin. 'My word, I shan't like to look at the Inspector's face when he hears about those false clues of yours. Good thing you've solved the mystery, that's all I can say. Let's hope that will cancel out the mischief you got into first.'

Pippin's voice was stern, but his eyes twinkled. 'Can't be really cross with you myself,' he said. 'Your clues put me where I could see the crime when it was just done—and now it looks as if I'll be able to show Goon up. He deserves it, browbeating that poor, queer-headed fellow into a false confession!'

The morning went on being more and more exciting. Alec Grant was collected from the theatre, where he was rehearsing with the others, who were most alarmed at Zoe's arrest. He put on a very bold face and pretended that he hadn't the least idea why Pippin wanted to question him.

He was very surprised to see all the children also crammed into the big car that Pippin had hired to take them over to see the Inspector. But nobody explained anything to him. The children looked away from him. Horrid, beastly thief—and how *could* he let Zoe and Boysie take the blame for something he himself had done?

Pippin telephoned to the Inspector before they left. 'Sir? Pippin here. About that Little Theatre job. I believe Mr. Goon's brought his two arrests over to you. Well, sir, can you hold things up for a bit? I've got some fresh evidence here, sir. Very important. I am bringing some one over to question—man named Alec Grant. Also, sir, I'm bringing—er—five children.'

'*What?*' said Inspector Jenks, thinking he must have misheard. 'Five *what*?'

'CHILDREN, sir,' said Pippin. 'You know, sir, you told me about them before I came here. One's a boy called Frederick Trotteville.'

'Oh, *really*?' said the Inspector. 'That's most interesting. So he's been working on this too, has he? Do you know what conclusions he has come to, Pippin?'

'Yes, sir, I know all about it,' said Pippin. 'Er—Mr. Goon didn't want me to work with him on this case, sir, so—er—well . . .'

'So you worked with Frederick, I suppose,' said the Inspector. 'Very wise of you. Well—I'll hold things up till you come.'

He called Goon into his room. 'Er, Goon,' he said, 'we must wait for about twenty minutes before proceeding with anything. Pippin has just phoned through. He's got fresh evidence.'

Goon bristled like a hedgehog. '*Pippin*, sir? He doesn't know a thing about this case. Not a thing. I wouldn't let him work with me on it, he's such a turnip-head. Course, he's only been with me a little while, but it's easy to see he's not going to be much good. Not enough brains. And a bit too cocky, sir, if you'll excuse the slang.'

'Certainly,' said the Inspector. 'Well, we will wait. Pippin is bringing a man for questioning.'

Goon's mouth fell open. 'A man—for questioning? But we've *got* the people who did the job now. What's he want to bring a man for? Who is it?'

'And he's also bringing five children, he says,' went on the Inspector, enjoying himself very much, for he did not like the domineering, conceited Mr. Goon. 'One of them is, I believe, that clever boy—the one who has helped us in so many mysteries—Frederick Trotteville!'

Goon opened and shut his mouth like a goldfish and for two minutes couldn't say a single word. He went slowly purple and the Inspector looked at him in alarm.

'You'll have a heart-attack one of these days, Goon, if you get so angry,' he said. 'Surely you don't mind Frederick coming over? You are quite sure you have solved the case yourself, and arrested the right people—so what is there to worry about?'

'I'm not worrying,' said Goon, fiercely. 'That boy—that toad—begging your pardon, sir—always interfering with the Law—always. . .'

'Now Goon, he *helps* the Law, he doesn't interfere with it,' said the Inspector.

Goon muttered something about toads and turnip-heads, and then subsided into deep gloom. Pippin coming—and all those dratted children. What was UP?

Pippin duly arrived with Alec Grant, the five children, and, of course, Buster. Goon's face grew even blacker when he saw Buster, who greeted him with frantic joy, as if he was an old friend, tearing round his feet in a most exasperating way.

'Ah, Frederick—so you're on the job again,' said the Inspector. 'Pleased to see you. Hallo, Larry—Pip—Daisy—and here's little Bets too. Have they turned you out of the Find- Outers yet, Bets?'

'Turned her out! I should think not,' said Fatty. 'If it hadn't been for Bets we'd never have hit on the right solution.'

There was a growl from Goon at this. The Inspector turned to him. 'Ah, Goon—you also think you have hit on the right solution, don't you?' he said. 'Your two arrests are in the other room. Now—what makes you think you have solved the case correctly, Goon? You were just about to tell me when I got Pippin's telephone call.'

'Sir, there's a confession here from Boysie Summers, the Pantomime Cat,' said Goon. 'Says as clear as a pike-staff that he did the job, with Zoe Markham to help him. This here's her handkerchief, found on the verandah on the night of the crime—Z, for Zoe, in the corner, sir.'

'Oh!' said Daisy. 'That's *my* old hanky, Inspector! And I put the Z in the corner, just for a joke. Didn't I, you others?'

The other four nodded at once. 'It's certainly not Zoe's,' said Daisy. 'She'd never have a dirty, torn old hanky like this. I should have thought Mr. Goon would have guessed that.'

Mr. Goon began to breathe heavily. 'Now look here!' he began.

'Wait, Goon,' said the Inspector, picking up the 'confession.' 'So this is what Boysie said, is it? Bring him in, Pippin. He and Zoe are in the next room. They can both come in.'

Pippin went to fetch Zoe and Boysie. Zoe was in tears, and so upset that she didn't even seem to see the five children. She went straight up to the Inspector and tapped the 'confession' he held in his hand.

'Not one word of that is true!' she said. 'Not one word! *He* forced Boysie to say things that weren't true. Look at Boysie—can you imagine him doing a crime like that, even with my help? He's nothing but a child, for all he's twenty-four. That policeman badgered him and terrified him and threatened him till poor Boysie was so frightened he said anything. Anything! It's wicked, really *wicked*!'

Boysie stood beside her. The children hardly knew him, out of his cat-skin. He did seem only a child—a child that trembled and shook and clutched at Zoe's dress. Bets felt the tears coming into her eyes.

'Well, Miss Markham,' said Inspector Jenks, 'we have here some one else for questioning. I think you know him.'

Zoe turned and saw Alec. 'Alec Grant!' she said. 'Did *you* do it, Alec? Alec, if you did, say so. Would you let poor Boysie be sent *right* off his head with this, if you could help it? You hated the manager. You always said so. Did *you* do it?'

Alec said nothing. The Inspector turned to Pippin. 'Pippin—will you say why you have brought this man here, please? '

Pippin began his tale. He told it extremely well and lucidly. It was plain to see that P.C. Pippin would one day make a very good policeman indeed!

The Inspector interrupted occasionally to ask a question, and sometimes Fatty had to put a few words in too. Goon sat with his mouth open, his eyes almost bulging out of his head.

Alec Grant looked more and more uncomfortable as time went on. When Pippin and Fatty between them related how the children had gone to Sheepridge and seen the different autograph in Julia's album—which Pippin placed before the Inspector as evidence—he turned very pale.

'So you think this man here got his twin-sister to impersonate him, whilst he slipped back to the theatre, doped Boysie, got into the cat-skin, took up a doped cup of tea to the manager, robbed the safe, and then pulled the skin on the sleeping Boysie again?' said Inspector Jenks. 'A most ingenious crime. We must get on to this man's twin-sister. We must pull her in too.'

'Here!' said Goon, in a strangled sort of voice. 'I can't have this. I tell you that man's not the culprit—he *didn't* do it. Haven't I got that confession there for you to see?'

And then poor Goon got a terrible shock. 'I *did* do it!' said Alec Grant. 'Exactly as P.C. Pippin described it. But leave my sister out of it, *please*! She knows nothing about it at all! I telephoned her and begged her to take my place at the concert, and she did. She's done that before when I've felt ill, and nobody has known. We're as alike as peas. I impersonate women, as you know–and who's to know the difference if my sister impersonates *me*? No one! Only these kids—they're too clever by half!'

Inspector Jenks took the 'confession' and tore it in half. 'There's a fire behind you, Goon,' he said, in a cold voice. 'Put this in, will you?'

And Goon had to put the wonderful 'confession' into the fire and watch it burn. He wished he could sink through the floor. He wished he was at the other end of the world. If ever cruelty and stupidity and conceit were punished well and truly, then they were punished now, in the person of Goon.

'I've got all the money,' said Alec. 'I meant to give it

back, really. It was just to give the manager a nasty shock-he's a mean old beast. If I'd known Boysie and Zoe were arrested I'd have owned up.'

'You *did* know,' said Pippin, quietly. 'No good saying that now.'

'Well,' said the Inspector, leaning back and looking at the children. 'Well! Once more you appear to have come to our rescue, children. I'm much obliged to you, Pippin, my congratulations—you handled this case well, in spite of being forbidden to work with Goon. Frederick, you are incorrigible and irrepressible—and if you place any more false clues I shall probably be forced to arrest you! You are also a very great help, and most ingenious in your tackling of any problem. Thanks very much!'

The Inspector beamed round at the five children and Pippin, including Zoe and Boysie in his smile. Bets slipped her hand into his. 'You don't *really* mean you'd arrest Fatty?' she said, anxiously. 'We were all as bad as he was with those clues and things, Inspector.'

'No. I was pulling his leg,' said the Inspector. 'Not that I approve of that sort of behaviour at all, you understand—very reprehensible indeed—but I can't help feeling that what you all did later has quite cancelled out what came before! And now, do you know what time it is? Two o'clock. Has any one had any lunch?'

Nobody had, and the children suddenly became aware of a very hollow feeling in their middles.

'Well, I hope you will do me the honour of lunching with me at the Royal Hotel,' said the Inspector. 'I'll get some one to telephone your families, who will no doubt be searching the countryside for you now! And perhaps Miss

Zoe would come too—and er—the Pantomime Cat?'

'Oh, thank you,' said Zoe, all smiles. 'Are we quite free now?'

'Quite,' said the Inspector. 'Goon, take this fellow Grant away. And wait here till I come back. I shall have a few words to say to you.'

Goon, looking like a pricked balloon, took Alec Grant away. Bets heaved a sigh of relief. 'Oh, Inspector Jenks, I was *so* afraid you'd ask Mr. Goon to come out to lunch too! '

'Not on your life!' said the Inspector. 'Oh, you're there too, Pippin. Go and get yourself a good meal in the police-station canteen, and then come back here and write out a full report of this case for me. And ring the children's parents, will you?'

Pippin saluted and grinned. He was very bucked with himself. He winked at Fatty and Fatty winked back. Aha! There would be a spot of promotion for Pippin if he went on handling cases like this.

'I've really enjoyed this mystery,' said Bets, as she sat down at a hotel table and unfolded a snowy-white napkin. 'It was very, very difficult—but it wasn't frightening at all.'

'Oh yes it was—to me and Boysie,' said Zoe, She filled a glass with lemonade and held it up to the children.

'Here's to you!' she cried. 'The Five Find-Outers—and Dog!'

The Inspector raised his glass too, and grinned. 'Here's to the great detectives—who solved the insoluble and most mysterious case in their career—the Mystery of the Pantomime Cat!'

Also available in the Mystery Series

THE MYSTERY OF THE BURNT COTTAGE

This is the first of Enid Blyton's thrilling mystery books. Fatty, Larry, Daisy, Pip, Bets—and Buster the dog—turn detectives when a mysterious fire destroys a thatched cottage in their village. Calling themselves the 'Five Find-Outers and Dog' they set out to solve the mystery and discover the culprit. The final solution, however, surprises the Five Find-Outers almost as much as Mr. Goon, the village policeman. They can hardly wait for the next mystery to come along!

THE MYSTERY OF THE DISAPPEARING CAT

The second book in the popular Mystery series in which the Find-Outers—Larry, Fatty, Daisy, Pip, Bets and Buster the dog—turn detectives again to solve a very puzzling mystery.

A valuable Siamese cat is stolen from next door and suspicion falls on the children's friend, Luke the gardener's boy. How can they find the real thief and clear Luke of blame, especially with Mr. Goon the policeman interfering as usual? The Find-Outers are plunged into the middle of a first class mystery with only the strangest of clues to work on.

THE MYSTERY OF THE SECRET ROOM

This is the third book in the Mystery series.

It is the Christmas holidays, and the Five are looking for mysteries. Then out of the blue Pip discovers a room, fully furnished, at the top of an empty house. Whose room is it? What is it used for? This is the problem that must be solved in *The Mystery of the Secret Room*. With the help of their friend Inspector Jenks, the Five Find-Outers eventually reach a solution in this most entertaining book.

THE MYSTERY OF THE SPITEFUL LETTERS

This is the fourth in the amusing adventures of the Five Find-Outers, and Dog. Fatty, Larry, Daisy, Pip and Bets are together once more for the Easter Holidays and quickly become involved in a very peculiar situation, trying to solve the mystery of the spiteful letters that arrive unsigned, for various people in Peterswood.

Mr. Goon, the policeman, tries to solve the mystery too, and comes up against Fatty, who in various disguises, manages to mystify the poor old policeman completely.

THE MYSTERY OF THE MISSING NECKLACE

The fifth book of the popular Mystery series, in which Fatty, Larry, Daisy, Pip, Bets—and Buster the dog, all play their parts as Find-Outers.

There are a great many clever burglaries going on and it is suspected that members of the gang have their meeting place somewhere in Peterswood. The children naturally determine to solve the mystery, and they tumble into other mysteries, too, in the process. Who is the old man on the seat? Who is Number Three? Where is the missing necklace? For once Mr. Goon, the policeman, defeats Fatty one strange night at the Waxworks Hall! But it all ends up most unexpectedly and amusingly with the children finally triumphant.

THE MYSTERY OF THE VANISHED PRINCE

Fatty, the Chief of the Five Finder-Outers, is very good at disguising himself so that even his friends do not recognise him. But it is when he comes back from a holiday and dresses up Pip, Bets, Larry and Daisy in Moroccan finery that trouble begins. What had started as a good joke turns into an exciting search for a missing Indian prince. This is the ninth Enid Blyton Mystery, and as always suspense and drama are mixed up with hilarity!

Enid Blyton's

THE MYSTERY

OF THE INVISIBLE THIEF

Enid Blyton's

THE MYSTERY

OF THE INVISIBLE THIEF

MAMMOTH

CONTENTS

1   ONE HOT SUMMER'S DAY

'DO you know,' said Pip, 'this is the fourth week of the summer holidays—the fourth week, mind—and we haven't even *heard* of a mystery!'

'Haven't even smelt one,' agreed Fatty. 'Gosh, this sun is hot. Buster, don't pant so violently—you're making me feel even hotter!'

Buster crawled into a patch of shade, and lay down with a thump. His tongue hung out as he panted. Bets patted him.

'Poor old Buster! It must be frightful to have to wear a fur coat this weather—one you can't even unbutton and have hanging open!'

'Don't suggest such a thing to Buster,' said Fatty. 'He'd look awful.'

'Oh dear—it's too hot even to laugh,' said Daisy, picturing Buster trying to undo his coat to leave it open.

'Here we are—all the Five Find-Outers—and Dog,' said Larry, 'with nothing to find out, nothing to solve, and eight weeks to do it in! Fatty, it's a waste of the hols. Though even if we had a mystery I think I'd be too hot to think about Clues and Suspects and what-nots.'

The five children lay on their backs on the grass. The sun poured down on them. They all wore as little as possible, but even so they were hot. Nobody could bear poor Buster near them for more than two seconds, because he absolutely radiated heat.

'Whose turn is it to fetch the iced lemonade?' said Larry.

'You know jolly well it's yours,' said Daisy. 'You always ask that question when it's your turn, hoping somebody will get it out of turn. Go and get it, you lazy thing.'

Larry didn't move. Fatty pushed him with his foot. 'Go on,' he said. 'You've made us all feel thirsty now. Go and get it.'

A voice came up the garden. 'Bets! Have you got your sun-hat on? And what about Pip?'

Bets answered hastily. 'Yes, Mother—it's quite all right. I've got mine on.'

Pip was frowning at her to warn her to say nothing about him. He had, as usual, forgotten his hat. But his mother was not to be put off.

'What about Pip? Pip, come and get your sun-hat. Do you want sunstroke *again*?'

'Blow!' said Pip, and got up. Larry immediately said what everybody knew he would say.

'Well, you might as well bring back the iced lemonade with you, old chap.'

'You're jolly good at getting out of your turn,' grumbled Pip, going off. 'If I'd been quick enough I'd have told you to get my hat when you got lemonade. All right, Mother. I'm COMING!'

The iced lemonade revived everyone at once. For one thing they all had to sit up, which made them feel much more lively. And for another thing Pip brought them back a bit of news.

'I say—do you know what Mother just told me?' he said. 'Inspector Jenks is coming to Peterswood this afternoon!'

'*Is* he?' said everyone, intensely interested. Inspector Jenks was a great friend of theirs. He admired the Five Find-Outers very much, because of the many curious mysteries they had solved. 'What's he coming for?' asked Fatty. 'I say—there's not a mystery on, is there?'

'No, I'm afraid not,' said Pip. 'Apparently his little god-daughter is riding in that gymkhana in Petter's Field this afternoon, and he's promised to come and see her.'

'Oh—what a disappointment,' said Daisy. 'I thought he might be on the track of some exciting case or other.'

'I vote we go and say how do you do to him,' said Fatty. Everyone agreed at once. They all liked the burly, good-looking Inspector, with his shrewd twinkling eyes and teasing ways. Bets especially liked him. Next to Fatty, she thought he was the cleverest person she knew.

They began to talk of the mysteries they had solved, and how Inspector Jenks had always helped them and encouraged them.

'Do you remember the Missing Necklace and how we found it?' said Larry. 'And that hidden house mystery—that was super!'

'The most exciting one was the mystery of the Secret Room, *I* think,' said Pip. 'Gosh—I shall never forget how I felt when I climbed that tree by the big empty house—looked into a room at the top and found it all furnished!'

'We've had some fun,' said Fatty. 'I only hope we'll have some more. We've never been so long in any holidays without a mystery to solve. The old brains will get rusty.'

'Yours could never get rusty, Fatty,' said Bets admiringly. 'The things you've thought of! And your disguises! You haven't done any disguising at all these hols. You aren't tired of it, are you?'

'Gosh, no,' said Fatty. 'But for one thing it's been too hot—and for another old Goon's been away, and the other bobby in his place is such a stodge. He never looks surprised at anything. I'll be quite glad whenGoon comes back and we hear his familiar yell of "You clear-orf!" Old Buster'll be pleased too—you miss your ankle-hunt, don't you, Buster?'

Bets giggled. 'Oh dear—the times Buster has danced round Mr. Goon's ankles and been yelled at. Buster really is wicked with him.'

'Quite right too,' said Fatty. 'I hope Goon comes back soon, then Buster can have a bit of exercise, capering round him.'

Buster looked up at his name and wagged his tail. He was still panting. He moved near to Fatty.

'Keep off, Buster,' said Fatty. 'You scorch us when you come near. I never knew such a hot dog in my life. We ought to fix an electric fan round his neck or something.'

'Don't make jokes,' begged Daisy. 'It's honestly too hot to laugh. I don't even know how I'm going to walk to Petter's Field this afternoon to see the Inspector.'

'We could take our tea, and ask the Inspector, plus god-daughter, to share it,' said Fatty.

'Brilliant idea!' said Daisy. 'We could really talk to him then. He might have a bit of news. You never know. After all, if there's any case on, or any mystery in the air, he's the one to know about it first.'

'We'll ask him,' said Fatty. 'Get *away*, Buster. Your tongue is dripping down my neck.'

'What we want, for a bit of excitement,' said Pip,' is a nice juicy mystery, and Goon to come back and make a mess of it as usual, while we do all the solving.'

'One of these days Goon will do all the solving and we'll make a mess of it,' said Daisy.

'Oh *no*,' said Bets. 'We couldn't possibly make a mess of it if Fatty's in charge.' The others looked at her in disgust—except Fatty, of course, who looked superior.

'Don't set Fatty off, for goodness sake,' said Pip. 'You're always hero-worshipping him. He'll be telling us of something wonderful he did last term, now.'

'Well, as a matter of fact, I forgot to tell you, but something rather extraordinary *did* happen last term,' said Fatty. 'It was like this . . .'

'I don't know the beginning of this story but I'm sure I know the end,' said Larry, gloomily.

Fatty was surprised, 'How can you know the end if you don't know the beginning?' he asked.

'Easily, if it's to do with you,' said Larry. 'I'm sure the end would be that you solved the extraordinary happening in two minutes, you caught the culprit, you were cheered and clapped to the echo and you had "As brilliant as ever" on your report. Easy!'

Fatty fell on Larry and soon they were rolling over and over on the grass with Buster joining in excitedly.

'Oh shut up, you two,' said Pip, rolling out of the way. 'It's too hot for that. Let's decide about this afternoon. Are we going to take our tea or not? If we are I'll have to go and ask my mother now. She doesn't like having it sprung on her at the last minute.'

Larry and Fatty stopped wrestling, and lay panting on their backs, trying to push Buster off.

'Yes, of course we're going to take our tea,' said Fatty. 'I thought we'd decided that. There'll be tea in the marquee in Petter's Field, of course, but it'll be stewing hot in there, and you know what marquee teas are like. We'll take ours and find the Inspector. He won't like marquee teas any more than we do, I'm sure.'

'There's a dog show as well as the gymkhana,' said Bets. 'Couldn't we enter Buster—or is it too late?'

'The only prize he'd win to-day is for the hottest dog,' said Fatty. 'He'd win that all right. Buster, keep *away* from me. You're like an electric fire.'

'We'd better go,' said Larry, getting up with a groan. 'It takes twice as long to get back home this hot weather—we simply crawl along! Come on, Daisy, stir yourself!'

Daisy and Larry went down the drive and up the lane to their own home. Pip and Bets didn't have to move because they were already at home! Fatty found his bicycle and put his foot on the pedal.

'Buster!' he called. 'Come on. I'll put you in my bike-basket. You'll be a grease-spot if you have to run all the way home.'

Buster came slowly up, his tongue out as usual. He saw the cook's cat in the hedge nearby, but he felt quite unable to chase it. It was just as well, because the cat felt quite unable to run away.

Fatty lifted Buster up and put him in his basket. Buster was quite used to this. He had travelled miles in this way with Fatty and the others.

'You'll have to take some of your fat off, Buster,' said Fatty, as he cycled down the drive. 'You're getting too heavy for words. Next time you see Goon you won't be able to dance round him, you'll only waddle!'

A bell rang in Pip's house, 'Lunch,' said Pip sitting up slowly. 'Come on—I hope it's salad and jelly—that's about all I want. Don't let's forget to ask Mother about a picnic tea for this afternoon. She'll probably be glad to get rid of us.'

She was! 'That's a good idea!' she said. 'Tell Cook what you want—and if you take drinks *please* leave some ice in the frig. You took it all last time. Yes—certainly a picnic is a very good idea—I shall have a lovely peaceful afternoon!'

2 AT THE GYMKHANA

THE five children, and Buster of course, met in Petter's field about three o'clock. The gymkhana had already begun, and horses were dashing about all over the place. Buster kept close to Fatty. He didn't mind passing the time of day with one or two horses in a field, but thirty or forty galloping about were too much.

'Anyone seen the Inspector?' asked Daisy, coming up with a big basket of food and drink.

'No, not yet,' said Fatty, getting out of the way of a colossal horse ridden by a very small boy. 'Is there any place in this field where there aren't horses tearing about! Buster will have a heart attack soon.'

'Look over there,' said Bets, with a giggle. 'See the woman who's in charge of that hoopla stall, or whatever it is? She might be Fatty dressed up!'

They all looked. They saw what Bets meant at once. The stall-woman had on a big hat with all kinds of flowers round it, a voluminous skirt, very large feet and a silk shawl pinned round her shoulders.

'Fatty could disguise himself like that beautifully!' said Daisy. 'Is she real—or somebody in disguise?'

'Inspector Jenks in disguise!' said Bets, with a giggle, and then jumped as somebody touched her on the shoulder.

'What's that you're saying about me?' said a familiar voice. All five of them swung round at once, their faces one big smile. They knew that voice!

'Inspector Jenks!' said Bets, and swung on his broad arm. 'We knew you were coming!'

'Good afternoon, sir,' said Fatty, beaming. 'I say, before anyone else gets hold of you—would you care to have a picnic tea with us—and bring your god-daughter too, of course. We've brought plenty of food.'

'So it seems,' said Inspector Jenks, looking at the three big baskets. 'Well, I wondered if I should see you here. Yes, I'd love to have tea with you—and so would Hilary—that's my small god-daughter. Well, Find-Outers—any more mysteries to report? What exactly are you working on now?'

Fatty grinned. 'Nothing, sir. Not a mystery to be seen or heard in Peterswood just now. Four weeks of the hols gone and nothing to show. Awful waste of time.'

'And Goon is away, isn't he?' said the Inspector. 'So you can't bait him either—life must indeed be dull for you. You wait till he comes back though— he'll be full of beans. He's been taking some kind of refresher course, I believe.'

'What's a refresher course?' asked Bets.

'Oh—rubbing up his police knowledge, refreshing his memory, learning a few new dodges,' said theInspector. 'He'll be a smart fellow when he comes back—bursting to try out all he's learnt. You look out, Frederick!'

'It does sound funny when you call Fatty by his right name,' said Bets. 'Oooh, Fatty—let's hope we don't have a mystery after all, in case Mr. Goon solves it instead of us.'

'Don't be silly,' said Pip. 'We can always get the better of Mr. Goon. It's a pity something hasn't happened while he's been away—we could have solved it before he came back, without any interruptions from him.'

'Here's my small god-daughter,' said the Inspector, turning round to smile at a small girl in jodhpurs and riding jacket. 'Hallo, Hilary. Won any prizes yet?'

Hilary sat on a fat little pony that didn't seem able to stand still. Buster kept well out of the way.

'Hallo, Uncle,' said Hilary. 'I'm going to ride now. I haven't won anything yet. Do you want to come and watch?'

'Of course,' said the Inspector. 'Let me introduce you to five friends of mine—who have helped me in many a difficult case. They want you and me to have a picnic tea with them. What about it?'

'Yes. I'd like to,' said Hilary, trying to stop her pony from backing on to an old gentleman nearby. 'Thank you.'

The pony narrowly missed walking on Buster. He yelped, and the restless little animal reared. Hilary slapped him and he tossed his head and knocked off the Inspector's trilby hat.

'Oh—sorry,' said Hilary, with a gasp. 'Bonny's a bit fresh, I'm afraid.'

'I quite agree,' said the Inspector picking up

his hat before Bonny could tread on it. 'All right, Hilary—I'll come and watch you ride now—and we'll all have tea together when you've finished.'

Hilary cantered off, bumping up and down, her hair flying out under her jockey cap. Buster was most relieved to see her go. He ventured out from behind Fatty, saw a friend he knew and trotted over to pass the time of day; but what with horses of all sizes and colours rushing about he didn't feel at all safe.

It was really a very pleasant afternoon. The policeman who had replaced Goon while he was on holiday stood stolidly in a shady corner, and didn't even recognize the Inspector when he passed. It is true that Inspector Jenks was in plain clothes, but Bets felt that *she* would recognize him a mile off even if he was wearing a bathing costume.

'Afternoon, Tonks,' said the Inspector, as they passed the stolid policeman. He leapt to attention at once, and after that could be seen walking about very busily indeed. The Inspector there! Was there anything up? Were there pick-pockets about—or some kind of hanky-panky anywhere? Tonks was on the look-out at once, and forgot all about standing comfortably in the shade.

Hilary didn't win a prize. Bonny really didn't behave at all well. He took fright at something and backed heavily into the judges, which made them look at him with much dislike and disfavour. Hilary was very disappointed.

She met them in a shady corner for tea, bringing Bonny with her. Buster growled. What—that awful horse again! Bonny nosed towards him and

Buster hastily got under a tent nearby, squeezing beneath the canvas.

Hilary was very shy. She would hardly say a word. She kept Bonny's reins hooked round one arm, which was just as well, as Bonny was really a very nosey kind of horse. Daisy kept a sharp eye on the baskets of food.

The Inspector talked away cheerfully. The children were disappointed that he had no cases to offer them, and no mystery to suggest.

'It's just one of those times when nothing whatever happens,' said Inspector Jenks, munching an egg-and-lettuce sandwich hungrily. 'No robberies, no swindlings, no crimes of any sort. Very peaceful.'

He waved his sandwich in the air as he spoke and it was neatly taken out of his hand by Bonny. Everyone roared at the Inspector's surprised face.

'Robbery going on nearby after all!' said Daisy. Hilary scolded Bonny, who backed away into the next picnic party. Buster put his nose out from under the tent canvas, but decided not to come out and join the party yet.

It was while all this was going on that the next mystery loomed up in the very middle of the picnic tea! Nobody expected it. Nobody realized it at first.

Pip happened to be looking down the field, where Mr. Tonks, the policeman, was standing beside the Red Cross Tent, having seen to somebody who had fainted in the heat. He stood there, mopping his forehead, probably feeling that he would be the next one to faint, when a man came quickly up to him. He looked like a gardener or handyman.

He spoke to Mr. Tonks, who at once took out his black note-book, licked his thumb and flicked over the pages till he came to an empty one. Then he began to write very earnestly.

Pip saw this, but he didn't think anything of it. But then Tonks walked over to where Inspector Jenks was sitting with the Five Find-Outers and Hilary.

'Excuse me for interrupting, sir,' he said. 'But there's been a daylight robbery in Peterswood. I'll have to go and investigate, sir. Seems pretty serious.'

'I'll come with you,' said the Inspector, much to the disappointment of the children. He glanced round. 'Sorry,' he said. 'Duty calls, and all that! I may not see you again, if I have to go straight back to my office. Thanks for a very fine tea. Good-bye, Hilary. You rode very well.'

He stepped straight back on to Bonny, who also backed and pulled Hilary right over with the reins. In the general muddle Fatty spoke to Mr. Tonks the policeman.

'Where was the robbery?' he asked.

'At Norton House,' said Mr. Tonks. 'Up on the hill, sir.'

'Don't know it,' said Fatty, disappointed. He stood up and spoke persuasively to the Inspector. 'I'll come along with you, sir, shall I? I—er—might be of a little help.'

'Sorry, Frederick—can't have you along just now,' said the Inspector. 'It'll be a plain enough job, I expect—rather beneath your powers! If it's not—well, you'll get going on it, no doubt!'

He went off with Tonks. Fatty stared after them gloomily. Now they would be first on the job—they would see everything, notice everything. And when Goon came back and took over from Tonks he would settle it all up and put a feather in his cap!

He sat down again. If only he could have gone to Norton House and had a snoop round himself! Now he really couldn't—the Inspector would be annoyed to see him there after he had said he didn't want him—and certainly the householders wouldn't allow him to look round all by himself, if he went after the Inspector had left.

'Never mind, Fatty,' said Bets, seeing how disappointed he was. 'It's only a silly little robbery, I expect. Nothing to bother about—no real mystery!'

Then something surprising happened. Hilary burst into tears! She wailed aloud and tears ran down her podgy cheeks.

'What's the matter? Do you feel sick?' asked Daisy, alarmed.

'No. Oh dear—it's *my* home that's been burgled!' wept Hilary. 'I live at Norton House. Uncle Jenks must have forgotten it's where I live. Oh, what shall I do?'

Fatty rose to the occasion at once. He put his arm round the weeping Hilary. 'Now now,' he said, producing an extremely clean white handkerchief, and wiping Hilary's face with it. 'Don't you worry. I'll take you home myself. I'll look after you. I'll even look all round your house to make sure there isn't a single robber left!'

'Oh, thank you,'said Hilary, still sniffing. 'I should hate to go home by myself.'

'We'd better wait a bit till your godfather has had time to look round himself,' said Fatty, who wasn't going to bump into the Inspector if he could help it. 'Then we'll go—and I'll soon see that everything is quite quite safe for you, Hilary!'

3 FATTY TAKES HIS CHANCE

THE others looked at Fatty in admiration. *Somehow* he always got what he wanted. Things always went right for him. He badly wanted to examine that burgled house, and he had been left behind by the Inspector and lo and behold, he could now go there, taking charge of Hilary, and nobody could say a thing against it!

'I can't go just yet,' sniffed Hilary. 'I've got to ride once more. You won't leave, will you? You *will* take me right home? You see, my parents are away, and there's only Jinny there—she's our housekeeper.'

Better and better! With no parents even to deal with, Fatty felt sure he could snoop as much as he wanted to. Larry and Pip looked at him rather jealously.

'We'll take Hilary home too,' said Larry.

'Better not,' said Fatty. 'Too many cooks etcetera, etcetera.'

Hilary looked at him, wondering what he meant. The others knew all right. Hilary's tears began to fall again. 'It's my riding prizes I'm thinking of,' she explained, between sobs. 'My cups, you know. I've won so many. The burglar might have taken them.'

This talk about prizes seemed rather surprising to the others, who had no opinion at all of either Hilary or Bonny as regards horsemanship. Fatty patted her on the shoulder and gave her his enormous handkerchief again.

'I'll come up to your room with you and see if your things are safe,' said Fatty, feeling very pleased to think of the first-hand examination he could make. 'Now don't cry any more, Hilary.'

Bets looked on a little jealously. That silly little Hilary! Why did Fatty make such a fuss of her? Surely he would be ashamed of her, Bets, if *she* fussed like that?

'I'll come too, Fatty,' she said. Fatty was about to say no, when he thought that probably it would be a good idea to let Bets come—Hilary could show her this, that and the other—and he could slip away unseen and snoop round by himself.

'Right, Bets,' he said. 'You can come—you'll be company for Hilary.' Bets was pleased. Now that silly little Hilary wouldn't have Fatty all to herself—she would see to that!

An enormously loud voice began calling over the field. 'Class 22, please take your places, Class 22.'

'That's my class,' said Hilary, scrambling to her feet. She pulled her cap straight and rubbed her eyes again. She brushed the crumbs off her jacket. Bonny neighed. He wanted to be off, now that he could see various horses moving about again. He had eaten as much tea as the others! He seemed to be an expert at nosing into baskets.

Hilary went off with Bonny, a podgy little figure with a tear-stained face. Fatty looked round triumphantly, winking at the others.

'I shall be in at the start, after all,' he said. 'Sorry you can't come, Pip, Larry and Daisy— but we can't all descend on the house. They'd smell a rat. Bets might be useful though, she can take up Hilary's attention whilst I'm looking round.'

Bets nodded. She felt proud to be in at the start with Fatty. 'Shall we go after Hilary's ridden in this show?' she asked. Fatty considered. Yes—Tonks and the Inspector should surely be gone by then.

So, after Class 22 had competed in jumping, and Hilary had most surprisingly won the little silver cup offered, Fatty, Bets and the rest moved off, accompanied by a suddenly cheerful Hilary.

She rode Bonny, who, now that he had won something, seemed a little more sensible. The others walked beside her, till they came to the lane where Larry and Daisy had to leave them. Then a little later Pip left them to go down the lane to his home. Fatty and Bets went on up the hill with Hilary. Buster kept sedately at Fatty's heels. He kept an eye on Bonny's legs and thought privately to himself that horses had been supplied with far too many hooves.

They came to Norton House. The Inspector's car was still outside. Blow! Fortunately Hilary didn't want to go in the front way. She wanted to take Bonny to the stables, which were round at the back.

Bonny was led into his stable. 'Don't you rub him down or anything before you leave him?' asked Fatty. 'I'd be pleased to do it for you, Hilary. You've had a tiring afternoon.'

Hilary thought that Fatty was the very nicest boy she had ever met in her life. Fancy thinking of things like that! She wouldn't have been so much impressed if she had known how desperately Fatty was trying to stay down in the stables till the Inspector had gone!

Fatty groomed the pony so thoroughly that even Hilary was amazed. Bets watched with Buster, rather bored. 'See if they've gone,' whispered Fatty to her, jerking his head towards the front garden. Bets disappeared. She soon came back. She nodded. Fatty straightened up, relieved. Now he could stop working on that fat, restless pony!

'Now we'll go to the house and find out exactly what happened,' said Fatty to Hilary. 'I expect your housekeeper is there. She'll tell us everything. Then you must show Bets all the prizes you have won. She'll love to see them. Won't you, Bets?'

'Yes,' said Bets, doubtfully.

'You must see them too, Fatty,' said Hilary. He nodded—also doubtfully.

'Come along,' said Hilary and they walked up a long garden path to the house. It was a nice house, square-built, with plenty of windows. Trees surrounded it, and it could not be seen from the road.

They went in at the back door. A woman there gave a little scream of fright. 'Oh, lawks! Oh, it's you Miss Hilary. I'm in such a state of nerves, I declare I'd scream if I saw my own reflection in a mirror!'

Fatty looked at her. She was a plump little woman, with bright eyes and a good-tempered, sensible mouth. He liked her. She sank down into a chair and fanned herself.

'I've heard about the robbery,' said Hilary. 'Jinny, this is a boy who's brought me home and this is a girl called Bets. They are friends of my godfather, Inspector Jenks.'

'Oh, *are* they?' said Jinny, and Fatty saw that they had gone up in her estimation at once. 'Ah, he's a fine man, that Inspector Jenks. So patient and kind. Went over everything, he did, time and time again. And the questions he asked me! Well there now, you'd never think anyone could pour them out like that!'

'It must have been a great shock for you, Jinny,' said Fatty, in his most courteous and sympathetic voice. He had a wonderful voice for that sort of thing. Bets looked at him in admiration. 'I was sorry for poor little Miss Hilary too. I felt I really must see her home.'

'That was real gentlemanly of you,' said Jinny, thinking that Fatty was just about the nicest boy she had ever met. 'She's nervous, is Miss Hilary. And I'll be nervous too, after this!'

'Oh, you don't need to be,' said Fatty. 'Burglars hardly ever come to the same place twice. Do tell us all about it—if it won't tire you too much.'

Jinny would not have been tired if she had told her story a hundred times. She began at once.

'Well, I was sitting here, half-asleep-like, with my knitting on my knee—about four o'clock it must have been. And I was thinking to myself, "I must really get up and put the kettle on to boil," when I heard a noise.'

'Oooh,' said Hilary faintly.

'What sort of noise?' asked Fatty, wishing he could take out his note-book and put all this down. Still, if he forgot anything, Bets would remember it.

'A sort of thudding noise,' said Jinny. 'Out there in the garden somewhere. Like as if somebody had thrown something out of the window and it had landed plonk in the garden.'

'Go on,' said Fatty, and Bets and Hilary listened, all eyes.

'Then I heard a cough upstairs somewhere,' said Jinny. 'A man's deep cough that was stifled quickly as if he didn't want to be heard. That made me sit up, I can tell you! "A man!" I ses to myself. "Upstairs and all! Can't be the master come back—anyway that's not his cough." So up I gets, and I yells up the stairs : "If there's anybody up there that shouldn't be, I'm getting the police!"'

She paused and looked at the others, gratified to see their intense interest.

'Very very brave of you,' said Fatty. 'What happened next?'

'Well—I suddenly sees a ladder outside,' said Jinny, enjoying herself thoroughly. 'The gardener's ladder, it looked like—run up against the wall leading to the Mistress's bedroom. And I thinks to myself, "Aha! Mister Robber, whoever you are, I'll see you coming down that ladder! I'll take good notice of you too! If you've got a bunion on your toe I'll notice it, and if you've got squint in your eye *I'll* know you again!" I know how important it is to notice what you can, you see.'

'Quite right,' said Fatty approvingly. 'And what *was* the robber like?'

'I don't know,' said Jinny, and she suddenly looked bewildered. 'He never came down that ladder after all!'

There was a pause. 'Well—how did he leave the house then?' asked Fatty. 'Did you hear him?'

'Never a sound,' said Jinny. 'I was standing in the hall, so I know he didn't come down the stairs—and there's only one set of stairs in this house. And there I stood, shivering and shaking I don't mind telling you—till I sees the telephone staring me in the face. And I grabs it and phones the police!'

'Go on,' said Fatty. 'What happened to the burglar? Was he still upstairs?'

'Well, just as I finished telephoning, who should come along but the baker and I yells to him, "Here you, come here and go upstairs with me. There's a burglar in the house." And the baker—he's a very very brave man for all he's so small—he came in and we went into every single room, and not a person was there. Not one!'

'He must have got out of another window,' said Fatty at last.

'He couldn't!' said Jinny triumphantly. 'They were all either shut and fastened, or there's a steep drop to the ground, enough to kill anyone taking a jump. I tell you, he had to come down the stairs or get down the ladder—and he didn't do either! There's a puzzle for you!'

'Well, he must still be there then,' said Fatty and Hilary gave a scream.

'He's not,' said Jinny. 'The Inspector, he looked into every hole and corner, even in the chest in your Ma's room, Miss Hilary. I tell you what *I* think—he made himself invisible! Oh, laugh if you like—but how else could he have got away without me seeing him?'

4 PLENTY OF CLUES

FATTY asked Jinny a great many questions, and she seemed very pleased to answer them. Hilary got bored. 'Come on upstairs and see my riding prizes,' she said. 'Jinny, *those* didn't get stolen, did they?'

'No, Miss Hilary dear—not one of them!' said Jinny comfortingly. 'I went to look, knowing as how you set such store on them. It's things like your Ma's little silver clock and some of the jewellery she left behind, and your father's cigarette box that have gone. All things from the bedrooms—nothing from downstairs that I can see.'

'Come on, Bets,' said Hilary, pulling Bets out of the room. 'Let's go upstairs. You come too, Fatty.'

Fatty was only too pleased. Hilary ran on ahead up the stairs. Fatty had a chance to whisper to Bets.

'You must pretend to be awfully interested, Bets, see? That will give me a chance to slip away and have a snoop round.'

Bets nodded. She was bored with the horsey little Hilary, but she would do anything for Fatty. They all went upstairs. Hilary took them into her little room. Bets was quite astonished to see the array of cups and other prizes she had won. She began to ask all kinds of questions at once, so that Fatty might slip away.

'What did you win this cup for? What's this? Why are there two cups exactly the same? What's this printed on this cup?'

Hilary was only too anxious to tell her. Fatty grinned. He was soon able to slip away, with Buster trotting at his heels. He went into all the bedrooms. He noticed that in most of the rooms the windows were shut and fastened as Jinny had said. In Hilary's parents' room the window was open. Fatty went to it and looked out. A ladder led down from it to the ground.

'That must be the ladder Jinny saw through the hall window,' thought Fatty. 'I saw it myself as we went to the stairs. How did that thief get down from upstairs without being seen, if Jinny didn't see him come down the stairs or the ladder? He can't be here still, because the stolen goods are gone—and anyway the place must have been thoroughly searched by the Inspector and Tonks.'

He went to see if there was any other window or balcony the thief could have dropped from unseen. But there wasn't.

Fatty concentrated his attention on the room from which the goods had been stolen. There were large dirty finger-marks on the wall by the window. Fatty studied them with interest.

'The thief wore gloves—dirty gloves too,' he thought. 'Well, he couldn't have been a very expert thief, to leave his prints like that! I'd better measure them.'

He measured them. 'Big-handed-fellow,' he said. 'Takes at least size eight and a half in gloves, probably nines. Yes, must be nines, I should think.

Hallo, he's left his glove-prints here too—on the polished dressing-table.'

There were the same big prints again showing clearly. Fatty looked at them thoughtfully. It should be easy to pick out this thief—he really had very large hands.

He went to the window again. He leaned out over the top of the ladder. 'He came up here by the ladder—didn't bother about the lower part of the house—he chucked the stuff out of the window—where did it land? Over there on that bed, I suppose. I'll go down and look. But yet he didn't get *down* by the ladder? Why? Was he afraid of Jinny spotting him as he went down? He knew she was in the hall because he heard her shouting.'

Fatty pondered deeply. How in the world had the thief got away without being seen? It was true he could have slipped out of any of the other windows, but only by risking a broken leg, because there was such a steep drop to the ground—no ivy to cling to, no balcony to drop down to. Fatty went round the top part of the house again, feeling puzzled.

He came to a boxroom. It was very small, and had a tiny window, which was fast-shut. Fatty opened it and looked down. There was a thick pipe outside, running right down to the ground.

'Now—*if* the window had been open instead of shut—and *if* the thief had been even smaller than I am—so that he could have squeezed painfully out of this tiny window—he might have got down to the ground from here,' thought Fatty. 'But the window's shut—and Jinny says all of them were,

Fatty leaned out over the top of the ladder

except the one with the ladder, and a few that nobody could leap from.'

He went downstairs, hearing Hilary still talking soulfully about her cups. He couldn't hear a word from Bets. Poor Bets! She really was a little brick.

'Who's that?' called Jinny sharply, as she heard Fatty come down the stairs.

'Only me,' said Fatty. 'Jinny it's a puzzle how that thief got away without being seen, isn't it? Especially as he must have been rather a big fellow, judging from the size of his hands. I've been looking at all the windows. There's only one that has a pipe running by it down to the ground—the one in the box room— a tiny window. Was that shut?'

'Oh yes,' said Jinny. 'The Inspector asked me that same question, sir. He said he found it shut too. And you're right—the thief couldn't possibly have squeezed out of that small window, he's too big. You should see his foot-prints out there on the bed—giant-size, I reckon!'

'I'll go and see, if you don't mind,' said Fatty. Jinny didn't mind at all—she was only too pleased to let Fatty do anything—a nice, polite boy like that! You didn't come across them every day, more's the pity!

Fatty went out into the garden. He went to where the ladder was raised up against the house. He looked at the bed below. There were quite a lot of foot-prints there—certainly the thief had a large foot as well as large hands! 'Wears a shoe about size eleven or twelve,' thought Fatty. 'Hm! Where's my measure?'

Fatty measured a print and recorded it in his note-book. He also made a note of the pattern of the rubber heel that the thief wore on his boots—it showed clearly in the prints.

Then he went to where the thief had thrown the stolen goods. They had been thrown well away from the ladder, and had fallen in a bush, and on the ground around. Fatty poked about to see if he could find anything. He felt sure he wouldn't, because the Inspector had already been over the ground—and Fatty had a great respect for Inspector Jenks' ability to discover any clue left lying about!

He came across a curious print—large, roundish, with criss-cross lines showing here and there. What could the thief have thrown out that made that mark? He went to ask Jinny.

'Ah, the Inspector, he asked me that too,' she said. 'And I couldn't tell him. There was nothing big taken as far as I know, sir. I've seen the mark too—can't think what made it! It's a queer mark —roundish like that, and so big—big as my largest washing-up bowl!'

Fatty had measured the queer print and drawn it in his book, with the little criss-cross marks on it here and there. Funny. What could it be? It must have something to do with the robbery.

He shut up his book. There was nothing more he could examine or find, he hadn't discovered anything that the Inspector hadn't—probably he hadn't discovered so much! If the Inspector had found anything interesting he would have taken it away. What a pity Fatty hadn't been on the spot with him when he came with Tonks!

'It won't be much of a mystery, I suppose,' thought Fatty, going upstairs with Buster to fetch Bets. 'Surely a thief as large as this one will be easily found and caught. I shouldn't be surprised if the Inspector hasn't got him already!'

This was rather a disappointing thought. Fatty went into Hilary's room and smiled when he saw poor Bets' bored face. She smiled back delightedly at him.

'Oh, Fatty—is it time to go? Hilary has been telling me all about her prizes.'

'Yes,' said Hilary, looking pleased with herself. 'Shall I tell *you* now, Fatty? See, this one was. . .'

'Oh, I've heard quite a lot, off and on,' said Fatty. 'You're wonderful, Hilary! To think you've won all those! You really must be proud.'

'Oh well—' said Hilary, trying to look modest. 'See this one I. . .'

Fatty looked at his watch and gave such a loud exclamation that Bets jumped and Hilary stopped, startled.

'Good gracious! *Look* at the time! I shall have to see your prizes another time Hilary. Bets, I must take you home—you'll get in an awful row if you're any later.'

Hilary looked disappointed. She had been quite prepared to go over the whole history of her riding prizes once again. Bets was overjoyed to think Fatty was at last going to leave.

'Thanks awfully, Hilary, for giving me such a lovely time,' said Bets politely but not very truthfully. Fatty patted Hilary on the shoulder and said it had been a real pleasure to meet her. Hilary beamed.

She went down to the front gate with them, and waved till they were out of sight. Bets heaved a sigh of relief when they at last turned a corner and the waving could no longer be seen.

'Oh, Fatty—did you find out anything? Is it a mystery?' she asked eagerly. 'Tell me!'

'I don't somehow think it is,' said Fatty. 'Just an ordinary little burglary, with one or two queer little touches—but I expect the Inspector and Tonks have got more information than I have, actually, as they were there first. I'll go and see Tonks, I think. He might let out something.'

'Why not ask the Inspector?' said Bets, as they turned down the lane to her home.

'Er—no—I think not,' said Fatty. 'I don't particularly want him to know I snooped round after all. Tonks is the one to question. I'll see him to-morrow. Tell Pip I'll be round at eleven o'clock.'

He took Bets right up to the door of her house and said good night. 'And thanks most awfully for doing your bit for me,' he said. 'I know you were bored—but I couldn't have gone without you and snooped round—you were a real help.'

'Then I don't mind being bored,' said Bets. 'Oh dear—I never never want to hear about riding prizes again!'

5 SOME INFORMATION FROM TONKS

FATTY went home and walked down to the shed at the bottom of the garden where he kept his most valuable possessions.

He cast an eye over the various chests and boxes in his closely-guarded shed. Here he kept his disguises—old clothes of various kinds, hats, boots and ragged scarves. Here was a box containing many curious things that he didn't want his mother either to find or to throw away!

False teeth to put over his own—false cheek-pads to swell out his face—eyebrows of all colours—wigs that fitted him and wigs that didn't—big and little moustaches. Oh, Fatty had a most interesting collection in this shed of his at the bottom of the garden!

He gazed at the array of belongings. 'I'd like to do a spot of disguising,' he thought. 'I will whenGoon comes back. It's not much fun doing it now unless there's a mystery on, or Goon to deceive. Wonder when he's coming back. I'll ask Tonks to-morrow.'

He went to see Tonks the very next morning, about ten o'clock. Buster ran beside his bicycle. Fatty had decided he really was too fat for words—exercise would be good for him. So poor Buster panted beside the bicycle, his tongue lolling out first on one side of his mouth and then on the other.

Fatty knocked at the door. 'Come in!' cried a voice and in went Fatty. He found Tonks poring over a sheaf of papers. The stolid policeman looked up and nodded.

'Ah—Master Frederick Trotteville, isn't it? Great friend of the Inspector's, aren't you? He was telling me yesterday some of the things you'd done.'

This seemed a very good beginning. Fatty sat down. 'I don't know if you're too busy to spare me a minute,' he said. 'I took Miss Hilary home last night, she was so scared, poor little thing—you know, the Inspector's god-daughter.'

'Oh—so that's what he meant when he suddenly said "My word—Norton House—that's Hilary's home,"' said the policeman. 'I didn't like to ask him.'

'I expect he didn't realize it was his goddaughter's house that had been burgled, when he went off with you,' said Fatty. 'Anyway, she was frightened and I took her home. I had a look round, of course—and I wondered if I'd found anything of use to you.'

'Shouldn't think so, sir,' said Tonks. 'Not that I'm much of a one for solving cases—never have been—but the Inspector was there, you see, sir, and there's nothing much *he* misses. Still, it's very nice of you to come along and offer to help.'

'Not at all,' said Fatty, in his most courteous voice. 'Er—did *you* find anything interesting?'

'Oh—just finger-prints—or rather, glove-prints—and foot-prints,' said Tonks. 'Same as you did, I expect. Pretty big fellow the thief seems to have been. Made a good getaway too—nobody saw him go, nobody met him down the hill—might have been invisible!'

Fatty laughed. 'That's what Jinny said. You'd have thought a big fellow like that, carrying a sack or parcel of some kind, would have been noticed, wouldn't you? Pity the baker didn't spot him when he arrived with the bread.'

'Yes. He never saw a thing,' said Tonks. 'I must say it was pretty brave of him to go upstairs with Jinny and look all round—he's a tiny little fellow, and wouldn't be any match for a big man. I went along to see him last night. He reckons his coming disturbed the thief. He hadn't really stolen very much, as far as I can make out.'

'Did anyone else come that afternoon—to Norton House, I mean?' asked Fatty.

'The postman, a woman delivering election leaflets and a man selling logs, according to Jinny,' said Tonks. 'We've seen them all—they didn't notice anything out of the way, not even the ladder. Anyway, they came a good time before the thief.'

'Where was the gardener?' asked Fatty.

'He'd gone off to take some tackle down to the gymkhana for Miss Hilary,' said Tonks. 'He came back just as all the excitement was over. The baker sent him off to tell me about the robbery, so down he went to Petter's Field again.'

Fatty fell silent. This was a queer kind of thief—big, clumsy, easy to see—and yet apparently invisible! Not a soul had noticed him.

'Did you find any other clues?' asked Fatty. Tonks looked at him doubtfully. He had already said rather a lot to this polite and quite helpful boy. But ought he to tell him everything?

'You needn't worry about what you tell me,' said Fatty, seeing at once that Tonks had something else to say and wasn't sure about it. 'I'm a friend of the Inspector's—you know that. All I do is help if I can.'

'Yes. I know that,' said Tonks. 'The Inspector said "Well, well—if *we* can't find the thief, Tonks, Master Frederick certainly will!"'

'Well, there you are,' said Fatty, grinning. '*You* haven't found him yet—so give me a chance, Tonks.'

The policeman produced two dirty bits of paper. He handed them to Fatty, who looked at them with much interest. One had scribbled on it:

2 Frinton.

The other was even shorter. It simply said,

1 Rods.

'What do they mean?' asked Fatty, studying the dirty little scraps of paper.

'Don't know any more than you do,' said Tonks, taking them back. 'Number 2, Frinton. Number 1, Rods. Looks like addresses of some sort. But I'm not going off to Frinton or Rods, wherever they are, to hunt for the thief! We found these bits of paper near the bush where the stolen goods had been thrown.'

'Funny,' said Fatty. 'Do you think they've really anything to do with this case? They look like scraps of paper torn up by someone and thrown away.'

'That's what I said,' agreed Tonks. 'Anyway, I'll have to keep them, in case they're important.'

Fatty could see there was nothing else to find out from Tonks. He got up. 'Well—I wish you luck in finding the thief,' he said. 'It seems to me the only way to spot him will be to snoop round everywhere till we see a man wearing size twelve shoes and size nine gloves!'

Tonks gave a sudden grin. 'Well—if Mr. Goon likes to do that, he's welcome. He's taking over the case when he comes back. Nice for him to have something to do in this dead-and-alive hole. I'm used to a big town—I don't like these quiet country places where the only thing that happens is a dog that chases sheep, or a man that doesn't buy his wireless licence.'

Fatty could have told Tonks how wrong he was. He could have told him of all the extraordinary and exciting mysteries that had happened in Peterswood— but he didn't, because of Tonks' unexpected piece of news about Goon.

'Did you say Mr. Goon was coming back?' he asked. 'When?'

'You sound pleased,' said Tonks. 'I did hear you didn't like one another! He's coming back this afternoon. I hand over then. I shan't be having any more to do with this case. Anyway Goon ought to put his hands on the thief soon enough—he can't be far away.'

Fatty glanced at the clock on the mantelpiece. He must go, or he would keep the others waiting. He had found out all he wanted to know—though it wasn't much help really. And Goon was coming back! Old Goon. Clear-Orf, with his bombastic ways and his immense dislike of all the Five Find-Outers and their doings—to say nothing of Buster.

Fatty shook hands solemnly with Tonks, assured him that it had been a great pleasure to meet him, and went off on his bicycle, with Buster panting once again near the pedals.

The others were waiting for him in Pip's garden. It was very hot again, and they lay on their backs, with iced lemonade in a patch of shade.

'Here's old Fatty,' said Pip, hearing his bicycle bell ringing as Fatty came at sixty miles an hour up the drive. 'How in the world can he ride at that pace when it's so hot?'

But Fatty was the bringer of news, and he didn't think once about the heat as he came riding up the garden path to the others. He flung his bicycle down and beamed round at them all.

'Goon's coming back,' he said. 'This afternoon! *And* he'll take over the case of the Invisible Thief— so we shall have some fun.'

Everyone sat up at once. 'That's good news,' said Larry, who always enjoyed their tussle of wits with Goon. 'Did you see Tonks then? Had he anything to say?'

Fatty sat down. 'Not much,' he said. 'He and the Inspector didn't really find out any more than I did. I'll tell you what I found out yesterday in a minute— unless Bets has already told you?'

No, Bets hadn't. She had thought that Fatty ought to tell everything—so he got out his notebook and went into all the details of the new case.

He told them of the setting-up of the ladder— the large foot-prints in the bed below—the equally large glove-prints in the bedroom above—the throwing out of the stolen goods—the apparently completely invisible getaway.

'Only two ways of escape—down the ladder or down the stairs,' said Fatty. 'And Jinny the housekeeper was standing in the hall, where she could see both—and she swears nobody came down either stairs or ladder.'

'Must have got out of another upstairs window then,' said Pip.

'All either fastened and shut, or too far from the ground,' said Fatty. 'There's only one that might have been used—and that is a tiny window in a boxroom— there was a fat pipe running by it to the ground. Anyone could have slithered down that—if he was tiny enough to get out of the window! But—the window was shut and fastened when Jinny went round the upstairs part of the house.'

'Hm—well, no thief could squeeze out of a window, hold on to a pipe, and then shut and fasten the window after him—from the inside!' said Pip. 'It's a bit of a puzzle, isn't it? Jinny's right—the man's invisible!'

'Well, if he is, he'll certainly perform again,' said Larry. 'I mean—an invisible thief has a great advantage, hasn't he!'

Fatty laughed. He showed them his note-book with the drawings of the foot-prints, the glove-prints—and the curious round-shaped print with the faint criss-cross marks.

'Can't imagine what made *that* mark,' he said. 'It was near the bush where the stolen goods were thrown. And look—can anyone make anything of this?'

He showed them the curious addresses—if they were addresses—that he had copied into his notebook too.

'Number 2, Frinton. Number 1, Rods,' he said. 'Those words and numbers were found on two separate dirty scraps of paper near the bush. What on earth do they mean?'

'Frinton,' said Bets, wrinkling her forehead in a frown. 'Wait a minute. That rings a bell, somehow. Frinton. Frinton. *Frinton*! Where have I heard that lately?'

'Oh—one of your friends sent you a post-card from Frinton-on-Sea, I expect, silly,' said Pip.

'No. Wait a minute—I'm remembering!' said Bets. 'It's that place down by the river—not very far from here, actually—the place where they take visitors— Frinton Lea!'

'Clever old Bets,' said Fatty, admiringly. 'There may be something in that. If we find a large-sized fellow slouching about there, we'll keep a watch on him.'

'What about Number 1 Rods,' said Larry.

Nobody could think up anything for that.

'We'll go round looking at the names of houses and finding out if anyone has that name,' said Fatty. 'Rods. It's a peculiar name, anyhow. Well Find- Outers—the Mystery has begun!'

6 THE SECOND ROBBERY

MR. GOON arrived back that afternoon, bursting with importance. His refresher course and the things he had learnt at it had given him completely new ideas about his job. Ah, he knew a lot more about the ways of wrong-doers now! He knew a good deal more about how to catch them. And he also knew an enormous amount about the art of disguising himself.

It was entirely because of Fatty that Mr. Goon had applied himself to the course given in the Arts of Disguise. Fatty had bewildered, puzzled, angered and humiliated poor Mr. Goon so many times because of his artful disguises. The times that boy had turned up as a red-headed cheeky telegraph boy—or a dirty old man—or even a voluble and rude old woman!

Mr. Goon gritted his teeth whenever he thought of them. Now—NOW—Mr. Goon himself knew a bit about disguises, and he had brought back with him quite a remarkable collection of clothes and other gadgets.

He'd show that fat fellow he wasn't the only one to use disguises. Mr. Goon patted his pocket as he travelled home in the motor-coach. Grease-paint—eyebrows—a beard—a wig—he was bringing them all back. He'd trick that toad properly. A real toad, that was what that boy was.

Mr. Goon was most delighted to hear about the new robbery from Tonks. Ah—here was something he could get his teeth into at once. With all the new things he had learnt he could tackle this fresh case easily—toss it off, so to speak, long before Fatty had even begun it.

He was a little dashed to find that Fatty had apparently already heard about it and was interested in it. 'That boy!' he growled to Tonks. 'Can't keep his nose out of anything!'

'Well, he couldn't very well help it this time,' said Tonks stolidly. 'He was there when I went and reported the robbery to the Inspector.'

'He would be,' said Goon, scowling. 'Look here, Tonks—I tell you this—if the Crown Jewels were stolen one dark night, that boy would somehow know all about it—he'd be there!'

'Rather far-fetched, that,' said Tonks, who thought Goon was a bit of turnip-head. 'Well, I'll be going. I've given you all the details—you've got those scraps of paper, haven't you? With those addresses on?'

'Yes. I'm going to do something about those at once,' said Goon pompously. 'I reckon if those places are watched, something'll come out—and watched they will be.'

'Right,' said Tonks. 'Well, good-bye, Mr. Goon. Good Luck.'

He went off and Goon heaved a sigh of relief. He sat down to look through the papers that Tonks had left.

But he hadn't been studying them long before the telephone bell rang. Goon took off the receiver and put it to his ear. 'Police here,' he said gruffly.

Someone spoke volubly and excitedly at the other

end. Goon stiffened as he listened—ah—another robbery—things were getting interesting!

'I'll be along, Madam. Leave everything as it is. Don't touch a thing,' commanded Goon, in his most official voice. He put on his helmet and went out to get his bicycle.

'And this time those interfering children won't be there to pester me,' he thought, as he cycled quickly along in the heat. 'I'll be in first on this.'

He cycled through the village, turned up a sideroad, and came to a house. He got off his bicycle, wheeled it in at the gate, and went up to the front door.

It was opened by Fatty!

Mr. Goon gaped. He scowled. He couldn't think of a word to say. Fatty grinned.

'Good afternoon, Mr. Goon,' he said, in his politest voice, a voice that always infuriated Mr. Goon. 'Come in. We've been expecting you.'

'What are *you* doing here?' said Mr. Goon, finding his voice at last. 'Tricking me? Getting me here for nothing? I thought it all sounded a bit funny on the phone—silly sort of voice, and silly sort of tale. I might have guessed it was one of your tricks—just to welcome me home I suppose! Well—you'll be sorry for this. I'll report you! You think because the Inspector is friendly to you, you can get away with anything! You think . . .'

'Woof!' said somebody—and Buster darted out in ecstasy, so pleased to hear the voice of his old enemy that he wagged his tail for joy! That was enough for Goon. He departed hurriedly, muttering as he went, his bicycle wobbling down the path.

'Well!' said Fatty, in surprise. 'What's up with him? He can't *really* think I'm hoaxing him! Larry, come here. Goon's gone off his head!'

Larry and Daisy appeared. They looked after the departing Goon, who was now sailing out of the gate.

'He's gone,' said Fatty. 'He came—he saw—and he didn't stay to conquer. What's up with him?'

'You'd have thought that with another splendid robbery, he'd have stayed like a shot,' said Daisy.

'Well, Miss Lucy reported it fully,' said Fatty. 'I heard her on the telephone.'

Somebody called out to them. 'Was that the police? Tell them to come in here.'

'It was Mr. Goon,' said Fatty. 'He came—but he went at once. Funny.'

'Well, thank goodness you and Larry and Daisy are here,' said Mrs. Williams. 'I don't know what I should have done without you.'

It had all happened very suddenly indeed. Fatty had gone to tea with Larry and Daisy that afternoon, as Pip and Bets had gone out with their mother. They had been having tea in the garden, when someone from the house next door began to call for help.

'Help! Robbers! Help! Help, I say!'

'Gosh—that's Mrs. Williams yelling,' said Larry, getting up quickly. 'Our next-door neighbour.'

'What's happened?' asked Daisy, half-frightened at the continual shouts.

'She's been robbed,' said Fatty. 'Come on—quick!'

All three climbed over the fence and appeared in

the next-door garden. Mrs. Williams saw them from a window and beckoned. 'Come in, quickly! I'm scared!'

They rushed in at the back door. There was no one in the kitchen. A heap of groceries lay on the table, and four loaves sat neatly side by side. A parcel stood by the door.

Fatty's quick eyes noted everything as he ran through the kitchen into the hall. 'Kitchen door open—the thief went in there, probably. Wonder if it's the same one as yesterday.'

Mrs. Williams was sitting on her sofa, looking rather white. She was a gentle grey-haired old lady, and she was very frightened. 'Get me my smelling salts out of my bag,' she said faintly to Daisy. Daisy got them and she held them to her nose.

'What happened, Mrs. Williams?' said Fatty.

'Well, I was having my afternoon rest in here,' said Mrs. Williams. 'And I suddenly heard the soud of heavy foot-steps upstairs. Then I heard the sound of a deep, hollow sort of cough—rather like a sheep makes, really.'

'A hollow cough?' said Fatty, at once, remembering that Jinny had also heard the same noise.

'Yes. I sat up, scared,' said Mrs. Williams. 'I crept out of this room and went into the hall. And suddenly someone gave me a push into the cupboard there, and in I went. The door was locked on me, and I couldn't get out.'

Just as she was speaking there came the sound of a key in the front door, and then the door was opened and shut. 'Who's that?' asked Fatty.

'Oh, that's Lucy, my companion—Miss Lucy,' said

Mrs. Williams. 'Oh, I'm glad she's back. Lucy, Lucy, come here. A dreadful thing has happened!'

Miss Lucy came in. She was a little bird-like woman with very sharp eyes, and a funny bouncy way of walking. She went to Mrs. Williams at once.

'What is it? You look pale!'

Mrs. Williams repeated again what she had told the children. They waited patiently till she came to where she had been locked in the cupboard.

'Well, there I was in the hall cupboard, and I could hear the thief walking about overhead again,' said Mrs. Williams. 'Heavy-footed too, and clumsy by the way he knocked things over. Then he came downstairs—I heard him clearly because the stairs pass over the hall cupboard—and I heard that awful sheep-like cough again.'

She stopped and shuddered.

'Go on,' said Fatty gently. 'How did you get out of the cupboard? Did the thief unlock it?'

'He must have,' said Mrs. Williams. 'I was so scared when I heard him coming downstairs that I must have fainted—and when I came round again, I found myself lying in a heap on all the boots and shoes and golf-clubs—and the door was unlocked! I tried it—and it opened.'

'Hmmmm!' said Fatty. 'Miss Lucy, you'd better telephone the police, I think—and I'll take a little look round. This is very—very—interesting!'

7   MR. GOON ON THE JOB

MISS LUCY ran to telephone the police at once and as we know, got on to Mr. Goon. Very excitedly and volubly she told him all that had happened, and then the household waited for Mr. Goon to arrive.

Fatty took a hasty look round while they waited. He was sure the thief was the same as the one who had been to Norton House the day before. For one thing—that deep, hollow cough—and for another, the heavy-footed clumsiness sounded as if they belonged to the same burglar.

Fatty ran upstairs. The first thing he saw in one of the bedrooms was a print on the wall, just by the door—a large glove-print! He flicked open his notebook and compared it with the measurements detailed there. Yes—pretty well exactly the same.

Now what about any foot-prints in the garden? The ground was so dry now that unless the thief obligingly walked on a flower-bed, he probably wouldn't leave any prints.

Fatty was just going out to see, when he caught sight of Mr. Goon coming up the front drive, and went to the door. *What* a shock it would be for Mr. Goon to see him! Fatty really enjoyed opening the door.

He was surprised when Mr. Goon dashed off so soon. Surely he couldn't be idiotic enough really to think that Fatty had hoaxed him? Well, well—if so, then he, Fatty, might as well get on with his job of snooping round. Mr. Goon wouldn't have let him do that if he had taken charge of the case, that was certain.

So Fatty made hay while the sun shone and slipped out into the garden, leaving Larry and Daisy to try and explain Mr. Goon's sudden departure to Mrs. Williams and Miss Lucy. They were most indignant.

Fatty went out through the kitchen door. He had decided that the thief had come in that way, as the front door had been shut. He went down the path that led from the kitchen. He saw a bed of flowers and walked over to it. The bed was underneath the sitting-room window, and it was in that room that Mrs. Williams had been asleep.

Fatty gave an exclamation. On the bed were a couple of very large foot-prints. The same ones as yesterday—he was sure of it! He flicked open his book again.

The bed was drier than the one he had examined the day before for prints, and the rubber heel did not show this time—but the large prints were there, plain to see.

'The thief came and looked in at the window,' thought Fatty. 'And he saw Mrs. Williams fast asleep. Hallo—here are some more prints—on this bed. Why did he walk here?

There didn't seem any reason why the thief had walked on the second bed—but it was clear that the prints matched the others. In fact, everything matched—the glove-prints, the foot-prints, the hollow cough. Would there also be any mark like that big, roundish one that Fatty had seen at Norton House?

He hunted about for one; and he found it! It was very faint, certainly, and the criss-cross marks could hardly be seen. The roundish print was by the kitchen door, on the dusty path there. Something had been stood there—what was it?

'Any scraps of paper this time?' wondered Fatty, rather struck by the way that everything seemed to be repeated in this second case of robbery. He hunted everywhere—but there were no scraps of paper this time.

He went indoors, and met Miss Lucy coming out to find him. 'Mr. Goon has just telephoned,' she said. 'I can't make him out. He wanted to know if there had been a *real* robbery here! Well, why didn't he stay and ask us about it when he came? He must be mad.'

Fatty grinned. Goon had evidently thought the whole thing over and decided that he had better find out for certain what the truth was—and to his disgust he had found that the robbery was real—it wasn't a trick of Fatty's after all!

'He's a bit of a turnip-head,' said Fatty cheerfully. 'Never mind. You tell him I'm on the job when he comes—he needn't worry about it at all. I've got it well in hand.'

Miss Lucy looked doubtfully at Fatty. She was getting a little bewildered, what with thieves, and policemen who arrived and departed all in the same minute, and boys who seemed to be acting like policemen ought to, but didn't.

Fatty pointed to the groceries on the table. 'Who took these in?' he asked. 'Have you a cook?'

'Yes. But she's off for the day,' said Miss Lucy. 'I left the back door open for the grocer's girl to leave the groceries in the kitchen—she often does that for us. The baker's been too, I see—and the postman, because there's a parcel by the door. Mrs. Williams has been in all the afternoon, but she likes a nap, so the tradesmen never ring when Cook is out. They just leave everything, as you see.'

'Yes, I see,' said Fatty thoughtfully. He gazed at the groceries, the bread and the parcel. Three people had come to the house in a short time. Had one of them noticed the thief hanging about anywhere? He must find out.

Mr. Goon arrived again, a little shame-faced. Miss Lucy let him in, looking rather severe. She thought a policeman who behaved like Goon was ridiculous.

'Er—sorry I didn't come in before,' said Mr. Goon. 'Hope I've not kept you waiting too long—urgent business, you know. By the way—that boy—has he gone? The fat boy.'

'If you mean young Master Trotteville, he is still here, examining everything,' said Miss Lucy coldly. 'He told me to tell you not to bother about the job. He's got it well in hand. I am sure he will recover the jewellery Mrs. Williams has had stolen.

Goon turned a curious purple colour, and Miss Lucy felt rather alarmed. She felt that she didn't want this peculiar policeman in the house at all. She tried to shut the front door—but Goon put his enormous foot in the crack at once.

Miss Lucy gave a faint shriek, and Mr. Goon took his foot out again, trying to think of something reassuring to say to this aggravating, bird-like creature.

Miss Lucy promptly shut the door and even put up the chain. Goon stared at the door, and went purple again. He walked ponderously round to the back door, where he found Fatty examining the path for footprints.

'Gah! ' said Mr. Goon, in a tone of deep disgust. 'Can't get rid of you! First you're at the front door, now you're at the back door. You be off. This here case has got nothing to do wih you. Nothing.'

'That's where you're wrong, Mr. Goon,' said Fatty in the mild, courteous voice that made Goon see red. 'I was called in to help. I've found out a lot already.'

Larry and Daisy heard Goon's infuriated voice and came out through the kitchen to listen. They stood at the back door, grinning.

'You here too?' said Goon, in even greater disgust. 'Can't you keep your noses out of anything? Now, you clear-orf, all of you, and let me got on with my work here. And just you call off that dog! '

Buster had now joined the trio, and was capering delightedly round Mr. Goon's feet.

'He's missed his ankle-hunting,' Fatty explained. 'Don't grudge him a little fun, Mr. Goon. And don't you kick him. If you do I won't call him off.'

Mr. Goon gave it up. He pushed past Larry

and Daisy, went into the kitchen, still pursued by a delighted Buster, and through the door into the hall. By a clever bit of work he managed to shut the door of the kitchen on Buster, who scraped at it, barking wildly.

'Well, he's gone to do a spot of interviewing,' said Fatty, sitting down on the kitchen door-step. 'He won't find the two ladies very pleased with him, I fear. He's rather started off on the wrong foot with them.'

'Fatty, have you found out anything interesting?' asked Larry eagerly. 'I saw you with your measuring tape, out of the window. What have you discovered?'

'I've discovered exactly the same as I discovered yesterday,' said Fatty. 'Except that I haven't found any bits of paper with names and numbers on. Look at those prints over there.'

Larry and Daisy examined them with interest. 'I know only one person in this village with feet big enough to fit those prints,' said Daisy. Fatty looked up at once.

'Who? Perhaps you've hit on the very person! There can't be many people with such enormous feet.'

'Well—it's Goon—old Clear-Orf!' said Daisy with a giggle. The others roared.

'You're right. His feet would certainly fit those prints!' said Fatty. 'Unfortunately he's about the only large footed person who's absolutely ruled out.'

'We'll certainly have to go about with our eyes on people's feet,' said Larry. 'It's the one thing the thief can't hide! He can stick his great hands in his pockets, and stop his hollow cough—but he can't hide his great feet!'

'No—you're right,' said Fatty. 'Well, let's not stop any more. Goon's had about enough of us for one afternoon, I should think.'

They climbed over the fence into Larry's garden. Buster squeezed through a hole.

'Gosh—I'd forgotten we were in the middle of tea,' said Fatty, pleased to see the remains of sandwiches and cakes on the grass. 'What's happened to some of these potted-meat sandwiches? Your cat's been at them, Larry.'

'Buster—on guard! ' said Larry at once, and Buster growled and looked round for the cat.

They finished their tea, talking about the two robberies. After a time Buster growled again and went to the fence. 'Must be Goon over the other side, doing a spot of detecting,' said Fatty with a grin. 'Let's go and see his turnip-brains at work.'

Goon was busy looking for prints and clues. He was most irritated to see three heads looking over the wall at him. They watched him solemnly as he measured and marked.

'Look! He's found a foot-print!' said Larry, in an admiring voice. The back of Mr. Goon's neck went scarlet but he said nothing.

'Now he's measuring it,' said Daisy. 'Oooh, isn't he *careful*?'

'Brains, Daisy, brains,' said Fatty. 'What can we do against brains like that?'

Mr. Goon felt as if he was going to burst. Those children! Toads! Pests! Always in his way, buzzing round like a lot of mosquitoes. He made a very dignified retreat into the kitchen, rather hurried at the end when he discovered that Buster had squeezed through the hole in the fence and was after him.

'Clear-orf! ' he shouted, slamming the door in Buster's face. 'You clear-orf!'

8 FATTY MAKES SOME PLANS

FATTY called a meeting down in his shed the very next day. Larry and Daisy arrived punctually, and Pip and Bets soon after. Buster greeted them all exuberantly, as if he hadn't seen them for years.

'This is a proper meeting,' announced Fatty. 'An official one, I mean. We've got our mystery all right—and we've got just under four weeks to solve it. That ought to be plenty of time!'

'Yes, it ought—for old hands like us! ' said Larry, grinning. 'Did you tell Pip and Bets all about yesterday's robbery next door to us? Do they know everything? '

'Yes. I went to tell them last night,' said Fatty. 'We've got to make plans this morning.'

'What? Lists of Suspects and so on? ' asked Bets eagerly.

'We haven't got a single suspect,' said Fatty. 'Not one! It's about the only mystery we've ever had with two crimes and no suspects at all. Most extraordinary. It's going to be difficult to get on with the case till we find a few suspects to enquire about.'

'We've got plenty of clues,' said Daisy. 'Foot-prints—glove-prints—coughs—bits of paper . . . .'

'What's your plan, Fatty? ' asked Pip. 'I bet you've got one.'

'Well, I have, as a matter of fact,' said Fatty modestly. 'It's like this—all we've got to go on at the moment is what we think the thief looks like—

big-footed, heavy-handed, clumsy, with a deep, hollow cough—and we've got two bits of paper possibly dropped by him—and if they are addresses or names, which they probably are, we must watch those addresses or people.'

'Yes,' said Larry. 'And what about asking the grocer, the baker and the postman if they saw any sign of a big-footed fellow yesterday afternoon, when they delivered their goods in our road? '

'I was coming to that,' said Fatty. 'It seems to me we must split up a bit and each do a job, as we usually do.'

'Oh dear,' said Bets. 'I'm really not much good by myself.'

'You're one of the best of us,' said Fatty warmly, and Bets blushed with pleasure. 'Who solved the mystery of the Pantomime Cat, I'd like to know? You did, Bets—oh yes you did—without your bright idea about it we'd never have solved it! So just you do your bit this time too.'

'Oh, I will, Fatty,' said Bets earnestly.

'Now you, Larry, go and interview the postman,' said Fatty. 'And you, Pip, go to the baker. If he's the same one that Jinny at Norton House called in to help her, the one who searched the upstairs rooms for her, all the better. He may have noticed something about the two cases that we haven't.'

'Right,' said Pip. 'I believe he is *our* baker too.'

'And you, Daisy and Bets, go and interview the grocer's girl,' said Fatty. 'Apparently it's a girl who delivers Harris's goods—that's the grocer. Go and get her to talk—listen to all she says—

remember it, and we'll piece together everything when we meet again.'

There was a silence. Everyone wondered what little job Fatty had kept for himself.

'What are *you* going to do? ' asked Bets.

'I 'm going to disguise myself,' said Fatty, and Bets gave a squeal of joy. 'And I'm going to go and watch Frinton Lea, just to see if any big-footed fellow lives there! If I watch the house all day long I may see something.'

'But Fatty—you'll be noticed if you stand outside all day long,' said Daisy. 'Besides—what about meals? '

'I've thought of all that,' said Fatty. 'Leave it all to me! I shan't tell you my disguise. When you've done your jobs you can come along and see if you recognize me. I'll be within fifty yards of the house all day long—visible to everyone—but I bet you anything you like that nobody will pay a moment's attention to me! '

They all stared at him. He stared back, his eyes twinkling. 'We shall spot you at once,' said Daisy.

'All right. Spot me, then,' said Fatty. 'Now, come on—let's get going. Clear-orf, all of you—and let me disguise myself! '

They all went off, laughing, wondering what Fatty was going to do. They were absolutely certain that they would spot Fatty at once. So would everyone else notice him, surely. How could anyone loiter outside a house all day long without being noticed? And what about meals? There was nowhere down by Frinton Lea where he could have even a snack. There were fields behind and the river ran just in front.

'I'm going back home to wait for the baker,' said Pip. 'He comes to us about twelve o'clock, I think.'

'Oh, that's an awfully good idea,' said Larry. 'I'll come with you, and wait for the parcel postman to come to your house too. Then we can keep each other company.'

'He may not come,' said Pip. 'We don't always have parcels.'

'I'll have to chance that,'said Larry. 'I don't feel like going to the post office and asking to interview the parcel postman there, in front of everyone! I half thought I'd have to do that at first!'

'What about the grocer's girl?' said Daisy. 'Do you have Harris for your grocer, Pip? If you do, Bets and I can be with you and Larry, and we can all be together.'

'No, we don't have Harris,'said Pip. 'Let me see now—what roads does the girl deliver to in the mornings? I've seen her somewhere. I know she only goes to your part of the town in the afternoon.'

'I know! She delivers down at the other end of the town,' said Bets suddenly. 'I was at Mrs. Kendal's once, with a message for Mother—and the grocer's girl came then. We could go and wait about for her there, Daisy.'

'Right. Come on,' said Daisy. 'Good-bye, boys— don't start playing a game and forget all about your job!'

'Don't be silly Daisy,' said Larry, quite annoyed. The boys went off to Pip's and the girls went off to the other end of the town.

They were lucky because they didn't have to wait very long. They sat in the small dairy near Mrs.Kendal's, eating ice-creams, keeping a watch for the grocer's van.

'There it is!' said Bets suddenly, and Daisy looked up, to see Harris's yellow van coming round the corner. It came to a stop nearby.

Daisy and Bets paid quickly for their ice-creams and hurried out. They were just in time to see the grocer's girl jump from the van, hurry to the back, undo the door, and drag out a big box piled with groceries.

'Let her go in with it first, and then we'll speak to her when she comes out,' said Daisy. They walked slowly to the back of the van. Then Bets saw that a little packet of soap powder had fallen out and was lying in the road.

'It must have fallen out of the girl's box,' she said to Daisy, and bent to pick it up just as the grocer's girl came out again, this time with her box empty.

'I say—you dropped this,'said Bets, holding it out.

'Oh, thanks very much,' said the girl gratefully. ' I missed it when I took the things in just now. I'm in an awful hurry this morning—had an interview with the police, you know. About the robbery at Mrs.Williams.'

This was just the opening the other two wanted. Daisy seized on it eagerly. 'Oh, did you really? Did you know that I and my brother lived next door to Mrs.Williams, and we rushed in to help her?'

'No! Well I never!' said the girl, astonished.

'I say, you dropped this,' said Bets

'Did you see anything of the thief? I hear he took quite a bit of Mrs. Williams' jewellery.'

'Did he?' said Daisy, who hadn't yet heard what exactly had been taken. '*You* went to the house yesterday afternoon too, didn't you? Did *you* see anything of the thief?'

'No, not a thing,' said the girl. 'I didn't see anyone at all. I think I must have come before he was there. I never saw or heard anything.'

'Did you see any loaves or any parcel in the kitchen when you went in?' asked Bets, wondering if the grocer's girl had gone to the house before the others.

'There were no loaves there when I went, and I didn't see any parcel,' said the girl, getting into her van. 'Mr. Goon asked me a lot of questions this morning—and I couldn't tell him a thing. To think I was there and might have brushed against the robber! Well, it just shows, doesn't it? '

Bets and Daisy didn't know exactly what it showed, but they nodded their heads.

'Sorry I can't stop,' said the girl. 'I'd love to hear what you did too—but I'm so awfully late. To think I didn't hear or see a *thing*. Bad luck, wasn't it?'

She drove off. Daisy and Bets looked at one another. 'Well, that was unexpectedly easy,' said Bets. 'It took us hardly any time. We may as well go back and see how the boys are getting on.'

So they went off to the boys, who were patiently waiting for the postman and the baker. They were swinging on the gate so as not to miss them. They looked most surprised to see Daisy and Bets so soon.

'We had an easy job,' said Daisy. 'But nothing came of it. The grocer's girl delivered her goods before the others, and she didn't see or hear anything suspicious at all.'

'Nobody ever seems to see this thief,' said Larry. 'They hear him and see his foot-marks and glove-marks, but they don't see him. I bet neither the postman nor the baker will have seen him, either.'

'Here *is* the postman!' said Daisy. "Look—coming up the road with his little cycle-van. Let's hope he's got a parcel for your house, Pip.'

The postman delivered two parcels next door. He came out again, mounted his saddle, and pedalled slowly to Pip's house. He stopped. He rummaged in his little van and produced a parcel.

'Mrs. Hilton,' he read out, and looked at the children. 'Any of you a Hilton?'

'Yes, I am,' said Pip, going over to the van. 'I'll take it to my mother. It'll save you a long ride up the drive and back.'

'Thanks,' said the postman. 'Sign for it, will you?'

Pip signed. 'I hope you won't bump into a thief to-day,' he said giving the postman back his stump of a pencil. 'I hear you almost ran into one yesterday!'

'Yes,' said the postman. 'Mr.Goon the policeman has been trying to find out if I saw him. I didn't. I went to the back door, as the Cook had told me to, so as not to disturb Mrs. Williams—and I saw all the groceries on the table, and I left my parcel by the door.'

'Were there any loaves on the table too?' asked Larry.

'Not so far as I remember,' said the postman. 'I just popped my hand in with the parcel and popped out again. I was in a hurry. I didn't see or hear anything at all. Off I went. I don't know whether the thief was there then or not—skulking round, maybe—or hiding in a bush.'

He began to pedal slowly away. The children watched him go.

'Nobody's much help,' said Pip. 'I never knew such a thief for not being noticed by anyone. You'd think they'd see his big feet, anyhow, wouldn't you?'

'Now we'll wait for the baker,' said Larry. 'Then we'll scoot off down to Frinton Lea and spot Fatty. I *bet* we spot him. Even if he's disguised himself as a tree we'll spot him.'

'Buck up baker!' said Bets, swinging on the gate. 'You're the last one left—and I guess you won't have noticed the thief either!'

9 THE PECULIAR FISHERMAN

THE baker arrived at last. He was a cocky little bantam of a man, with a rather high voice, and a silly way of clearing his throat. He left his van at the bottom of the road and came along carrying his basket on his arm.

'Hallo, kids,' he said, as he came up to the gate. 'Having a swing-swong, eh?'

'Shall we take the bread to our cook for you?' asked Pip.

'Well—there are thieves about, you know!' said the baker, pretending to look scared. 'My word—I nearly ran into one yesterday, up at Mrs Williams's. Did you hear tell about that?'

'What happened?' asked Larry, thinking it would be a good thing to let him talk.

'Well, nothing really so far as I'm concerned,' said the baker. 'I goes up there as usual, carrying my bread on my arm in my basket, like I always does. I knocks on the kitchen door before I remembers that Cookie is out. I sees the groceries on the table, and a parcel by the door, and I says, "Ah, the grocer girl's been and left her things, and so's the postman. Now it's your turn, baker!"'

He grinned at them as if he had said something rather clever.

'And so I looks at the note Cookie's left for me, and I sees as how she wants four loaves,' went on the cocky little baker. 'And I pops them down, and out I goes.'

And you didn't see or hear anything of the thief at all then,' said Larry, disappointed.

'No. Nothing,' said the baker. 'All I see is some big foot-prints on a bed.'

'Ah—you saw those!' said Pip and Larry together. The baker looked surprised.

'What do *you* know about them? ' he said. 'Yes, I see them—and I thinks—ah, somebody's been walking their big feet all over the beds. Maybe the window-cleaner or somebody. And off I goes.'

'That means that the thief must either have come and gone, or was still there, hiding somewhere whilst you were delivering your bread,' said Larry. 'Gosh—you might easily have seen him. What a pity you didn't.'

'I never seen him the other day either, at Norton House,' said the baker in his high, rather silly voice. 'I heard Jinny shouting and in I went—but we didn't see no thief at all.'

'Funny,' said Pip, puzzled. 'Well, baker—if you like to give me your basket I'll take it up to our cook and let her see what bread she wants. It will save you a long walk up the drive.'

He held out his hand for the basket, but the baker backed away and shook his head.

'No thanks. I don't want boys messing about with my nice clean bread,' said the baker. 'I'm particular I am. I'm the only baker in Peterswood that covers his bread up with a clean cloth.'

'Oh, all right,' said Pip. 'Take it yourself. I'm sure I don't want to lug it all the way to the back door. It looks pretty heavy to me.'

The baker went in at the gate and walked up

the drive like a little strutting bantam. The children watched him and laughed. 'What a funny little fellow,' said Bets. 'So proud of his clean bread too. You'd think he would keep his hands clean as well, if he's as clean as all that! They're filthy!'

They watched him disappear round the bend of the drive, looking spruce and smart in his little white coat, breeches, and small-sized, highly polished boots with polished gaiters above.

'Most disappointing,' he said, as he came back again. 'No thief to-day anywhere. I don't mind telling you I'm on the look-out now. Anyone suspicious and I tell the police! I promised Mr. Goon that. I go into nearly everyone's house, and I'm keeping my eyes open for him. He thinks there'll be more robberies soon!'

'Really?' said Larry politely. The little baker strutted back to his van whistling.

'Very pleased with himself, isn't he?' said Larry. 'I don't think I like him much.'

'Now let's go down to Frinton Lea and see if we can find Fatty,' said Bets, jumping off the gate.

'Yes, let's,' said Daisy, pleased. 'We've done our bits now—not that we've found out anything.'

They walked down the lane to the river, then along the river-path that led to Frinton Lea. They soon came in sight of it. It was a big rambling house, once built by rich people, and now owned by someone who ran it for paying guests.

Boats slid by on the water. Fishermen sat by the bank, stolid and patient, almost like bits of the scenery. Each had his little camp-stool, and each hunched himself over his rod, watching his float like a cat watching a mouse-hole.

'I've never seen any of these fishermen catch a fish yet,' said Bets stopping by one.

'Sh!' said the fisherman angrily, and Bets went away, alarmed.

'You'll frighten away the fish he doesn't catch,' said Pip with a laugh. 'For goodness sake don't go and disturb a fisherman again!'

They passed two labourers in a field, and then came to Frinton Lea. They looked about expectantly for a heavily disguised Fatty. Was he anywhere about?

At first they could see nobody—and then, sitting in a little boat, not far from the bank, was a hunched-up figure, silently fishing. He had on most extraordinary clothes.

His hat was a large cloth cap with a rather loud check pattern. His scarf was a curious sickly green. His coat was very tight blue alpaca, and he wore red braces that showed in front where the coat fell open.

The children stared at this peculiar figure. It took one look at them and then glanced away.

'There's *Fatty*!' said Pip. 'But what a getup! It's not so much a disgise as a fancy-dress. What's he thinking of to dress like that!'

'He must have got some reason for it,' said Daisy. 'Fatty never does anything without a reason. What braces!'

'Did you see his face when he looked round at us?' said Larry with a laugh. 'Fierce eyebrows and a fierce moustache, and he must have got his cheek-pads in again, his face looks so fat.'

'I do wish he would look at us properly,' said Bets, who simply couldn't recognize Fatty at all.

'Don't be silly,' said Pip. 'He hopes we shan't recognize him, the goof.'

Still the fisherman in the boat didn't look in their direction. He fished stolidly. Then he coughed.

'Jolly good cough,' said Pip in a loud voice. The fisherman took no notice.

'Psssssst!' Larry said to him and still he didn't so much as turn his head. Any ordinary fisherman would certainly have lost his temper by now and ordered them away. It was most decidedly Fatty.

'Don't be goofy!' called Pip in a low voice.

'We've spotted you!' said Daisy, also keeping her voice low. 'It was easy!'

The fisherman obstinately refused to look in their direction. After a little more 'Pssssssting' and attempts to make him turn round, the four gave it up.

'We'll walk home and come back afterwards,' said Larry. 'It's getting late. Fatty's an ass.'

They walked home, had their lunches and came back again. Perhaps Fatty would be more amenable this afternoon.

'The boat's gone,'said Daisy. 'Oh no—look, it's there by the bank. And the fisherman is sitting on the grass, eating his lunch. *Now* we can get him to talk!'

They went up to him and sat down solemnly. He took a hurried look at them and then swallowed a mouthful so quickly that he choked.

'Bad luck,' said Larry, sympathetically. 'Caught many fish?'

'No,' said the fisherman in a strangled sort of voice. He got up suddenly and went to his boat.

'Psssst!' said Larry. The fisherman clambered hurriedly into his boat, making it rock up and down. Larry was about to go to his help, meaning to whisper a few stinging remarks into Fatty's ear, when Bets caught hold of him and pulled him back. He looked down at her in surprise.

She looked up at him and shook her head, her eyes wide and frightened. She nodded towards the fisherman's boots. They were enormous—and so were his hairy hands!

Larry stopped with a jerk. Gosh—it wasn't Fatty after all! Of course it wasn't. Who was it then? And why had he behaved so queerly?

'Big feet—enormous hands!' whispered Bets. 'It's the thief! It is, Larry—it must be! That's why he's tried to shake us off. He's afraid we're on his track.'

The fisherman had pushed off into the river again. He sat now with his back to the children, hunched up as before. They gazed at him silently. How could they possibly have thought he was Fatty?

'What are we to do?' asked Daisy in a low voice. 'We ought to tell Fatty. But where is he? Is he somewhere near—in disguise? We can't let the thief go now we've found him! Where *is* Fatty? I simply can't see him anywhere!'

10 TELEPHONE CALL TO GOON

LARRY thought hard. He was the head of the Five when Fatty was not there. What was the best thing to do?

'If only we could spot Fatty!' he groaned. 'I'll tell you what we'd better do. Pip, you and Bets stay here and keep an eye on the thief. Daisy and I will wander about a bit and see if we can spot Fatty. He said he'd be within fifty yards of Frinton Lea, so he will be.'

'Right,' said Pip and he and Bets settled down on the grassy bank. The other two walked off down the path. The fisherman heard their footsteps and turned cautiously round to see who it was.

'See him look round?' whispered Bets. 'He hoped we'd gone! Then I bet he was going to row to the shore and escape.'

It was rather dull sitting and watching the fisherman. He didn't catch a single fish. He just sat there with his rod, seemingly asleep.

But he wasn't. He suddenly gave a nasty hollow cough. Bets clutched Pip.

'Did you hear that? I'm sure it's the thief, now. He coughed just like sheep barking—just like Mrs. Williams said he did. I wish he'd do it again.'

He didn't. He slumped back in the boat and appeared to be asleep. But he wasn't, because whenever anyone came by he turned and gave a quick look.

Not many people came by, however. The postman cycled by with some letters. The telegraph boy came once, whistling loudly as he turned in at Frinton Lea. The fisherman turned to give him a quick look, and the children eyed him well too, wondering if he could possible be Fatty. But he wasn't. He was too thin. There was only one thing about himself that Fatty could not hide—his plumpness!

A nursemaid came by with a pram, and then the little baker appeared with his basket of bread. He had to leave his van a good way away because there was no road right to the river, only a path.

He recognized Pip and Bets, as he walked up with his cocky little stride. 'Hallo, hallo, *hallo*!' he said in his high, sparrow-like voice. 'Here we are again! How many loaves to-day, Mister? Caught any thieves yet?'

Pip thought it was silly of the baker to talk to him as if he was about six years old. He merely jerked his head at him and turned away. But the baker was not to be put off.

He came up and gazed at the fisherman in the boat. 'There's a nice easy job! ' he chattered on. 'Sitting in the sun with water lapping all round you, having a nap away from everyone else. Nobody to disturb you. No heavy basket to carry. My, why aren't I a fisherman?'

The fisherman had already turned his head once to glance at the baker. Now he took no notice. The baker called out to him.

'Hey, there! Caught any fish?'

The fisherman did not turn round. 'Not yet!' he said in a curious deep voice.

The baker stood and talked away to Pip and Bets, but they took as little notice of him as the fisherman. They thought he was silly. He went at last, carrying his basket of bread through the gate of Frinton Lea.

'Silly little idiot,' said Pip. 'He's too big for his boots. He's got such a high opinion of himself that he just can't see he's a nuisance.'

'Well, let's move a little way off till he comes out again and goes,' said Bets, so they got up and walked in the opposite direction. The baker soon came out, gave them a wave and strutted off on his spindly legs to his van.

'I wonder how Larry and Daisy are getting on,' said Bets. 'I hope they've found Fatty. It's maddening not to have him just at this important moment.'

Larry and Daisy had wandered all round Frinton Lea, but they hadn't seen Fatty. They had felt sure they had got him once—when they had seen a woman sitting on a stool, painting a picture of the river. She was rather big and had untidy hair and a hat that hid her face. Daisy nudged Larry.

'That's Fatty, surely! See—that woman painting. It would be a fine way of sitting and watching a house—to pretend to be an artist.'

'Yes. It might be Fatty,' said Larry. 'We'll stroll over and see.'

The woman looked up at them as they came and stood beside her. At once Daisy and Larry knew she was not

Fatty. Her nose was far too small. Fatty could make his nose bigger—but he certainly couldn't make it smaller!

'No go,' said Larry gloomily. 'Dash it all! Where on earth is he?'

'He might be one of those fishermen,' said Daisy. 'Look—sitting solemnly fishing on the bank. That one over there looks most like Fatty—the way he's sitting somehow. And he's got a position that gives him a very good view of Frinton Lea.'

'That's the one who said "Sh", to Bets,' said Larry. 'We'd better be careful, or he'll shush us too. Walk up very very quietly.'

So they walked up softly—so very softly that the fisherman didn't hear them coming at all. They looked at his hands—hands were always a give-away, because they couldn't very well be altered. But the fisherman wore gloves. They looked at his feet—he wore Wellingtons! He also wore a large shady hat that hid his face.

The fisherman had no idea at all that anyone was just behind him. He suddenly opened his mouth and gave a bored yawn—and that gave the game away at once! It was Fatty's yawn! Fatty always yawned loud and long, and this was Fatty all right.

Larry sat down beside him with Daisy on the other side. 'Fatty!' said Larry in a low voice. 'We've found the thief.'

The fisherman immediately became Fatty, and gave a low whistle. He looked down at Larry and Larry felt quite startled. The eyes were Fatty's, but that was all!

They sat down beside Fatty

Fatty had his false teeth in, the ones that slid over his own, and he had also done something peculiar to his eyebrows. He wore a silly little moustache, and these things made him look a different person altogether. But his eyes were the same, direct and clear and shrewd.

'What did you say?' asked the fisherman, in Fatty's own voice. Larry repeated what he had said.

'See that fellow over there in the boat?' said Larry. 'Well, he's the thief! You should see his enormous feet and hands—and he's got a cough like a sheep, too. He's the one, Fatty. I bet he lives at Frinton Lea. We've found him!'

Fatty was silent for a moment. 'Are you sure about it?' he said at last. 'Well, I'll sit here and keep an eye on him and you go and telephone to Goon.'

'Telephone to *Goon*?' said Larry, surprised. 'Why should we let *him* know? We're not working with *him*, are we?'

'You do as I say,' said Fatty. 'If he's not in, telephone again after a while. Tell him all about the awful fellow in the boat. He'll be thrilled. Tell him I'm keeping an eye on him till he comes down to arrest him.'

Larry and Daisy were puzzled. They looked at Fatty, but his face was so different, with its protruding teeth and moustache and eyebrows that they could not tell what he was really thinking.

'All right,' said Larry, getting up, puzzled that Fatty did not show more excitement. He went off with Daisy to find Bets and Pip.

'I believe old Fatty's quite jealous because we found the thief before he did,' said Larry. 'Pretty tame ending to the mystery anyway—handing the thief over to Goon like this!'

Daisy was disappointed too. It wasn't like Fatty to be jealous. They went to Bets and Pip and sat down beside them. They told them in a whisper what they were to do.

'We'll *all* go and telephone,' said Daisy, 'I'm fed up with messing about here now. Fatty says he'll keep an eye on the thief out there. He can see him from where he is.'

They left the river and walked back up to the town. They decided to go to the post office to telephone—but alas, Goon was not in. His charwoman answered the telephone. She didn't know where he was, but said he had left a note to say he would be back by half-past four at the latest.

'Blow! It's only about a quarter *to* four now', said Larry. 'Let's go and get some ice-cream and lemonade, and wait for a bit.'

So they had ice-creams—two each—and iced lemonade in the little sweet-shop. That took them about half an hour. Then they strolled across to the telephone box to try their luck again.

This time Goon answered the telephone himself. Larry looked round at the others. 'He's in,' he said. 'Good!'

'Police here,' said Goon's voice sounding gruff and sharp. 'What is it?'

'Mr. Goon! It's Laurence speaking, Frederick Trotteville's friend,' said Larry. 'I've something to report—

about that robbery case—the two cases, I mean.'

'Well—go on,' said Goon sharply.

'We've found the thief,' said Larry, unable to keep the excitement out of his voice. 'We saw him to-day.'

'Where?' asked Mr. Goon.

'In a boat just opposite Frinton Lea,' said Larry. 'He's been there ages. Probably he lives at the boarding-house. You remember there was a scrap of paper with Frinton on it?'

There was a peculiar noise at the other end. 'What did you say?' said Larry, but Goon was silent. Larry went on eagerly.

'He's a frightful-looking fellow, Mr. Goon. We recognized him because of his colossal feet and huge hands. He's very ugly—puffy cheeks, rather protruding eyes—and he's got a cough like a sheep—just like Mrs. Williams and Jinny said. If you go down to the river now, you'll catch him. Fatty's keeping his eye on him for you.'

Larry paused. Goon didn't seem to be taking this in. 'Mr. Goon—are you going to arrest him?' asked Larry.

A loud snort came down the telephone—then a bang. Goon had put down his receiver so hard that surely he must have chipped it!

'He's rung off,' said Larry amazed. 'Whatever's the matter with him?'

11   A TEA-PARTY—AND A
BRAIN-WAVE

LARRY and the others stepped out of the telephone box
into which they had all crowded. Larry repeated the
conversation. They were very puzzled.

'Better go back and tell Fatty,' said Larry at last.
'It's quite obvious that Goon doesn't believe us. So
we shall have to do something about it now. I've a
good mind to ring up the Inspector.'

'No. Don't do that till we've asked Fatty,' said
Bets. 'It seems to me there's something funny about
all this. Let's go back to Fatty.'

'Why—there he is!' said Daisy suddenly, and sure
enough, there *was* Fatty! He was himself now, very
spruce and clean, with Buster trotting delightedly at
his heels.

The others poured out of the post-office and stared
in astonishment at Fatty, who grinned back.

'Fatty! Have you left him? How did you get home
and change so quickly? What's happened?' asked
Larry.

'Oh, he went immediately you left,' said Fatty. 'So
I left too, of course.'

'Did you follow him? Where did he go?' asked
Daisy.

'No. I didn't follow him,' said Fatty. 'There wasn't
any point in doing so—I knew quite well where he
was going. Did you telephone Goon?'

'Yes. He was out the first time—but we got him

the second time,' said Larry. 'I told him all about the frightful fellow in the boat—all the details, of course—and he just gave a snort and banged the receiver down. I suppose he didn't believe me.'

Fatty suddenly began to laugh. He laughed as if he had been keeping it in for some time. He exploded, held on to the railings, and laughed till the tears came into his eyes. Bets began to laugh too. He looked so funny, and his laughter was really infectious.

'What's the *matter*?' said Larry suspiciously. 'What's the joke? You're acting most peculiarly to-day, Fatty. So is Goon.'

'Yes. You're right about *him*,' said Fatty, wiping his eyes. 'Oh dear—I'd have given anything to see Goon's face when you rang him up and told him what a hideous fellow he was, with his big feet and hands and protruding eyes!'

The others stared, puzzled at first—and then a great light dawned on them. Larry sank down on to a wooden bench by the bus-stop. He felt suddenly weak.

'Gosh! You don't mean to say—you don't *really* mean to say that that frightful fisherman in the boat was *Goon*—Goon himself!"

'Well—think back to him,' said Fatty. 'How you could all fall for that ridiculous disguise of his I really don't know. You ought to be ashamed of yourselves. Why, Goon himself stuck out a mile in that frightful get-up. And you actually go and think he's the thief!'

'Oh, Fatty—*I* put the idea into the others' heads,' said Bets as if she was going to burst into tears. 'I saw his big feet—and hands—oh, Fatty!'

'You beast, Fatty—you told us to go and telephone to Goon—and we've gone and described him to himself!' said Daisy, full of horror. 'Oh, Fatty—you really are a beast.'

'Serves you right,' said Fatty unfeelingly, and began to laugh again. 'Fine lot of detectives you are, I must say—go and hunt for a thief and pick on the only policeman of the village, in disguise! As Goon would say—Gah!'

'No wonder he snorted and banged the receiver down,' said Daisy, still more alarmed. 'I say—I hope he won't go round and complain to our parents again.'

'He won't,' said Fatty. 'He doesn't know whether you really fell for his disguise or not. If he thinks you did he'll be very bucked to think he took you in. If he thinks you saw through his disguise and were pulling his leg when you phoned, he'll feel a bit of an idiot. He won't say a word either way. He'll only snort.'

'He won't be very fond of us now,' said Pip.

'He never was,' said Fatty. 'All the same, I was surprised to see him there this morning. I spotted him at once out in that boat.'

'You would!' said Larry, half-annoyed, and half-admiring.

'When I saw him I knew he'd had the same idea as we had about Frinton Lea,' said Fatty. 'And what's more he'll probably go and snoop outside Rods now, wherever that is.'

'Do you think it's much good snooping round either Frinton Lea or Rods, wherever that is?' asked Larry.

'No, I don't think I do,' said Fatty, considering the point. 'It's only just that we can't afford to leave any clue unexplored. If we do, it's bound to be the only one that might lead us to the solution! Anyway, I had a bit a luck this afternoon, just before you came to talk to me, Larry and Daisy.'

'What?' asked Larry. 'You're a lucky beggar, Fatty—you always have any bit of luck that's going.'

'I was sitting fishing, when that artist woman came by,' said Fatty. 'I expect you saw her. My hat blew off at that very moment and she picked it up for me. I began to talk her—and it turned out that she lived at Frinton Lea!'

'Golly!' said Larry. 'So you asked a few leading questions, I suppose?'

Fatty grinned. 'I did! And I found out that the only man staying at Frinton Lea has been very ill and is only just allowed to get up. So we can rule him out as the thief, who must be an agile fellow, to say the least of it!'

'Oh—well, that's good,' said Daisy. 'Your day hasn't been wasted, Fatty. You didn't see the thief, but you did find out he wasn't at Frinton Lea.'

'Your day wasn't wasted either,' said Fatty, beginning to laugh again. 'I hope I don't think of you telephoning old Goon when I'm having dinner with my parents to-night. I shall choke if I do.'

'What about tea?' said Bets. 'I'm getting hungry.'

'You've just had two ice-creams and a lemonade!' said Pip.

'Well, they don't make any difference,' said Bets. 'You don't eat those, you just swallow them. Anyway, we'd better go home quickly, or we shall be too late for tea.'

'I'll treat you all,' said Fatty generously. 'I've got enough money on me.' He pulled out a handful of change and examined it. 'Yes, come on. We'll go to Oliver's and have meringues and chocolate slices—in celebration of finding the thief-who-wasn't.'

Everyone laughed. Bets took Fatty's arm. Dear, generous Fatty—he always seemed to have plenty of money, but he always shared it round. Bets squeezed his arm affectionately.

'The mystery's getting on, isn't it? ' she said. 'We've ruled out Frinton Lea. Now we've got to find out what Number 1, Rods is, and rule that out too.'

'Well, we shan't be much further on with the mystery, silly, if we keep examining our clues and finding they're no good,' said Pip, exasperated with his small sister. 'Anyway, Number 1, Rods sounds more like a note made by somebody going fishing than anything else.'

'It's an idea,' said Fatty, taking them all into Oliver's. They sat down and ordered lemonade, egg-sandwiches, meringues, chocolate éclairs and chocolate slices. Bets' mouth began to water.

'I never know whether to eat as quickly as possible so as to enjoy everything before I stop feeling hungry, or to eat slowly and taste every single bit,' said Bets, eyeing the pile of delicious-looking cakes.

'Idiot,' said Pip scornfully. 'You stop feeling hungry as soon as you've eaten a certain amount, whether you've eaten it quickly or not.'

'You eat how you like, Bets,' said Fatty, who always stuck up for Bets when her brother ticked her off. They all began on their tea, having a friendly argument as to whether the meringues were better than the éclairs. The dish was soon empty, and Fatty, after examining his money again, called for a fresh supply.

'About this Rods place,' said Fatty. 'It's either the name of a house, shortened—or else it's the name of a family, either complete or shortened. I've never heard of anyone called Rods though.'

'How could we find out?' wondered Larry. 'We could look in the telephone book for names beginning with Rod or Rods.'

'Yes, that's a good idea,' said Daisy. taking her second éclair. 'And we've got a street directory at home, with everyone's house in it, and the name or number.'

'You're talking good sense,' said Fatty, sounding pleased. 'Anyone got an idea for finding a person with enormous feet? Apart from examining the feet of everyone we meet, I mean. I've rather ruled that out—it would be frighful to look at nothing but feet, feet all day long wherever we go.'

Bets giggled. 'And even if we find someone with colossal feet we can't very well stop them and say, "Excuse me, may I see the pattern of the rubber heels you're wearing? "'

'No, we can't,' said Pip. 'But I say—I tell you what we *could* do—I've just thought of it. It's a brain-wave! '

'What?' asked everyone together.

Pip dropped his voice. One or two people in the shop seemed rather too interested in what they were all saying, he thought.

'Why can't we go to the cobbler's—there *is* only one in Peterswood now the other fellow's gone—and ask if he ever has size twelve books in for repair, and if so, whose are they?'

There was a little silence after this remarkable suggestion. Then Fatty solemnly reached out and shook hands with Pip.

'First class!' he said. 'Brilliant! Talk about a brain-wave! Go up top, Pip. That really *may* lead us somewhere!

12   FATTY, THE COBBLER—AND GOON

THE next day they set to work to follow out the suggestions made at the tea-shop. Daisy and Larry said they would look up the streets directory and read down every single street to see if there was a house name beginning with Rod or Rods.

Pip and Bets were to look in the telephone directory for names. Fatty was to go to the cobbler's. Nobody particularly wanted to do that, because they couldn't think how to go about it without making the cobbler think they were either mad or silly.

'I'll manage it,' said Fatty. 'I'll think of a way. And for goodness sake don't get taken in again by any disguise of Goon's—he's been studying hard, I can see, on his refresher course, and goodness knows what he'll produce next.'

'I shall just look at his feet,' said Bets, 'and if they're enormous I'll know they belong to Goon!'

Fatty considered carefully how to approach the cobbler. He was known to be a hot-tempered man who would stand no nonsense at all. He would have to go to him with a sensible idea of some sort. But what?

Fatty remembered an old second-hand shop he had once seen in Sheepridge. He tried to remember if they sold boots. Yes, he had an idea they did. In that case it would be a good idea to catch the bus to Sheepridge, look in the second-hand shop and buy the biggest pair there—they would presumably want mending, and he could take them to the cobbler. Fatty felt certain that with that opening he could soon find out if the cobbler had any customers with really enormous feet.

' Then I'll get their names, and see if any of them might be the thief,' he thought. So off he went to catch the bus to Sheepridge. He found the second-hand shop, and, feeling as if he wanted to hold his nose because of the musty, dusty smell, he went inside.

There was a special box for boots and shoes. Fatty turned them all over, and at the bottom he found what he wanted—a pair of elevens, down at heel and with a slit in one side.

He bought them for a shilling and went off with them, pleased. He caught the bus back to Peterswood and went home. He debated whether or not to disguise himself, and then decided that he would, just for practice.

He went down to his shed and looked round at his things. An old tramp? He was rather good at that. Yes—that wouldn't be a bad idea at all—he could wear the frightful old boots too! They would make him limp but what did that matter? It would look all the more natural.

Fatty began to work deftly and quickly. He hoped his mother wouldn't come and look for him. She would be scared to see a dirty old tramp in the shed. After about half an hour the door opened, and the tramp came out and peered round cautiously.

He looked dreadful. Fatty had blacked out two of his front teeth, and had put in one cheek-pad so that it looked as if he had tooth-ache on the right side of his face. He had put on grey, untrimmed eye-brows, and had stuck on a bristly little grey moustache. His face was lined with dirty creases and wrinkles. Fatty was an adept at creasing up his face! His wig was one of his best—grey straggling hair with a bald patch in the middle.

Fatty had laughed at himself when he looked in the long glass he kept in his shed. What a tramp! He wore holey old golves on his hands, dirty corduroy trousers, an equally dirty shirt—and the boots!

Fatty could only hobble along in them, so he took an ash-stick he had cut from the hedge on one of his walks to help him along. He stuck an old clay pipe in the corner of his mouth and grinned at himself. He felt really proud, and for half a minute wondered if he should present himself at the back door and ask for a crust of bread from the cook.

He decided not to. The last time he had done that the cook had screamed the place down, and his mother had very nearly caught him. He went cautiously out of the shed to the gate at the bottom of the garden. He was not going to risk meeting any of his household.

The old tramp hobbled down the road, sucking at his empty pipe, and making funny little grunting noises. He made his way to the cobbler's and went inside the dark little shop.

The cobbler was at the back, working. He came into the shop when the bell rang. 'What do you want?' he said.

'Oooh-ah,' said Fatty, taking his pipe out of his mouth. ' It's my boots, Mister. They hurt me something crool.

Too small they are, and they want mending too. You got any bigger ones to sell?'

The cobbler bent over his counter to look at Fatty's feet. 'What size are they—elevens or twelves?' he said. ' No, I haven't got that size to sell. It's a big size.'

The old tramp gave a peculiar wheezy laugh, ' Ah, yes, it's big. I was a big man once, I was! I bet you haven't got anyone in this here neighbourhood that's got feet bigger than mine!'

' There's two people with big feet here,' said the cobbler, considering. ' There's Mr. Goon the policeman and there's Colonel Cross—they're the biggest of all. I charge them more when I sole their boots—the leather I use for their repairs! Do you want me to mend your boots?'

'Ay, I do—if you can get me another pair to put on while you mend these,' said the old tramp, and he gave his wheezy laugh again. ' Or couldn't I borrow a pair of Colonel Cross's—have you got a pair in to mend?'

'No, I haven't—and you wouldn't get 'em if I had,' said the cobbler sharply. ' Get along with you! Do you want to get me into trouble?'

'No no,' said the old tramp. ' Do his boots have rubber heels on? '

The cobbler lost his temper. ' What's that to do with you? Coming in here wasting my time! You'll be wanting to know if the butcher has brown or black laces next. Be off with you, and don't come back again.'

'That's all right, sir, that's all right,' wheezed the old man, shuffling to the door, where he stopped and had a most alarming coughing-fit.

'You stop smoking a clay pipe and you'll get rid of that cough,' said the cobbler, bad-temperedly. Then he saw someone else trying to get past the coughing tramp. 'Get out of my shop and let the next person come in.'

The next person was a burly man with a little black moustache, a dark brown face, dark glasses and big feet.

He pushed past the old tramp. 'Give me room,' he said, in a sharp voice. Fatty pricked up his ears at once. He knew that familiar voice—yes, and he knew that unfamiliar figure too—it was Goon!

'Goon! In *another* disguise!' thought Fatty in amazement and mirth. 'He's done better this time—with dark glasses to hide his frog-eyes, and some stuff on his red face to make it look tanned.'

He looked at the burly Goon. He wore white flannel trousers and shirt with no tie, and a red belt round his portly middle. On his feet were enormous white shoes.

'Why the disguise?' wondered Fatty. 'Just practising, like me? Or is he going to snoop round somewhere? Perhaps he has found out where or who Rods is. I'd better stand by and find out.'

He shuffled out and sat down on a wooden bench, just outside. He strained his ears to see if he could catch any words. What was Goon doing in the cobbler's? Surely he hadn't got the same bright idea as Pip had had—of asking about repairs to large-size boots!

Goon had! He was very pleased about it. He had made up a nice little story to help him along.

'Good morning,' he said to the cobbler. 'Did my

brother leave his boots here to be mended? He asked me to come in and see. Very large size, twelves or thirteens.'

'What name?' asked the cobbler.

'He didn't give his name,' said Mr. Goon. 'Just left the boots, he said.'

'Well, I haven't any boots as big as that here,' said the cobbler. 'I've only got two customers with feet that size.'

'Who are they?' asked Goon.

'What's that to you?' said the cobbler, impatiently. 'Am I going to waste all my morning talking about big boots?'

'I know one of your customers is Mr. Goon,' said Mr. Goon. 'I know Mr. Goon very very well. He's a great friend of mine. Very nice fellow.'

'Oh, *is* he? Then you know him better than I do,' said the cobbler. 'I've got no time for that pompous old bobby.'

Mr. Goon went purple under his tan. 'Who's your other customer?' he asked, in such an unexpectedly fierce voice that the cobbler stared. 'The one with big feet, I mean. You'd better answer my question. For all you know I might have been sent here by Mr. Goon himself!'

'Bah!' said the cobbler, and then thought better of it. 'The other fellow is Colonel Cross,' he said.

'Does he have rubber heels?' asked Mr. Goon and was immediately amazed by the cobbler's fury.

'Rubber heels! How many more people want to know if he has rubber heels! What do I care? Go and ask him yourself!' raged the cobbler, going as purple as Mr. Goon. 'You and that old tramp are a pair, you are!'

'What old tramp?' asked Goon in surprise.

'The one you pushed past at the door—with feet as big as yourself!" raged the cobbler. 'Clear out of my shop now. I've got work to do. Rubber heels!'

Goon went out with great dignity. He longed to tell the cobbler who he was—what a shock for him that would be. What was it he had called him? 'A pompous old bobby!' Goon put that away in his memory. One day he would make the cobbler sorry for that rude remark!

Now, what about this tramp with big feet? Where was he? He might be the thief! There didn't seem many people with enormous feet in Peterswood as far as he could find out—only himself and Colonel Cross. He would have to enquire about Colonel Croos's boots—see if they had rubber heels—though it wasn't very likely that Colonel Cross went burgling other people's houses.

Goon blinked in the bright sunshine, quite glad of his dark glasses. Where was that tramp? Well—what a piece of luck—there he was, sitting on the bench nearby!

Goon sat down heavily beside him. Fatty took one look and longed to laugh. He saw Goon looking at his big old boots. Ah—they had roused his suspicions. Well, Fatty was quite prepared to sit there as long as Goon—and to have a bit of fun too. He stuck his big boots out well in front of him. Come on, Goon—say something!

13   A LITTLE BIT OF FUN

Goon hadn't the slightest idea that he was sitting next to Fatty. He looked through his dark glasses at the dirty old man. Could he be the thief? He tried to see his hands, but Fatty was still wearing the holey old gloves.

'Want some baccy? ' said Goon, seeing that Fatty's clay pipe was empty.

Fatty looked at him and then put his hand behind his ear.

'*Want some baccy*? ' said Goon a little more loudly.

Still Fatty held his hand behind his ear and looked enquiringly at Goon, sucking at his dirty old pipe, and squinting horribly.

'WANT SOME BACCY?' roared Goon.

'Oh, ah — yes — I've got a bad back-ache,' answered Fatty. 'Oooh, my back-ache. Somethink crool, it is.'

'I said, "WANT SOME BACCY?" ' yelled Goon again.

'I heard you the first time,' said Fatty, with dignity. 'I'm having treatment for it at the horspital. And for me pore old feet too.'

He gave a long, wheezy cough and rubbed the back of his hand over his nose.

'You've got big feet!' said Goon loudly.

'Oh, ah—it's a nice sunny seat,' agreed the old tramp. 'I allus sits here of a mornin'.'

'I said—"you've got BIG FEET,"' shouted Goon.

'You're right. Not enough meat these days,' said the

tramp, and coughed again. ' 'Taint right. Meat's good for you.'

Goon gave it up. 'Silly old man,' he said in his ordinary voice, thinking that the tramp was absolutely stone deaf. Most surprisingly the old fellow heard him.

'Here! Who are you calling a silly old man?' said the tramp fiercely. 'I heard you! Yes, I did! Think I was deaf, didn't you? But I heard you!'

'Now now—don't be silly,' said Goon, alarmed at the disturbance the tramp was making. 'Be calm.'

'Harm! Yes, I'll harm you!' said the tramp, and actually raised his stick. Goon retreated hurriedly to the other end of the bench and debated with himself. This old chap couldn't be the thief. He was deaf, his feet were bad, and he had backache. But where had he got those boots? It might be as well to follow him home and find out where he lived. It was no good asking him, that was plain. He'd only make some silly reply. So Goon took out his own pipe and proceeded to fill it, and to wait until the old tramp moved off.

Fatty was also waiting for Goon to move off, because he wanted to see if the policeman had discovered who or where Rods was. So there they both sat, one sucking an empty pipe, the other pulling at a lighted one. The smoke from it almost choked poor Fatty.

And then he saw Larry, Daisy, Bets and Pip coming down the street! Thank goodness they hadn't got Buster, who would certainly have smelt out Fatty at once and greeted him with joy. Buster was safely locked up in the shed, and was no doubt still scraping hopefully at the door.

Fatty sank his chin down on his chest, hoping that none of the four would recognize him. It would be maddening if they did, and came over to him and gave the game away to Goon.

They didn't recognize him. They gave him a mere glance, and then rested their eyes on Goon.

They walked by, giving backward glances at the disguised policeman, who pulled at his pipe desperately, praying that the four would go away. Thank goodness that fat boy was not with them. He'd have spotted him at once, disguise or no disguise.

The four children stopped at the end of the street because Bets was pulling at Larry's sleeve so urgently. 'What is it, Bets?' asked Larry.

'See that big man sitting on the bench by the dirty old tramp?' said Bets. 'I'm sure it's Goon! I'd know his big hairy hands anywhere. He's in disguise again—a better disguise this time, because his eyes are hidden. You just simply can't mistake those when you see them.'

'I believe Bets is right,' said Daisy, looking back. 'Yes—you can see it's Goon—the way he sits, and everything. It *is* Goon!'

'Let's have a bit of fun with him then,' said Pip. 'Come on, let's. He won't know if we've spotted him or not, and he'll be in an awful fix.'

Bets giggled. ' What shall we do?'

'Oh nothing much—just go up to him innocently and ask him footling questions,' said Larry. 'You know—what's the time, please? Have you got change for sixpence? Where does the bus start?'

Everyone laughed. ' I'll go first,' said Pip. He walked up to the bench. Fatty saw him coming, and felt alarmed.

Surely Pip hadn't recognized him. It looked as if he was going to speak to him. No—Pip was talking to Goon!

'Could you please tell me the time?' Pip asked innocently. Goon scowled. He pulled out his big watch.

'Ten to twelve,' he said.

'Thanks awfully,' said Pip. Fatty was astonished. Pip had his own watch. What was the point? Gosh! —could the others have recognized Goon after all—and have made up their minds to have some fun with him?

Larry came next. 'Oh—could you possibly give me change for sixpence, sir?' he asked Goon politely. Fatty almost choked, but his choke was lost in Goon's snort.

'No. Clear-orf,' said Goon, unable to stop himself from using his favourite expression.

'Thanks very much,' said Larry, politely and went off. Fatty got out his handkerchief, ready to bury his face in it if any of the others came along with a request. He hadn't bargained for this.

Up came Daisy. 'Could you tell me, please, if the bus stops here for Sheepridge?' she asked.

Goon nearly exploded. These kids! Here he was, in a perfectly splendid disguise, one good enough to prevent anyone from knowing him, one that should be an absolute protection against these pests of children—and here they all were, making a bee-line for him. Did they do this sort of thing to everybody? He'd have to report them—complain to their parents!

'Go and look at the bus time-table,' he snapped at Daisy.

'Oh, thank you very much,' she said. Fatty chortled again into his handkerchief and Daisy looked at him in surprise. What a queer old man.

Bets was the last to come. ' Please, have you seen our little dog, Buster?' she asked.

'No,' roared Goon. 'And if I do I'll chase him out of town.'

'Oh, thanks very much,' said Bets politely, and departed. Fatty was nearly dying of laughter, trying to keep back his guffaws. He had another coughing fit in his handkerchief and Goon looked at him suspiciously.

'Nasty cough of yours,' he said. Poor Fatty was quite unable to answer. He prayed that the others wouldn't come to ask any more questions.

Goon was debating with himself again. With those children about, pestering him like this, he'd never get anywhere. Had they seen through his disguise? Or was this kind of thing their usual behaviour? He saw Daisy bearing down on him and rose hurriedly. He strode off in the direction of the police station. He could bear no more.

Fatty collapsed. He buried his face in his handkerchief and laughed till he cried. Daisy looked at him in alarm. ' Are you all right?' she said timidly.

Fatty recovered and sat up. ' Yes, thanks, Daisy,' he said in his normal voice, and Daisy stood and stared at him, her mouth open in amazement.

'Fatty!' she whispered. 'Oh, *Fatty*! We recognized Goon—but we didn't know the tramp was you! Oh, Fatty!'

'Listen,' said Fatty. 'I don't want to have to change out of this disguise—it takes ages to take off and put on—and I want to see if Goon has found out anything about Rods. He's using his brains over all this, you know. Thought about going to see the cobbler and everything, just as we did. I don't want him to get ahead of us. I think I'd better trail him to-day.'

'All right,' said Daisy, sitting down near to him, and speaking in a low voice. ' You want us to get you some lunch, I suppose? There's a bus stop near Goon's house. You could sit there and eat your lunch and read a paper—and watch for Goon at the same time.'

'Yes—that's what I'll do,' said Fatty. ' I feel somehow as if Goon's got going on this. If he's going to get ahead of us I want to know it.'

'I couldn't find the streets directory this morning,' said Daisy, talking straight out in front of her, so that nobody would think she was talking to an old tramp. 'Larry's borrowing one this afternoon. Pip found two names in the telephone directory that might help—one is Rodney, the other is Roderick. The Rodneys live up on the hill and the Rodericks live near you.'

'Oh yes—I remember now,' said Fatty. 'Well, we can rule the Rodericks out, I think. There's only an old lady, a Mrs. Roderick, and a young one, a Miss. There's no one there who wears size twelve shoes. I don't know about the Rodneys though.'

'Shall I and the others go and see if we can find out anything at the Rodneys? ' said Daisy. ' We could go this afternoon. Mother knows them, so I could easily go on some excuse.'

'There's a jumble sale on in the town,' said Fatty. 'Couldn't you go and ask for jumble? *Especially* old boots—large size if possible as you know an old tramp who wears them!'

Daisy giggled.' 'You do have bright ideas, Fatty,' she said. 'I suppose you're the old tramp who wears them! Yes, I'll go and ask for jumble. Bets can go with me. I'll go over to the others now. They're standing there wondering what on earth I'm doing, talking to myself!'

They were certainly very surprised to see Daisy sitting down after Goon had so hurriedly departed, apparently murmuring away to herself. They were just about to come over when she left the bench and went to them.

' What's up with you?' asked Larry. Daisy smiled delightedly. ' That was Fatty!' she whispered. ' Don't recognize him, for goodness sake. We've got to get some lunch for him somehow, because he thinks Goon is on the track of something and he wants to trail him.'

The four marched solemnly past Fatty on the bench, and each got a wink from the dirty old tramp.

' We're going off to get lunch,' said Daisy loudly, as if she was speaking to Larry. But the tramp knew quite well that she was speaking to *him*!

14 A VERY BUSY AFTERNOON

FATTY shuffled his way to the bus-stop bench near Goon's house. He let himself down slowly as if he indeed had a bad back. He let out a grunt. An old lady on the bench looked at him sympathetically. Poor old man! She leaned across and pressed a sixpence into his hand.

Fatty was so taken-aback that he almost forgot he was a tramp. He remembered immediately though, and put his finger to his forehead in exactly the same way that his father's old coachman did when he came to see him.

' Thank you kindly,' he wheezed.

There was no sign of Mr. Goon. He had gone hurriedly into the back-door of his house, and was now engaged in stripping off his disguise. He was going out in his official clothes this afternoon—P.C. Goon—and woe betide any cobblers or others who were rude to him!

Soon Daisy came slipping back with a picnic-lunch, done up in a piece of neswpaper. Fatty approved of that touch! Just what he *would* have his lunch in if he really was an old tramp. Good for Daisy! His troop were coming along well, he considered.

Daisy sat down on the bench, bending over to do up her shoe. She spoke to Fatty out of the corner of her mouth. 'Here's your lunch. Best I could get. Larry's looked up the names of houses in the directory he borrowed. There's only one beginning with Rod, and that's one called Rodways, down by Pip's house. '

'Thanks. You go to the Rodneys about the jumble with Bets, and tell Larry and Pip to go to Rodways and snoop,' said Fatty. 'Find out if there's anyone there with large feet, who *might* be the thief. Rodways is only a little cottage, isn't it?'

'Yes,' said Daisy. 'All right. And you're going to trail Goon, aren't you, to see if he's up to something? We'll meet at your shed later.'

She laced up her shoe, sat up and whispered goodbye. Then off she went—and behind her she left the newspaper of food. 'Very clever!' thought Fatty, opening it. ' Good old Daisy.'

He had a very nice lunch of egg sandwiches, tomato sandwiches and a large slice of fruit cake. Daisy had even slipped in a bottle of ginger beer with an opener! Fatty ate and drank everything, and then put his clay pipe back into his mouth again. He opened the newspaper, which was that day's, and began to read very comfortably.

Goon went into his little front room and sat down to go through some papers. He glanced out of the window, and saw the old tramp on the bench.

'Turned up again like a bad penny!' said Goon to himself. ' Well, I can certainly keep an eye on him if he sits there. Still, he can't be the thief—he's too doddery.'

The tramp read his paper and then apparently fell asleep. Goon had his lunch, did a little telephoning and then decided to go on with his next job. He looked at his notes.

Frinton Lea. He had crossed that out. What with watching it all day and enquiring about it, he had come to the conclusion that he could wash that out. Now for the other people or places—the Rodericks— the Rodneys—and that house down the lane—what was it called—Rodways. One of them must be the Rods on this scrap of paper. 'Rods. It's some sort of clue, that's certain. Good thing those children don't know about these bits of paper. Ha, I'm one up on them there.'

Poor Mr. Goon didn't know that Tonks had shown them to Fatty, or he wouldn't have been nearly so pleased! He put his papers together, frowned, thought of his plan of campaign, and got up heavily, his great boots clomping loudly as he went out into the hall.

The old tramp was still on the bench. ' Lazy old thing!' thought Mr. Goon. He wheeled his bicycle quickly to the front, got on it and sailed away before Fatty could even have time to sit up!

' Blow!' said Fatty. 'He's out of disguise—and on his bike. I'm dished! I never thought of his bike. I can't trail him on that.'

He wondered what to do. Well, the others were taking care of the Rodneys and the house called Rodways. He'd better go and find Colonel Cross's house. As he was apparently the only other person in Peterswood who wore size twelve or thirteen shoes, he certainly must be enquired into!

Goon had shot off to the Roderick's first. There he found out what Fatty already knew—that there was no man in the house at all. Right. He could cross that off.

He went to see the Rodneys—and the very first things he saw there were two bicycles outside the front fence—girls' bicycles, with Daisy and Bets just coming out of the gate towards them!

Those kids again! What were they doing *here*? And whatever were they carrying? Goon glared at them.

' Good afternoon, Mr. Goon,' said Daisy, cheerfully. ' Want to come and buy a pair of shoes at the jumble sale?'

Goon eyed the four or five old pairs of boots and shoes wrathfully. ' Where did you get those?' he said.

' From Mrs. Rodney,' answered Daisy. ' We're collecting for the jumble sale, Mr. Goon. Have *you* got anything that would do for it? An old pair of big boots, perhaps?'

' Mrs. Rodney let us look all through her cupboard of boots,' said Bets, 'and she gave us these.'

Goon had nothing to say. He simply stood and glared. The Rodneys! So these pests of kids had got on to that clue too—they were rounding up the Rods just as he was—but they were just one move in front of him.

He debated whether to go in or not now. Mrs. Rodney might not welcome somebody else enquiring after shoes. He cast his eye again on the collection of old boots and shoes that Daisy and Bets were stuffing into their bicycle baskets.

Daisy saw his interest in them. ' No. None size twelve,' she said with a giggle. 'Size ten is the very largest the Rodneys have. That will save you a lot of trouble, won't it, Mr. Goon.'

' Gah!' said Mr. Goon, and leapt angrily on his bicycle. Interfering lot! And how did they know about the Rods, anyway? Had Tonks shown those scraps of paper? He'd bite Tonks' head off, if he had!

He rode off to Rodways, the cottage down the lane that led to the river. He was just putting his bicycle against the little wall when he noticed two more there—boys' bicycles this time. Well, if it was any of those little pests' bikes, he'd have something to say!

Larry and Pip were there. They had stopped outside the cottage, apparently to have a game of ball—and one of them had thrown the ball into the cottage garden.

' Careless idiot!' Pip shouted loudly to Larry. ' Now we'll have to go and ask permission to get the ball!'

They went in and knocked at the door, which was wide open. An old woman, sitting in a rocking-chair, peered at them from a corner of the room inside.

' What do you want?' she asked, in a cracked old voice.

' We're so sorry,' said Larry, politely. 'Our ball went into your garden. May we get it?'

' Yes,' said the old woman, beginning to rock herself. ' And just tell me if the milkman's been, will you? If he has, the milk-bottle will be outside. And did you see the baker down the lane?'

' No, we didn't,' said Pip. 'There *is* a bottle out here on the step. Shall I bring it in?'

Yes, thank you kindly,' said the old woman.

' Put it in the larder, there's a good lad. That baker! He gets later every day! I hope I haven't missed him. I fall asleep, you know. I might not have heard him.'

Larry looked round the little cottage. He saw a big

sou'wester hanging on a nail, and an enormous oil-skin below it. Aha! Somebody big lived here, that was certain.

' What a big oilskin!' he said to the old woman. 'Giant-size!'

' Ah, that's my son's,' said the old woman, rocking away hard. ' He's a big man, he is—but kind and gentle—just like a big dog, I always say.'

Pip had pricked up his ears too, by this time. ' He must be enormous,' he said. ' Whatever size shoes does he wear? Sixteens!'

The old lady gave a cackle of laughter. ' Go on with you! Sixteens! Look over there, on that shelf—those are my son's boots—there's a surprise for you!'

It *was* a surprise—for the shoes were no more than size sevens, about Larry's own size! The boys looked at them in astonishment.

' Does he really only wear size seven?' said Larry. ' What small feet he has for such a big man.'

' Yes. Small feet and small hands—that's what my family always have,' said the old woman, showing her own mis-shapen but small feet and hands. Pip looked at Larry. Rodways was definitely ruled out. The thief didn't live here!

Someone came up the path and called in. ' Granma! Baker-boy here!'

'Gosh—it's that awful little peacock of a baker again!' said Pip, in disgust. 'We can't seem to get rid of him.'

'One loaf as usual, baker!' called the old lady. 'Put it in my pan for me.'

The baker put down his basket, took a loaf, and strutted in. He saw the two boys, and smiled amiably. 'Here we are again! Come to see old Granma?'

'What a big oilskin!' Larry said to the old woman

He flung the bread into the pan in the larder and strutted out again. He picked up his basket and went off, whistling, turning out his feet like a duck.

'Now you go and look for your ball,' said the old woman, settling herself comfortably! 'I can go to sleep now I know the milk and the bread have come.'

They went out, found their ball, and Larry threw it out into the road. There was an angry shout.

'Now then, you there! What you doing, throwing your ball at me?'

Mr. Goon's angry red face appeared over the hedge. The boys gaped in surpirse. 'Golly—did it hit you, Mr. Goon?' said Pip, with much concern. 'We didn't know you were there.'

'Now look here—what are you *here* for?' demanded Mr. Goon. 'Everywhere I go you're there before me. What are you playing at?'

'Ball,' said Larry, picking up the ball and aiming it at Pip. It missed him, struck the wall, bounced back, and struck Mr. Goon on the helmet. He turned a beetroot colour, and the boys fled.

'Toads!' muttered Mr. Goon, mopping his hot neck. 'Toads! Anyone would think this was their case! Anyone would think they were running the whole show. Under my feet the whole time. Gah!'

He strode up the path to the front door. But the old lady had now gone fast asleep, and did not waken even when Mr. Goon spoke to her loudly. He saw the oil skin on the peg, and the same thought occurred to him, as had occurred to the two boys. Big oil skin— Big man—Big feet—The thief!

He crept in and began to look round. He fell over a

shovel and the old woman awoke in a hurry. She saw Mr. Goon and screamed.

'Help! Help! Robbers! Thieves! Help, I say!'

Mr. Goon was scared. He stood up, and spoke pompously. 'Now, madam, it's only the police come to call. What size shoes does your son take?'

This was too much for the old woman. She thought the policeman must be mad. She began to rock herself so violently that Mr. Goon was sure the chair would fall over.

He took one last look round and ran, followed by the old woman's yells. He leapt on his bicycle and was off up the lane in a twinkling. Poor Mr. Goon— he was no match for an angry old woman!

15 MOSTLY ABOUT BOOTS

FATTY had gone off to find Colonel Cross's house. It was a pleasant little place not far from the river. Sitting out in the garden was a big man with a white moustache and a very red face.

Fatty studied him from the shelter of the hedge. He looked a bit fierce. In fact, very fierce. It was quite a good thing he was asleep, Fatty thought. Not only asleep, but snoring.

Fatty looked at his feet. Enormous! The cobbler was right—the Colonel certainly wore size twelve or thirteen boots. Fatty thought he could see a rubber heel on one of them too. Goodness—suppose he had at last hit on the right person! But Colonel Cross didn't look in the least like a thief or burglar. Anything but, thought Fatty.

Fatty wished he had a small telescope or longsighted glasses so that he could look more closely at the rubber heel. He didn't dare to go crawling into the garden and look at the heels. The colonel was certainly very fast asleep, one leg crossed over the other—but he might be one of these light sleepers that woke very suddenly!

The Colonel did wake suddenly. He gave an extra loud snore and woke himself up with a jump. He sat up, and wiped his face with a table-cloth of a handkerchief. He certainly was enormous. He suddenly caught sight of Fatty's face over the hedge, and exploded.

'Did you wake me up? What are you doing there? Speak up, man!'

'I didn't wake you, sir,' said Fatty, in a humble voice. 'I was just looking at your feet.'

'Bless us all—my feet? What for?' demanded the Colonel.

'I was wishing you had an old pair of your boots to give me,' said Fatty, very humbly. 'I'm an old tramp, sir, and tramping's hard on the feet. Very hard, sir, And I've big feet, sir, and it's hard to get boots to fit me—cast-off boots, I mean.'

'Go round and ask my housekeeper,' said the colonel gruffly. 'But see you do something in return if there's an old pair to give you! Hrrrrr-umph!'

This was a wonderful noise—rather like a horse makes. Fatty stored it away for future use. Hrrrrr-umph! Fine! He would startle the others with it one day.

'Thank you, sir. I'll chop up wood or do anything if I can have a pair of your boots!' he said.

He left the hedge and went round to the back door. A kindly faced woman opened it.

'Good day, Mam, the colonel says have you got a pair of his old boots for me,' asked Fatty, his hat in his hands, so that his straggly grey hair showed.

'Another old soldier!' sighed the housekeeper. 'There's not a pair of boots—but there may be an old pair of shoes. And even so they're not really worn-out yet! Dear, dear—the colonel only came back yesterday and here he is giving his things away as usual!'

Fatty pricked up his ears. 'Where has he been?' he asked.

'Oh, India,' said the woman. 'And now he's home for the last time. Arrived by air yesterday.'

'Ah,' thought Fatty, 'then that rules out the colonel. Not that I really thought it could be him—he doesn't look in the least like a burglar! Still, all suspects have to be examined, all clues have to be followed.'

The woman came back with a pair of old shoes. They had rubber heels on. Fatty's eyes gleamed when he saw them. The pattern of the heels looked extremely like the pattern he had drawn in his note-book! How queer!

'Did you say you often give you master's shoes away?' he asked.

'Not only shoes—anything,' she said. 'He's fierce, you know, but he's kind too—always handing out things to his old soldiers. But since he's been away I've sent his things to the Jumble Sales each year.'

'My—I hope you didn't send any of this size boots or shoes!' said Fatty jokingly. 'They would have done fine for me!'

'I sent a pair of boots last year,' said the woman, 'they would just have done for you. But who would buy such enormous ones I *don't* know. I said to Miss Kay when she asked me for them, "Well there now, you can have them, but you won't sell them, I'll wager!"'

Fatty made a mental note to find out Miss Kay and asked her if she remembered who bought the big boots belonging to the colonel. It might have been the thief!

'The colonel said I was to do a job for you,' said Fatty remembering.

'Well now, you go and weed that bed out in the garden,' said the housekeeper. 'I can't seem to get down to it. He's asleep again. I can hear him snoring, so you won't disturb him.'

'I'll be pleased to do it,' said the old tramp and shuffled off. The housekeeper stared after him. He seemed so feeble that she felt rather guilty at having asked him to weed that bed!

Fatty knelt down and began to weed. He spent a pleasant ten minutes pulling out groundsel and chickweed, and in sorting out the thoughts in his head. He was beginning to think that the clues of 2. Frinton and 1. Rods were not clues at all—simply bits of paper blown by chance into Norton House garden. The real clues were the big footprints and glove-prints—and perhaps the queer print with the criss-cross marks on it.

Still, if the colonel's boots led him to the thief who bought them, the scraps of paper would have come in useful after all. Fatty thought swiftly as he weeded.

He heard the sound of bicycle tyres on the lane outside. The sound stopped as someone got off the bicycle. A head looked cautiously over the hedge. Fatty looked up at the same moment.

Goon was peering over the hedge! He saw Fatty at the same moment as Fatty saw him, and gave a startled grunt. That tramp! He'd left him asleep on the bench outside his house—and now here he was weeding in the colonel's garden. Goon couldn't believe his eyes.

Fatty nodded and smiled amiably. Goon's eyes nearly dropped out of his head. He felt very angry.

Everywhere he went there was somebody before him—first those girls, then those boys, now this deaf old, dirty old tramp. If Goon had been a dog he would have growled viciously.

'What *you* doing here?' said Goon, in a low, hoarse voice.

'Weeding,' answered Fatty, forgetting to be deaf. 'Nice job, weeding.'

'Any cheek from you,' began Goon, forgetting not to wake the colonel. But it was too late. Colonel Cross awoke once more with a jump. He sat up and mopped his forehead. Then he caught sight of Goon's brilliant red face over the top of the hedge. Goon was still addressing Fatty.

'What you doing in this neighbourhood? ' Goon was saying aggressively.

The colonel exploded. 'What's that! What's that! Are you addressing me, my man? What are *you* doing, I should like to know! Hrrrrrumph!'

The last noise startled Goon very much. Fatty chortled as he weeded.

'It's all right, sir. I was speaking to that tramp,' said Goon, with dignity. 'I—er—I had occasion to speak sternly to him this morning, sir. Can't have loiterers and tramps around—what with robberies and things.'

'I don't know what you're talking about,' said Colonel Cross. 'Go away. Policemen should know better than to come and wake me up by shouting to tramps who have been given a job in my garden.'

'I came to have a word with you, actually, sir,' said Goon, desperately. 'Privately.'

'If you think I'm going to get up and go indoors and hear a lot of nonsense from you about robberies and tramps and loiterers you're wrong.' said the old colonel fiercely. 'If you've got something to say, say it here! That old tramp won't understand a word.'

Fatty chortled to himself again. Goon cleared his throat. 'Well–er—I came, sir—just to ask you about your boots!'

'Mad,' said the colonel, staring at Goon. 'Mad! Must be the weather! Wants to talk about my boots! Go away and lie down. You're mad!'

Goon was afraid to go on with the matter. He wheeled his bicycle down the lane, and waited a little while to see if the old tramp came out. He meant to have a word with him! Ho! He'd teach him to cheek him in the colonel's garden!

Fatty finished the bed and tiptoed out, because the colonel was once more asleep. He said good day to the housekeeper, and went off down the path with the old pair of shoes slung round his neck. He was longing for a moment to open his note-book and compare the pattern of those rubber heels!

He didn't see Mr. Goon till he was almost on top of him. Then the policeman advanced on him, with fire in his eye. He stopped short when he saw the enormous pair of shoes slung round Fatty's neck.

To think he'd come all the way down there to talk politely to the colonel about his boots, and had been ordered off and told he was mad—and this dirty old tramp had actually begged a pair, and was wearing them round his neck! Shoes that might be Great Big Clues!

'Give me those!' ordered Goon, and grabbed at the shoes. But the feeble, shuffling old tramp twisted cleverly out of the way, and raced off down the road as if he was a school-boy running in a race.

As indeed he was! Fatty put on his fastest speed, and raced away before Mr. Goon had recovered sufficiently from his surprise even to mount his bicycle.

Fatty turned a corner and hurled himself through a hedge into a field. He tore across it, knowing that Goon couldn't ride his bicycle there. He would have to go a long way round to cut him off!

Across the field, over the stile, across another field, down a lane, round a corner—and here was the front gate of his own house! Into the gate and down the path to the shed. The cook caught a brief glimpose of a tramp-like figure from the kitchen window and then it was gone. She hardly knew if she had seen it or not.

Fatty sank down in the shed. panting and then got up again to lock the door. Phew! What a run! Goon was well and truly left behind. Now to examine the rubber heels.

16   ON THE TRACK AT LAST!

FATTY pulled out his note-book and turned over its pages eagerly till he came to the drawings he had made of the foot-prints. He glued his eyes to his sketch of the pattern of the rubber heels shown in one of the prints.

'Line going across there, two little lines under it, long one there, and three lines together,' he noted. Then he compared the drawn pattern with the rubber heel on one of the shoes.

'It's the same!' he said exultingly. 'The absolute same! That proves it—although it is not the colonel, it's somebody who wears his old boots—somebody who bought a pair last year at Miss Kay's jumble sale. I'm on the track at last!'

He was thrilled. After all their goings and comings, their watchings and interviewings which seemed to have come to nothing, at *last* they had something to work on. Something Mr. Goon hadn't got!

Fatty did a solemn little jig round his shed. He looked very comical indeed, for he was still disguised as a tramp. He carried one of the big shoes in each hand and waved them about gracefully, as if he was doing a scarf or flower dance.

He heard a sound at the window, and stopped suddenly. Was it Goon? Or his mother?

It was neither. It was Larry's grinning face, enjoying the spectacle of the old tramp's idiotic dance. Fatty rushed to the door and unlocked it.

All the others were there, smiling to see Fatty's excitement.

'What is it, Fatty? You've got good news,' said Daisy, pleased.

'I must get these things off,' said Fatty, pulling off his grey wig and suddenly appearing forty years younger. 'Phew—a wig's jolly hot this weather! Now, report to me, all of you, while I make myself decent.'

They all made their reports. First the girls, who giggled when they told him of the boots and shoes they had got from the Rodneys for the jumble sale. 'We've taken them already to give to Miss Kay, the person who's running it,' said Daisy. 'Oh dear—if you could have seen Goon's face when he saw us staggering out with loads of shoes and boots! Anyway, there's nobody at the Rodneys with big feet, so that's another clue finished with. I don't somehow think those scraps of paper meant anything.'

'Nor do I,' said Larry. '*We* got mixed up with old Clear-Orf too—he arrived at Rodneys when we were there. He nearly had a heart-attack when he saw us, he was so furious! We really thought we'd got something at that place, though, when we saw a colossal sou'wester and oilskin hanging up. But no—the owner wears small-size shoes after all!'

'Now tell us what *you* did down at Colonel Cross's,' said Daisy expectantly. 'Go on, Fatty!'

Fatty related his tale with gusto, and when he came to the bit where he had looked up from his weeding and had seen Goon's face glowering over the hedge, with the sleeping colonel between them, the others went off into fits of helpless laughter.

'Oh, Fatty—if only I'd been there!' said Daisy. 'What about the shoes? Tell us.'

Fatty told them everything, and proudly displayed the shoes. 'And now the greatest news of all!' he said, turning up the shoes suddenly so that they displayed the rubber heels. 'See the rubbers? Well look!'

He placed his note-book down beside one of the shoes, so that the drawing and the rubber heel were side by side. The children exclaimed at once.

'It's the same pattern! The very same! Golly, we're getting somewhere now. But surely—it can't be the colonel who's got anything to do with the robbery?'

'No,' said Fatty, and explained about how a pair of his boots had been sent to last year's jumble sale. 'And *if* we can find out who bought them, I think we've got our hands on the thief!' said Fatty exultingly. 'We shall find that the person who bought them is somebody else with big feet—somebody the cobbler doesn't know about because probably the fellow mends his own boots. We're on the track at last!'

Everyone felt thrilled. They watched Fatty become his own self again, rubbing away the greasy lines on his face, removing his eyebrows carefully, sliding his aching feet out of the stiff old boots he wore. He grunted and groaned as he took off the boots and rubbed his sore feet.

'I had three pairs of socks on,' he said, 'because

the boots are so big and stiff—but even so I bet I'll limp for days!'

'You do everything so thoroughly, Fatty,' said Bets admiringly, watching him become the Fatty she knew.

'Secret of success, Bets,' said Fatty with a grin. 'Now then—what do we do next? I feel that our next move is very very important—and it's got to be done quickly before old Goon gets another move on.'

Daisy gave a little giggle when she remembered how they had seen through Goons's disguise that morning, and pestered him. Poor old Clear-Orf! 'Please can you tell us the time?' 'Please can you give change for sixpence?' Oh dear—however dared they be such pests!

'Anyone know Miss Kay?' asked Fatty, putting on his shoes and lacing them up. 'She apparently ran the jumble sale last year. Is she running it this year?'

'Yes,' said Daisy. 'She's the one we took the Rodneys' shoes to. But, Fatty, we can't very well go barging up to her and ask her straight out who bought those boots of the colonel's last year—she'd think it awfully queer.'

'I'm not thinking of doing any barging or blurting out of silly questions,' said Fatty with dignity. 'I've got a very fine idea already—no barging about it!'

'Of *course* Fatty's got a good idea,' said Bets, loyally. 'He always has. What is it, Fatty?'

'I'm simply going to present our very finest clue to Miss Kay for her jumble sale—the colonel's big shoes—and mention casually that perhaps the person who bought them last year, whoever he was might like to buy the same size again this year!' said Fatty. 'Same kind of rubber heels and all!'

Everyone gazed admiringly at him. That was about the best and most direct way of getting the vital information they wanted, without arousing any suspicion at all! Trust Fatty to produce an idea like that.

'Jolly good, Fatty,' said Pip, and the others agreed.

'Let's have tea now,' said Fatty, looking at the time. 'I'll go and see if I can get something out of our cook. You come with me, Bets, because she likes you—and we'll take it out under that tree over there and have a picnic, and relax a bit after all our hard work to-day.'

He and Bets went off together. They came back with an enormous tea on two trays, and an excited Buster. The cook had looked after him all day, and kept him from following Fatty; now he was wild with delight to be with his friends again.

'It's a marvel both the trays haven't crashed,' said Fatty, putting his down carefully. 'I never knew such a dog for getting under your feet when you're carrying anything heavy. Get away from that cake, Buster. Daisy, do stop him licking it all over. There'll be no icing left. Oh golly, now he's stepped on the buns.'

Bets caught Buster and held him down beside her. 'He can't help dancing about, he's so pleased we're back,' she said. 'See what lovely things we've brought you all! I feel we've earned a good tea!'

They talked over their day as they ate, giggling whenever they thought of poor Mr. Goon and his despair at finding them just in front of him, wherever he went.

'I'm going down to Miss Kay's this evening,' said Fatty. 'Taking the shoes! Oh, wonderful, magnificent shoes, that will solve the mystery for us! And before seven o'clock comes I'll be back with the name of the thief! A little telephoning to the Inspector—and a little explaining—and we shall be able to let Goon know tomorrow that the case is closed—the mystery is solved—as usual, by the Five Find-Outers—and dog!'

'Hip, hip, hurrah!' said Pip. 'I say, Bets—*don't* give Buster any more of those potted-meat sandwiches—I want some too! Fatty, stop her. Buster's fat enough as it is. If he gets much fatter he won't be able to help in any more mysteries. Not that he's *really* helped in this one much!'

'Now you've made him put his tail down,' said Bets, and gave him another sandwich. 'Oh, Fatty, do let me come with you to Miss Kay's. You know who she is, don't you? She's the cousin of that horrid little baker—the one who always tries to be funny.'

'She's just as silly as he is,' said Daisy. 'I told you that we took the Rodneys' boots and shoes to her this afternoon. She's got a dreadful collection of things there. Honestly I think jumble is awful. She was very pleased with the boots and shoes. She says they go like hot cakes at a sale.'

'Well, I think I'll go now,' said Fatty, getting up

and brushing the crumbs from his front. 'Coming, Bets? Yes, you can come too, Buster.'

Bets, Buster and Fatty went out. Fatty carried the colonel's shoes wrapped in a bit of brown paper.

'Well, so long!' said Fatty cheerfully. 'Get out the flags for when we come back—we'll bring you the name of the thief!'

17 A BITTER DISAPPOINTMENT

FATTY and Bets walked off to Miss Kay's with Buster trotting at their heels. They kept a sharp look out for Mr. Goon. Fatty felt sure that he had guessed who the old tramp was that afternoon, and he didn't particularly want to meet him just then.

Miss Kay lived in a tiny cottage next to her cousin and his wife. Bets hoped they wouldn't see the little baker. 'I get so tired of trying to smile at his silly jokes,' she said to Fatty. 'Look—here we are—don't you think it looks like a place where jumble is taken? Daisy and I thought so, anyway.'

Bets was right. The cottage and its little garden looked untidy and 'jumbly,' as Bets put it. A broken-down seat was in the little front garden, and a little, much-chipped statue stood in the centre. The gate was half off its hinges, and one of its bars had gone. The curtains at the window looked dirty and didn't match.

'I should think Miss Kay buys most of the jumble for herself!' whispered Bets, nodding at the broken seat and chipped statue.

Miss Kay looked a bit of a jumble herself, when she opened the door to them. She was as small and sprightly as her baker-cousin, but not nearly so neat and spruce. 'She's all bits and pieces,' thought Bets, looking at her. 'Hung about with all the jumble nobody else buys—bead necklaces, a torn scarf, a belt with its embroidery spoilt, and that awful red comb in her hair!'

Miss Kay seemed delighted to see them. '*Do* come in!' she said, in a kind of cooing voice. 'It isn't often I get a nice young gentleman to see me. And this dear little girl again too—you came this afternoon, didn't you, dearie?'

'Yes,' said Bets, who didn't like being called 'dearie' by Miss Kay.

'And what have you brought me *this* time, love?' asked Miss Kay, leading the way into a little room so crowded with furniture that Fatty had great difficulty in finding where to step. He knocked over a small table, and looked down in alarm.

'I'm so sorry,' he said, and bent to pick up the things that had fallen. Miss Kay bent down at the same time and their heads bumped together.

'Oh, sorry,' said Fatty, again. Miss Kay gave a little giggle, and rubbed her head.

'Oh, it's nothing! My cousin says I've got a wooden head,so a bump never matters to me!' She gave another silly little giggle, and Bets smiled feebly.

'This kind little girl brought me *such* a lot of nice things for the Jumble Sale, this afternoon,' chattered Miss Kay. 'And I'm hoping *you've* brought something too. *What's* in that parcel?'

She put her head on one side, and her comb fell out. She gave a little squeal and picked it up. 'Oh dear—I seem to be falling to bits! You know, that cheeky cousin of mine says one day I'll be a bit of jumble myself, and be sold for sixpence. He, he, he!'

Fatty felt rather sick. He didn't like the baker, her cousin, but he liked Miss Kay even less. He opened his parcel and took out the shoes. All he wanted to do now was to get information he needed, and go!

Miss Kay gave another squeal. 'Oh! *What* an enormous pair of shoes! Are they *yours*? That's just a joke of course, I didn't mean it. I'm such a tease aren't I! My, it's quite a good pair, though.'

'It's a pair of Colonel Cross's,' said Fatty. 'He sent a pair of boots last year too. I thought perhaps the same person who had feet big enough to fit last year's boots would probably like to buy these. Do you know who it was?'

Bets' heart began to beat fast. She looked breathlessly at Miss Kay. She and Fatty waited for the name. What would it be?

'Oh, they weren't sold last year,' said Miss Kay. 'There was *quite* a little mystery about them! Really, it gave me *quite* a shock. You see . . .'

'What do you mean—they weren't sold?' asked Fatty, determined to keep her to the point.

'Well, love—they just *disappeared*!' said Miss Kay, speaking with bated breath as if she hardly wanted anyone to hear. 'Disappeared! One night they were here, ready for the sale—and the next morning they were gone!'

'Were they stolen?' asked Fatty bitterly disappointed.

'Oh yes—no doubt about it,' said Miss Kay. 'Funny thing is, nothing else was taken at all—just those big boots. They were under that table over there—where I've put all the boots and shoes this year—and the thief went there, chose out the big boots and went off with them. I'd marked them with a price and everything. As a matter of fact I hoped to sell them to that nice policeman of ours—Mr. Goon. But they just went one night.'

'Who stole them—do you know?' asked Fatty. 'Is there anyone you know who has big feet, who might think of stealing them? It must surely be someone in the village—how else would they know you had a pair of enormous boots here that would fit them? They knew where to find them too—under that table in your cottage!'

Miss Kay gave another little squeal. 'How very clever you are, love! As clever as that nice Mr. Goon. No, I don't know who took the boots—and I don't know anyone with enormous feet either, who could wear them.'

'Did Mr. Goon know about it?' asked Fatty.

'Oh no. My cousin said that as I'd only marked the boots at a shilling, it wasn't worth taking up the time of the police over a pair of jumble boots,' said Miss Kay. 'He's very good like that, my cousin is. He gave me six pence towards the stolen boots and I gave sixpence myself, and we put the shilling into the Jumble Box, so the Sale didn't lose by it. I do hope you think I was right.'

'Quite right,' said Fatty, bored with all this niggling over jumble boots, and wild to think that their wonderful idea was no good. The boots had been stolen—and nobody knew who had taken them. Nobody even seemed to know anyone with outsize feet. There seemed to be a dearth of large feet in Peterswood. It was really most annoying. He seemed to run into a blank wall, no matter what clue he followed. Fatty felt very down in the dumps.

'I think, on the whole, I won't leave these big shoes here,' said Fatty, wrapping them up again. 'I mean— if there are thieves about here who have an urge for enormous boots and shoes, these might disappear as well. I'll bring them down to you on the day of the Jumble Sale, Miss Kay.'

Fatty wasn't going to leave his precious shoes, with their rubber heels, at Miss Kay's now that he hadn't got the information he wanted! It would be a waste of his clue. He was quite determined about that.

Miss Kay looked as if she was going to burst into tears. Fatty hurriedly went to the door with Bets before this disaster happened. He saw someone in the next garden—the little baker, Miss Kay's cousin. He groaned. Now there would be another volley of silly talk.

'Hallo, hallo, *hallo*!' said the baker genially. 'If it isn't Master Frederick Trotteville, the great detective. Solved the mystery of the robbery yet, young man?'

Fatty always hated being called 'young man' and he especially disliked it from the little baker. He scowled.

Bets spoke up for him. 'He's nearly solved it. He soon will. We just want to find the name of the man with big feet, that's all. We almost got it to-night.'

'Shut up, Bets,' said Fatty in a low and most unexpectedly cross voice. Bets flushed and fell silent. But the little baker made up for her sudden silence.

'Well, well, well—we shall expect to hear great

things soon! I suppose the same man did both the robberies? I saw his prints all right! Me and Mr. Goon we had a good old chin-wag over it—ah, Mr. Goon will get the thief all right—before you do, young man! He's on the track, yes, he's on the track. Told me so when I left his bread to-day. Those were his very words. "I'm on the track, Twit," he said, just like that.'

'Interesting,' said Fatty in a bored voice, and opened the gate for Bets to go through. The little baker didn't like Fatty's tone of voice. He strutted up to his own gate and stood there, going up and down on his jeels in rather an insolent manner, leering at Bets and Fatty.

' "Interesting!" you says—just like that! Pride goes before a fall, young man. You watch your step. I've heard a lot about you from Mr. Goon.'

'That's enough, Twit,' said Fatty in such a stern, grown-up voice that Bets jumped. So did Twit. He altered his tone at once.

'I didn't mean no harm, sir. Just my joke, like. Me and my cousin, Miss Kay, we do like a joke, don't we, Coz?'

Coz was apparently Miss Kay, who was standing by her front gate, smiling and listening, bobbing up and down on her heels just like her cousin.

'Guard your tongue, Twit,' said Fatty, still in his grown-up voice. 'You'll get yourself into trouble if you don't.'

He walked off with Bets, angry, disappointed and rather crestfallen. Twit and Miss Kay watched them go. Twit was red in the face and angry.

'Insolence!' he said to his cousin. 'Young

upstart! Talking to me like that! I'll learn him. Thinks himself no end clever, does he? Ah, Mr. Goon's right—he's a toad, that boy.'

'Oh, don't talk like that!' said Miss Kay fearfully. 'You'll lose your customers!'

Bets slipped her hand through Fatty's arm as they went home. 'Fatty,' she said, 'I'm awfully sorry for what I said to Twit. I didn't think it mattered.'

'Well, I suppose it doesn't,' said Fatty, patting Bets' hand. 'But never talk when we're solving a mystery, Bets. You just might give something away—though it seems to me that Twit must know pretty well everything from Goon—they sound like bosom friends!'

'Are you very disappointed, Fatty?' asked Bets, very sad to see Fatty so down in the dumps. It wasn't a bit like him.

'Yes, I am,' said Fatty. 'We've come to a dead end, little Bets. There's no further clue to follow, nothing more to do. We'll have to give it up—the first mystery we've ever been beaten by!'

And, in a mournful silence, the two went dolefully down to the shed to tell the miserable news.

18   THE THIRD ROBBERY

FOR a day or two the Five Find-Outers were very much subdued. It was horrid to have to give up —just when they had thought the whole thing was going to be solved so quickly and successfully too!

Fatty was quite upset by it. He worried a lot, going over and over all the clues and the details of the two robberies, trying to find another trail to follow. But he couldn't. As he had said to Bets, they had come to a dead end, a blank wall.

The weather broke and the rain came down. What with that and Fatty looking so solemn, the other four were quite at a loose end. They got into mischief, irritated their parents, and simply didn't know what to do with themselves.

Fatty cheered up after a bit. 'It's just that I *hate* being beaten, you know,' he said to the others. 'I never am, as a matter of fact. This is the first time— and if anybody feels inclined to say, "Well, I suppose it's good for you, Fatty," I warn them, don't say it. It *isn't* good for me. It's bad .'

'Well, do cheer up now, Fatty,' said Daisy. 'It's really awful having you go about looking like a hen out in the rain! As for poor old Buster, I hardly know if he's got a tail these days, it's tucked between his legs so tightly. It hasn't wagged for days!'

'Hey, Buster! Good dog, Buster! Master's all right now!' said Fatty suddenly, to the little Scottie. He spoke in his old cheerful voice, and Buster leapt up as if he had been shot. His tail wagged nineteen to the dozen, he barked, flung himself on Fatty and then went completely mad.

He tore round and round Pip's playroom as if he was running a race, and finally hurled himself out of the door, slid all the way down the landing and fell down the stairs.

The children screamed with delight. Buster was always funny when he went mad. Mrs. Hilton's voice came up the stairs.

'Pip! Fatty! Come and catch Buster. He seems to have gone off his head. Oh—here he comes again. What is the matter with him!'

Buster tore up the stairs at sixty miles an hour, slid along the landing again and came to rest under a chair. He lay there, panting, quite tired out, his tail thumping against the floor.

Everyone felt better after that. Fatty looked at his watch. 'Let's go to Oliver's again and have a splash— I could do with three or four meringues.'

'Ooooh, yes—*I've* got some money to-day,' said Larry, pulling out a ten-shilling note. 'It's one my uncle Ted gave me weeks ago and I couldn't think where I'd put it for safety. I found it to-day in my tie-box.'

'We'll all go shares,' said Pip. 'I've got two bob, and Bets has got a shilling.'

'Right,' said Fatty. 'The more the merrier. Come on. I'll just telephone to my mother to tell her we're going to Oliver's.'

They went off, feeling happier than they had done for days. Buster's tail had appeared again and was wagging merrily as he ran along with them.

His master was all right again—life was bright once more!

They stayed a long time over their tea, talking hard, and eating equally hard. Nobody said a word about the mystery. They weren't going to remember defeat when éclairs and meringues and chocolate cake were spread in front of them! That would be silly.

Feeling rather full, they walked back to Fatty's , and went down the garden to the shed. Buster trotted on ahead. He surprised them all by suddenly barking urgently and loudly.

'What's up, Buster?' shouted Fatty, beginning to run. Larry raced down the path with him. Whatever could Buster be barking about like that?

Pip and Larry came to the shed. The door was wide open, though Fatty always left it shut and locked. Fatty ran in, amazed. He looked round.

His things were all in a muddle! Clothes had been dragged down from the pegs, drawers in a chest had been emptied, and everywhere was mess and muddle. Someone had been there and turned everything upside down.

'My money's gone, of course,' said Fatty in exasperation. 'I'd got two pounds I was saving for Mother's birthday—why did I leave it here! I never do leave money in the ordinary way. Blow!'

'Anything else gone?' asked Larry. Pip, Daisy and Bets crowded into the untidy shed. Bets burst into tears, but nobody took any notice of her, not even Fatty.

'My knife's gone—that silver one,' said Fatty. 'And that little silver case I kept odds and ends in.

And yes—my cigarette case is gone, the one I use when I'm disguised. Well, the thief is welcome to that! I suppose he thought it was silver, but it isn't. It's Woolworth!'

'Oh, Fatty!' wailed Bets. 'What's happened? Has a robber been here? Oh, what shall we do?'

'Shut up, Bets,' said Pip. 'Behaving like a baby as usual. Go home if you can't be any help.'

Bets stopped wailing at once. She looked at Fatty but he was completely engrossed in checking up his belongings.

She went outside to swallow her tears and be sensible—and then she suddenly saw something that made her stare. She yelled loudly.

'Fatty! FATTY! Come here, quick!'

Fatty appeared at top speed, the others behind him. Bets pointed to the muddy path near the shed. On it were clear foot-prints—enormous ones!

'Gosh!' said Fatty. 'It's our robber again. The very same one—look at the marks his rubber heels made— the same pattern as before.'

'Will there be glove-prints too?' asked Daisy excitedly, and she went back into the shed.

'Shouldn't think so,' said Fatty following. 'There's no wall-paper or distemper to show them up.'

'Well, look—there they are!' said Daisy, pointing triumphantly. And sure enough, there were two large glove-prints showing clearly on the looking glass that Fatty had in his shed!

'He likes to leave his mark, doesn't he?' said Larry. 'You'd almost think he was saying, "This is the robber, his mark!"'

'Yes,' said Fatty thoughtfully. 'Well, it's the same fellow all right. He hasn't got away with a great deal, thank goodness—but what a mess!'

'We'll soon clear it up,' said Bets, eager to do something for poor old Fatty.

'Let's take a very very careful snoop round before we move *anything*,' said Fatty. 'The Mystery has come right to our very door—it's all alive-oh again. We may perhaps be able to solve it this time.'

'I suppose you're not going to inform the police!' said Larry with a laugh.

'No. I'm not,' said Fatty very firmly. 'First thing I'm going to do is to measure up the footprints to make absolutely certain they're the same ones that we saw before—at Norton House and at Mrs. Williams's.'

They were, of course, exactly the same. No doubt about it at all. The glove-prints were the same too.

'We can't find out whether there was a hollow cough this time,' said Pip, 'because there was nobody here to hear it. I suppose there aren't any scraps of paper, are there, Fatty?'

'None,' said Fatty. 'But there weren't at Mrs. Williams's either, you know. I'm beginning to think that they really had nothing to do with the robberies. They don't really link up with anything.'

Daisy went wandering off down the path a little. She came to another print by the side of the path, almost under a shrub. She called Fatty.

'Look!' she said. 'Isn't this queer print like the ones you found in both the other robberies?'

Fatty knelt to see. On the wet ground under the shrub the mark was quite plain—a big roundish print with criss-cross lines here and there.

'Yes,' said Fatty puzzled, turning over the pages of his note-book to compare his drawing with the print. 'It's the same. I cannot *imagine* what makes it—or why it appears in all the robberies. It's extraordinary.'

They all gazed down at the strange mark. Pip wrinkled his forehead. 'You know—somehow I feel as if I've seen it somewhere else besides the robberies. Where could it have been?'

'Think, Pip, ' said Fatty. 'It might help.'

But Pip couldn't think. All he could say was that he thought he had seen it somewhere on the day when they all went interviewing.

'That's not much help,' said Fatty with a sigh. 'We were all over the place that day. Now we'd better put everything back. I can't see that we can find any more clues. As a matter of fact it seems as if this robbery is almost an exact repetition of the others—large foot-prints, glove-prints, strange unknown print, and small goods stolen.'

They hung up the clothes, and put back everything into the chest of drawers. They kept a sharp look-out for any possible clue, but as far as they could see there was none at all.

'How did the thief get down to the shed?' asked Larry. 'Did he get in through the back gate leading into the lane, do you think? It's not far from the shed. Or did he come down the path from the house?'

'Well—if he made that queer mark under the shrub, it rather looks as if he came from the house,' said Fatty. 'On the other hand, the large footprints are only round and about the shed—I didn't find any on the path up to the house, did you?'

'No,' said Larry. 'Well, it's more likely he would have come quietly in through the back-gate down by the shed—he wouldn't be seen then. It's very secluded down here at the bottom of the garden—can't be seen from the house at all.'

'All the same, I think we'd better ask the cook and the house-parlourmaid if they saw anyone,' said Fatty. 'They just might have. And we'll ask who has been to the house this afternoon too. Any tradesman or visitor might have seen somebody.'

'Yes. Good idea,' said Larry. 'Come on—let's go and find out.'

19   THE WARNING

THE house-parlourmaid was out, and had been out all the afternoon. The cook was in, however, and was rather surprised to see all the five children and Buster trooping in at her kitchen door.

'Now don't you say you want tea,' she began. 'It's a quarter to six, and. . .'

'No, we don't want tea,' said Fatty. 'I just came to ask you a few things. Someone's been disturbing my belongings in the shed at the bottom of the garden. I wondered if you had seen anyone going down the path to the shed this afternoon.'

'Goodness,' said the cook alarmed. 'Don't tell me there's tramps about again. I thought I saw a very nasty-looking fellow slipping down that path the other day.'

Fatty knew who *that* was all right. So did the others. They turned away to hide their grins.

'No—it's to-day I want to know about,' said Fatty. 'Did you see anyone at all?'

'Not a soul to-day,' said the cook. 'And I've been sitting here at this window all the time!'

'You didn't have forty winks, I suppose?' asked Fatty, with a smile. 'You do sometimes.'

'Well, maybe I did for a few minutes,' said the cook, with a laugh. 'I get right sleepy in the afternoons, when it's hot like this. Still, I was awake enough all right when the tradespeople came.'

'Who came?' asked Larry.

'Oh, the usual ones,' said the cook. 'The girl

with the groceries, the milkman, the baker—and let me see, did the gasman come? No, that was this morning.'

'Anyone else?' asked Fatty.

'Well, Mr. Goon called,' said the cook, 'and he asked for your mother, but she wasn't in. So he went away again. He came at the same time as the baker did. They had a good old talk together too, out in the front garden. I heard them. Mr. Goon bumped into the baker just as he was leaving.'

'I bet they had a good talk about Bets and me,' said Fatty to the others. 'Anyone else call, Cook?'

'Not that I know of,' she said. 'I didn't have any talk with the baker—he's too much of a saucy one for me—I just left a note on the table to tell him how many loaves to leave. And I didn't see the milkman either—he knows how much to leave. I saw the grocer's girl, and she was in a hurry as usual.'

'I wonder what Goon wanted,' said Fatty as they left the kitchen to walk down to the shed again. 'I bet he wants to know if I was the old tramp the other day. As if Mother would know!'

They were just walking out of the scullery door when Daisy stopped suddenly and looked down at the ground.

'Look!' she said, and pointed.

They all looked—and there, just by the scullery door, in a wet patch of ground, was the same roundish mark that they had seen under the shrub! The same as they had seen at the other two robberies as well.

'Gosh!' said Fatty staring down. 'The thief

did actually come to the scullery door then! He must have made that mark—but why?'

'Your cook said nobody else came except the people she mentioned,' said Larry. 'It seems to me as if the thief came here, peeped in and saw the Cook asleep and went down to the shed to do his dirty work.'

'The why didn't he leave large foot-prints here?' said Daisy. 'There's only small ones going to and from the bottom of the garden. I looked. There's no large ones at all—no larger than size seven, anyway.'

'It beats me!' said Pip.

It beat them all. Now there had been three separate robberies, all obviously done by the same man, who left exactly the same marks each time—and yet he had never once been seen, though he must really be a very big fellow indeed.

'He's invisible—that's how he can do all these things!' said Daisy. 'I mean—surely *some*body would have seen him *one* of the times. But all he does is to come and go, and leave behind him foot and glove-prints, and do just what he likes! He must be laughing up his sleeve at all of us.'

'It *can't* be old Goon, can it?' said Bets hopefully. 'He has large feet and hands, and he *has* got a hollow, sheep-like cough, and he really does hate you, Fatty. He came here to-day too—why couldn't he have slipped down and been spiteful, turning all your things upside down and making a mess?'

'I daresay he'd *like* to,' said Fatty, 'but remember he was away at the time of the first robbery—

and honestly I don't think he's ass enough to do such idiotic things—I mean, it's sheer dishonesty, robbing people like this, and Goon wouldn't risk his job and his pension. No, rule that right out, Bets.'

'Are you going to ask the milkman and the others if they saw anyone?' asked Bets. Fatty shook his head.

'No. I'm pretty certain now that if the milkman, the baker or the grocer's girl had seen anyone here this afternoon, wandering about in large-size boots they would have told Cook. Anyway, I'm not interviewing that cocky little baker again—wouldn't he be pleased if he knew I'd been robbed! He'd rub his little hands like anything, and rock to and fro on his toes and heels with glee.'

'Yes, he would,' said Bets, rocking to and fro as she remembered how he had gone up and down on his heels. 'Nasty little man. I hope he doesn't hear about this.'

'No one is to,' said Fatty firmly. 'I'm not going to have Goon strolling down the garden and fingering everything in my shed. How he'd love to look through my make-up box, and pick up all my moustaches and eyebrows and wigs!'

'Well, none of us will say a word about this afternoon's do,' said Larry. 'We'll keep the thief guessing! He'll wonder whyever there's no news of his last robbery.'

'The thief burst the lock on your door, Fatty,' said Bets. 'How will you lock it to-night?'

'I'll slip out and buy a padlock,' said Fatty. 'That will be the easiest thing to do to-night— put a padlock on the door. I'll come with you when you go home. I can get one at the garage—that stays open till seven.'

So, at ten to seven Fatty and the others strolled up the lane to the garage in the village. They bought a strong little padlock, and came out, examining it.

A voice behind them made them jump. It was Mr. Goon, starting out on his first night-round.

'Ho! A padlock! Maybe you'll need that, Master Frederick! You'd better be careful.'

Everyone swung round in astonishment. 'What do you mean, Mr. Goon?' said Fatty.

'I've had notice that you'll be the next on the robbery-list,' said Goon importantly. 'I came to warn your mother this afternoon. Just you see that everything is well-locked up to-night, windows fastened and everything. And have that there pesky little dog of yours in the front hall.'

'What *is* all this about?' said Fatty, hoping that nobody would blurt out anything about the robbery that had already happened that afternoon. 'What nonsense, Mr. Goon!'

Mr. Goon swelled up a little, and Bets was sure one of his uniform buttons was about to spring off. He fumbled in his breast-pocket and brought out his little note-book. He undid the elastic strap and ran through the pages. Everyone watched in silence.

He took out a scrap of dirty paper, and handed it to Fatty. 'There you are. If that isn't a plain warning I don't know what is. 'Course, you don't need to take no notice of it at all—and anyway I'll be sure to be round two or three times to-night to see as everything is all right round at yours.'

Fatty took the scrap of paper. On it, printed in uneven lettering, were three words:

TROTVILLS NEXT—Bigfeet

Fatty silently passed it round to the others. They knew what Goon didn't know—that the warning was too late. Bigfeet the robber, had already been to the Trottevilles!

'There you are!' said Goon, enjoying the interest he was causing. 'The impertinence of it! Good as saying "Fat lot of good you are—I'll tell you where I'm going to strike next." Signing himself Bigfeet too. He's got some sauce!'

'Goon, have you got the other scraps of paper on you?' asked Fatty. 'The ones found at Norton House, with 2, Frinton and 1, Rods on? It would be useful to compare them.'

Goon gave a scornful little snort. 'Think I didn't compare them, Mr. Smarty? 'Course I did. But this here note's in printed capitals and the others aren't. Can't see any likeness at all.'

'I think you're wrong, Mr. Goon,' said Fatty suddenly speaking like a grown-up again. 'And if you like I'll show you the likeness.'

'Gah,' said Goon in disgust. 'Think you know everything, don't you? Well, I tell you I've compared the three scraps of paper, and this one's different.'

'I don't believe it,' said Fatty.

That stung Mr. Goon and he glared. He felt in the little pocket of his note-book and produced the other two notes. He showed them to Fatty, together with the third one. 'See? No likeness at all!' he said triumphantly.

'I'm not thinking of the words written on the papers,' said Fatty. 'I'm thinking of the *paper* they're written *on*. It's exactly the same. Whoever wrote the first notes, wrote this one too. So those first scraps of paper *were* clues after all—though they led to nothing.'

Mr. Goon stared at the scraps of paper. Fatty was right. They had obviously been torn from the same note-book or sheets of paper—they were all rather yellowed and the surface was a little fluffy.

Mr. Goon cleared his throat. He felt a little awkward. That boy! Always putting him in the wrong. He put the scraps back into his pocket-book.

He cleared his throat again. 'Think I didn't notice that?' he said. 'Why, it hits you in the eye!'

'It didn't seem to have given you a very hard blow then,' said Fatty. 'Well, I'm not heeding that warning, Mr. Goon—so you can sleep in peace to-night! There will be no robbery at the Trottevilles, I can tell you that!'

20 MOSTLY ABOUT GOON

THE five children, with Buster, went on their way, Fatty thinking deeply. The others respected his thoughts and said nothing. They came to the corner where they had to part with Larry and Daisy.

'Any orders, Fatty?' said Larry respectfully.

'Er—what? Oh, orders. No, none,' said Fatty, coming out of his trance. 'Sorry to be so goofy all of a sudden. But it's queer, isn't it—that warning, I mean. Why did the thief send it? He must be jolly sure of himself—though, of course, he might have sent it to Goon *after* he'd done the job. I just don't understand it.'

'When did Goon get it?' said Daisy. 'I didn't hear him say. Did you ask him?'

'No. I was so surprised to find that the third scrap of paper was the same as the first two, which meant they really did have something to do with the thief, that I didn't ask any of the questions I should,' said Fatty vexed. 'That means I'll have to go back and get a little more information. Goon will be pleased!'

'Is the mystery on again?' asked Bets.

'Very much on, Bets,' said Fatty. 'Oh very much! Blow Bigfeet! I shall dream about him to-night. It really is a puzzle how that fellow can get about without being noticed—I mean, there's all of us on the watch, and Goon, and the baker, and the grocer's girl, and goodness knows how many other people too, looking for a large-footed man—and yet the fellow has the nerve to walk up the road to my house, go in at one of the front gates, walk up to the scullery door, and all the way down to the shed, and then out again with his stolen goods—and not a single soul sees him.'

'He *must* be invisible!' said Bets quite convinced.

'The Case of the Invisible Thief—or the Mystery of Bigfeet the Robber!' said Fatty. 'It's a funny case this—lots of clues all leading nowhere.'

They said good-bye and parted. Fatty went back to Mr. Goon's house. He must find out where that paper had been put when it was delivered, and what time it was sent.

He came to Mr. Goon's house. Goon was back again, and was spending an interesting ten minutes trying on a supply of new moustaches that had arrived by post that day.

He was sitting in front of the mirror, twirling a particularly fine moustache when he heard the knock at the front door. He peered out of the window. Ah— that fat boy. Goon grinned to himself.

He crammed a hat down on his head, frowned, twisted his new moustaches up, and leaned out of the window.

'What do you want?' he asked in a deep, rather sinister voice. Fatty looked up and was extremely startled to see the scowling, moustached face above him. In a trice he recognized Goon—there was no mistaking those frog-like eyes. However, if Goon wanted to think he could make himself unrecognizable by adding a moustache and a scowl, Fatty was quite willing to let him.

'Er—good evening,' said Fatty politely. 'Could I speak to Mr. Goon? Or is he busy? '

'He's busy,' said the face, in a hollow voice and the moustache twitched up and down.

'Oh, what a pity. It's rather important,' said Fatty.

'I'll see if he'll see you,' said the face, and disappeared. Fatty chuckled. The door opened half a minute later, and Mr. Goon appeared, minus scowl and moustache. Actually he felt quite amiable for once. His disguise had deceived that fat boy—ha, Fatty wasn't as clever as he thought he was!

'Good evening, Mr. Goon,' said Fatty. 'Did your friend tell you I wanted to see you.'

'He did,' said Goon. 'What do you want?'

'I forgot to ask you how you got that third note and when,' said Fatty. 'It might be important.'

'I don't know how *or* when it came,' said Mr. Goon annoyingly.

'Well—when did you find it?' asked Fatty.

'I was going through some papers in the office,' said Goon, 'and I was lost in them—very important papers they were, see. Well, the milkman and the baker came and left the bread and the milk as usual—and when I came into the kitchen to get myself a cup of tea, I picked up the bottle of milk—and there was the note on top of it!'

'Thank you,' said Fatty. 'So you don't really know what time it came except that it must have come after the milkman and baker. Did you hear *them* come?'

As Mr. Goon had been fast asleep all the afternoon he had heard no one at all, but he wasn't going to tell Fatty that.

'I expect I heard them come,' he said. 'But when I read through official papers—very important ones too—I get lost in them. I daresay the tradesmen came about the usual time—three o'clock or so.'

'Thanks,' said Fatty. 'That's all I wanted to know. You came along to my house then, to give us the warning? Our cook told me you came.'

'Yes. I came along at once,' said Goon. 'As was my bounden duty. Pity you won't take no notice of that warning. Still, I'll be along to-night all right.'

'As is your bounden duty!' said Fatty. 'Well, I'll be off. I'm sorry to have disturbed that friend of yours, Mr. Goon.'

'Oh, he won't mind,' said Goon, most gratified to find that Fatty apparently hadn't recognized who the 'friend' was.

'Good-looking fellow, isn't he?' said Fatty, innocently. Goon agreed instantly.

'Yes, quite. Fine moustaches,' he said.

'Very very fine,' said Fatty. 'Actually they are what made him good-looking. Without those, he'd have been very plain indeed, in fact, quite ugly. Don't you agree?'

And before poor Goon could find his tongue Fatty had gone. That boy! Slippery as an eel in all he said and did. Now, exactly what did he mean by those last remarks?

Fatty walked home, deep in thought again. He had his supper by himself because his parents were out, and didn't even notice what a delicious meal the cook had prepared for him, much to her disappointment. He was thinking so very hard.

He went up to his own room after his meal and tried to read a very thrilling mystery story; but his own mystery was much more interesting to him, and after a bit he pushed the book aside and fell into thought again.

'What I can't understand is that all the different clues we have *ought* to fit together like a jigsaw puzzle and make a definite picture of the thief,' said Fatty to himself. 'And they don't. They just don't. And yet if I could find out how to fit them together I could solve the mystery at once—who the thief is— how he gets about unseen—why he doesn't care whether his prints are all over the place or not—how he gets away with his goods without fear of being detected with them—and above all why he sent that warning. That's so boastful, somehow—he must be very very certain of himself and his powers.'

He fell asleep immediately he got into bed, and then woke up worrying again. Half asleep and half awake he lay there with his mind milling round and round all the clues and details. Things got mixed up in his half-sleeping mind—the milkman's cart and the warning note on the milk-bottle—the baker's basket and pairs of large boots—hollow coughs and large moustaches—there was no end to the pictures that came and went in his mind.

Then Buster began to bark! Fatty awoke properly and sat up. 'Gosh! Did that warning mean the thief was coming to the *house*?' thought

Fatty, dragging on his dressing-gown. He had imagined that it meant the robbery in the shed. He shot downstairs and opened the front door to let Buster out. The dog had run straight to the door and scraped at it.

'Well, if the thief's outside, you'll give him a shock, Buster,' said Fatty. Buster shot out and disappeared into the front garden. There came an agonized yell.

'Get out! Clear-orf! Clear-orf, I say!'

Fatty collapsed into laughter. It was poor old Goon out there, solemnly 'doing his bounden duty' in the middle of the night. He had come to see that the Trotteville's house was not already burgled.

'Buster! Come here!' yelled Fatty, and the yell woke his parents, the cook and house-parlour-maid at once. Everyone crowded on to the landing.

'Frederick! What *is* all this disturbance?' called his father, coming downstairs. Buster was now in Fatty's arms, struggling to go again. Oh, the joy of being let out in the middle of the night and finding Goon's ankles at his mercy! What a wonderful surprise it had been to Buster.

Mr. Goon loomed up in the doorway, very angry. 'You set that there dog on me,' he began. 'And me doing my duty, and guarding your property.'

Mrs. Trotteville had no time for Mr. Goon. 'What does he want?' she called down to Fatty.

'I don't really know,' said Fatty. 'What exactly did you say you wanted, Mr. Goon?'

'I don't want anything, as you very well know,' said Mr. Goon, in a real temper. 'I was just doing my duty, what with that warning and all. . . .'

Mr. Goon loomed up in the doorway, very angry

'What's he talking about?' said Mr. Trotteville coming up to the front door.

'About a warning,' said Fatty.

'What warning?' asked Mr. Trotteville, quite at sea.

'Why, that warning from Bigfeet,' said Mr. Goon, in surprise not realizing that Fatty had said nothing to his parents.

'Bigfeet! Is he mad?' said Mr. Trotteville. 'Look here, Goon, you come along in the morning and talk about big feet all you like—but not in the middle of the night. You go home to bed.'

Goon snorted, and was about to say something very cutting when Mr. Trotteville firmly shut the door. 'Is he mad?' he asked Fatty.

'Not more than usual,' said Fatty. 'Well, if he comes again I'll let Buster out—he won't come very often after that!'

But Goon didn't come again. He walked off wrathfully, thinking of all the things he would like to do to that young toad—yes, and to that pest of a dog too.

'And me doing my bounden duty,' he said to himself. 'Well, let 'em be robbed good and proper— good and proper, is what I say!'

21 PIP PLAYS A TRICK

THE next morning Fatty felt very gloomy again. He ate his breakfast in complete silence, much to his mother's surprise.

'Do you feel quite well, Frederick?' she asked him.

'What, Mother? Oh yes—I'm all right,' said Fatty. 'Just thinking, that's all.'

'I hope you haven't got mixed up in one of those awful mystery affairs again,' said Mrs. Trotteville.

Fatty said nothing. He *was* mixed up in one—and he was completely at a loss about it! Three different robberies—one in his own shed—heaps of clues—and no solution at all, unless he made up his mind that the thief was invisible, which was obviously impossible.

'The worst of it is he's laughing up his sleeve at us the whole time,' thought Fatty, in exasperation. 'I feel that it's someone who knows us. Do we know *him*? And he's so jolly certain of himself and his ability to get away unseen that he even has the cheek to warn us where he's going to commit the next robbery.'

He thought of his visit to Miss Kay, and his high hopes when he went there. If only those boots hadn't been stolen, everything would have been so easy.

'Frederick, you really must go and get your hair cut this morning,' said Mrs. Trotteville. 'It's far too long.'

'All right, Mother,' said Fatty, who had been expecting this suggestion for the last two weeks. He knew his hair was rather long, but it made disguises a bit easier if his hair was long and he wasn't going to wear a wig. He could pull it about a bit, and make it go different ways under a hat.

'Ring up and make an appointment,' said Mrs. Trotteville, ' then you won't have to wait for ages.'

When the others came at ten o'clock to meet in Fatty's shed, and see if anything further had happened, they were met by a gloomy Fatty.

'Got to go and get my hair cut,' he said. 'I'll be back in about half an hour. You can either wait for me here or go and have you first ice-cream of the day while I'm at the hairdresser's.'

'All right,' said Larry. 'Anything further happened?'

'Nothing much—except that Goon came in the middle of the night to see if we'd been burgled or not—and I really thought it might be the thief and let old Buster out. Gosh, he was thrilled to find Goon's ankles out there!'

Everyone laughed, and Fatty cheered up a bit, 'Well, what are you going to do? Wait here?' asked Fatty.

'Yes. I think we will,' said Larry. 'We're all a bit short of cash to-day. We'll laze here under the trees till you come back. Don't be long.'

Fatty went off, still looking gloomy. The others looked at one another. It was not very nice when Fatty was in low spirits. It didn't often happen but when it did it cast a definite gloom over the party.

'I wish we could do something to cheer Fatty up,' said Bets.

'Well—let's play a trick on him or something,' said Pip.

'Too hot,' said Larry. 'Not enough time, either. He'll be back so soon.'

Pip wandered into Fatty's shed. He looked round. He did badly want to play a trick that would make Fatty laugh. He wondered what he could do —dress up and disguise himself so that Fatty wouldn't know him? No, there wasn't time to do that properly.

His eyes fell on the enormous pair of shoes that Fatty had got from Colonel Cross's housekeeper, and had refused to leave with Miss Kay. There they were, hanging on a peg by their laces. Pip looked at them— and an idea came into his head!

He grinned. Gosh, he certainly *had* got an idea— one that would make Fatty and the others sit up properly. He would enjoy himself over this idea. Talk about a little bamboozling!

He took off his rubber shoes and slipped them into his pocket. He took down the big shoes and pulled them on. They slip-slopped about on his feet, but he could just walk in them. Pip went cautiously out of the shed unseen by the others, who were on the other side of a bush.

He knew Fatty would come back through the garden-gate not far from the back of the shed. He also knew that there was a bed there that had just been dug over and prepared by the gardener for lettuces.

Pip walked painfully over to the nice smooth

bed. He took a few steps this way on the earth, and a few steps that way. Then he stopped to see his footwork—marvellous! It looked for all the world as if Bigfeet the thief had visited them once again, and left his giant-size foot-prints plainly to be seen!

Pip grinned again. He took a few more steps, treading as hard as he could. Then he walked quietly back to the shed, took off the shoes, and put on his own once more. He'd like to see old Fatty's face when he came back and saw those foot-prints!

He walked out to the others. 'Shall we go and meet Fatty?' he said. 'Come on. He'd be pleased. It's only a little way.'

'All right,' said Larry, and Bets and Daisy agreed at once.

'I can see Mrs. Trotteville in the front garden,' said Pip, peering through the trees. 'We'd better go and say how-do-you-do to her.'

He didn't want to take the others past his beautifully prepared foot-prints. He wanted the full glory of them to burst on everyone at once. He hugged himself gleefully.

They said a few polite words to Mrs. Trotteville and then escaped. They walked almost to the hairdresser's before they met Fatty. He came towards them looking very smooth-headed indeed. Buster trotted as usual at his heels.

'Hallo—come to meet me?' said Fatty, pleased. 'Right. Ice-creams for everyone in return!'

'Oh no, Fatty,' said Daisy. 'You're always spending your money on us.'

'Come on,' said Fatty, and they went to have

ice-creams. Pip sat as patiently as he could with his. He hoped everyone would hurry up. Suppose the gardener went down to that bed and raked over the foot-prints! His trick would be ruined.

They finished their ice-cream at last, and walked back to Fatty's. Pip wished they would hurry, but they wouldn't, of course!

'We'll go in the garden-gate way,' said Fatty, as Pip had hoped he would say. 'It's nearer.'

They all went in. The bed with the foot-prints was not very far from the gate. Bets was running ahead with Buster when she suddenly saw them. She stopped at once, amazed.

Then Fatty saw them. He stopped dead and stared as if he couldn't believe his eyes. Larry and Daisy looked down in astonishment.

'Gosh!' said Fatty. 'What do you make of *that*! Fresh-made too!'

Pip grinned, and tried to hide it—but nobody was looking at him at all. Their eyes were glued to the enormous foot-prints.

'I *say*! The thief's been here—while we were gone!' said Daisy. 'Just those few minutes!'

'There's the gardener over there—we'll ask him who's been here,' said Fatty. But the gardener shook his head.

'Nobody came down the garden while I've been working here,' he said. 'And I've been here a matter of an hour or more. Never saw a soul!'

'Invisible as usual!' groaned Fatty. 'I just can't make it out. He comes and goes as he likes, does what he likes—and nobody ever sees him.'

He took out a magnifying-glass and bent to look closely at the prints. He frowned a little, and then got out his note-book. He opened it at the drawings there. Then he straightened up.

'This is queer,' he said. 'I don't understand it. These prints are the same size—and the rubber-heel pattern is the same—but the print isn't *quite* the same. The thief didn't wear the same boots.'

'Clever old Fatty!' thought Pip. 'He even spotted that the prints were made by those big shoes, and not by big boots worn by the real thief. He really is a marvel!'

The five children walked to the trees and sat down. Pip kept his head turned away because he simply couldn't help grinning all over his face. What a joke! How marvellous to see the others taken in like this—all serious and solemn and earnest!

'It beats me,' said Fatty. 'It absolutely beats me. Running all over the bed like that for apparently no reason at all. He must be mad as well as a thief. I mean—what's the point? Just to show off, I suppose.'

Pip gave a little snort of laughter and tried to turn it into a cough. Bets looked at him in surprise. 'What are you grinning for?' she asked. 'What's the joke?'

'No joke,' said Pip, trying to straighten his face. But a moment later his mouth twisted into broad smiles again and he was afraid he was going to laugh out loud.

'At any moment I shall expect to see foot-prints suddenly walking in front of me now,' said

Fatty gloomily. 'I've really got the things on my mind.'

Pip gave a squeal and burst into laughter. He rolled over on the ground. He laughed till he almost burst his sides. The others looked at him in amazement.

'Pip! What's the joke?' demanded Fatty.

'It's—er—oh dear—I can't tell you,' stuttered Pip, and rolled over again.

'He's gone potty,' said Larry, in disgust. Fatty looked at Pip hard. He poked him with his foot.

'Shut up now, Pip—and tell us what the joke is,' he said. 'Go on—you've been up to something. What is it?'

'Oh my—it's those foot-prints,' gasped Pip. 'I took you all in beautifully, didn't I!'

'What do you mean?' cried everyone, and Fatty reached out and shook Pip.

'I made them!' said Pip, helpless with laughter. 'I put on those big shoes and made those prints myself!'

22 MEETING AT HALF-PAST TWO

LARRY, Daisy and Bets fell on Pip and pummelled him till he cried for mercy. Buster joined in and barked madly. Only Fatty did nothing. He just sat as if he was turned to stone.

The others realized at last that Fatty was not joining in Pip's punishment. They sat up and looked at him. Pip wiped his streaked, dirty face.

Fatty sat there as if a thunderbolt had struck him. He gazed out through the trees with such a tense concentration that it really impressed the others. They fell silent.

'Fatty! What are you thinking about?' asked Bets timidly at last. He turned and looked at them all.

'It's Pip's joke,' he said. 'Gosh—to think I never guessed how the thief did it! Pip's solved the mystery!'

The others gaped in surprise.

'How do you mean?' asked Larry at last.

'Can't you see even *now*?' said Fatty impatiently. 'What did Pip do to make us think he was a large-footed thief? He took off his small shoes and put on big ones—and simply danced about over that bed in them. But he's no more got big feet than Bet's here! Yet we all fell for his trick.'

'I'm beginning to see,' said Pip.

'And we fell for the thief's trick, which was exactly the same!' said Fatty. He smacked himself hard on the knee. 'We're mutts! We're too feeble for words!

We've been looking for a bit-footed fellow, and the real thief has been laughing at us all the time—a fellow with small feet—and small hands too!'

'Oh—do you mean he wore big gloves over his hands?' asked Bets. 'To make people think he had both big hands *and* big feet?'

'Of course. He probably wore somebody's big old gardening gloves,' said Fatty. 'And no wonder he left so many clear marks—he *meant* to! He didn't *want* to be careful! The more prints the merrier, as far as he was concerned.'

Light was beginning to dawn very clearly in everyone's mind now. All that hunting for large-footed, burly, big-handed men! They should have looked for just the opposite.

But who *was* the thief? They knew now he wasn't big—but that didn't tell them the name of the robber.

'I suppose that deep cough was put on too,' said Larry. 'What about those scraps of paper, Fatty? Do they really belong to the mystery?'

'I think so,' said Fatty frowning. 'I'm beginning to piece things together now. I'm. . *gosh*!'

'What?' said everybody together.

'I think I know who it is!' said Fatty, going scarlet with excitement.

'Who?' yelled everyone.

'Well—I won't say yet in case I'm wrong,' said Fatty. 'I'll have to think a bit more—work things out. But I think I've got it! I think so!'

It was most exasperating that Fatty wouldn't say

any more. The others stared at him, trying to read his thoughts.

'If I'm right,' said Fatty, 'all our clues, including the scraps of paper, belong to the mystery—yes, even that queer roundish print with the criss-cross marks. And I believe I know how it was that the thief was able to take those big boots about without anyone ever seeing them—and remove the stolen goods too, without anyone ever guessing. Golly, he's clever.'

'Who *is* it?' asked Bets, banging Fatty on the shoulder in excitement.

'Look—I want to go and think this out properly,' said Fatty getting up. 'It's important I should be sure of every detail—very important. I'll tell you for certain this afternoon. Meet here are half-past two.'

And with that Fatty disappeared into the shed with Buster and shut the door! The rest of the company looked at each other in irritation. Blow Fatty! Now they would have to puzzle and wonder for hours!

Fatty opened the door and stuck out his head for one moment. 'If I can think of everything, so can you. You know just as much as I do! You use your brains too, and see what you can make of it all!'

'I can't make *any*thing,' said Pip kicking at the grass. 'The only thing I'm pleased about is that my trick set old Fatty on the right track. I think he's right, don't you? About the thief wearing boots too big for him?'

'Yes. I think he is,' said Daisy, and everyone agreed. She got up. 'Well, come on—Fatty doesn't want us mooning round if he's really going to solve

everything and have it all cut and dried. My word—
I do hope he thinks it all out before Goon does.'

They all thought hard during the hours that
followed. Fatty thought the hardest of all. Bit by bit
he pieced it all together. Bit by bit things became
clear. Of course! All those odd clues did fit together,
did make a picture of the thief—and it could only be
one thief, nobody else.

Fatty did a spot of telephoning early that afternoon.
He telephoned Inspector Jenks and asked him if he
could possibly come along at half-past two that
afternoon. The Inspector was interested.

'Does this by any chance mean that you have
solved the latest mystery—the mystery of the Big-
Footed Thief?' he asked.

'I hope so, sir,' said Fatty modestly. 'May I ask
Mr. Goon to come along too, sir? He'll be—er—quite
interested too.'

The Inspector laughed. 'Yes, of course. Right, half-
past two, and I'll be there, at your house.'

Mr. Goon was also invited. He was astonished and
not at all pleased. But when he heard that the
Inspector was going to be present, there was no help
for it but to say yes, he'd be there too. Poor Goon—
how he worried and puzzled all the rest of the
morning. Did it mean that fat boy had got ahead of
him again?

At half-past two the Inspector arrived. Mrs.
Trotteville was out, as Fatty very well knew. Then
Mr. Goon arrived. Then the rest of the Find-Outers
came, amazed to see Inspector Jenks and Mr. Goon
sitting in the little study with Fatty.

'Why this room?' asked Bets. 'You never use it for visitors. Is it something to do with the mystery, Fatty?'

'Not really,' said Fatty, who was looking excited and calm all at once. Mr. Goon fidgeted, and the Inspector looked at Fatty with interest. That boy! What wouldn't he give to have him as a right-hand man when he was grown-up! But that wouldn't be for years.

'We're all here,' said Fatty, who had got Buster under his chair so that he wouldn't caper round Mr. Goon. 'So I'll begin. I may as well say at once that I've found out who the thief is.'

Mr. Goon said something under his breath that sounded like 'Gah!' Nobody took any notice. Fatty went on.

'We had a few clues to work on—very large foot-prints that were always remarkably well-displayed—and very large glove-prints, also well displayed so that nobody could possibly miss them. We also had two scraps of paper with 2, Frinton on one and 1, Rods on the other. We had also a curious roundish mark on the ground, and that was about all.'

'Now—the thing was—nobody ever saw this thief coming or going, apparently, and yet he must have been about for everyone to see—and he apparently had the biggest feet in Peterswood, with the exception of Mr. Goon here and Colonel Cross.'

Poor Mr. Goon tried to hide his feet under his chair, but couldn't quite manage it.

'Well, we examined every single clue,' said Fatty. 'We followed up the hints on the scraps of paper and went to Frinton Lea. We went to houses and families whose names began with Rod. We visited the cobbler for information about big shoes and he told us about Colonel Cross. Both Mr. Goon and I went to see the colonel—not together, of course—I was doing a spot of weeding, I think, Mr. Goon, when you arrived, wasn't I?'

Goon glared but said nothing.

'Well, it was Colonel Cross who put us on the track of where the thief might have got his big boots,' went on Fatty. 'He gives his old ones to jumble sales! And we learnt that he had given a pair to Miss Kay last year for the jumble sale. We guessed that if we could find out who bought them, we'd know the thief!'

Goon made a curious noise and turned it into a throat-clearing.

'We had a shock then, though,' said Fatty. 'The boots hadn't been sold to anyone, they had been stolen! By the thief, of course, for future use! But that brought us to a dead-end. No boots, no thief. We gave up!'

'And then Pip played a trick and showed you how the thief did it!' called out Bets, unable to contain herself. Fatty smiled at her.

'Yes. Pip's trick made me realize that the thief was playing *us* a trick too—the same as Pip's trick! He was wearing very large boots over his small shoes in order to make enormous prints that would make us think he was a big fellow—and the same with his gloves.

'Ha!' said the Inspector, 'Smart work, Frederick. Very smart!'

'So then I had to change my ideas and begin thinking of a *small* fellow instead of a very big one!' said Fatty. 'One who came unquestioned to our houses, whom nobody would suspect or bother about.'

Mr. Goon leaned forward, breathing heavily. The others fixed their eyes on Fatty in excitement. *Now* he was going to tell them the name of the thief!

But he didn't. He paused, as if he were listening for something. They all listened too. They heard the click of a gate and footsteps coming along the path that led along the study-wall to the kitchen.

'If you don't mind, sir, I'll introduce you to the thief himself,' said Fatty, and he got up. He went to the door that led from the study into the garden and opened it as a small figure came by.

'Good afternoon,' he said. 'Will you come in here for a minute? You're wanted.'

And in came a small, strutting figure with his basket on his arm—little Twit the baker!

23 WELL DONE, FATTY!

'TWIT!' said Mr. Goon, and half-rose from his chair in amazement. The Inspector looked on, unmoving. All the children gaped, except Fatty, of course. Buster flew out at Twit barking.

'Down, Buster, back under my chair,' ordered Fatty, and Buster subsided.

Twit looked round in surprise and alarm. 'Here! What's all this?' he said. 'I got my work to do.'

'Sit down,' said the Inspector. 'We want you here for a few minutes.'

'What for?' blustered Twit. 'Here, Mr. Goon, what's all this about?'

But Goon didn't know. He sat stolidly and said nothing. He wasn't going to get himself into any trouble by appearing to be friendly with Twit!

'Twit,' said Fatty, 'I've got you in here for reasons of my own. Put your basket down—that's right. Take off the cloth.'

Twit sullenly took off the cloth. Loaves of bread were piled in the basket. Another cloth lay beneath them.

'Take out the loaves and put them on the table,' said Fatty. 'And the cloth under them too.'

'Now what's all this?' said Twit, again, looking scared. 'I got my work to do, I tell you. I'm not messing about with my loaves.'

'Do as you're told, Twit,' said the Inspector.

Twit immediately took out his loaves and laid

them on the table. Then he took out the cloth beneath them. Fatty looked into the bottom of the basket. He silently took out four things that lay closely packed there—two large boots and two large gloves!

He set them on the table. Twit collapsed on a chair and began to tremble.

'This is how he managed to go about, carrying the boots and gloves, ready for any chance he might have for a little robbery!' said Fatty. 'He never knew what afternoon he might find an easy chance —perhaps nobody in the house except a sleepy maid or mistress—which, as we know, he did find.'

Fatty picked up one of the boots and turned it over. He showed the Inspector the rubber heel. 'I expect, sir, you took a drawing of the foot-print on the beds at Norton House,' he said, 'or Tonks did—and so you will see that the rubber heels on these boots and in your drawing are the same. That's proof that the thief wore these boots that Twit has in his basket.'

Fatty turned to the trembling Twit. 'Will you give me your note-book—the one you put down any orders or telephone calls in?' he said. Twit scowled, but put his hand into his pocket and brought out a little pad of cheap paper.

Fatty took it. Then he spoke to Goon. 'Have you got those two scraps of paper on you, Mr. Goon?'

Mr. Goon had. He produced them. Fatty compared them, and the warning note too, with the paper on the pad. The paper was exactly the same, cheap, thin and with a fluffy surface.

'Those two scraps of paper you found at Norton House, sir, were bits that Twit had made notes on to remind him of the amount of bread to leave—two loaves for Frinton Lea, and one loaf for Rodways. He apparently makes notes of his orders, and slips them into his basket to remind him. The wind must have blown them out in the garden at Norton House.'

'Gah!' breathed Goon, again, staring at the pad of paper and the notes. 'I never thought of that—orders for loaves!'

'Nor did I,' confessed Fatty. 'Not until I began to piece all the clues together properly and found that they added up to the same person— Twit here!'

'Wait a minute,' said Larry. 'How do you explain the thing that puzzled us so tremendously in the Norton House robbery—how did the thief—Twit, that is—come downstairs without being seen by Jinny.'

'That was easy,' said Fatty. 'He simply squeezed himself out of that little window in the boxroom and slid down the pipe to the ground. He's small enough to do that without much difficulty.'

'Yes—but wait, Fatty—that window was *shut* when I and Tonks went round the house,' said the Inspector. 'He couldn't have escaped through there, and shut it and fastened it from the outside —balanced on the pipe!'

'He didn't shut it *then*,' said Fatty with a grin. 'He simply shinned down the pipe, ran to where he had thrown the stolen goods, stuffed them in his basket under the cloth, slipped off the big boots that he had put on over his own small ones—and then went as bold as brass to the back-door—appearing there as Twit the baker!'

'And when he went upstairs to look for the thief with Jinny, he carefully shut and fastened the little window he had escaped from!' said Larry suddenly seeing it all. 'Gosh, that was smart. *He* was the thief—and he came indoors after the robbery and pretended to hunt all round for the robber—and we all thought he was so brave!'

'Gah!' said Goon, looking balefully at Twit. 'Think yourself clever don't you? Stuffing everybody up with lies—making yourself out a hero, too—looking for a thief who was standing in your own shoes!'

'He certainly pulled wool over everyone's eyes,' said Fatty. 'It was a pretty little trick, and needed quite a lot of boldness and quick thinking. It's a pity he doesn't put his brains to better use.'

'Fatty—what about that funny, roundish mark—the one with criss-cross lines?' asked Bets. 'Was that a clue too?'

'Yes,' said Fatty, with a grin. 'Come out for a minute and I'll show you what made that mark. I could have kicked myself for not thinking of it before!'

They all crowded to the door except Twit who sat nervously picking at his finger-nails. Fatty carried the basket to the door. He set it down in a damp part of the path. Then he lifted it up again.

'Look! It's left a mark of its round shape—and little criss-cross basket-lines!' cried Daisy. 'Oh, Fatty—how clever you are!'

'Golly—*I* saw that mark outside Rodways Cottage.' suddenly said Pip. 'Larry, don't you remember—when we were in that cottage with the old woman? The baker came, and left his basket outside to go and put the loaves in the pan. And after he had gone I noticed the mark his basket had left, and it reminded me of something—of course, it was the drawing in Fatty's book!'

'That's it,' said Fatty. 'That mark was always left where a robbery was committed—because Twit had to stand his basket somewhere, and if he stood it on a dusty path or a damp place, the heavy basket always left a mark. That's why we found those roundish marks at each robbery! If we'd guessed what they were we would soon have been on the track!'

They were now back in the room. Fatty replaced the loaves in the basket, wrapped up in their cloths.

'No wonder Twit was always so particular about putting cloths over his loaves to keep them clean,' he said. 'They were very convenient for hiding whatever else he had there—not only the boots and gloves, but also anything he stole!'

'Quite smart,' said the Inspector. 'Carried the things he needed for his robbery, as well as his loaves, and also had room for stolen goods too—all under an innocent white cloth. Where did you get all these bright ideas from, Twit?'

Twit said nothing, but gazed sullenly at his

smartly-polished little boots, with their highly-polished gaiters.

'Where did you get the big boots from, Twit?' asked Fatty. 'Oh, you don't need to bother to answer. Your cousin, Miss Kay, runs the jumble sale, doesn't she—and she had the boots given to her for it last year—and you saw them and took them. Goodness knows how many times you've carried those boots round in your basket, hoping to find a chance to wear them and play your big-footed trick!'

'I never stole them,' said Twit. 'I paid for them.'

'Yes—you paid sixpence!' said Fatty. 'Just so that everyone would think you were a kind, generous fellow, paying for jumble-sale boots that had been stolen! I heard all about it, and it made me wonder. It didn't seem quite in keeping with what I knew of you.'

Mr. Goon cleared his throat. 'I take it you are certain this here fellow is the thief, sir?' he said to the Inspector.

'Well, what do *you* think of the evidence, Goon?' said the Inspector, gravely. 'You've been on the job too, haven't you? You must have formed opinions of your own. No doubt you too suspected Twit.'

Mr. Goon swallowed once or twice, wondering whether he dared to say yes, he *had* suspected Twit. But he caught Fatty's eye on him, and decided he wouldn't. He was afraid of Fatty and his sharp wits.

'Well, no, sir—I can't say as I suspected the baker,'

he said, 'though I was coming to it. Master Trotteville got just one move ahead of me, sir. Bad luck on me! I've tried out all the dodges I learnt at the refresher course, sir—the disguises and all that . . . and . . .'

'Mr. Goon! Have you really disguised yourself?' said Fatty, pretending to be amazed. 'I say—you weren't that dirty old tramp, were you? Well, if you were, you took me in properly!'

Goon glared at Fatty. That old tramp! Why, surely it was Fatty himself who had gone shuffling round in tramp's clothes—yes, and eaten his lunch under Mr. Goon's very windows. Gah!

'Take Twit away, Goon,' said Inspector Jenks, getting up. 'Arrange with him to find someone to take the bread round, or nobody will have tea this afternoon. Twit, I shall be seeing you later.'

Twit was marched out by Mr. Goon, looking very small beside Goon's burly figure. All his strut and cockiness were gone. He was no longer a little bantam of a man, peacocking about jauntily—he looked more like a small, woebegone sparrow.

Inspector Jenks beamed round, and Buster leapt up at him. 'Very nice work, Find-Outers,' he said. 'Very nice indeed. In fact, as my niece, Hilary, would say— smashing! Now, what about a spot of ice-cream somewhere? I'm melting.'

'Oooh yes,' said Bets, hanging on to his arm. 'I knew you'd say that, Inspector! I felt it coming!'

'My word—you'll be as good as Fatty some day, guessing what people think and do!' said the Inspector. 'Well, Frederick, I'm pleased with you—pleased with all of you. And I want to hear the whole story, if you don't mind—from beginning to end.'

So, over double-size ice-creams, he heard it with interest and delight.

'It's a curious story, isn't it?' said Fatty, when they had finished. 'The story of a cocky, little man who thought the world of himself—and was much too big for his boots!'

Bets gave a laugh and had the last word. 'Yes! So he had to get size twelve and wear those, Fatty—but they gave him away in the end.'

'They did,' said Fatty. 'Well, that's another mystery solved—and here's to the next one! May it be the most difficult of all!'

Enid Blyton's

THE
MYSTERY
OF THE HIDDEN HOUSE

MAMMOTH

CONTENTS

1 THE FAT BOY AT THE STATION

'IT's to-day that Fatty's coming back,' said Bets to Pip. 'I'm so glad.'

'That's the sixth time you've said that in the last hour,' said Pip. 'Can't you think of something else to say ?'

'No I can't,' said Bets. 'I keep on feeling so glad that we shall soon see Fatty.' She went to the window and looked out. 'Oh Pip—here come Larry and Daisy up the drive. I expect they will come to the station to meet Fatty too.'

'Of course they will,' said Pip. 'And I bet old Buster will turn up as well! Fancy Fatty going away without Buster-dog!'

Larry and Daisy walked into Pip's play-room. 'Hallo, hallo!' said Larry, flinging his cap on a chair. 'Won't it be nice when Fatty's back? Nothing ever seems to happen unless he's around.'

'We aren't even the Five Find-Outers without him,' said Bets. 'Only four—and nothing to find out!'

Larry, Daisy, Fatty, Pip and Bets called themselves the Five Find-Outers (and Dog, because of Buster). They had been very good indeed at solving all kinds of peculiar mysteries in the various holidays when they came back from boarding-school. Mr. Goon, the village policeman, had done his best to solve them too, but somehow the Five Find-Outers always got a little ahead of him, and he found this very annoying indeed.

'Perhaps some mystery will turn up when Fatty

comes,' said Pip. 'He's the kind of person that things always happen to. He just can't help it.'

'Fancy him being away over Christmas!' said Daisy. 'It was queer not having Fatty. I've kept him his presents.'

'So have I,' said Bets. 'I made him a note-book with his full name on the cover in beautiful lettering. Look, here it is—Frederick Algernon Trotteville. Won't he be pleased?'

'I shouldn't think he will,' said Pip. 'You've got it all dirty and messy, carrying it about.'

'I bought him this,' said Daisy, and she fished a box out of her pocket. She opened it and brought out a neat little black beard. 'It's to help him in his disguise.'

'It's a lovely one,' said Pip, fingering it, and then putting it on his chin. 'How do I look?'

'Rather silly,' said Bets, at once. 'You look like a boy with a beard—but if Fatty wore it he would look like an elderly man at once. He knows how to screw up his face and bend his shoulders and all that.'

'Yes—he's really most frightfully clever at disguises,' said Daisy. 'Do you remember how he dressed up as Napoleon Bonaparte in the waxwork show last hols?'

They all laughed as they remembered Fatty standing solemnly among the waxworks, as still as they were, looking exactly like one.

'That was a super mystery we solved last hols,' said Pip. 'I hope one turns up these hols too. Any one seen Mr. Goon lately?'

'Yes, I saw him riding his bicycle yesterday,' said Bets. 'I was just crossing the road when he came round the corner. He almost knocked me down.'

'What did he say? Clear orf?' said Pip, with a grin.

Clear-Orf was the nickname that the children gave to Mr. Goon the policeman, because he always shouted that when he saw them or Buster, Fatty's dog.

'He just scowled like this,' said Bets, and screwed up her face so fiercely that every one laughed.

Just then Mrs. Hilton, Pip's mother, put her head in at the door. 'Aren't you going to the station to meet Frederick?' she said. 'The train is almost due!'

'Gosh! Yes, look at the time!' cried Larry, and they all sprang to their feet. 'He'll be there before we are if we don't hurry.'

Pip and Bets dragged on coats and hats, and the four of them went thundering down the stairs like a herd of elephants. Crash, went the front door, and Mrs. Hilton saw them racing down the drive at top speed.

They got to the station just as the train was pulling in. Bets was terribly excited. She hopped about first on one foot, then on the other, waiting for Fatty's head to pop out of a carriage window. But it didn't.

The train stopped. Doors were flung open. People jumped down to the platform, some with bags that porters hurried to take. But there was no sign of Fatty.

'Where is he?' said Bets, looking upset.

'Perhaps he's in one of his disguises, just to test us,' said Larry suddenly. ' I bet that's it! He's dressed himself up and we've got to see if we can spot him. Quick, look round and see which of the passengers he is.'

'Not that man, he's too tall. Not that boy, he's not tall enough. Not that girl, because we know her. Not those two women, they're friends of mother's. And there's Miss Tremble. It's not her. Golly, which can he be?'

Bets suddenly nudged Larry. 'Larry, look—*there's* Fatty! See, that fat boy over there, pulling a suit-case out of the very last carriage of all.'

Every one stared at the fat red-faced boy at the end of the

train. 'Yes! That's old Fatty! Not such a good disguise as usual, though—I mean, we can easily spot him this time.'

'I know! Let's pretend we *haven't* spotted him!' said Daisy, suddenly. 'He'll be so disgusted with us. We'll let him walk right by us without saying a word to him. And then we'll walk behind him up the station slope and call to him.'

'Yes—we'll do that,' said Larry. 'Here he comes. Now—pretend not to know it's Fatty, every one!'

So when the plump boy walked down the platform towards them, carrying his bag, and a mackintosh over his arm, the others didn't even smile at him. They looked right through him and beyond him, though Bets badly wanted to run up and take his arm. She was very fond of Fatty.

The boy took no notice of them at all. He marched on, his big boots making a clattering noise on the stone platform. He gave up his ticket at the barrier. Then he stopped outside the station, put down his bag, took out a red-spotted handkerchief and blew his nose very loudly.

'That's how Mr. Goon blows his!' whispered Bets in delight. 'Isn't Fatty clever! He's waited for us to go up to him now. Don't let's! We'll walk close behind him, and when we get out into the lane, we'll call to him.'

The boy put his handkerchief away, picked up his bag and set off. The four children followed closely. The boy heard their feet and looked back over his shoulder. He scowled. He put down his bag at the top of the slope to rest his arm.

The four children promptly stopped too. When the boy picked up his bag and walked on again, Larry and the others followed at his heels once more.

The boy looked back again. He faced round, and said, 'What's the big idea? Think you're my shadows, or somethink?'

Nobody said anything. They were a little taken-aback. Fatty looked so very spiteful as he spoke. 'You clear-orf,' said the boy, swinging round again and going on his way. 'I don't want a pack of silly kids following me all day long.'

'He's better than ever!' whispered Daisy, as the four of them walked on at the boy's heels. 'He quite scared me for a minute!'

'Let's tell him we know him,' said Pip. 'Come on! We can help to carry his bag then!'

'Hey! Fatty!' called Larry.

'Fatty! We came to meet you!' cried Bets and caught hold of his arm.

'Hallo, Fatty! Have a good Christmas?' said Daisy and Pip together.

The boy swung round again. He put down his bag. 'Now, look here, who do you think you're calling Fatty? Downright rude you are. If you don't clear-orf straight away I'll tell my uncle of you. And he's a policeman, see?'

Bets laughed. 'Oh, Fatty! Stop being somebody else. We know it's you. Look, I've got a note-book for your Christmas present. I made it myself.'

Looking rather dazed, the boy took it. He glanced round at the four children. 'What's all this, that's what I want to know!' he said. 'Following me round—calling me names—you're all potty!'

'Oh, Fatty, *please* be yourself,' begged Bets. 'It's a wizard disguise, it really is—but honestly we knew you at once. As soon as you got out of the train, we all said, 'That's Fatty!'

'Do you know what I do to people who call me names?' said the boy, looking round fiercely. 'I fight them! Any one like to take me on?'

'Don't be silly, Fatty,' said Larry, with a laugh. 'You're going on too long. Come on, let's go and find Buster, I bet he'll be pleased to see you. I thought he'd be at the station to meet you with your mother.'

He linked the boy's arm in his, but was shaken off roughly. 'You're potty,' said the boy again, picked up his bag and walked off haughtily. To the surprise of the others he took the wrong road. The way he went led to the village, not to his mother's house.

They stared after him, shaken and puzzled. A little doubt crept into their minds. They followed the boy at a good distance, watched him go to the village, and then, to their enormous surprise, he turned in at the gate of the little house where Mr. Goon, the policeman, lived.

As he turned in, he saw the four children at a distance. He shook his fist at them and went to knock at the door. It opened and he went in.

'It *must* be Fatty,' said Pip. 'That's exactly the way he would shake his fist. He's playing some very deep trick on us indeed. Gosh—what's he doing going to Mr. Goon's house?'

'He's probably playing a trick on Mr. Goon too,' said Larry. 'All the same—I feel a bit puzzled. We didn't get even a wink from him.'

They stood watching Mr. Goon's house for a little while and then turned to go back. They hadn't gone very far before there was a delighted barking, and a little black dog flung himself on them, licking, jumping and barking as if he had suddenly gone mad.

'Why, it's Buster!' said Bets. 'Hallo, Buster! You've just missed Fatty. What a pity!'

A lady was coming down the road, and the two boys raised their caps to her. It was Fatty's mother, Mrs. Trotteville. She smiled at the four children.

'I thought you must be somewhere about when Buster

suddenly tore off at sixty miles an hour,' she said. 'I'm going to meet Frederick at the station. Are you coming too?'

'We've already *met* him,' said Larry, in surprise. 'He was in a frightfully good disguise, Mrs. Trotteville. But we spotted him at once. He's gone to Mr. Goon's house.'

'To Mr. *Goon's* house,' said Mrs. Trotteville, in amazement. 'But whatever for? He telephoned me to say he had just missed the train, but was getting one fifteen minutes later. Did he catch the first one then? Oh dear, I wish he wouldn't start putting on disguises and things—and I do hope you won't all begin getting mixed up in something horrid as soon as Frederick comes home. *Why* has he gone to Mr. Goon? Surely something odd hasn't turned up already?'

This was an idea. The children stared at one another. Then they heard the whistle of a train. 'I must go,' said Mrs. Trotteville. 'If Frederick isn't on that train, after telephoning me he'd missed the other, I shall be very angry indeed!'

And into the station she went, with all the children following.

2   HULLO, FATTY!

THE train drew in. People leapt out—and Bets suddenly gave a shriek that made every one jump in fright.

'There is Fatty! Look, look! And he isn't in disguise either. Fatty! Fatty!' Fatty swung little Bets off the ground as she and Buster flung themselves on him. He grinned all over his good-natured face. He kissed his mother and beamed round at every one. 'Nice of you to come and meet me. Gosh, Buster, you've made a hole in my trousers. Stop it!'

Mrs. Trotteville was very pleased to see Fatty, but she looked extremely puzzled. 'The children said they had already met you once—in some disguise or other,' she said.

Fatty was astonished. He turned to Larry. 'What do you mean? I haven't arrived till now!'

The four children looked very foolish. They remembered all they had said to the other boy. Was it possible that it hadn't been Fatty after all—well, it couldn't have been of course, because here *was* Fatty, arriving on the next train. He couldn't possibly be on two trains at once.

'We've made complete idiots of ourselves,' said Larry, going red. 'You see...'

'Do you mind walking out of the station before the porters think we are waiting for the next train?' said Mrs. Trotteville. 'We're the last on the platform as it is.'

'Come on,' said Fatty, and he and Larry set off with his bag between them. 'We can talk as we go.'

Bets took his mackintosh. Pip took a smaller bag and Daisy took a parcel of magazines. They were all extremely glad to see the real Fatty, to hear his determined voice, and see his broad grin.

'You see,' began Larry again, 'we didn't know you'd missed the first train so we came down to meet you—and we thought you might be in disguise—so when a plumpish boy got off the train, we thought he was you!'

'And we didn't say anything at first, just to puzzle you, as we thought,' said Pip. 'We followed this boy out of the station and he was frightfully fed up with us.'

'And then we called to him, and said, "Fatty!"' said Bets. 'And you see, he *was* fat—and he swung round and said he fought people who called him rude names.'

'Golly! I wonder he didn't set on you all!' said Fatty. 'You might have known I wouldn't say things like that to you, even if I *was* disguised. Where does he live?'

'He went to Mr. Goon's house,' said Daisy. 'He said Old Clear-Orf was his uncle.'

'Gracious! You've put your foot in it properly!' said Fatty. 'Goon *has* got a nephew—and I bet he's asked him to stay with him. Won't he be wild when he knows how you greeted him!'

'It's a great pity,' said Mrs. Trotteville, who had been listening to all this with astonishment and dismay. 'He must have thought you were very rude. Now Mr. Goon will probably complain about the behavior of you children again.'

'But, Mother can't you see that...' began Fatty.

'Don't begin to argue, please, Frederick,' said Mrs. Trotteville. 'It seems to me that you will have to go and explain to Mr. Goon that the others thought his nephew was you.'

'Yes, Mother,' said Fatty in a meek voice.

'I do want you to keep out of any mysteries or problems these holidays,' said Mrs. Trotteville.

'Yes, Mother,' said Fatty. Mrs. Trotteville heard a suppressed giggle from Bets and Daisy. They knew perfectly well that Fatty didn't mean a word he was saying. Who could keep him out of a mystery if he even so much as smelt one? Who could imagine that he would go and explain anything to Mr. Goon?

'Don't say "Yes, Mother," and "No, Mother" like that unless you mean it,' said Mrs. Trotteville, wishing she didn't feel annoyed with Fatty almost as soon as she had met him.

'No, Mother. I mean, yes, Mother,' said Fatty. 'Well—I mean whatever you want me to say, Mother. Can the others come to tea?'

'Certainly not,' said Mrs. Trotteville. 'I want to have a little chat with you and hear all your news—and then you have your bag to unpack—and soon your father will be home, and...'

'Yes, Mother,' said Fatty, hastily. 'Well, can the others come round afterwards? I haven't seen them at all these hols. I've got presents for them. I didn't send them any at Christmas.'

The mention of presents suddenly made Bets remember that she had given her precious notebook to the fat boy. She bit her lip in horror. Gracious! He had put it into his pocket! She hadn't asked for it back, because she had been so scared when he had offered to fight them all, that she had forgotten all about the note-book.

'I gave that boy the present I had made for you,' she said, in a rather shaky voice. 'It was a note-book with your name on the front.'

'Just what I want!' said Fatty, cheerfully, and gave Bets a squeeze. 'I'll get it back from that boy, don't you worry!'

'Now, just remember what I say,' warned Mrs. Trotteville, as they came to her gate. 'There's to be no silly feud with that boy. He might be very nice.'

Every one looked doubtful. They were as certain as they could be that any nephew of Mr. Goon's must be as awful as the policeman himself. Buster barked loudly, and Bets felt sure he must be agreeing with them in his doggy language.

'Mother, you haven't said if the others can come round this evening,' said Fatty, as they went in at the gate.

'No. Not this evening,' said Mrs. Trotteville, much to every one's disappointment. 'You can meet them tomorrow. Good-bye children. Give my love to your mothers.'

Fatty and Buster disappeared up the path with Mrs. Trotteville. The others outside the gate looked gloomily at one another and then walked slowly down the road.

'She might have let us have just a *little* chat with Fatty.' said Larry.

'We made an awful noise last time we went to Fatty's,' said Bets, remembering. 'We thought Mrs. Trotteville was out, do you remember—and played a dreadful game Fatty made up, called Elephant-Hunting...'

'And Mrs. Trotteville was in all the time and we never even heard her yelling at us to stop because we were making such a row,' said Pip. 'That was a good game. We must remember that.'

'I say, do you think that boy *was* Mr. Goon's nephew?' said Daisy. 'If he tells Mr. Goon all we did we'll get a few more black marks from him!'

'He'll know who we are,' said Bets dolefully. 'That boy's got the note-book I made—and there's Fatty's name on it. And, oh dear, inside I've printed in my best printing, headings to some of the pages. I've printed "CLUES," "SUSPECTS," and things like that. So Mr. Goon will know we're looking out for another mystery.'

'Well, silly, what does that matter?' demanded Pip. 'Let

him think what he likes!'

'She's always so scared of Old Clear-Orf,' said Daisy. 'I'm not! We're much cleverer than he is. We've solved mysteries that he hasn't even been able to *begin* solving.'

'I hope Mr. Goon won't come and complain to our parents about our behaviour to that boy,' said Pip. 'Honestly, we must have seemed a bit dotty to him. Goon will probably think we did it all on purpose—made a set at the boy just because he was his nephew.'

Pip's fear of being complained about was very real. He had strict parents who had very strong ideas about good and bad behaviour. Larry and Daisy's parents were not so strict and Fatty's rarely bothered about him so long as he was polite and good mannered.

But Pip had had some angry tickings-off from his father and two or three canings, and he and Bets were always afraid of Mr. Goon coming to complain. So, when they arrived home that afternoon to tea, they were horrified to hear from their maid, Lorna, that a Mr. Goon had been ringing up their mother ten minutes before.

'I hope as how you haven't got into mischief,' said Lorna, who liked the children. 'He says he's coming to see your Ma to-night. She's out to tea now. I thought I'd just warn you in case you've gone and got yourselves into trouble.'

'Thank you awfully, Lorna,' said Pip and went to have a gloomy tea in the play-room alone with Bets, who also looked extremely down in the dumps. How *could* they have thought that boy was Fatty? Now that she came to think of it Bets could quite clearly see that the boy was coarse and lumpish— not even Fatty could look like that!

The two children decided to warn Larry and Daisy, so they rang them up.

'Gosh!' said Larry. 'Fancy listening to tales from that

clod of a nephew about us! I don't expect my mother will pay much attention to Mr. Goon. But yours will! Horrid old man. Cheer up. We'll meet to-morrow and discuss it all.'

Pip and Bets waited for their mother to come in. Thank goodness their father was not with her. They went down to greet her.

'Mother,' said Pip, 'We—er—we want to tell you something. Er—you see...'

'*Now,* what mischief have you got into?' said Mrs. Hilton impatiently. 'Have you broken something? Tell me without all this humming and hawing.'

'No. We haven't broken anything,' said Bets. 'But you see, we went to meet Fatty at the station...'

'And there was a fat boy we thought was Fatty in one of his disguises,' went on Pip, 'so we followed him up the road, pretending not to know him...'

'And then we called out "Fatty" to him, and told him we knew him—and he was angry, and...'

'And what you mean is, you made a silly mistake and called a strange boy Fatty, and he was annoyed,' said Mrs. Hilton, making an impatient tapping noise on the table. 'Why *must* you do idiotic things? Well, I suppose you apologized, so there's not much harm done.'

'We didn't actually apologize,' said Pip. 'We really thought he *was* Fatty. But he wasn't. He was Mr. Goon's nephew.'

Mrs. Hilton looked really annoyed. 'And now I suppose I shall have that policeman here complaining about you again. Well, you know what your father said last time, Pip—he said...'

The door opened and Lorna came in. 'Please Madam, there's Mr. Goon wanting to see you. Shall I show him in?'

Before Mrs. Hilton could say yes or no, the two children had opened the French windows that led to the garden and had shot out into the darkness. Pip wished he hadn't gone, as soon as he was out there, but Bets clutched him so desperately that he had shot off with her. A great draught of icy air blew into the sitting-room behind them.

Mrs. Hilton closed the garden door, looking cross. Mr. Goon came into the room, walking slowly and pompously. He thought Mr. and Mrs. Hilton were proper parents—they listened to him seriously when he made complaints. Well, he was going to enjoy himself now.

'Sit down, Mr. Goon,' said Mrs. Hilton, trying to be polite. 'What can I do for you?'

3   ERN

PIP and Bets went round to the kitchen door and let themselves in. The cook was out and Lorna was upstairs. They fled past the big black cat on the hearthrug and went up to their play-room.

'I should have stayed,' said Pip. 'I haven't done anything wrong. It was silly to run away. It will make Mother think we really are in the wrong.'

'Hark! Isn't that Daddy coming in?' said Bets. 'Yes, it is. He'll walk straight in on top of them, and hear everything too!'

Mr. Goon seemed to stay a long time, but at last he went. Mrs. Hilton called to Pip.

'Pip! Bring Bets down here, please. We have something to say to you.'

The two children went downstairs, Bets quite plainly scared, and Pip putting on a very brave face. To their surprise their parents did not seem angry at all.

'Pip,' said his mother, 'Mr. Goon came to tell us that he has his nephew staying with him. He says he is a very nice lad indeed, very straightforward and honest—and he says he would be glad if none of you five led him into trouble. You know that every holidays you seem to have been mixed up in mysteries of some kind or other—there was that burnt cottage—and the disappearing cat—and...'

'And the spiteful letters, and the secret room, and the missing necklace,' said Pip, relieved to find that apparently Mr. Goon hadn't done much complaining.

'Yes. Quite,' said his father. 'Well, Mr. Goon doesn't want

his nephew mixed up in anything like that. He says he has promised the boy's mother to look after him well these holidays, and he doesn't want you dragging him into any mystery or danger...'

'As if we'd *want* to do that!' said Pip, in disgust. 'His nephew is just a great clod. We don't want to drag him into anything—we'd like to leave him severely alone.'

'Well, see you do,' said his mother. 'Be friendly and polite to him, please. Apparently you were very rude and puzzling to him to-day—but as Pip had already explained to me the mistake you made, I quite saw that you didn't really mean to be rude. Mr. Goon was very nice about that.'

'We won't drag his nephew into anything,' said Pip. 'If we find a mystery we'll keep it to ourselves.'

'That's another thing I want to say to you,' said his father. 'I don't like you being mixed up in these things. It is the job of the police to solve these mysteries and to clear up any crimes that are committed. It's time you five children kept out of them. I forbid you to try and solve any mysteries these holidays.'

Pip and Bets stared at him in the greatest dismay. 'But I say—we belong to the Five Find-Outers,' stammered Pip. 'We *must* do our bit if a mystery comes along. I mean, really... why, we couldn't possibly promise to...'

'Mr. Goon has already been to see Larry and Daisy's parents,' said Mrs. Hilton. 'They have said that they too will forbid their children to get mixed up in any mysteries these holidays. Neither you nor they are to look for any, you understand?'

'But—but suppose one comes—and we're mixed up in it without knowing?' asked Bets. 'Like the missing necklace mystery.'

'Oh, one won't come if you don't look for it,' said

Mr. Hilton. 'Naturally if you got plunged into the middle of one without your knowledge nobody could blame you—but these things don't happen like that. I just simply forbid you to look for any mystery these holidays, I forbid you above all to allow Mr. Goon's nephew to get mixed up in anything of the kind.'

'You can go now,' said Mrs. Hilton. 'Don't look so miserable! Any one would think you couldn't be happy without some kind of mystery round the corner!'

'Well,' began Pip, and then decided to say no more. How could he explain the delight of smelling out a mystery, of making a list of Clues and Suspects, of trying to fit everything together like a jigsaw puzzle till the answer came, and the picture was complete?

He and Bets went out of the room and climbed up the stairs to their play-room. 'Fancy Larry and Daisy being forbidden too,' said Pip. 'I wonder if Mr. Goon went to Fatty's people too?'

'Well, I shouldn't think it would be any good forbidding Fatty to get mixed up in anything,' said Bets.

Bets was right. It wasn't any good. Fatty talked his mother and father over to his point of view under the very nose of Mr. Goon.

'I've been very useful indeed to Inspector Jenks,' he told his parents. 'You know I have. And you know I'm going to be the finest detective in the world when I'm grown up. I'm sure if you ring up the Inspector, Mother, he will tell you not to forbid me to do anything I want to. He trusts me.'

Inspector Jenks was a great friend of the children's. He was chief of the police in the next town, head of the whole district. Mr. Goon was in great awe of him. The children had certainly helped the Inspector many times in the way they had tackled various mysterious happenings.

'You ring up the Inspector, Mother,' said Fatty, seeing that the policeman didn't want Mrs. Trotteville to do this at all. 'I'm sure he'll say Mr. Goon is wrong.'

'Don't you bother the Inspector, Mrs. Trotteville; *please,*' said Mr. Goon. 'He's a busy man. I wouldn't have come to you if it hadn't have been for this young nephew of mine— nice fellow he is, simple and innocent—and I don't want him led into all sorts of dangers, see?'

'Well, I'm sure Frederick will promise not to lead him into danger,' said Mrs. Trotteville. 'It's the last thing he would want.'

Fatty said nothing. He was making no promises. He had a kind of feeling that it would be good for Mr. Goon's nephew to be led into something if he was as simple and innocent as the policeman made out. Anyway, all this was just to make sure that the Five Find-Outers didn't solve another mystery before Mr. Goon did! Fatty could see through *that* all right! Mr. Goon, not feeling very satisfied, departed ponderously down the garden-path, annoyed to find that his bicycle had suddenly developed a puncture in the front tyre. It couldn't possibly have been anything to do with That Boy, who had been in the room all the time—but Mr. Goon thought it was a very queer thing the way unpleasant things happened to him when he was up against Frederick Algernon Trotteville!

The Five Find-Outers met at Fatty's the next day. Buster gave every one a hilarious welcome. 'Now!' he barked. 'We are all together again. That's what I like best.'

But four of them, at least, looked gloomy. 'That spoilsport of a Goon,' said Larry. 'We were just waiting for you to come home and find another mystery to solve, Fatty. Now we're forbidden even to look for one.'

'All because of that goofy nephew of Mr. Goon's,' said Daisy.

'Well—*I'm* going to do exactly as I've always done,' said Fatty. 'Look out for a mystery, find my clues and suspects, fit the pieces together—and solve the whole thing before Mr. Goon even knows there's anything going on. And I'll tell you exactly what I'm doing the whole time!'

'Yes—but we want to *share* it,' said Pip. 'Share it properly, I mean—not just look on whilst you do it all. That's no fun.'

'Well, I don't suppose anything will turn up these hols at all,' grinned Fatty. 'Can't expect something *every* time, you know. But it would be rather fun to pretend we're on to something and get Goon's nephew all hot and bothered about it, wouldn't it? He'd say something to Goon, who wouldn't know whether to believe it or not—and he'd get into a mighty stew, too,'

'That's a wizard idea,' said Larry, pleased. 'Really wizard. If we can't find a mystery ourselves, we'll make up one for that boy. That'll serve Goon right for trying to spoil our fun!'

'Let's come and see if we can find the boy.' said Fatty, 'I'd be interested to see what sort of a fellow you mistook for me in disguise! Must be jolly good-looking, that's all I can say!'

They all went to the village. They were lucky, because just as they came in sight of Mr. Goon's house his nephew came out, wheeling his uncle's bicycle, having been ordered by Goon to take it to the garage and get the puncture mended.

'There he is!' said Bets excitedly. Fatty looked and an expression of deep disgust came over his face. He gazed at the Find-Outers in disappointment.

'Well! *How* you could think that boy was me—even in *disguise,* I really don't know! He's an oaf! A clod! A lump! Not a brain in his head. Good gracious, surely I don't look in the *least* like him?'

Fatty looked so hurt that Bets put her arm in his and

squeezed it. 'Fatty! Don't be upset. We thought it was one of your clever disguises.'

The boy wheeled his bicycle towards them. He stopped when he saw them, and to their surprise he grinned.

'Hallo! I know all about your mistake yesterday. You got me properly hot and bothered. I told my uncle and he spotted it was you. Said you called yourself the Find-Outers, or some such thing. He said you were a set of cheeky toads.'

'What's your name?' asked Pip.

'Ern,' said the boy.

'*Urn?*' said Bets in surprise, thinking of the great tea-urns her mother had at mothers' meetings.

'SwatIsaid,' said Ern.

Nobody understood the last sentence at all. 'I beg your pardon? What did you say?' asked Larry politely.

'I said "SwatIsaid,"' said Ern, impatiently.

'Oh—he means "It's what I said,"' explained Daisy to the others.

'Course it is—short for Ernest, see?' said Ern. 'I got two brothers. One Sid, short for Sidney the other's Perce, short for Percy. Ern, Sid and Perce—that's us.'

'Very nice,' murmured Fatty. 'Ern suits you marvellously.'

Ern looked pleased. 'And Fatty suits you,' he said, handsomely. 'Right down to the ground it does. And Pip suits him too—bit of a pip-squeak, isn't he? Wants to grow a bit, I'd say.'

The Find-Outers thought these remarks were out of place from Ern. He was getting a bit too big for his boots.

'I hope you'll have a nice holiday with your uncle,' said Bets, suddenly very polite.

Ern made a curious chortling noise. 'Oooh! My uncle! His high-and-mighty-nibs! Says I mustn't get led into danger by you! Well, you see here—if you get hold of any mysteries you just tell me, Ern Goon. I'd like to show my uncle I've got better brains than his.'

'That wouldn't be very difficult,' said Fatty. 'Well, Ern— we'll certainly lead you to any mysteries we find. I expect you know that your uncle has forbidden us to solve any ourselves these hols—so perhaps you could take our place and solve a mystery right under his nose?'

Ern's rather protruding eyes nearly fell out of his head. 'Jumping snakes! Do you mean that? Lovaduck!'

'Yes. We'll provide you with all sorts of clues,' said Fatty, solemnly. 'But don't you go and tell your uncle in case he gets angry with us.'

'You bet I won't,' said Ern.

'Oh, Ern—can I have back that note-book I gave you by mistake yesterday?' said Bets, suddenly. 'It wasn't meant for you, of course. It was meant for Fatty.'

'I was going to use it for my portry,' said Ern, looking disappointed. He took it out and held it for Bets to take. 'I love portry.'

'What's portry?' asked Bets, puzzled.

'Portry! Lovaduck, don't you know what's portry. It's when things rhyme, like.'

'Oh—you mean poetry,' said Bets.

'SwatIsaid,' said Ern. 'Well, I write portry.'

This was so astonishing that nobody said anything for a moment.

'What sort of poetry—er, I mean portry?' asked Fatty.

'I'll recite you some,' said Ern, looking very pleased with himself. 'This here one's called "The Pore Dead Pig." He cleared his throat and began :

'How sad to see thee, pore dead pig,
When all...'

'Look out — here's your uncle!' suddenly said Larry, as

Ern chatted to the others

a large dark—blue figure appeared in Mr. Goon's little front garden. A roar came from him.

'What about my BIKE! Didn't I tell you I wanted it right back?'

'So long!' said Ern, hurriedly, and shot off down the street at top speed. 'See you later!'

4   FATTY IS MYSTERIOUS

ERN soon became a terrible bore. He lay in wait for the
Find-Outers every day, and pestered them to tell him if they
had smelt out any mystery yet. He kept wanting to recite his
'portry.' He shocked the five children by his very low opinion
of his uncle, Mr. Goon.

'We've got a low opinion of Old Clear-Orf ourselves,'
said Larry, 'but really, to hear Ern speak of his uncle any
one would think he was the meanest, slyest, greediest, laziest
policeman that ever lived!'

Ern was always bringing out dreadful tales of his uncle.
'He ate three eggs and all the bacon for his breakfast, and he
didn't leave me nothing but a plate of porridge,' said Ern.
'No wonder he's bursting his uniform!'

'My uncle isn't half lazy,' he said another time. 'He's
supposed to be on duty each afternoon, but he just puts his
head back, shuts his eyes and snores till tea-time! Wouldn't
I like the Inspector to come along and catch him!'

'My uncle says you all want locking up for a few days,
you're just a set of cheeky toads,' said Ern, yet another time.
'He likes *your* mother and father, Pip—but he says Fatty's
people are just the...'

'Look here, Ern—you oughtn't to repeat what your uncle
says about us or our people,' said Fatty. 'It's a rotten trick.
You know jolly well Mr. Goon wouldn't tell you all these
things if he thought you were going to repeat them.'

Ern gave one of his chortles. 'Lovaduck! What do you
suppose he says them for? 'Course he wants me to tell you
them! Nice easy way for him to be rude to you.'

'Really?' said Fatty. 'Well, two can play at that game. You tell your uncle we think he's a...'

'Oh don't, Fatty,' said Bets, in alarm. 'He'll only come round and complain again.'

'He can't complain to *your* parents about what *I* say,' said Fatty.

'Oh yes, he can,' said Pip. 'You should just see him walking into our house like a flat-footed bull-frog, as pompous as a...'

Ern gave such a loud chortle that every one jumped. Pip stopped in a hurry.

'That's a good one, that is!' said Ern. 'Lovaduck, I'd like to see Uncle Theophilus when I tell him that!'

'If you repeat that I'll fight you!' said Pip, furious with himself for saying such a silly thing in front of Ern. 'I'll knock your silly nose off, I'll...'

'Shut up, Pip,' said Fatty. 'You can't even box. You ought to learn boxing at school like I do. You should just see me box! Why, last term I fought a chap twice my size, and in five minutes I...'

'Had him flat on his back!' finished Larry 'with a couple of black eyes and a squashed ear.'

Fatty looked surprised. 'How do you know?' he said. 'Have I told you before?'

'No, but your stories always end in some way like that,' grinned Larry.

'Found any mystery yet?' inquired Ern, who didn't like to be left out of the talk for long. Fatty at once looked secretive.

'Well,' he said, and hesitated. 'No, I don't think I'd better tell you, Ern. You'd only split to your uncle. You just can't keep your mouth shut.'

Ern began to look excited. 'Come on! You've got

something, I know you have. You said you'd tell me if you was on to a mystery. Lovaduck! Wouldn't it be a sell for Uncle if I got on to a mystery and solved it before he got a sniffofit.'

'What was that last word?' asked Fatty. Ern had a curious habit of running some of his words together. 'Sniffofit? What sort of a fit is that? Does your uncle go in for fits?'

'Sniffofit!' repeated Ern. 'Can't you understand plain English? Sniffofit.'

'He means "sniff of it" said Daisy.

'SwatIsaid,' said Ern, looking sulky.

'Swatesaid,' said Fatty at once to the others. They giggled. Ern scowled. He didn't like it when the others made fun of him. But he soon cheered up.

'Go on—you tell me about this mystery you've got,' he begged Fatty.

Fatty, of course, knew of no mystery at all. The holidays, in fact, stretched dull and dreary in front of him, with not a hint of any mystery anywhere. Only Ern promised a little fun and excitement. Fatty looked mysterious.

He began to speak in a whisper. 'Well,' he said, 'it's like this.' He stopped and looked over his shoulder as if there were people listening. Ern began to feel thrilled.

Then Fatty shook his head firmly. 'No, Ern. I can't tell you yet. I don't think I'd better. I'm only at the beginning of things. I'll wait till I know a little more.'

Ern could hardly contain his excitement. He clutched Fatty's arm. 'Look here, you've *got* to tell me !' he hissed. 'I won't breathe a word to Uncle. Go on, Fatty, be a sport.'

The others watched Fatty, trying not to laugh. They knew he hadn't anything to tell. Poor old Ern — he just swallowed everything he was told.

'I'll wait till I've a bit more to tell,' said Fatty. 'No, it's no good, Ern. Not even the others know anything yet. The time hasn't come yet to develop the case.'

'Lovaduck! That sounds good,' said Ern, impressed. 'All right, I'll wait. I say — do you think I ought to get a note-book and write down in it the things young Bets here wrote down in yours — the one she gave you for a present ?'

'It wouldn't be a bad idea,' said Fatty. 'You've a note-book in your pocket, I see — bring it out and we'll show you what to write.'

'No. That's my portry note-book,' said Ern. 'Can't write nothing in that except portry.' He took it out and flicked over the pages. 'Look — I wrote a pome last night — proper good pome it was too. It's called ''The Pore Old Horse.'' Shall I read it to you ?'

'Well, no — not now,' said Fatty, looking at his watch and putting on a very startled expression. 'My word — look at the time. Sorry, old horse — pore old horse — but we can't stop to-day. Another time perhaps. Get a note-book, Ern, and we'll set down in it all you ought to have in a proper mystery note-book.'

The five went off with Buster, grinning. Ern went back to his uncle, pondering whether to repeat Pip's words to his uncle — what were they now? Flat-footed bull-frog. That was good, that was. Good enough to put into a pome !

'Ern and his pomes and portry !' giggled Daisy. 'I wish I could get hold of that portry book — I'd write a poem in it that would make Old Clear-Orf sit up !'

'Quite an idea !' said Fatty, and put it away in his mind for future use. 'Now, Find-Outers, we'd better plan what sort of wild-goose chase we're to send Ern on! We can't possibly disappoint him. We've got to give him a bit of excitement.'

They went to Pip's play-room and began to plan. 'It wouldn't be a bad idea to practise a few disguises,' said Fatty thoughtfully. 'It doesn't look as if we're going to have much fun these hols, so we might as well make our own.'

'Oh, yes — *do* let's practise disguises,' said Bets, thrilled.

'We're going to have a good time with old Ern,' chuckled Fatty. 'Now, let's plan. Anybody got any ideas?'

'Well — what about a mystery kidnapping or something like that?' said Larry. 'Men who kidnap rich men's children and keep them prisoner. We might get Ern to try and rescue them.'

'Or we might have mysterious lights at night flashing somewhere, and send Ern to see what they are,' said Bets.

'Go on. We're getting some good ideas,' said Fatty.

'Or what about a robbery — with the loot hidden somewhere — and Ern has to find it ?' suggested Daisy.

'Or a collection of clues to puzzle Ern. You know how we once put a whole lot of clues down for Clear-Orf,' said Pip. 'My word — I'll never forget that.'

Every one laughed. Fatty tapped his knee thoughtfully with his pencil. 'Jolly good ideas, all of them,' he said. 'Super, in fact. I vote we try and use all of them. Might as well give Ern good measure. And if old Goon gets excited about it too, so much the better. I bet Ern won't be able to keep it dark. Goon will know there's something up — but he won't know how much is pretence and how much isn't. We'll have them both on a string !'

'It won't be as good as a real mystery, but it will be great fun !' Said Bets, hugging herself. 'It will serve Mr. Goon right for coming to complain to Daddy and Mother ! And for trying to do *us* out of a mystery these hols.'

'Not that there's even a shadow of one at the moment,' said Daisy.

'Well, now, let's get down to it,' said Fatty. 'Ern will come complete with his note-book next time we see him, I'm sure of that. We'll put down the usual headings — Clues, Suspects, Progress and so on. Then we'll begin providing a few clues. We'd better let him find them. He'll get awfully bucked if he thinks he's better at spotting things that we are. I'll make up some kind of story, which I won't tell you now, so that it will seem quite fresh to you. You can listen with large eyes and bated breath!'

'What's bated breath?' asked Bets. 'Do we breathe fast, or something ?'

'No — we just hold it, silly,' said Pip. 'And don't you go and give the game away, Bets. It would be just like you to do that !'

'It would *not,*' said Bets, indignantly. 'Would it, Fatty?'

'No. You're a very good little Find-Outer,' said Fatty, comfortingly. 'I bet you'll bate your breath best of any one. Hallo, what's that ?'

'The dinner-bell,' said Pip, gloomily. 'It always goes when we're in the middle of something.'

'Spitty,' said Fatty, and got up.

'What do you mean — *spitty* ?' said Larry.

'He means ''It's a pity !'' said Bets with a giggle.

'SwatIsaid,' said Fatty, and got up to go.

5 IN FATTY'S SHED

THE next day Ern got a message that filled him with excitement. It was a note from Fatty.

'Developments. Must talk to you. Bottom of my garden, twelve o'clock. F.T.'

Mr. Goon saw Ern goggling over this note and became suspicious at once. 'Who's that from ?'

'One of my friends.' said Ern haughtily, and put it into his pocket.

Mr. Goon went a purple-red. 'You show it to me,' he said.

'Can't,' said Ern. 'It's private.'

'What do you mean — *private* !' snorted Mr. Goon. 'A kid like you don't know what private means. You give me that note.'

'But Uncle — it's only from Fatty to say he wants to see me,' protested Ern.

'You show that note to me !' shouted Mr. Goon, and Ern, scared, passed it over. Mr. Goon snorted again as he read it.

'Gah ! All a lot of tommy-rot ! Developments indeed ! What does he mean by that ?'

Ern didn't know and he said so several times, but his uncle didn't believe him. 'If that there cheeky toad is up to his tricks again, I'll skin him !' said Mr. Goon. 'And you tell him that, see ?'

'Oh, I will, Uncle,' said Ern, trying to edge out of the room. 'I always tell them what you say. They like to hear. But it's not right of Pip to say you're a flat-footed bullfrog, I did tell him that.'

Before the purple Mr. Goon could find his tongue to say what he thought of this, Ern was out of the house and away. He mopped his forehead. Lovaduck — his uncle was a hot-tempered chap all right. Anyway, he hadn't forbidden him to go; that was something !

He arrived at the bottom of Fatty's garden and heard voices in the shed there. It was Fatty's work-room and play-room. He had made it very comfortable indeed. On this cold winter's day he had an oil-stove burning brightly and the inside of the shed was warm and cosy. A tiger-skin was on the floor, old and moth-eaten but looking very grand, and a crocodile skin was stretched along one side of the shed-wall. The Five Find-Outers were trying to roast chestnuts on top of the oil-stove. They had a tin of condensed milk and were each having a dip in it with a spoon as they talked.

Ern looked in at the window. Ha ! They were all there. Good ! He knocked at the door.

'Come in!' called Fatty, and Ern went in. An icy draught at once came in with him.

'Shut the door,' said Daisy. 'Oooh! What a draught. Hallo, Ern. Did you enjoy your egg for breakfast?'

Ern looked surprised. 'Yes. But how did you know I had an egg for breakfast ?'

'Oh — we're doing a bit of detecting for practice this morning,' said Daisy. The others tried not to laugh. Ern had spilt a good bit of his egg down the front of his jacket at breakfast, so it was not a difficult bit of detecting !

'Sorry you had to leave in such a hurry to come here,' said Fatty, solemnly.

Ern looked even more surprised. 'Lovaduck ! Is that another bit of detecting ? How'd you know I left in a hurry ?'

Ern had no hat and no coat, so *that* wasn't a very difficult bit of detecting either. Nobody explained to Ern how they knew about his breakfast or his hurry, and he sat down feeling rather puzzled.

'Perhaps you'd like to tell me what *I* had for breakfast,' said Fatty to Ern. 'Go on — do a bit of detecting too.'

Ern looked at Fatty's solemn face, but no ideas about breakfast came into his mind. He shook his head. 'No. I can see this sort of thing wants a lot of practice. Coo, I wasn't half excited when I got your note this morning. My uncle saw me reading it.'

'Did he really?' said Fatty with interest. 'Did he say anything?'

'Oh, he got into a rage you know, but I soon settled *that.*' said Ern. 'I just told him what I thought of him. "Uncle," I said, "this is a private note. It's none of your business, so keep out of it." Just like that.'

Every one looked at him admiringly but disbelievingly. 'And what did he say to that ?' asked Pip.

'He began to go purple,' said Ern, 'and I said ''Now calm yourself, Uncle, or you'll go pop. And don't go poking your nose into what I do with my friends. It's private." And then I walked out and came here.'

'Most admirable !' said Fatty. 'Sit down on the tiger-skin rug, Ern. Don't be afraid of the head and the teeth. He's not as fierce now as he was when I shot him in the Tippylooloo Plain.'

Ern's eyes nearly fell out of his head. 'Lovaduck ! You been tiger-shooting? What about that thing up on the wall ? Did you shoot that too ?'

'That's crocodile skin,' said Bets, enjoying herself. 'Let me see, Fatty — was that the third or fourth crocodile you shot?'

Ern's respect for Fatty went up a hundredfold. He gazed

about him with the greatest awe. He looked at the fierce head of the tiger-rug, and felt a bit scared of it, even though it was no longer alive. He moved a little way from the snarling teeth.

'You said in your note there were developments,' said Ern, eagerly. 'Are you going to tell us anything to-day ?'

'Yes. The time has come for us to ask you to do something,' said Fatty, in a solemn voice that sent a thrill down Ern's spine. 'I am uncovering a very mysterious mystery.'

'Coo,' said Ern, in a hushed voice. 'Do the others know ?'

'Not yet,' said Fatty. 'Now listen all of you. There are strange lights flashing at night over on Christmas Hill !'

'Oooh,' said Ern. 'Have you seen them ?'

'There are rival gangs there,' said Fatty, in a grave voice. 'One is a kidnapping gang. One is a gang of robbers. Soon they will get busy.'

Ern's mouth fell open. The others, although they knew it was all Fatty's make-up, couldn't help feeling a bit thrilled too. Ern swallowed once or twice. Talk about a mystery ! This was a whacker !

'Now the thing is — can we get going, and find out who they are and their plans, before they start their robbing and kidnapping ?' said Fatty.

'*We* can't, said Bets, in a dismal voice. 'We've been forbidden to get mixed up in any mystery these hols.'

'So have we,' said Larry and Daisy together. 'Yes, it's bad luck,' said Fatty. 'I'm the only one who can do anything — but I can't do it alone. That's why I've got you here this morning, Ern. You must help me.'

Ern took in all this rather slowly, but with the utmost excitement and delight. He swelled out his chest proudly.

'You can count on me,' he said, and made his voice deep

and solemn. 'Ern's with you ! Coo! I feel all funny-like. I bet I'd write a good pome with this sort of feeling inside me !'

'Yes. It could begin like this,' said Fatty, who could reel off silly verse by the mile.

> 'There's a mystery a-moving
> Away on Christmas Hill,
> Where kidnappers and robbers
> Are waiting for the kill.
> But when kidnappers are napping
> And robbers are asleep,
> We'll pounce on them together
> And knock them in a heap !'

Every one laughed. No one could reel off verse like Fatty. Ern gaped and couldn't find a word to say. *Why,* that was wonderful portry ! To think Fatty could say it all off like that !

He found his voice at last. 'Lovaduck ! Did you make all that up out of your head just this minute ? It takes me hours to think of a pome — and even when I do, it won't rhyme for ages. You must be one of them queer things — a genius.'

'Well — you never know,' said Fatty, trying to look modest. 'I remember having to write a poem — er, I mean pome — for class one day, and forgetting all about it till the master pounced on me and asked for mine. I looked in my desk, but of course it wasn't there because I had forgotten to write one. So I just said 'Sorry, sir, it seems to be mislaid — but I'll recite it if you like.' And I stood up and recited six verses straight off out of my head. What's more, I got top marks for it.'

'I don't believe you,' said Pip.

'Well, I'll recite it for you now if you like,' said Fatty, indignantly, but the others wouldn't let him.

'Stop boasting,' said Larry. 'Let's get down to work. How

did we get on to this poem-business anyway ? You'll have Ern wanting to recite next !'

Ern would have been only too willing to oblige, but most unfortunately in his hurried departure from his uncle's house he had left his portry note-book — a very grand one, with black covers, and elastic band, and a pencil down the back.

'Mr. Goon's got one like that,' said Bets. 'Did he give you that ?'

Mr. Goon would not even have dreamed of giving his nephew one of his precious note-books, provided for him by the Inspector. Ern licked the end of the pencil and looked round triumphantly. 'Give it me ! I should think not ! I pinched it out of his drawer.'

There was a horrified silence. 'Then you'll jolly well give it back,' said Fatty. 'Or *you'll* be pinched one day. You're disgusting, Ern.'

Ern looked hurt and astonished. 'Well, he's my uncle, isn't he ? It won't hurt him to let me have one of his note-books — and I'm going detecting, aren't I? You're very high-and-mighty all of a sudden.'

'You can think us high-and-mighty if you like,' said Fatty, getting up. 'But we think *you're* very low-down to take something out of your uncle's drawer without asking him.'

'I'll put it back,' said Ern, in a small voice. 'I wouldn't have taken it for my portry — but for detecting, well, somehow I thought that was different. I kind of thought I *ought* to have it.'

'Well, you think again,' said Fatty. 'And put it back before you get into trouble. Look — here's a note-book of mine you can have. It's an old one. We'll tell you what to write in it. But mind — you put that black one back as soon as ever you get home !'

'Yes, I will, Fatty,' said Ern, humbly. He took the old

note-book Fatty held out to him, and felt about in his pocket for a pencil, for he did not feel he dared to use the one in the black note-book now. Fatty might get all high-and-mighty again.

'Now,' said Fatty, 'keep this page for clues. Write the word down — Clues.'

'Clues,' said Ern, solemnly, and wrote it down. The word 'Suspects' came next. 'Coo,' said Ern, 'do we have Suspects too ? What are they ?'

'People who *might* be mixed up in the mystery,' said Fatty. 'You make a whole list of them, inquire into their goings-on, and then cross them off one by one when you find they're all right.'

Ern felt very important as he put down the things Fatty told him. He licked his stump of a pencil, and wrote most laboriously, with his tongue sticking out of the corner of his mouth all the time.

Buster suddenly growled and cocked up his ears. Fatty put his hand on him. 'Quiet, Buster,' he said. He winked at the others. 'I bet it's Old Clear-Orf snooping round,' he said. Ern looked alarmed.

'I wonder he dares to come snooping after Ern, considering the way he got ticked off by Ern himself this morning,' said Fatty, innocently. 'If it *is* your uncle, Ern, you'd better send him off at once. Bit of cheek, tracking you down like this !'

Ern felt even more alarmed. A shadow fell across the cosy room, and the Find-Outers and Ern saw Mr. Goon's head peering in at the window. He saw Ern with a note-book. Ern looked up with a scared face.

'You come on out, Ern,' boomed Mr. Goon. 'I got a job for you to do !'

Ern got up and went to the door. He opened it and out

shot Buster in delight. He flew for Mr. Goon's ankles at once, barking madly.

'Clear-orf !' yelled Mr. Goon, kicking out at Buster. 'Here you, call off your dog ! Ern, hold him ! He'll take a bit out of my ankle soon ! Clear-orf, you pestering dog !'

But it was Mr. Goon who had to clear-orf, with Buster barking at him all the way, and Ern following in delight. 'Go on, Buster !' he muttered under his breath. 'Keep it up ! Good dog then. Good dog !'

6   ERN GETS INTO TROUBLE

THE Five Find-Outers were very pleased with their little bit of work that morning. 'We'll keep Ern busy,' said Fatty. 'And as I'm pretty sure he'll let everything out to Goon — or Goon will probably dip into Ern's note-book — we shall keep *him* busy too !'

'It's a pity Mr. Goon came and interrupted our talk this morning,' said Bets, getting up to go. 'We were just getting on nicely. Fatty, what's the first clue to be ?'

'Well, I told Ern that this morning,' said Fatty. 'Mysterious lights flash on Christmas Hill at night ! Ern will have to go and find out what they are.'

'Will you go with him ?' asked Bets.

'No. I'll be flashing the lights,' said Fatty with a grin. The others looked at him enviously.

'Wish we could come too,' said Larry. 'It's maddening to be forbidden to do anything these hols.'

'Well, you're not forbidden to play a trick on somebody,' said Fatty, considering the matter. 'You're forbidden to get mixed up in any mystery or to go and look for one. You're not looking for a mystery, and there certainly isn't one, so I don't see why you and Pip can't come.'

The others' faces brightened. But Bets and Daisy were soon disappointed. 'The girls can't come out these cold nights,' went on Fatty. 'We'll have to find something else for them to do. Look here — I'll do a bit of disguising the first night Ern goes mystery hunting — and you two boys can do the light-flashing. I'll let Ern discover me crouching in a ditch or something, so that he really will think he's happened on some robber or other.'

'Yes — that would be fine !' said Larry. 'When shall we do it ?'

'Can't do it to-night,' said Fatty. 'We may not be able to get in touch with Ern in time. Tomorrow night, say.'

'Wasn't Ern funny when you spouted all that verse,' said Larry, with a grin. 'I don't know how you do it Fatty, really I don't. Ern thinks you're the world's wonder. I wonder if Sid and Perce are just as easy to take in as Ern. Are we going to meet again to-day ?'

'If I can get my mother to say you can all come to tea, I'll telephone you,' said Fatty. 'I don't see why I can't go and buy a whole lot of cakes, and have you to tea down here in the shed. We'd be nice and cosy, and we could make as much noise as we liked.'

But alas for Fatty's plan, an aunt came to tea, and he was made to go and behave politely at tea-time, handing bread and butter, jam and cakes in a way that Ern would have admired tremendously.

Ern was not having a very good time with his uncle. He had tried in vain to replace the note-book he had taken, but Mr. Goon always seemed to be hovering about. Ern didn't mean to let his uncle see him put it back !

He kept trying to go into his uncle's office, which was next to a little wash-place off the hall. But every time he sauntered out into the hall, whistling softly as if he hadn't a care in the world, his uncle saw him.

'What you want ?' he kept asking. 'Why are you so fidgety ? Can't a man have forty winks in peace without you wandering about, and whistling a silly tune ?'

'Sorry, Uncle,' said Ern, meekly. 'I was just going to wash my hands.'

'What, *again* ?' said Mr. Goon, disbelievingly. 'You've

washed them twice since dinner already. What's this new idea of being clean ? I've never known you wash your hands before unless I told you.'

'They feel sort of — sticky,' said Ern, rather feebly. He went back into the kitchen, where his uncle was sitting in his arm chair, his coat unbuttoned, and his froggy eyes looking half-closed and sleepy. Why didn't he go to sleep as he usually did ?

Ern sat down. He picked up a paper and pretended to read it. Mr. Goon knew he was pretending, and he wondered what Ern was up to. He didn't want to wash his hands ! No, he wanted to go into his uncle's office. What for ? Mr. Goon thought deeply about the matter.

A sudden thought came into his mind. Aha ! It was that cheeky toad of a boy, Frederick Trotteville, who had put Ern up to snooping about his office to see if any mystery was afoot. The sauce ! Well, let him catch Ern snooping in his desk, and Ern would feel how hard his hand was ! He began to hope that Ern *would* do a bit of snooping. Mr. Goon felt that he would quite like to give somebody a really good ticking-off ! He was in that sort of mood what with that dog snapping at his ankles and making him rush off like that in front of Ern.

He closed his eyes. He pretended to snore a little. Ern rose quietly and made for the door. He stopped in the hall and looked back. Mr. Goon still snored, and his mouth was half open. Ern felt he was safe.

He slipped into the office, and opened the drawer of the desk. He slid the note-book into the drawer — but before he could close it a wrathful voice fell on his ears.

'Ho ! So that's what you're doing — snooping and prying in my private papers ! You wicked boy — my own nephew too, that ought to know better.'

Ern felt a sharp slap across his left cheek, and he put up his hand. 'Uncle ! I wasn't snooping ! I swear I wasn't.'

'What were you doing then ?' demanded Mr. Goon.

Ern stood and stared at his uncle without a word to say. He couldn't possibly own up to having taken the note-book — so he couldn't say he was putting it back ! Mr. Goon slapped poor Ern hard on the other cheek. 'Next time I'll put you across my knee and deal with you properly !' threatened Mr. Goon. 'What are you snooping for ? Did that cheeky toad of a boy tell you to hunt in my desk to see what sort of a case I was working on now ? Did he tell you to find out any of my clues and give them to him ?'

'No, Uncle, no,' said Ern beginning to blubber in fright and pain. 'I wouldn't do that, not even if he told me to. Anyway, he knows the mystery. He's told me about it.'

Mr. Goon pricked up his ears at once. What ! Fatty had got hold of another mystery ! What could it be ? Mr. Goon could have danced with rage. That boy ! A real pest he was if ever there was one.

'Now, you look here,' he said to Ern, who was holding his hand to his right ear, which was swollen with the slap Mr Goon had given it, 'you look here ! It's your duty to report to me anything that boy tells you about this mystery. See ?'

Ern was torn between his urgent wish to be loyal to Fatty, the boy he admired so tremendously, and his fear that Mr. Goon might really give him a thrashing if he refused to tell anything Fatty told him.

'Go on,' said his uncle. 'Tell me what you know. It's your bounden duty to tell a police officer everything. What's this here wonderful mystery ?'

'Oh — it's just lights flashing on Christmas Hill,' stammered poor Ern, rubbing his tear-stained face. 'That's about all I know, Uncle. I don't believe Fatty knows much more. He's given me a note-book — look. You can see what's written down in it. Hardly anything.'

Mr. Goon frowned over the headings. He began to plan. He could always get this note-book from Ern — and if the boy refused to give it to him, well then, as an officer of the law he'd get it somehow — even if he had to do it when Ern was asleep. He gave it back to Ern.

'I've got a good hard hand, haven't I, Ern ?' said Mr. Goon to his nephew. 'You don't want to feel it again, do you ? Well, then, you see you report to me all the goings-on that those kids get up to.'

'Yes, Uncle,' said Ern, not meaning to at all. He backed away from his uncle. 'There aren't any goings on just now. We hadn't planned anything, Uncle. You came and interrupted us.'

'And a good thing too,' said Mr. Goon. 'Now you can just sit down at the kitchen table and do some holiday work, see ? Time you did something to oil those brains of yours. I'm not going to have you tearing about with those five kids and that dog all day long.'

Ern went obediently to the kitchen and settled down at the table with an arithmetic book. He had had a bad report from his school the term before, and was supposed to do a good bit of holiday work. But instead of thinking of his sums he thought about the Find-Outers, especially Fatty, and the Mystery, and Flashing Lights, and Kidnappers and Robbers. Lovaduck ! How exciting it all was.

Ern was worried because his uncle wouldn't let him go out. He couldn't get in touch with the others if he didn't go out. Suppose they went to look for those flashing lights and didn't let him know ? Ern felt he simply couldn't *bear* that.

All that day he was kept in the house. He went to bed to dream of tigers, crocodiles, Fatty reciting verse and somebody kidnapping his uncle. When he awoke the next morning he began to plan how to get into touch with the others.

But Mr. Goon had other plans. 'You can take down all those files in those shelves,' he said. 'And clean up the shelves and dust the files, and put them back in proper order.'

That took Ern all the morning. Mr. Goon went out and Ern hoped one of the Find-Outers would come, but they didn't. In the afternoon Mr. Goon settled himself down to go to sleep as usual. He saw Ern looking very down in the dumps and was pleased. 'He won't go snooping again !' he thought. 'He knows what he'll get if he does !'

And Mr. Goon went peacefully off to sleep. He was awakened by a thunderous knocking at the door. He almost leapt out of his chair and Ern looked alarmed.

'Shall I go, Uncle ?' he said.

Mr. Goon did not answer. He went to the door himself, buttoning up his uniform. That knocking sounded official. It might be the Inspector himself. People didn't usually hammer on the door of a police officer like that. They'd be afraid to !

Outside stood a fat old woman in a red shawl. 'I've come to complain,' she began, in a high, quavering voice. 'The things I've put up with from that woman ! She's my next-door neighbour, sir, and she's the meanest woman you ever saw. She throws her rubbish into my garden, sir and she always lights her bonfire when the wind's blowing my way, and ...'

'Wait, wait,' said Mr. Goon, annoyed. 'What's your name and where do ...'

'And only yesterday she called me a monster, sir, that was the very word she used, oh, a wicked woman she is, and it's myself won't stand it any longer. Why, last week her dustbin ...'

Mr. Goon saw that this would go on for ever. 'You can

put in a written complaint,' he said. 'I'm busy this afternoon,' and he shut the door firmly.

He settled himself down in his chair again, but before two minutes had gone, here came such a knock at the door that it was a wonder it wasn't broken down. Mr. Goon, in a fury, leapt up again and almost ran to the door. The woman was there again, her arms folded akimbo over her chest.

'I forgot to tell you, sir,' she began, 'when I put my washing out last week this woman threw a pail of dirty water over it, and I had to wash it all again, and ...'

'Didn't I tell you to put in a written report ?' roared Mr. Goon. 'Do as you're told, woman !' And again he shut the door, and stamped into the kitchen, fuming.

No sooner had he sat down than the knocker sounded again. Mr. Goon looked at Ern. 'You go,' he said. 'It's that woman again. Tell her what you like.'

Ern went, rather scared. He opened the door and a flood of words poured over him. 'Oh, it's you this time, is it ? Well, you tell your uncle, what's the good of me putting in a written report, when I can't read nor write? You ask him that. You go in and ask him that!'

And then, to Ern's enormous astonishment, the red-shawled woman dug him in the chest, and said in a whisper, 'Ern! Take this ! Now, tell me to go away, quick !'

Ern gaped. That was Fatty's voice, surely. Coo, was this Fatty in one of his disguises ? Wonderful ! Fatty winked hugely, and Ern found his voice.

'You clear-orf !' he cried. 'Bothering my uncle like this ! I won't have it ! Clear-orf, I say !'

He slammed the door. Mr. Goon, in the kitchen, listened in astonishment. Why, Ern had been able to get rid of the woman far more quickly than he had. There must be something in the boy after all.

Ern was quickly reading the note Fatty had pushed into his hand :

'To-night. Watch for lights on Christmas Hill. Hide in ditch by mill. Midnight. Report tomorrow.'

Ern stuffed the note into his pocket, too thrilled for words. It was beginning ! He was plunging into a Mystery ! And he wouldn't tell his uncle a single word. That Fatty ! Fancy having the cheek to dress up like that and come thundering on his uncle's front door. Ern went into the kitchen, quite bemused.

'So you got rid of that woman ?' said his uncle. 'Well, let's hope she won't come hammering again.'

She didn't. She went home to Fatty's house, slipped out of her things in Fatty's shed — and there was Fatty himself, taking off the woman's wig he wore, and rubbing away the wrinkles he had painted on his face. He chuckled. 'That took Goon in properly ! My word, Ern's face was a picture when he saw it was me !'

7   MYSTERIOUS HAPPENINGS ON CHRISTMAS HILL

ERN was in such a state of excitement all the rest of the day that his uncle couldn't help noticing it. He stared at Ern and wondered. What was up with the boy ? He hadn't seen or heard from the others. Then why was he so excited ? He couldn't keep still for a minute.

'Stop fidgeting, Ern !' said Mr. Goon sharply. 'What's the matter with you ?'

'Nothing, Uncle,' said Ern. Actually Ern was a bit worried about something. He knew Christmas Hill all right — but he didn't know where this mill was that Fatty had written of in his letter. How could he find out ? Only by asking his uncle. But would his uncle smell a rat if he began talking about the mill ?

He decided to get a map of the district out of the book-case and study it. So when Mr. Goon was answering the telephone, Ern slid the map from the shelf, opened it and looked for the mill. Oh yes — there it was — on the right of the stream. If he followed the stream he couldn't help coming to the mill. Ern shivered in delight when he thought of creeping out all by himself that night. He marked where the mill was, and then with his pencil followed the way he would go, right up to the mill.

Mr. Goon's eyes looked sharply at the map as he came back into the room 'What you studying ? He asked.

'Oh — just looking at a map of this district to see if I can go for a good walk somewhere,' said Ern. He put the map back, and felt the little note in his pocket. Nothing would make him show it to Mr. Goon. Ah, that was a clever trick of Fatty's getting him a message through, right under Mr. Goon's nose!

Mr. Goon knew there was something up, especially when Ern said he would pop off to bed early. That wasn't like Ern ! He watched him go, and then took out from the shelf the map that he had seen Ern using. He at once saw the pencilled path from the village of Peterswood to the old mill on Christmas Hill.

'So that's where something's going on !' said Mr. Goon to himself. 'Lights flashing on Christmas Hill — which means somebody's there that's got no business to be. And the person to look into this is P.C. Goon. There's no time like the present, either. I'll go to-night !'

Quite a lot of people were preparing to go to Christmas Hill that night ! Pip and Larry were going, complete with torches, and red, blue and green coloured paper to slip over the beam now and again. Fatty was going, of course, to give Ern a fright. Ern was going — and so was Mr. Goon. A real crowd !

Mr. Goon didn't go to bed that night. It wasn't worth it. He planned to slip off at about half-past eleven, very quietly so as not to wake Ern.

Ern, as a matter of fact, was wide awake, listening to the church clock striking the half-hours. He shivered with excitement in his warm bed. He didn't hear Mr. Goon go quietly out of the front door and pull it to behind him. He quite thought his uncle was in bed and asleep, as he usually was at that hour.

About two minutes after Goon had gone from the house Ern got up. He was fully dressed. He took his torch and tried it. Yes, it was all right. Bit faint, but it would last. He pulled on a coat, stuffed a scarf round his neck, and put on his big cap. He trod quietly down the stairs, hoping not to wake up his uncle — who by this time was plodding softly up Christmas Hill.

Fatty was already by the mill, hidden safely under a bush. Larry and Pip were some distance away, each with a torch and directions to begin shining them here and there, to and fro, every few minutes, in the direction of the mill. The hill was a desolate, deserted place, and the wind was very cold as it swept across it that night.

Mr. Goon wished he was safe home and warm in bed. He plodded along quietly, thinking of comforting things like oil-stoves and hot cocoa and hot water-bottles. And quite suddenly he saw a light flashing not far from him !

Mr. Goon sank down on the hillside beside a hedge. So that toad of a boy was right. There *was* something going on after all on Christmas Hill ! What could it be ?

He watched intently, almost forgetting to breathe. A red light — flash-flash ! A green one — flash-flash-flash ! And gracious, there was another light farther up the hill — a blue one, flash !

Larry and Pip were enjoying themselves, flashing hard, hoping that Ern was seeing the flashes and marvelling. Fatty was waiting impatiently for Ern. Where was he ? All this flashing was being wasted if Ern wasn't seeing it. Surely he hadn't gone to sleep in bed when he had been told to come to the mill ?

Then Fatty heard a sigh as if some one was letting out a big breath. Ah — that must be Ern. He must be hiding somewhere nearby. Perhaps he didn't quite know where the mill was.

Flash-flash-flash ! The lights winked out over the hill. Mr. Goon wondered if they were being flashed in the Morse code, but after trying hard to puzzle out any letters being flashed he gave it up. Who were these signallers ? Were they flashing to somebody in the old deserted mill ? Mr. Goon thought about the mill. It was almost ruined. He was positive there was nothing to be found there but rats and owls.

Mr. Goon moved his cramped legs and a twig cracked sharply under him. He held his breath again ! Would any one hear that ? He listened and heard nothing. The lights went on and on flashing merrily. Most extraordinary. Mr. Goon debated whether or not to tell the Inspector about it. He decided not to. He'd better get to the bottom of things before that cheeky Frederick Trotteville did.

The lights stopped flashing. They had been going strong for twenty minutes, and now Larry and Pip were so cold that they decided to make their way home. They would meet Fatty again in the morning, and hear what had happened to him and Ern. They chuckled as they thought of Ern, discovering Fatty crouching in a ditch, and wondered what he would do. Run away, probably.

When the lights stopped flashing Mr. Goon moved very cautiously from the hedge. He went down into some kind of ditch and tried to get a safe footing. Fatty heard him scraping about and had no doubt at all but that it was Ern, watching lights flashing with wonder and fear.

Well, if Ern wasn't going to discover *him,* he had better discover Ern ! He would leap on him and give him the fright of his life ! They would have a good old rough and tumble !

Fatty crept towards Mr. Goon. He decided to make a few noises first. So he made a mewing noise like a cat. Mr. Goon stopped, surprised. A cat ? Out here on Christmas Hill, with not a building near ! Poor thing !

'Puss, puss, puss !' he called. Then he heard an unmistakable clucking. 'Cluck-luck-luck-luck-luck ! *Cluck-*luck-luck-luck-luck !'

A hen ! Who could it belong to ? Mr. Goon frowned. It must have escaped from somewhere — but where ? There was no farm for miles !

Fatty then mooed like a cow. He was a good mooer and could even startle cows. He startled Mr. Goon extremely, much more than he had ever startled cows. Mr. Goon almost jumped out of his skin. A cow now ! Visions of Christmas Hill suddenly populated in the middle of night with cows, cats and hens came into Mr. Goon's mind. He couldn't understand it. For one moment he wondered if he could be dreaming.

But he was too cold to be dreaming. He scratched the side of his cheek and puzzled about the cow. He ought to take a cow away from this bitter-cold hill. He felt for his torch, and shone it all around, trying to find the cow. Fatty, crouched under a nearby bush, giggled. He thought it was Ern trying to see the cow, the cat and the hen. He debated weather to grunt like a pig or to wail like a baby.

He wailed, and Mr. Goon froze to his very marrow. He was petrified. What else was abroad on this dark hill to-night ? Whatever there was he wasn't going to waste any more time looking for it. He turned to run, and another wail made him shake at the knees.

Fatty stood up when he heard the noise of somebody running away. He couldn't let Ern go like that ! He must go after him, pounce on him and pummel him — and then he'd let him go — and perhaps Ern would spin such a wonderful tale to Old Clear-Orf about queer mysteries up on Christmas Hill that it would bamboozle the policeman completely.

So Fatty padded after My. Goon. The policeman was terrified to hear somebody after him. He caught his foot on a root and fell flat on his face. Fatty fell over him and began to pummel him. He was thoroughly enjoying himself.

But Ern seemed curiously strong ! Fatty found himself heaved off, and a strong arm bent him back. A familiar voice grated in his ear. 'Ho, you would, would you ? You comealonga me !'

Now it was Fatty's turn to get a shock. Gracious, it was *Goon,* not Ern. Fatty freed himself as soon as he could and shot off down the hill, praying that Goon would not be able to put on his torch quickly enough to spot him.

His head was spinning. That was *Goon.* Why was *he* there ? Where was Ern ? He went cold when he thought of what Mr. Goon would say if he found out that it was Fatty who had leapt on him like that.

Mr. Goon fumbled for his torch, but it was broken in the rough and tumble. He was no longer frightened. He felt victorious. He had frightened off that fellow who had attacked him, whoever it was.

'He must have been a big chap,' thought Mr. Goon, 'a big hefty strong chap. And I heaved him off as easy as winking. Flung himself on me, he did, like a ton of bricks ! And me down flat on my face, too. Not a bad night's work, really.'

He made his way cautiously down the hill. He heard no more curious noises. Nobody else attacked him. He puzzled over the night's happenings and tried to sort them out.

'Flashing lights — all colours — in two different places. A cat, a hen, a cow and something that wailed in a horrible manner. And a great giant of a fellow who attacked me out of the dark. That's something to go on ! Can't make head nor tail of it now, but I'll get to the bottom of it !'

Fatty made his way home too. Larry and Pip were already home and in bed, hugging rather lukewarm hot-water bottles. They were longing to see Fatty in the morning and to know what had happened to Ern. Had he been frightened of the lights ? What did he do when he found Fatty crouching in the ditch ?

Where *was* Ern ? *He* was having a little adventure all on his own !

8   ERN HAS AN ADVENTURE TOO

ERN, most unfortunately, had followed the wrong stream, so that it did not, of course, lead him to the mill on Christmas Hill. It meandered through frosty fields, and didn't go anywhere near a hill at all. Ern was rather astonished that he had no climbing to do, but he clung to the stream hoping that sooner or later it would take him uphill.

If he had cared to flash his torch on the water he would have seen that the stream was going exactly the same way as he was, and could on no account be expected to run uphill, but Ern didn't think about that. He just went on and on.

He felt that it must be past midnight, and still there was no sign of a mill, and no sign of Chrismas Hill either. He couldn't imagine where he was. He stumbled on over the frosty bank beside the little stream, following in curves.

Soon it was about half-past twelve. Ern paused and considered things. He must be going the wrong way. The others wouldn't have waited for him. They would probably have gone home after watching for the lights.

'I'd better go back,' said Ern, shivering. 'It's too cold. I don't care what the others say, I'd better go back.'

And then Ern suddenly saw a light ! He was not expecting one and was extremely astonished. It suddenly shone out from some distance away and then faded. Could it possibly be part of the Mystery ?

Then he heard a noise. He listened. It was a low purring noise, like a car. It came from the same direction as the light he had seen. He couldn't see the car at all, but it must have passed down some path or lane not very far from him, because the purring of the engine grew louder and then faded again as the car was driven farther and farther away.

'Why didn't it have lights ?' wondered Ern. He stood there, waiting and listening and then decided to move on a little farther down the stream. He went cautiously, not liking to put on his torch.

Then he heard footsteps — soft footsteps walking nearby, crunching quietly over the frosty ground. Two pairs of footsteps — or was it three ? No, two.

A voice spoke softly in the darkness. 'Goodnight, Holland. See you later.'

There was an answering mumble, and then no other noise except departing footsteps. It sounded as if the two men had gone different ways.

Ern shivered with excitement and cold. He wished the others were there. Why weren't they ? This must be part of the Mystery Fatty had talked about. Then Fatty should have been there to share it with him. Were those men kidnappers or robbers or what ?

Ern turned back. He put up his coat-collar and tightened his scarf, for now he was meeting the wind. He kept close to the stream and walked over the frosted grass as fast as he could. Ooooh ! It was cold !

He came at last to the bridge he knew, that crossed the stream and led into a little lane. He went up the lane, turned into the village street and made his way quietly to his uncle's house. He had been wise enough to take the back-door key with him. He stole round to the back, and let himself in.

Mr. Goon was now in bed, fast asleep and snoring. He didn't even know that Ern was out ! He had crept-upstairs, undressed, and got into bed with hardly a sound, not wanting to let Ern know he had been out at midnight. He didn't want him to guess he had been up to Christmas Hill, probing the

Mystery !

It took Ern a long time to go to sleep. To begin with he was very cold, and the bed wouldn't seem to warm up. And then he was puzzled by what he had seen and heard. It wasn't much — but it didn't make sense somehow. He thought he couldn't be a very good detective. That boy Fatty would have guessed a whole lot of things if he had been with Ern that night. Ern was quite sure of that.

Neither Mr. Goon nor Ern said a word to each other of their midnight escapades. Mr. Goon had a bruise on his cheek where his face had struck a stone when he had fallen. Ern had a scratch across his forehead where a bramble had scraped him. They both looked tired out.

'You do what you like to-day, Ern,' said Mr. Goon, who felt that probably Ern might pick up a few Clues from Fatty about the Mystery, and pass them on to him — or if he wrote them down in his note-book he could get them when Ern was asleep and read them.

'Thanks, Uncle,' said Ern, perking up at once. Now he would be able to go and see the others and hear what had happened.

He went round to Fatty's shed, but Fatty wasn't here. However, there was a message up on the door. 'Gone to Pip's. Join us there.'

Guessing correctly that the message was for him Ern went up to Pip's. Bets saw him from the window and waved to him.

She opened the windows. 'Don't go to the front door. Come in the garden door at the side of the house, and wipe your feet for goodness' sake !'

Ern did as he was told. He forgot to take off his cap when he got into the house, and when he met Pip's mother she stared at him disapprovingly and said, 'Please take your cap off. Where are your manners?'

Ern blushed bright red and fled upstairs. He pulled his cap off so hurriedly that his hair stood straight up.

'Hallo,' said Fatty, when he came in at the play-room door. 'You saw the massage then. What happened to you last night ? You went to sleep and didn't wake up in time to come, I suppose ?'

'I didn't go to sleep at all !' said Ern, indignantly. 'I got up and followed the stream — but it didn't lead me to Christmas Hill, or to any mill. I don't know where it led me to. But I saw the mysterious light all right.'

'You didn't,' said Larry. 'Pip and I and Fatty were up on the hill and saw them. You couldn't *possibly* have seen any flashing lights if you weren't up on the hill.'

'Well, I did then,' said Ern, looking annoyed. 'You weren't with me. You don't know *what* I saw !'

'Did you tell your uncle that we had told you to go to the mill on Christmas Hill last night ?' demanded Fatty.

''Course I didn't,' said Ern, even more annoyed. 'He was in bed and snoring !'

'He wasn't,' said Fatty. 'He was up on Christmas Hill.'

Ern didn't believe him at all. 'Oh, goanborlyered!' he said in a disgusted voice.

The Find-Outers looked inquiringly at him. What did this peculiar word mean ? 'What did you say then ?' asked Fatty, interestedly. 'Is it Spanish or something ?'

'I said "Goanborlyered," ' repeated Ern. 'And fry your face too !'

The second part of what he said threw light on the first part. 'Oh ! he said "Go and boil your head !"' explained Daisy.

'SwatIsaid,' said Ern looking sulky.

'Swatesaid,' said Fatty. 'What's the matter Ern ? Why

don't you believe me when I say your uncle was up on the hill last night ?'

'Because I heard him snoring like billyoh when I got in, that's all,' said Ern.

'Did you hear snoring like billyoh when you went out ?' asked Fatty. Ern considered, frowning hard.

'No. Can't say I did. He *might* have gone out without me hearing him, and come back before I did.'

'That's about what he did then,' said Fatty. 'But what I can't make out is — why did he go up ? How did he know anything about meeting at the mill on Christmas Hill ?'

'He might somehow have got hold of the note you gave Ern when you disguised yourself as the red-shawled woman,' said Daisy. 'He'd know then.'

'Yes. I suppose that's what he must have done—if Ern was silly enough to give him the chance,' said Fatty.

'Well, I didn't' said Ern. 'What you all getting at me this morning for ? I got up, didn't I, and I tried to get to Christmas Hill ? I must have followed the wrong stream, that's all. I looked up the mill in the map and I saw that if I could follow the stream that runs down by it, I'd get there all right. But it was dark and I couldn't see anything. But I tell you I did see a light.' Every one felt certain that Ern was making this up, just as they had made up their flashing lights ! Ern went on trying to impress the others that he really was telling the truth.

'I was standing by the stream, see. And I saw this light. It just shone out once and then faded. Then I heard a purring noise and a car came by somewhere — and it hadn't any lights on. That was queer, and I thought may be it was all part of the mystery too.'

The others were listening now. Ern went on, warming up a little. 'Well then, after the car had gone I heard footsteps

— two pairs — and then I heard one man say to the other "Good-night Holland. See you later" or something like that. And after that I turned back and went home.'

There was a silence. Every one believed Ern now. If he had been making up his tale he would have pretended that he had seen many lights, heard more than one car and more that two men. Because it was a simple story, it seemed as if it might be true.

'Have you told your uncle this ?' asked Fatty at last.

'No,' said Ern. There was a pause. Then Ern remembered something. 'I put that note-book back,' he said, 'and Uncle found me just shutting the drawer. He said I was snooping round to find out things for you, and he hit me twice. See my ear ?'

He showed the children his ear, which was still swollen. Bets felt very sorry for him. Horrible Mr. Goon !

'I'm not telling my uncle a thing now !' said Ern. 'Hitting me like that when I was doing something decent.'

'You shouldn't have taken the note-book in the first place,' said Fatty. 'Then you wouldn't have had to put it back and you wouldn't have been discovered and got those blows. You deserved what you got, in case you think you didn't.'

Ern scowled, partly because he knew Fatty was right and partly because he didn't like having it said to him in such a candid manner. But Fatty always did say what he thought, and nothing would stop him.

'Look here,' said Ern, suddenly, 'which mystery is the real one ? The one you mean, with flashing lights on Christmas Hill — or mine, down by the stream ? Or are they both real ?'

Fatty rubbed his nose. He didn't quite know what to say. His had been made up, but he didn't want to admit that. Neither did he want Ern to think there might be any mystery in what *he* had seen and heard the night before, in case there really *was*. If there was, Fatty didn't want Ern blundering into it and telling his uncle everything.

'I suppose,' said Ern, answering his own question, 'the mystery up on the hill's the real one — or else uncle wouldn't have gone up there, would he ?'

'He must have thought there was something going on there,' agreed Fatty.

'And there was,' said Pip, with a little giggle.

'Well, Ern, what about you going up on Christmas Hill to see if you can find a few clues in daylight,' said Fatty. 'They would be a help.'

'What sort of clues ?' asked Ern, looking cheerful again.

'Oh—cigarette ends, buttons, footprints, anything like that,' said Fatty. 'You just never know. A real detective can usually find no end of clues.'

'I'll go up about three,' said Ern. 'Uncle will be having his afternoon snooze then. Well — I'd better be going. I'll bring any clues to you if I find them. So long !'

9   LOTS OF CLUES FOR ERN !

THE Find-Outers looked at each other when Ern had disappeared. 'What do you think, Fatty ?' said Larry. 'Anything in what he said ?'

'I don't know,' said Fatty slowly. 'It seems a bit queer, doesn't it — a light in the middle of the night — a car suddenly appearing without lights — and then voices. What did he say the one man said to the other ?'

' "Good-night, Holland. See you later," ' said Larry.

'Yes, that's it. Wonder how Ern managed to remember the name Holland, and if he heard it right,' said Fatty.

'Any good having a snoop along the stream to see if we can spy anything?' asked Larry.

'Not allowed to,' said Pip at once.

'Well — it's not a mystery *yet*, and may never *be,*' said Larry. 'So I don't see why we shouldn't at least go for a walk along the stream.'

'With Ern ?' asked Bets.

'I don't know,' said Fatty. 'He'll probably go and tell everything to Goon. Still, Goon has got plenty to think of at the moment. He's seen masses of lights on Christmas Hill, heard a cow, a hen, a cat and a baby up there, and struggled with an unknown attacker. Quite a nice little mystery for him to be getting on with !'

He others laughed. They had roared at Fatty's account of what had happened the night before, and his amazement at finding the person by the hedge was Goon, not Ern.

'I think one of the best things we can do is to go up to Christmas Hill before three o'clock, and drop a nice meaty lot of clues,' said Fatty. 'Ern will find them and glory in them — probably write some portry about them. And if he hands them over to Goon so much the better !'

So, in great glee, the Five Find-Outers and Buster set off up Christmas Hill, taking with them what they thought would do for Clues. It was a fine sunny day, but cold, and they got nice and warm going up the hill. Their parents were pleased to see them going out. Nobody liked all the five indoors. Some noisy game always seemed to develop sooner or later.

'Here's where I fought Goon last night,' said Fatty, showing where he and Goon had rolled in the ditch. 'I got an awful shock when I found it was Goon. He's strong, you know. He almost caught me. What a row I'd have got in if he'd seen it was me !'

'Let's put a clue here,' said Larry. 'A torn-off button with bit of cloth attached. Very good clue !'

'Where did you get it ?' said Daisy. 'You'll get into trouble if you tore it off one of your coats.'

'Idiot ! I tore it off the old coat that's hung in the garage for ages,' said Larry, and threw the brown button down, with its bit of brown cloth attached to it. 'Clue number one.'

'Here's Clue number two,' said Pip, and put down a bit of paper, on which he had scribbled a telephone number. 'Peterswood 0160.'

'Whose number's that ?' asked Fatty at once.

'Oh, nobody's, said Pip. 'I just made it up.'

'Your finger-prints will be on it,' said Fatty, who always thought of things like that.

'No they won't,' said Pip. 'I tore it out of a new note-book, with gloves on my hands, and I've carried it in my gloved hands all the way. So there !'

'You're getting quite clever,' said Fatty, pleased. 'Right. That's Clue number two. Here's Clue number three.'

He threw down a cigar-stump that he had taken from his father's ash-tray.

'That's a good clue,' said Larry. 'Robber smokes Corona cigar. Mr. Goon will love that if he gets it from Ern.'

'I've got a clue too,' said Bets. 'A red shoe-lace, broken in half and dirtied !'

'Yes. very good, Bets,' said Fatty approvingly. 'I like the way you've dirtied it. Ern will be thrilled to pick that up.'

They went on a little way farther, nearer the mill. Daisy still had her clue to dispose of. It was a very old ragged handkerchief with 'K' embroidered in one corner.

'K,' said Fatty. 'I can't think of any one we know beginning with K. Whose was it ?'

'Don't know,' said Daisy with a laugh. 'I picked it up by the hedge that runs by Pip's garden !'

'I hope the wind won't blow any of our clues away,' said Larry anxiously.

'I don't expect so,' said Fatty. 'It's a calm day. Come on, let's get back before we meet Ern coming up here'

They ran down the hill. At the bottom they met Mr. Goon labouring along on his bicycle, very angry because his snooze had been interrupted by a call about a stolen dog. When he saw the children at the bottom of Christmas Hill, he stopped in suspicion.

'What you been doing up there ?' he asked.

'Having a lovely walk. Mr. Goon,' said Fatty, in the polite voice that always sent Mr. Goon into a frenzy. Buster, who had been left some way behind with his nose in a rabbit-hole, now came rushing up in delight.

'If you don't want that dog of yours kicked, you keep him off,' said Mr. Goon fixing them all with a protruding eye. 'And if I was you — I'd keep away from Christmas Hill.'

'Oh, Mr. Goon but why ?' asked Fatty, in such an innocent voice that Mr. Goon began to go purple. That cheeky toad !

'It's such a nice hill to run down,' said Pip.

'Now, don't *you* start !' said Mr Goon, slowly swelling up in rage. 'And take my advice — don't you go up Christmas Hill again !'

'Can we come down it ?' asked Larry, and the others went off into shouts of laughter to see Mr. Goon trying to work this out.

'Any more sauce from you,' he began, 'and ...'

At this moment Buster, who had been struggling for all he was worth in Fatty's arms, leapt right out of them almost on top of Mr. Goon. The policeman hurriedly got on his bicycle. 'You clear-orf !' he shouted to Buster and the children too. He kicked out at Buster and nearly fell off his bicycle. He rode up the lane at top speed, trying to shake him off, and almost collided with Ern, who was on his way to search for clues up Christmas Hill.

'Out of my way !' yelled Mr. Goon, nearly running over Ern's toes. Buster ran between Ern's legs and he fell over at once. In joy and delight Buster stopped to sniff round this fresh person, and found it was Ern. He leapt on him and began to lick him, whilst Mr. Goon pedalled thankfully up the road, getting redder and redder as he went.

'Your uncles's in a bit of a rage,' said Fatty. 'It's not good for him to ride a bike at such a speed. You ought to warn him. It must be bad for his heart.'

'It would be, if he had one,' said Ern. 'Well, I'm going to do what you said — hunt for clues. You coming too ?'

'No, we've got to get home,' said Fatty. 'I hope you find a few, Ern. Let us know if you do. That's the sign of a good detective, you know, to be able to spot clues.'

Ern glowed. If there were any clues to be found on the

Out of my way

hill, he'd find them ! He badly wanted Fatty to admire him. He took out his note-book and opened it.

'I wrote a pome about last night,' he said. 'It's called ''The Dark, Dark Night''.'

'Fine !' said Fatty, hastily. 'Pity we can't wait and hear it. Don't be too long before you go up the hill, Ern, or you'll find yourself in the dark dark night up there again. Follow the stream and you'll come to the mill.'

They parted, and Ern put his note-book away. He took out his other note-book, the one Fatty had given him. He opened it at the page marked 'CLUES.' How he hoped to be able to make a list there before the afternoon was done.

The others went home. Fatty was rather silent. Bets walked close beside him, not interrupting his thoughts. She knew he was trying to puzzle out something.

'Pip, have you got a good map of the district ?' said Fatty, as they came to Pip's house. 'If you have I'll just come in and have a squint at it. Somebody's borrowed ours.'

'Yes. Dad keeps one in the map-shelf,' said Pip. 'But for goodness sake put it back when you've finished with it.'

''Course I will,' said Fatty, and they went in. Pip found the map and they took it upstairs. Fatty put his finger on Peterswood, their village. He traced the way up to the mill, up the stream on Christmas Hill. Then he traced another way, alongside another stream, that at first ran near the first one and then went across the fields.

'I think this must be the stream Ern went by last night,' he said. 'Let's see where it flows past. Nothing much, look ! Just fields.'

The others all bent over the map, breathing down Fatty's neck. They watched his finger go along the stream. It came to where a thick wood was marked. In the middle of the wood some kind of building was shown.

'Now I wonder what building that is,' said Fatty, thoughtfully. 'Any one been along that way ?'

Nobody had. Nobody even knew the wood very well, though they had sometimes passed it. Not one of them had known there was any building in the wood.

'We'll ask about it,' said Fatty, getting up. 'Golly, I must go. I'm supposed to be going out to tea with mother. Awful thought. You know, I do believe there may be something in Ern's story. Cars that leave a wood in the middle of the night without lights need a bit of looking into.'

The others looked excited. 'Is it a mystery, Fatty ?' asked Bets eagerly. 'Do say it is ! Wouldn't it be funny if we did tumble into the middle of a real mystery just because we invented one for Ern.'

'It would,' said Fatty. 'Well, we shall see. Won't Ern be thrilled when he finds all those clues ? He'll come rushing along to-morrow !'

'I hope I shan't giggle,' said Bets.

'You dare !' said Pip. 'Good-bye, Fatty. Behave yourself at tea, and be a dear well-mannered child !'

'Oh, goanborlyered !' said Fatty, rudely, and off he went, with shouts of laughter following him.

10   MR GOON AND ERN

ERN had a simply wonderful time up on Christmas Hill, collecting clues. It was a lovely afternoon and he walked slowly up the hill, his eyes on the ground. He felt important. The beginnings of a 'Pome' swam into his mind, as he looked up and saw the sun sinking redly in the west.

'Pore dying sun that sinks to rest,' thought Ern, and felt excited and pleased. That was a good line, a very good one indeed. Ern never wrote a cheerful 'pome'. They were all very very sad, and they made Ern feel deliciously sad too.

He walked on, his eyes on the ground, thinking about the dying sun. He suddenly saw a piece of rag fluttering and picked it up. Nobody could tell what colour it had been. Ern looked at it. Was it a clue ? He pondered over it. He wished he was like Fatty, able to tell at a glance what things were clues and what weren't.

He put it into his overcoat pocket. Fatty would know. He cast his eyes on the ground again. Aha ! What was this in the ditch ? A button ! Yes, with a bit of brown cloth attached to it. Surely that was a clue ? Ern looked at the ground in the ditch, and noted the broken twigs and the way the frosty ground was rubbed and scraped. 'Been somebody here !' thought Ern in excitement. 'And this button's off his coat. That's a Fat Clue, a really Meaty one.'

He put that in his pocket too. He was feeling really thrilled now. Two clues already !

He found the broken shoe-lace. He found the cigar-end and sniffed at it in a very knowing manner. 'Ha ! A good cigar ! Whoever was here has money to spend. I'm getting on. I see a man with a brown coat with brown buttons, smoking a good cigar, and wearing reddish laces in his shoes. I don't know about that bit of rag. That doesn't fit in somehow.'

He picked up an empty cigarette packet. It had held Players cigarettes. 'Coo! He smokes cigarettes as well !' said Ern, feeling cleverer and cleverer. That went into his pocket too. He was getting on ! Who would have thought there were so many clues left carelessly lying about like that ? No wonder detectives went hunting for them after a robbery.

He picked up a broken tin next. It looked as if it had possibly been a tin of boot polish, but it was so old and rusty that there was no telling what it might have been. Anyway it went into his pocket too.

Then he found Pip's bit of paper blowing about. Ern picked it up. 'Lovaduck ! Now we're getting hot ! This is somebody's telephone number — in Peterswood too. I'm really getting hot ! Pity Fatty didn't come up with me — we'd have had a fine time collecting clues !'

He then found Daisy's ragged old handkerchief, embroidered with 'K' in the corner. This seemed a first-class clue. 'K !' he thought. 'K for Kenneth. K for Katie. Or it might be a surname of course. Can't tell.' That went into his pocket as well.

After that he only found two more things that seemed worth picking up. One was a burnt match, the other was the stub of a pencil. It had initials cut into it at the end. E.H.

With a pocketful of interesting clues Ern went down the hill again. It was getting dark. He would have liked to stay longer and find more clues but he couldn't see clearly any longer. Anyway he had done well, he felt.

When he got home his uncle was out. Ern got himself some tea, then took out his note-book and opened it at the page marked 'Clues'.

He sharpened his pencil and set to work to put down a list of all the things he had found.

CLUES

1. Piece of rag.
2. Brown button with bit of cloth.
3. Broken shoe-lace, reddish colour.
4. End of good cigar.
5. Empty cigarette packet (Players).
6. Broken tin, very rusty.
7. Bit of paper with telephone number.
8. Ragged handkerchief, 'K' in corner.
9. Burnt match.
10. Pencil, very short, E.H. on it.

'Look at that', said Ern, in satisfaction. 'Ten clues already ! Not a bad bit of work. I'd make a good detective. Lovaduck ! Here's uncle !'

Mr. Goon could be heard coming into the little hall, and a familiar cough sound. In haste Ern swept all the clues into his pocket, and was just stuffing his note-book away when his uncle came in. Ern looked so guilty that Mr. Goon was suspicious at once. Now what had that boy been up to ?

'Hallo, Uncle,' said Ern.

'What you doing sitting at an empty table, doing nothing ?' said Mr. Goon.

'I'm not doing anything.' said Ern. Mr. Goon gave a snort.

'I can see that. What you been doing this afternoon?'

'I've been for a walk,' said Ern.

'Where ?' said Mr. Goon. 'With those five kids ?'

'No, by myself,' said Ern. 'It was such a nice afternoon.'

Ern was not in the habit of taking walks by himself, and Mr. Goon looked at him suspiciously again. What *was* the boy up to ? How much did he know ?

'Where did you go ?' he asked again.

'Up Christmas Hill,' said Ern. 'It — it was awfully nice up there. The view, you know, Uncle.'

Mr. Goon sat down ponderously in his armchair and gazed solemnly at Ern. 'Now, you look here, my boy,' he said, you're Up To Something with those pestering kids. Ho, yes, you are, so don't try to say you aren't. Now, you and me, we must work together. We're uncle and nephew, aren't we ? In the interests of the Law we must tell each other all the Goings-On.'

'What Goings-On ?' asked Ern, in alarm, wondering how much his uncle knew. He was beginning to feel frightened. He put his hand into his pocket to feel the clues there. He mustn't tell his uncle about them. He must keep them all for Fatty and the others.

'You know quite well what the Goings-On are,' said Mr. Goon, beginning to remove his boots. 'Up Christmas Hill ! Didn't you tell me about the lights flashing there ?'

'Yes,' said Ern. 'But that's all I told you, Uncle. What other Goings-On do you mean ?'

Mr. Goon began to lose his temper. He stood up in his stockinged feet and advanced on poor Ern, who hadn't even a chance of getting up from his chair and backing away.

'I'm going to lose my temper with you, Ern,' said Mr. Goon. 'I can feel it. And you know what happened last time, don't you ?'

'Yes, Uncle. But please don't hit me again,' begged Ern.

'I got a cane somewhere,' said Mr. Goon, suddenly, and began to rummage about in a cupboard. Ern was terrified. He began to cry. He was terribly ashamed of himself, because he knew quite well that not even little Bets would give away her friend, but he knew he was going to. He was a coward ! Poor Ern.

When he saw his uncle bringing out a very nasty-looking yellow cane, he blubbered even more loudly.

'Now, you stop that noise,' said Mr. Goon. 'You're not hurt yet, are you ? You be a good boy, and work with me, and everything will be fine. See ? Now you tell me what that boy, Frederick, told you.'

Ern gave in. He hadn't any courage at all. He knew he was a poor weak thing, but he couldn't seem to help it.

'He said there were two gangs,' blubbered Ern. 'Kidnappers was one gang. Robbers was the other.'

Mr. Goon stared at Ern in surprise. This was news! 'Go on!' he said disbelievingly. 'Kidnappers and robbers! What next !'

'And lights flashing on Christmas Hill,' went on Ern. 'Well, I don't know about that, Uncle. I haven't seen any lights there at all.'

Mr. Goon had though ! He looked thoughtfully at Ern. That bit of the tale was true, anyway — about the lights flashing, because he had seen them himself the night before — so the other part might be true, too. Kidnappers and robbers! Now *how* did that boy Frederick get to know these things ? He brooded about Fatty for a little while and thought of quite a lot of things he would like to do to him.

It was very very necessary to make sure that Ern told him everything in future. Mr. Goon could see that. He decided it would be best not to frighten Ern any more. He must win his friendship ! That was the line to follow.

So, to Ern's enormous surprise, Mr. Goon suddenly patted him on the shoulder, and gave him his large handkerchief to wipe his eyes. Ern looked up in surprise and suspicion. Now what was Uncle up to ?

'You were right to tell me, Ern, all that you've heard from those kids,' said Mr. Goon, in a kindly voice. 'Now you and

me can work together, and we'll soon clean up this mystery
— and we'll get no end of praise from Inspector Jenks.
You've met him, haven't you ? He said he thought you were
a fine boy, and might help me no end.'

This wasn't true at all. Inspector Jenks had hardly glanced
at Ern, and if he had he certainly wouldn't have said such
nice things about him. Poor Ern didn't shine in public at all,
but looked very awkward and stupid.

Ern was relieved to see that his uncle was going to be
friendly after all. He watched him put away the cane.
Lovaduck ! That was a near squeak. All the same Ern was
very much ashamed of giving away all that Fatty had told
him. Now his uncle would solve the mystery himself, arrest
all the men and Fatty and the other Find-Outers wouldn't
have any fun.

'Anything else you can tell me, Ern ?' said Mr. Goon,
putting on his enormous slippers.

'No, Uncle,' said Ern, wishing he hadn't got a pocketful
of clues. He was glad he hadn't tried to wipe his eyes with
his own handkerchief — he might have pulled out a whole
lot of clues with it !

'What did you go up Christmas Hill this afternoon for ?'
asked Mr. Goon, lighting his pipe.

'I told you. For a nice walk,' said Ern, looking sulky again.
When would his uncle stop all this ?

Mr. Goon debated whether to go on cross-examining Ern
or not. Perhaps not. He didn't want to make the boy obstinate.
When he was safely asleep in bed that night he would get
Ern's note-book out of his pocket and see if he had written
anything down in it. Mr. Goon picked up the paper and settled
down for a read. Ern heaved a sigh of relief, and wondered if
he could slip out to see the others.

It was about six o'clock now — but Ern felt that he simply

must tell Fatty all about the clues.

'Can I go out for a bit, Uncle ?' he asked, timidly. 'Just to slip round and have a talk with the others ? They might have a bit of news for me.'

'All right,' said Mr. Goon, turning a friendly face to Ern. 'You go. And get all you can out of them and then tell me the latest news. See ?'

Ern lost no time. He pulled on his coat, took his cap and scarf and fled out of the house. He made his way to Pip's, because he remembered that Fatty was going out to tea that day.

He was lucky enough to find all the Find-Outers gathered together in Pip's play-room, under strict instructions from Mrs. Hilton to take off their shoes if they wanted to play any games that meant running across the room. Fatty had just arrived, having dropped in on his way home with his mother, who was seeing Mrs. Hilton for a few minutes downstairs.

'I say !' said Ern, bursting in suddenly. 'I've got ten clues for you ! What do you think of that for a good day's work ! I've got them all here !'

'Lovaduck !' said Fatty. 'Smazing ! Simpossible ! Swunderful ! Let's have a look, Ern, quick !'

11   ERN'S CLUES

ERN pulled everything out of his pocket. When Bets saw all
the things there that the Find-Outers had so carefully put on
Christmas Hill for Ern to find, she wanted to giggle. But she
saw Fatty's eye on her, and she didn't.

'See ?' said Ern, proudly. 'Cigar-end. That means
somebody with money. And look here — he smokes
cigarettes too — see this empty packet ? And look — we
want to look for somebody with a brown coat. And ..'

'This is a very remarkable collection of clues, Ern,' said
Fatty, solemnly. 'I can see that Mr. Goon's brains have been
passed on to you. You take after him ! A very remarkable
afternoon's work.'

Ern was thrilled. Praise from Fatty was praise indeed. He
showed every clue he had.

'Course, some of them mayn't be clues at all,' he admitted
handsomely. 'I see that.'

'You're right,' said Fatty. 'You think of everything Ern.
This is all most interesting. It will help us tremendously.'

'Will it really ?' said Ern, delighted. Then his face clouded
over. 'I got something awful to tell you,' he said.

'What ?' asked every one, curiously.

'I went and gave the game away to my uncle,' said Ern,
dismally. 'He took a cane out of the cupboard and I could
see he was gong to use it one me — so I went and told him
about the kidnappers and the robbers up of Christmas Hill.
You needn't call me a coward. I know that all right.'

He looked so completely miserable that the Five Find-

Outers wanted to comfort him. Even Buster felt the same and put his front paws up on Ern's knee. Ern looked down at him gratefully.

'Well,' said Fatty, 'certainly it wasn't a brave thing to do, Ern, to give away somebody else's secret — but Mr. Goon and a cane must have been a very frightening pair. We won't tick you off.'

'He told me I must work with him,' said Ern, brightening up a little, as he saw the the Find-Outers did not mean to cast him off. 'He said we were uncle and nephew, and we ought to work together. I've got to tell him anything that happens.'

Fatty considered this. It suited him very well to have Goon told all the things that didn't matter. It would serve him right for threatening poor Ern with the cane. Fatty did not like the streak of cruelty in Mr. Goon.

'Well, there's something in that,' said Fatty. 'Yes, quite decidedly there's something in that. Families ought to work together. We shan't complain any more if you pass on any news to you uncle, Ern.'

'But I don't want to !' protested Ern at once. 'I want *you* to solve things, not uncle. I don't want to work with uncle.'

'Poor Ern !' suddenly said Bets. She could see very clearly how Ern was torn in two — he dearly wanted to work with the Find-Outers and be loyal to them — and he was terribly afraid he would have to help his uncle instead, because he was so frightened of him. All Ern needed was a little courage, but he hadn't got it.

'You'd better show these clues to your uncle,' said Fatty. 'Hadn't he, Larry ? If they are going to work together, Goon had better know about these. He'll think that Ern has done a fine piece of work.'

'I don't want to show him the clues,' said Ern, desperately. 'I tell you, I found them for you, not for uncle.'

'Well, do what you like,' said Fatty. 'We shan't mind whether you show them or not. I suppose you wrote them all down in your note-book ?'

'Oh yes,' said Ern, proudly, and showed his long list. Fatty nodded approvingly.

'You didn't tell your uncle about how you went out alone last night, did you ?' he said. 'It was very important that Goon shouldn't know that. Ern shook his head.

'No. Course I didn't. I'm not telling him things he can't possibly guess. He'd be very angry if he knew I'd slipped out like that.'

'Tell us again about your little adventure,' said Fatty. So Ern obligingly told it. He used almost the same words as before, and all the Find-Outers felt that he was telling the exact truth.

'Are you certain that one man addressed the other as "Holland ?" asked Fatty.

'Oh yes. You see we did Holland in geography last term,' said Ern. 'So I knew the name all right.'

Well, what certainly seemed to fix the name. That might be very useful, thought Fatty. He got up to go, hearing his mother calling him from downstairs. Larry and Daisy got up too.

'There's mother ready to go,' said Fatty. 'Come on, Ern — you'd better go too.'

'I thought of a fine pome this afternoon,' said Ern, getting up. 'About the Dying Sun.'

'We haven't time to hear it now,' said Daisy.

'Spitty,' said Fatty. Every one but Ern knew what this meant. Ern looked at him in surprise.

'Spitty ?' he said, ' What do you mean ?'

'You heard me,' said Fatty. 'SPITTY !'

Bets went off into giggles. There came another call from

downstairs. Fatty hurried to the door.

'He meant "It's a pity," ' giggled Bets.

'SwatIsaid,' said Fatty and disappeared with Larry and Daisy.

Ern, still rather bemused over the curious word Fatty had suddenly used, followed the three downstairs. He slipped out of the garden-door unseen. He didn't want to meet Mrs. Hilton, Pip's mother. He was scared of her in case she found fault with his manners again. He tore home to his uncle's house, hoping there was something nice for supper.

A delicious smell of bacon and eggs met him as soon as he got in. Ern stood and sniffed. Lovaduck ! Uncle was doing himself proud to-night. Ern wondered if he was going to get any bacon and eggs, or whether he would have to sup on bread and cheese.

'Hurry up, young Ern !' called Mr. Goon, in a jovial sort of voice that Ern had never heard before. 'I've fried you an egg and a bit of bacon. Hurry up !'

Ern hurried up. There was not only bacon and eggs but a bowl of tinned peaches and creamy custard. Ern took his place hungrily.

'Well ? Did you see those kids ? Get any news from them?' inquired Mr. Goon, affably, piling eggs, bacon and toast on to Ern's plate.

'No. There wasn't any news, Uncle,' said Ern.

'But you must have talked about something,' said Mr. Goon. 'What did they say to you ?'

Ern racked his brains to think of something harmless to tell his uncle. He suddenly remembered something.

'I told them you said we were to work together,' he said.

'You shouldn't have told them that,' said Mr. Goon, crossly. 'Now they won't tell you a thing !'

'Oh yes they will. They said it was right that an uncle and

nephew should work together,' said Ern, shovelling egg and bacon into his mouth. 'And what's more, Fatty said I took after *you,* Uncle. He said you'd passed your brains on to *me.*'

Mr. Goon looked most disbelievingly at Ern. He felt certain that Fatty didn't think much of any brains he possessed, and if he did he certainly wouldn't say so. He was just pulling Ern's leg. Mr. Goon wished in exasperation that Ern wasn't so simple.

'He didn't mean that, see?' said Mr. Goon. 'He can't think much of your brains, Ern. You know you haven't got any to speak of. You think of your last school report.'

Ern thought instead of the remarkable set of clues he had found that afternoon. He smiled. 'Oh, I've got brains all right, Uncle. You wait and see.'

Mr. Goon felt that he was about to lose his temper again. He just simply couldn't be more than ten minutes with Ern without feeling annoyed and aggravated. His ears turned red, and Ern saw them and felt uncomfortable. He knew that was a danger sign. What *could* he have said now to annoy his uncle ?

He ate his peaches and custard in silence, and so did Mr. Goon. Then, still in silence, Ern did the washing-up and after that got out his books to do some work. Mr. Goon, trying to look pleased so as not to make Ern obstinate, sat reading his paper again. He looked up approvingly as Ern sat down to work.

'That's right, my boy. That's the way to get brains like mine. A bit of hard study will make a lot of difference to you.'

'Yes, Uncle,' said Ern, resting his head on his hands as if he was learning something. But Ern was going over his clues, one by one. He was thinking of robbers and kidnappers. He was up on Christmas Hill, waiting for desperate men to do desperate deeds. Oh, Ern was far far away from his geography book on the kitchen table !

He went to bed early because he was tired. He fell asleep at once, and did little snores like Mr. Goon's big ones. Mr. Goon heard them from downstairs and rose quietly. Now to get Ern's note-book and see what he had written in it ! If Ern wouldn't tell him everything Mr. Goon meant to find it out. No harassing thoughts of being mean or deceitful entered Mr. Goon's mind. He thought himself in duty-bound to sneak Ern's note-book from his pocket !

Ern did not stir when Mr. Goon tiptoed in. His uncle slipped his hand into the coat-pocket and found the note-book at once. He felt the trousers and decided to take them downstairs and see what was crowding up the pockets.

He sat down at the table to study Ern's note-book. It fell open at the page headed 'Clues.' Mr. Goon's eyes grew round as they saw the long, long list.

'Look at that ! All them clues and never a word to me about them. The young limb ! I'd like to skin him !'

He read down the list. Then an idea occurred to him and he put his hand into Ern's trousers' pocket. Out came the ten clues, tumbling on the table. Mr. Goon took a deep breath and stared at them.

A button and a bit of cloth ! Now that was a very very important clue. And this cigar-end. Expensive ! Mr. Goon sniffed it. He picked up the clues one by one and considered them carefully. Which of them would have any real bearing on the happenings up on Christmas Hill ?

Should he tell Ern he had found the clues or not ? No, better not. Ern might tell Fatty and the others, and they would have plenty to say about Mr. Goon's methods of getting hold of things. Mr. Goon took a little snipping of the cloth attached to the button so that he would have a piece to match up with the coat, should he be fortunate enough to meet any one wearing it. He took a note of the Peterswood number. Whose was it ?

He rang up the telephone exchange to find out. The number belonged to a Mr. Lazarinsky. Ha — that sounded most suspicious. Mr. Goon made a mental note to keep an eye on Mr. Lazarinsky. So far as he knew, the man was a harmless old fellow who spent most of his time growing roses and chrysanthemums. But you never know. That might be a cover for all kinds of dirty work.

Mr. Goon replaced everything in Ern's pockets, the note-book as well. Ern didn't stir when he tiptoed out of the bedroom. Mr. Goon felt that he had done a good evening's work. He wondered how much Fatty knew about this curious mystery. It was funny that the Inspector hadn't sent him word of any possible goings-on in Peterswood.

Well, it would be a real pleasure to Mr. Goon to open the Inspector's eyes, and show him that dirty work could go on under his very nose, in his own district — without people guessing anything. But he, Mr. Goon knew ! He'd soon clear everything up — and perhaps this time he really *would* get promotion.

But even Mr. Goon couldn't help feeling that this was rather doubtful !

12   A LITTLE INVESTIGATION

FATTY had been making a few inquiries. What was that building in the middle of the little wood ? He asked his mother, who had never even heard of it. He asked the postman, who said it wasn't on his round but he thought it was a ramshackle old place that had been used in the last war.

He found a directory of Peterswood, but it did not mention the building — only the wood, which it called Bourne Wood. The little stream that flowed through Peterswood was called the Bourne, so Fatty imagined the wood was named after it.

He didn't seem to be getting very far. He decided that it would be a very good idea to walk out to the wood and have a look round. So, the next morning, he went round to Larry and Daisy, collected them, and then went to fetch Pip and Bets. Buster came, of course, full of delight to think there was a walk for him.

'I thought we'd follow the stream, just like Ern did,' said Fatty. 'Then, when we come to about where he thought he was, we'll have a look round to see where that light he saw could have come from.'

The others were thrilled. 'Now mind !' said Fatty, '*you* are only going for a walk. Nothing to do with any mystery, so keep your minds easy. I'm the one that is mystery hunting !'

They all laughed. 'Right,' sid Pip. 'But if we do happen to spot anything we'll tell you, Fatty !'

Ern had not appeared so far, so they all set off without him. Fatty thought it was best, anyhow. They didn't want to let Ern think there was any real mystery in what he had seen the other night, in case he said anything to Mr. Goon. Let

Mr. Goon concentrate on Christmas Hill and imaginary kidnappers and robbers !

They crossed the little bridge, and went along the bank beside the stream. It was still frosty weather and the grass crunched beneath their feet. The little stream wound in and out, and bare willow and alder trees grew here and there on its banks. The scene was a maze of wintry fields, dreary and desolate.

The stream wound endlessly through the fields. Here and there Fatty pointed to where Ern must have stumbled the other night, for marks were clearly to be seen on the frosty bank.

After some time Bets pointed to the left. 'Look ! Is that the wood over there ?'

'Can't be,' said Pip. 'It's on our left instead of straight ahead.'

'I expect the stream winds to the left then,' said Fatty. And so it did. It suddenly took a left-hand bend and ran towards the dark wood.

The wood was made upon evergreen trees, and stood dark and still in the wintry air. Because the fir and pine trees still kept their foliage, dark green and thick, the wood somehow looked rather sinister.

'The trees are crouched together as if they are hiding something !' suddenly said Bets. Every one laughed.

'Silly !' said Pip. But all the same they knew what Bets meant. They stood by the stream and looked at the wood. It did not seem very little now that they were near it . It seemed large and forbidding.

'I don't like it,' said Daisy. 'Let's go back.'

But she didn't mean that, of course. Nobody would have gone back just as they had got there. They were all filled with curiosity to know what was so well hidden in those trees !

They followed the stream again until they had almost reached the wood. Not far off was a narrow lane, almost a cart-track, it was so rough.

Fatty stopped. 'Now, he said, ' we know that a car went by not far from Ern, when he stood by the stream. It seems to me that the car must have gone down that lane. It must lead to the road that goes to Peterswood. I saw it in the map.'

'Yes, said Larry. 'And this little lane or track must come from the middle of the wood — from whatever building is there. Let's go to the track and follow it.'

'Good idea,' said Fatty. 'Hey, Buster, come along. There can't be any rabbits down that hole — it's far too small !'

Buster left the rat-hole he was scraping at and ran to join them. They all jumped across the little stream, Buster too, and went towards the narrow track. They squeezed through the hedge and found themselves in a very small lane indeed, hardly wide enough to take a full-sized car !

'There are car tracks each side of the lane,' said Fatty, and the others saw tyre marks — many of them, all running almost on top of one another because the lane was so narrow. Two cars could not possibly pass.

'Come on — we'll go up the lane,' said Fatty. Then he lowered his voice. 'Now, not a word about anything except ordinary things. And if we're stopped, be surprised, scared and innocent. Don't say anything we don't want people to hear — we don't know when we may be overheard.'

A familiar thrill went through the Find-Outers as they heard Fatty's words. The mystery was beginning. They were perhaps walking into it. They had been forbidden to — but how could they tell, until they had walked into one, that a mystery was really and truly there ?

The track wound about almost as much as the stream had

done. Buster ran ahead, his tail wagging. He turned a corner ahead and then the children heard him barking.

They ran to see why. All they saw was a big pair of iron gates set into two enormous stone posts. A bell hung at one side. On each side of the posts stretched high walls, set with glass spikes at he top.

'Gracious ! Is this the building ?' said Bets in a whisper. Larry frowned at her, and she remembered she mustn't say anything unless it was quite ordinary. So she began to talk loudly about a game she had had for Christmas. The others joined in. They came near to the gates and then saw that a small lodge was on the other side.

They went to the great gates and pressed their faces to the wrought-iron work. Beyond the gates lay a drive, much better kept than the lane outside. Tall, dark trees lined the drive, which swept out of sight round a bend. There was no sign of any building.

Fatty looked and looked. 'That building, whatever it is, must be jolly well hidden,' he thought. ' wonder what it was used for in the last war. Some hush-hush stuff, I suppose. Well, it looks as if it's pretty hush-hush now, tucked away in this wood, guarded by this enormous wall, and these gates. I wonder if they're locked.'

He pushed against them. They didn't budge. The others tried too, but nobody could open them. Fatty thought they must be locked on the other side.

He glanced at the bell. Should he ring it ? Yes, he would ! He could always ask the way back to Peterswood, and make that the excuse for ringing. Somebody at the little lodge nearby would probably answer.

So, to the others' delight, Fatty pulled at the bell. A jangling noise came from above their heads, and they saw a bell ringing by one of the stone posts. Buster barked. He was startled by the bell.

'I'm going to ask the way,' said Fatty. 'We're lost. See !'

Somebody peered out of one of the little windows of the dark lodge. Then the door opened and a man came out. He was dressed like a gamekeeper, and had on a corduroy coat, trousers tucked into boots and a belt round his waist. He looked surly and bad-tempered.

'What do you want ?' he shouted. 'You can't come in here. Go away !'

Fatty promptly rang the bell again. Bets looked scared. The man came striding to the gates, looking black as thunder.

'You stop ringing that bell !' he shouted. 'What's the matter with you ? This is private, can't you see that ?'

'Oh !' said Fatty, looking innocently surprised. 'Doesn't my uncle, Colonel Thomas, live here ?'

'No, he doesn't,' said the man. 'Go away, the lot of you, and take that dog with you.'

'Are you *sure* he doesn't live here ?' persisted Fatty, still looking disbelievingly. 'Well, who does then ?'

'Nobody ! The house is empty, as anybody knows. And I'm here to see the kids and tramps don't get in and spoil the place, see ? So get away quickly !'

'Oh — couldn't we just see round the garden,' begged Fatty, and the others, taking his cue, joined in. 'Yes, do let's, please !'

'I'm not going to stand here arguing all afternoon with a pack of silly kids,' said the man. 'You clear off at once. Do you know what I keep for people that come here and pry ? A great big whip — and maybe I set my dogs on them.'

'Aren't you afraid of living here all alone ?' said Bets, in an innocent voice.

'In one minute more I'll open these gates and come out and chase you with my whip,' threatened the man — and he looked so terribly fierce that Fatty half-thought he might be as good as his word.

'Sorry to have bothered you,' he said, in his politest voice. 'Could you tell us the way back to Peterswood ? We came over the fields, and we might lose our way going back. We haven't any idea where we are. What's this place called ?'

'You just go and follow the lane, and you'll come to Peterswood all right,' said the man. 'And good riddance to you ! Waking me up and bringing me out here for nothing. Be off with you !'

He turned to go back to his lodge. The children set off down the narrow track.

'What a very very sweet-natured fellow,' said Larry, and they all laughed.

'Pity we couldn't get in,' said Pip, in a low voice to Fatty. Fatty nudged him to keep quiet. Pip saw somebody riding up the track. It was a postman on his bicycle.

'Good afternoon,' said Fatty, at once. 'Could you tell us the time, please ?'

The postman got off his bicycle, undid his coat and looked at a watch in his pocket.

'Stopped !' he said. 'Don't know what the matter is with this old watch of mine. Just won't go now !'

'It's a nice old watch, isn't it,' said Fatty. 'Are you going up to those iron gates ? We've just been there too, but the man at the lodge won't let us in.'

'He's the caretaker,' said the postman, putting back his watch and buttoning up his coat. 'Proper bad-tempered fellow too. 'Course he wouldn't let you in ! He's there to stop children and tramps and trippers from spoiling the place. It belongs to an old fellow who won't live there himself, and asks such an enormous price for the place that nobody will buy it.'

'Really ?' said Fatty, with interest. 'Is he ever here ?'

'Not that I know of,' said the postman. 'The only letters I ever take are for Peters the gate-keeper — the man you saw. He has too many for me ! It's a job cycling out all this way each day to take letters to one man ! Well — sorry not to be able to tell you the time. Bye-bye !'

He cycled off again, whistling. Fatty looked very pleased. 'Trust a postman for being able to tell you all you want to know !' he said, in a low voice. 'A queer story, isn't it ? A great big place, apparently unlet and empty, surrounded by an enormous wall, with one surly man to guard the place — and *he* has a lot of letters ! That last bit strikes me as queer.'

The children went down the lane, talking quietly. They all felt sure they had hit on their next mystery. But so far they couldn't make head or tail of it !

13   A LITTLE PORTRY

ERN was not told anything about the walk to the wood. He wanted to know, however, what were the steps that Fatty was going to take in the mystery of Christmas Hill.

'Well,' said Fatty, looking mysterious, 'word has come to me that a big robbery will be done in the next few days, and that the robbers on Christmas Hill will hide the loot in the old mill.'

Ern's eyes almost dropped out of his head. 'Coo !' he said, and couldn't say any more.

'The thing is — who's going to look for the loot after the robbery ?' said Fatty, seriously. 'I can't let any of the others, because they're forbidden to do things like looking for loot — and at the moment I've got other things in hand — tracking down the kidnappers, for instance.'

'Coo,' said Ern again, in awe. An idea shone brilliantly in his mind. 'Fatty ! Why don't you let *me* find the loot ? I could go and search the old mill for you. Lovaduck ! I'd be awfully proud to find the swag.'

'Well — I *might* let you,' said Fatty. He turned to the others. 'What about it.' Find-Outers ? Shall we let him in on this and give him a chance of finding the loot ? After all, he did a lot of hard work finding those clues.'

'Yes. Let him,' said the others, generously, and Ern beamed and glowed. Whatever next ! This was life, this was — creeping out at dead of night — hunting for clues up on the hill next day — and now searching for hidden loot. What exciting lives the Find-Outers led ! Ern felt honoured to belong to their company. He felt he could write a 'pome' about it all. A line came into his head.

'The dire dark deeds upon the hill.' What a wonderful beginning to a 'pome.' Ern took out his portry note-book and wrote down the line before he could forget it.

'See that ?' he said triumphantly to the others. 'The dark dire deeds upon the hill. That's the beginning of a new pome. That's real portry, that is.'

> 'The dark dire deeds upon the hill
> Strike my heart with a deadly chill,'

began Fatty.

> 'The robbers rob and the looters loot,
> We'd better be careful they don't all shoot,
> They're deadly men, they're fearful foes,
> What end they'll come to, nobody knows !
> Oooh, the dark dire deeds upon the hill
> Strike my heart with a deadly chill !'

This poem was greeted with shrieks of delighted laughter by all the Find-Outers, even Buster joining in the applause. Fatty had reeled it off without stopping.

Only Ern didn't laugh. He listened solemnly, with open mouth, to Fatty's recitation, admiration literally pouring out of him.

'Fatty ! You're a *reel* genius. Why, you took my first line and you made up the whole pome without stopping. I'd never have thought of all that, if I'd sat down the whole day long.'

'Ah — that's the secret,' said Fatty, wickedly. 'You don't sit down — you just stand up and it comes. Like this :

> 'Oh have you heard of Ernie's clues,
> Ernie's clues, Ernie's clues,
> A broken lace, our Ernie found,
> A smoked cigar-end on the ground,
> A match, a packet, and a hanky,

Honest truth, no hanky-panky !
A rag, a tin, a pencil-end,
How very clever is our friend !'

Fatty couldn't go on because the others were laughing so much. Ern was even more impressed. But he felt down in the dumps too. He could never, never write pomes like that. How did Fatty do it ? Ern determined to stand up in his bedroom that night when he was alone and see if portry rolled out of him as it did out of Fatty.

'You're marvellous,' he said to Fatty. 'You ought to be a poet, you reelly ought.'

'Can't,' said Fatty. 'I'm going to be a detective.'

'Couldn't you be both ?' said Ern.

'Possibly, but not probably,' said Fatty. 'Not worth it ! Any one can spout that sort of drivel.'

Ern was astonished. Could Fatty realy think that was drivel ? What a boy !

'Well, to come back to what we were talking about,' said Fatty, 'we've decided, have we, to let our Ern look for the loot ?'

'Yes,' chorused every one.

'Right,' said Fatty.

'When do I look for it ?' said Ern, almost quivering with excitement. 'To-night ?'

'Well, it's not usual to look for loot before the robbery has been committed,' said Fatty, his face very serious.

'But if you think there's a chance of finding it before it's put there, you go on and do it, Ern.'

Bets gave a giggle. Ern worked all this out and blushed. 'Yes. I see what you mean. I won't go looking till after the robbery. But when will the robbery be ?'

'The papers will tell you,' said Fatty. 'You look in your uncle's papers each morning, and as soon as you see that the robbery has been done, you'll know it's time to hunt in the old mill. And if you want to tell your uncle about it, we've no objection.'

'I don't want to,' said Ern. 'Well, I must be going. Lovaduck ! You're a one for spouting portry, aren't you ? I can't get over it. So long !'

He went, and the others began to laugh. Poor old Ern. His was a wonderful leg to pull ! Larry suddenly saw his 'portry note-book' left on the table.

'Hallo ! He's left this. Fatty, write something in it ! Something about Goon. Go on !'

'I'll write a "pome" about Goon himself, in Ern's handwriting,' said Fatty, begining to enjoy himself. He could imitate any one's writing. Bets thought admiringly that really there wasn't anything that Fatty couldn't do — and do better than any one else too ! She stood close beside him and watched him.

He found a page in the book, and borrowed a pencil from Pip. 'Ern will be simply amazed to find a poem about his uncle written in his own book in his own handwriting,' said Fatty. 'He'll certainly think he must have written it himself — and he won't know when ! Golly, I wish I could be there when he finds it !'

He began to write. As usual the words flowed out straightaway. No puzzling his brains for Fatty, no searching for a rhyme ! It just came out like water from a tap.

'TO MY DEAR UNCLE

'Oh how I love thee, Uncle dear,
Although thine eyes like frogs' appear,
Thy body is so fat and round,
Thy heavy footsteps shake the ground.
Thy temper is so sweet and mild
'Twould frighten e'en the smallest child,

And when thou speakest, people say,
"Now did we hear a donkey bray ?"
Dear Uncle, how...'

'Fatty! Ern's coming back !' said Bets, suddenly. Her sharp ears had heard footsteps. 'Shut the book, quick.'

Fatty shut the book and slid it over the table. He picked up Buster and began to play with him. The others crowded round, laughing.

Ern's head came round the door. 'Did I leave my portry note-book here ? Oh yes, I did. Silly of me. Good-bye all.'

He took his book and disappeared. 'What a pity you couldn't finish the poem, Fatty,' said Daisy. 'It was such a good one — especially all the thees and thys. Just the kind of thing Ern would write.'

'And I suppose, as usual, you got top marks for it ?' said Pip, who only believed half of the extraordinary stories that Fatty told. As a matter of fact most of them were perfectly true. The rest were almost true but rather exaggerated. Fatty certainly had a remarkable career at school, and had caused more laughter, more annoyance and more admiration than any other boy there.

'I say, Fatty — poor old Ern may have to wait weeks to look for his loot,' said Daisy.

'No, he won't,' said Fatty. 'Haven't you noticed that there's a robbery reported nearly every day in the paper ? It's about the commonest crime there is. There'll be one to-morrow, or the next day, don't you worry ?'

Fatty got out his own note-book, in which he kept particulars of whatever mystery the Find-Outers were trying to solve. He glanced down his notes.

'This is a very difficult case,' he said to the others. 'There doesn't seem much we can do to find out anything. I've hardly got anywhere. I've found out that that building in the wood is called Harry's Folly, but nobody seems to know why. And the name of the man who is supposed to own it is Henry White — a very nice, common, insignificant name. I can't find out where he lives — all I've heard is that he lives abroad — which doesn't help us much !'

'We know that one of the men who was near the place was called Holland,' suggested Bets.

'Yes,' said Fatty, giving Bets a pat on the shoulder. 'That's a good point. I was just coming to that. As the men were walking, it looks as if they lived in or near Peterswood — though according to Ern, they said good-night to one another near him and went different ways. So it's likely that one might have been the caretaker, and the other was Holland. In which case Holland was walking home.'

Every one sat and thought. 'Where's your telephone directory, Pip ?' said Fatty. 'Let's see if there are any Hollands in it.'

Pip fetched it. They all crowded round Fatty as he looked up the H's. 'Here we are,' he said. 'Holland. A.J. Holland. Henry Holland. W. Holland & Co., Garage proprietors, Marlow. Three Hollands.'

'Have to look them all up, I suppose,' said Larry. 'Lists of Suspects ! Three Hollands and one caretaker, called Peters !'

'Correct !' said Fatty. He looked thoughtfully at the directory. 'We'd better begin a bit of detecting again,' he said.

'Well, we're in on this,' said Larry at once. 'We *still* don't know if it's a mystery, so there's no harm in asking about the Hollands.'

'I believe my mother knows some people called Holland,' said Pip suddenly. 'I'll find out. Where do they all live, by the way ?'

'Two in Peterswood, and the garage fellow at Marlow,' said Fatty. 'Well, Pip, you be responsible for finding out about one lot of Hollands. Larry and Daisy find out about the other — and I'll bike over to Marlow and smell out the Hollands there.'

They all felt very cheerful now that there was something definite to do. 'I think I'll go in disguise,' said Fatty, who always welcomed a chance to put on one of his disguises. 'I'll go as Ern ! I bet I could make myself up to be exactly like him, now I know him so well.'

'Why — you were quite annoyed with us for thinking Ern was you when we met him at the station,' said Daisy.

'I know. Still, I think I can put on a disguise that would deceive even old Goon, if he wasn't too near !' chuckled Fatty. 'Well, Find-Outers we'll do a spot of work to-morrow. Come on Buster. Stop chewing the rug and come and have your dinner !'

14   SOME GOOD DETECTING

QUITE a lot of things happened the next day. For one thing there was the report of a big robbery in the daily papers. Ern could hardly believe his eyes when he saw the headlines ! Fatty was right. There was the robbery. Coo !

Mr. Goon was astonished to see Ern poring over the paper, reading details on the front page, and the back page too, quite forgetting his breakfast.

'What's up ?' he said. 'Give me the paper. Boys shouldn't read at meal-times.'

Ern handed it over, his head in a whirl. It had happened ! The robbery was committed. Soon the loot would be in the old mill — and he'd find it. He'd be a hero.His uncle would admire him tremendously and be very sorry indeed for all the hard things he had said. Ern sat in a happy dream all through his breakfast, much to the surprise of his uncle.

Mr. Goon read about the robbery too — but he didn't for one moment think it had anything to do with Ern or himself. Robberies didn't concern him unless they were in his own district. He wondered why Ern looked so daft that morning. Had he found any more clues, or got any more news ?

No, said Ern — he hadn't. He felt guilty when he remembered how he was going to fiNd the loot, without telling his uncle anything about it — but he wasn't going to split on Fatty any more. He was going to behave like a real Find-Outer !

The Find-Outers were busy that day. Pip and Bets had laid their plans very carefully, hoping not to arouse their parents' suspicions when they asked about the Hollands.

'We'll talk about people who have queer names,' decided Pip. 'I'll remind you of a girl you used to know whose surname is Redball — you remember her ? Then you say "oh yes — and do you remember those people called Tinkle ?" or something like that. And from that we'll go on to people with names of towns or countries — and when we get to the name Holland, I'll ask mother if she knows people of that name.'

'Yes, that would be a safe way of finding out,' said Bets, pleased. So they began at breakfast time.

'Do you remember that girl you used to know — she had such a funny name,' said Pip, 'Redball, I think it was.'

'Oh yes,' said Bets. 'That *was* a queer name. I remember somebody else with a funny name too — Tinkle. Don't you remember, Pip ?'

'Yes. It must be queer to answer to a name like that,' said Pip.

'You get used to it,' said his mother, joining in unsuspectingly.

'Some people have names of countries and towns,' said Pip. 'There's a composer called Edward Germany, isn't there ?'

'Edward *German*,' corrected his father, 'not Germany. Plenty of people are called England and I have known an Ireland and a Scotland too.'

'Have you known a Holland ?' asked Bets. This was going much better than they had hoped !

'Oh yes,' said Mrs. Hilton at once. 'I know a Mrs. Holland quite well.'

'Is there a Mr. Holland ?' asked Pip.

'Yes, I think so,' said Mrs. Hilton, looking rather surprised. 'I've never seen him. He must be an old man by now, because Mrs. Holland is a very old lady.'

'Did they have any children ?' asked Pip, ruling out old Mr. Holland at once, because it didn't seem very likely that he would be engaged in any sort of mystery if he was so old.

'Well — their children would be grown up by now,' said his mother.

'Was there a boy ?' asked Bets. 'A boy who would be a man now ?'

Mrs. Hilton felt surprised at these last questions. 'Why all this sudden interest in the Hollands ?' she asked.

'What are you up to ? You're usually up to something when you begin this sort of thing.'

Pip sighed. Mothers were much too sharp. They were like dogs. Buster always sensed when anything was out of the ordinary, and so did mothers. Mothers and dogs both had a kind of second sight that made them see into people's minds and know when anything unusual was going on. He kicked Bets under the table to stop her asking any more questions.

She understood the kick, though she didn't like it, and tried to change the subject. 'I wish I had another name, not Hilton,' she said. 'A more exciting name. And I wish people would call me Elizabeth, not Bets.'

'Oh *no*,' said her father. 'Bets suits you. You are a proper little Bets.'

So the subject was changed and nothing more was said about the Hollands. But Pip and Bets were rather downcast because they hadn't found out what Fatty would want to know.

They went up to the play-room. Lorna the maid was there, dusting. 'It's a pity we didn't find out anything more about the Hollands,' said Bets. 'Oh — hallo, Lorna.

'The Hollands ?' said Lorna. 'What do you want to know about them for ? There's not much to know ! My sister's in service with old Mrs. Holland.'

Well ! Who would have thought that Lorna knew all about the Hollands ! She told them in half a minute all they needed to know.

'Poor old Mrs. Holland, she's all alone now that her husband's dead,' said Lorna. 'She had two daughters, but they're both living in Africa — and her son was killed in the last war but one. So she's nobody to care for her at all.'

Pip and Bets thought this was very sad. They also thought that their Mrs. Holland, at any rate, didn't belong to the family of Hollands that Fatty was looking for.

'I wonder how Larry and Daisy are getting on,' said Pip.

They were getting on quite well ! They had decided to ask their postman if he knew of any Hollands. He was a great friend of theirs. So they swung on their front gate that morning and waited till he came.

'Well, aren't you cold, out here so early ?' said the postman, when he came. 'Expecting something special ?'

'Only our circus tickets,' said Larry, truthfully. 'Ah — I bet they're in this envelope.'

He and the postman then had a very interesting talk about the various circuses they had both seen.

'Well, I must be off,' said the postman at last, and he turned to go.

As if he had only just thought of it, Larry called after him. 'Oh — half a minute — do you know any one called Holland in Peterswood ?'

'Holland — let me see now,' said the postman, scratching his rough cheek. 'Yes, there are two. One's in Rosemary Cottage. The other's in Hill House. Which one do you want ?'

'One with a man in it,' said Daisy.

'Ah — then you don't want old Mrs. Holland of Rosemary Cottage,' said the postman. 'Maybe you want the Hollands of Hill House. There's a Mr. Holland there — but I did hear

Larry called after the postman

he's in America at the moment. Yes, that's right, he is. I keep taking post cards from America to the house for all the children. Five of them and little monkeys they are too !'

'Thank you,' said Larry, as a loud knocking came from behind him. It was his mother knocking on the window for him to come in to breakfast. He and Daisy fled indoors. It didn't look as if either of the Peterswood family of Hollands was the right one. Perhaps the Marlow Holland was the one they wanted !

Fatty was out on his bike when the other Find-Outers went to find him. 'Gone over to Marlow, I expect,' said Larry. 'Well, we'll wait for him. He's left the oil-stove on in his shed. We'll wait there.'

So they sat down in the cosy shed. Buster was not there. He had gone with Fatty, sitting upright as usual in Fatty's bicycle basket. Fatty had set off soon after breakfast before his mother could plan any jobs for him to do. It was not very far to Marlow — hardly three miles. The wind was cold, and Fatty's cheeks grew redder and redder.

He had made himself up just like Ern, enormous cap and all ! Ern had teeth that stuck out, so Fatty had inserted his set of false celluloid teeth, which were very startling when displayed in a sudden grin. But they did make him look like Ern. He had put on a wig of rather untidy, coarse hair, very like Ern's, an old mack, and corduroy trousers. He wished the others could see him !

Buster was used to Fatty's changed appearances by now. He never knew when his master was going to appear as an old woman, a bent old man, an errand boy or a correct young man ! But Buster didn't mind. Fatty always smelt the same, whatever he wore, so Buster's nose told him the truth, even if his eyes didn't.

Holland's garge was in a road off the High Street. Fatty

cycled to find it. He saw it from a distance and then dismounted. Taking a quick look round to make sure that nobody saw him, he let all the air out of one of his tyres, so that the wheel bumped dismally on the ground.

Fatty then put on a doleful expression and wheeled his bicycle to Holland's Garage. He turned in at the big entrance. There were a good many men working about on different cars, but nobody took any notice of him.

Fatty saw a boy about his own age washing down a car near the back of the garage. He went up to him.

'Hallo, chum,' he said, 'any chance of getting my bike mended here ? Got a puncture.'

'Not just now,' said the boy. 'I do the punctures usually, but I'm busy.'

'Oh come on ! Leave the washing alone, and do my bike for me,' said Fatty. But the boy was keeping an eye on a little window let into the wall of the wooden office near him. Fatty guessed correctly that the Boss might be in there.

'Can't do it yet,' said the boy, in a low tone. 'I say is that your dog in the basket ! Isn't he good !'

'Yes. He's a fine dog,' said Fatty. 'Come on Buster, you can get down now !'

Buster leapt out of the basket, and ran to the hose. He barked at it and the boy gave him a spraying, which delighted Buster's heart.

'This is quite a big garage, isn't it ?' said Fatty, leaning back against the wall. 'And a lot of men working in it. You must be pretty busy.'

'We are,' said the boy, still vigorously hosing the car. 'Busier than any other garage in the district.'

'I wouldn't mind taking a job in a garage myself,' said Fatty. 'I know a bit about cars. Any chance of a job here ?'

'Might be,' said the boy. 'You'd have to ask Mr. Williams

there — he's the foreman. The Boss would want a look at you too.'

'Who's the Boss ?' asked Fatty.

'Mr. Holland, of course,' said the boy, his eye still on the window nearby. 'He owns this garage and another one some miles away. But he's usually here. Slave-driver, I call him.'

'Bad luck,' sympathized Fatty.

At that moment another dog ran into the garage, and Buster darted at him. Whether Buster thought this was his own particular garage for the moment or not Fatty didn't know — but Buster certainly acted as if he thought it was ! He caught the other dog by the back of the neck, and immediately a terrific howling, snarling and barking filled the place.

The little window near Fatty and the boy flew up at once. 'Who does that black dog belong to ?' said a harsh voice.

'To this boy here, Mr. Holland, sir,' said the garage boy, scared.

'What's your name ?' demanded Mr. Holland of Fatty, who was too surprised not to answer.

'Frederick Trotteville of Peterswood,' he said. 'What's the fuss about, sir ?'

'I won't have dogs fighting in my garage,' snapped the man. 'I shall report your dog to the police if you bring him in here again. What have you come for ? I've seen you chattering to this boy here for ages, making him do his work carelessly !'

'I came to ask if I could have my bike puncture mended,' said Fatty. He eyed Mr. Holland, wondering whether to take a shot in the dark. He decided that he would.

'I want to ride over to a place called Harry's Folly, sir. It's got some fine iron gates, I'm told, and I'm interested in them, sir. Do you happen to know the best way to get to

Harry's Folly ?'

Fatty paused for breath, watching Mr. Holland's face.

Mr. Holland had certainly heard of Harry's Folly ! He started a little when Fatty mentioned it, and a peculiar expression came over his face. Then his face smoothed out, and he answered immediately.

'Harry's Folly ! No, I've never heard of it. We can't mend your bike here now. We're too busy. Clear off and take your dog with you.'

Fatty winked at the boy, who was now hosing the wheels of the car very very well indeed. He called Buster.

'Hey, Buster ! Come on !'

Buster left the fascinating hose and ran to Fatty's feet.

Fatty wheeled his bike slowly out of the garage. He had a very satisfied expression on his face.

He was sure he had found the right Mr. Holland ! He had seen the little start the man gave at the mention of Harry's Folly. He knew the house all right — then why did he deny all knowledge of it ?

'Very very fishy,' decided Fatty, wheeling his bicycle into another side road. He pumped up the tyre swiftly, put Buster into the basket, and rode home, pleased with himself. Frederick Algernon Trotteville, you certainly are a good detective, Fatty told himself.

Back at the garage Mr. Holland sat in his office, quite silent. He took down a telephone directory and found the name Trotteville in it, and the address. He dialled a number and spoke to somebody.

'That you Jack ? Listen — what was the name of that kid who cleared up the Missing Necklace affair ? Smart lad, you remember ? Ah, I thought so. It may interest you to know he's just been here — complete with a dog called Buster — and he told me he wanted to bike to a place called Harry's

Folly ! What do you make of that ?'

Somebody evidently made a lot of it at the other end of the telephone, for Mr. Holland listened intently for a few minutes. Then he spoke in a low voice, very near the mouthpiece.

'Yes, I agree with you. Kids like that must be dealt with. Leave it to me !'

FATTY cycled back to Peterswood, his mind hard at work. So Mr. Holland was connected with Harry's Folly — and something was going on there, though Fatty couldn't imagine what ! And Mr. Holland didn't want people to know that he knew Harry's Folly — very peculiar altogether !

'Shall I ring up Inspector Jenks ?' wondered Fatty. 'Or shall I just jog along on my own for a bit and try to solve the mystery ? I'd like to do that. Funny to think of old Goon getting all excited about an imaginary mystery, and here are the Find-Outers on the edge of a real one again !'

He came to Peterswood. He stopped and put Buster down. The little Scottie bounded gleefully along by the bicycle.

In the distance Mr. Goon loomed up, on his way to talk severely to somebody who had let their chimney get on fire. To his enormous surprise he saw somebody he thought was Ern riding a bicycle not far off. Mr. Goon stopped and stared. He simply couldn't believe this eyes.

'I've left Ern at home, clearing out my shed,' he thought. 'And I told him to clean my bike too. And now there he is, riding my bike, calm as a cucumber. I'll tell him off ! Can't trust that boy at all, not for one minute !'

He hurried towards Fatty. Fatty spotted him, and rode into a side-street, waving merrily. He couldn't help hoping that Mr. Goon would think he was Ern. Mr. Goon, of course, hadn't any doubt of it at all. He was feeling very angry.

'Ern !' he called. 'ERN !'

Fatty took no notice, but rode slowly. Mr. Goon hurried after him, his face going purple. That boy ! Waving to him like that, cheeky as a monkey !

'ERN ! YOU COME HERE !'

'Ern' rode round the corner and Mr. Goon lost sight of him. He almost burst with rage. He retraced his steps and went back down the road, thinking of all the things he would do to Ern when he next saw him. To his astonishment Ern actually appeared before him again, at the end of the street, and waved to him.

Mr. Goon nearly had a fit. Fatty, of course, was dying of laughter at the sight of Mr. Goon's face, and could hardly keep on his bicycle. He pedalled out of sight, tears running down his cheeks, almost helpless with laughter.

Once more he cycled round the block of houses and swam into Mr. Goon's sight and out again. Mr. Goon had now reached the pitch of shaking his fist and muttering, much to the amazement of all the passers-by. Fatty decided that he really would fall off his bicycle with laughing if he saw Mr. Goon again, and regretfully pedalled home to tell the Find-Outers all that had happened.

But Buster, having spotted Mr. Goon, thought it would be much more fun to trot at this heels than to go with Fatty. So he went behind him, sniffing at his trousers till the policeman felt him and turned in aggravation.

'Now you clear-orf,' said Mr. Goon, exasperated. 'First it's Ern cheeking me, and now it's you ! Clear-orf I say, or I'll kick you into the middle of next week.'

Buster didn't clear-orf. He capered round Mr. Goon, making playful little darts at his legs as if he wanted him to have a game. Mr. Goon was so worked up that he backed straight into a street-sweeper's barrow and almost knocked it over.

The sweeper sent Buster away by frightening him with his broom. Buster trotted down the street pleased with himself. He certainly was a dog worthy of a master like Fatty !

Mr. Goon finished his errand, gradually getting less purple, and then walked home. Now to deal with Ern !

Ern had done a remarkably good morning's work. He had cleaned out the shed thoroughly, and now he was just finishing cleaning Mr. Goon's bicycle. He was trying to think of some portry as he worked.

The next-door neighbour, Mrs. Murray, thought that Mr. Goon had a very hard-working boy for a nephew. Every time she hung out her washing, there he was, working away. She called over the fence.

'You're a good boy, you are ! You haven't stopped working one minute since you began !'

Ern beamed. Mrs. Murray went indoors. Mr. Goon arrived, and walked down the little garden to where Ern was working by the shed, polishing the bicycle handles.

'Ho !' said Mr. Goon, in an awful voice, 'so you thought you could sauce me, did you ? What do you mean by it, riding round the village on *my* bike, cheeking me like that ?'

Ern couldn't make out what his uncle was talking about at all. He stared at him, puzzled.

'What do you mean, Uncle ?' he said. 'I've been here all the time. Look, the shed is clean and tidy — and I've almost finished your bike.'

Mr. Goon looked. He was most surprised to see the shed so neat and tidy, and certainly his bicycle looked very spick and span.

'Ern, it's no good you denying it,' he said, his face going red, on its way to turning purple. 'I saw you — and you waved at me. I called you and you didn't come. What's more, you were riding my bike, and I don't allow that.'

'Uncle. I tell you I've been here all the morning,' said

Ern, in an aggrieved voice. 'What's the matter with you ? Haven't I done all you said ? I tell you I didn't ride your bike. You've made a silly mistake.'

Mr. Goon was now purple. He raised his voice. 'I won't have you cheek me, Ern, see ? You were out on my bike, and you cheeked me ? I tell you ...'

Mrs. Murray popped her head over the fence. She had heard everything, and she meant to put in a word for that hard-working boy, Ern.

'Mr. Goon,' she said, and the policeman jumped. 'Mr. Goon ! That boy hasn't left this garden. A harder-working boy I never did see in all my life. You ought to be proud of a boy like that instead of accusing him of things he never did. I say to you, Mr. Goon, that boy hasn't budged from his place. I've been in and out with my washing, and I know. You leave that nephew of yours alone, or there's things I'll tell round to every one. Ah, you may be an officer of the law, Mr. Goon, but you don't deceive *me* ! I remember when ...'

Mr. Goon knew that there was absolutely no way of stopping Mrs. Murray once she had begun. He was afraid of what she might say in front of Ern. So he put on a very dignified face, said 'Good morning to you, Mam,' and marched indoors. Retreat was always the best policy when Mrs. Murray was on the warpath !

'You stick up for yourself, lad,' said Mrs. Murray. 'Don't you let him go for you like that !'

A voice bellowed from the kitchen. 'ERN !'

Ern dropped his duster and ran. However mistaken his uncle might be, he was still an uncle with a cane in the cupboard, and Ern thought he had better keep on the good side of both.

Mr. Goon said no more about Ern riding his bike. An uncomfortable thought had come into his mind. He was wondering if that boy who looked like Ern could possibly have been Fatty up to his tricks. Ern must certainly have been in the garden all the time if Mrs. Murray said so. Her tongue was sharp and long but it told the truth.

'Have you seen those kids to-day yet ?' asked Mr. Goon. 'Got any more news for me ?'

'You know I haven't been out, Uncle. I've just told you so,' said Ern. 'I'd like to go and see them this afternoon though.'

Ern was longing to discuss the robbery with the Find-Outers. He had got the paper again as soon as his uncle had gone out, and read every single detail. The jewels those thieves had taken ! Coo ! There ought to be a fine bit of loot up at the old mill to-night ! Ern was thrilled at the thought.

'How that boy Fatty knows these things just beats me,' thought Ern. 'He's a wonder, he is ! I wish I could be like him. I'd do anything in the world for Fatty !'

A good many people felt like that about Fatty. However annoying, boastful or high-handed he was people always admired him and wanted to do things for him, especially other boys. He was head and shoulders above them in brains, boldness and courage, and they knew it.

Ern rushed round to the Find-Outers immediately after his dinner. They were at Fatty's down in the cosy shed. He had been telling them all his adventures of the morning. They had admired the things he had found out at Holland's garage and had roared with laughter at the way he had played a trick on Goon, pretending to be Ern.

'I expect Ern will be along soon,' said Fatty, opening a daily paper. 'Any one see the account of this big robbery ? Ern will be sure to think it's the one we meant !'

Larry and Daisy had seen it, but not Pip or Bets. They all pored over it, and Ern chose a very good moment to come into the shed.

'Hallo !' he said beaming round. 'I say — you're looking at the story of the robbery ! You're a marvel, Fatty, to know it was going to be done so soon. I can't think why you don't tell the police beforehand, when you know these things.'

'They wouldn't believe me,' said Fatty, truthfully. 'Well, Ern — there should be plenty of fine loot up in the old mill soon !'

'I'm going to-night,' said Ern, solemnly. 'It's awfully good of you to let me, Fatty.'

'Don't mention it,' said Fatty. 'Spleshure.'

'Pardon ?' said Ern.

'SPLESHURE !' said Fatty, loudly.

The others laughed. 'What's he say ?' said Ern, puzzled.

'He means, "It's a pleasure," explained Bets, giggling.

'Swatesaid !' chorused the Find-Outers together.

'Funny way of talking you have sometimes,' said Ern to Fatty, seriously. 'I say, my uncle wasn't half queer with me this morning. Said he saw me riding his bike and cheeking him when all the time I was cleaning out his shed.'

'Must be mad,' said Fatty. 'Well, Ern — the best of luck to you to-night. I hope the swag won't be too heavy for you to carry.'

'Coo !' said Ern, in alarm. 'I never thought of that !'

16 UNPLEASANT NIGHT FOR ERN

ERN passed the rest of the day in a state of excitement. His uncle couldn't think what was the matter with him.

'Thinking out some more of your wonderful portry, I suppose,' he said, scornfully.

'No, I'm not,' said Ern, and he wasn't. He was thinking of what he was going to do that night. There would be a small moon. That would help him to find the way properly this time without making a mistake. Would the loot be too heavy ? Well, if it was he'd go twice to fetch it !

Ern went to bed early again. Mr. Goon felt that Something was Up. Ern knew something that he hadn't passed on to his uncle. Drat the boy !

He listened at Ern's door when he went up to bed himself. If Ern was asleep he'd creep in and get that note-book again. But Ern wasn't asleep. He was tossing and turning, because Mr. Goon could quite well hear the bed creak.

Mr. Goon undressed and got into bed, meaning to lie awake till Ern was asleep. But somehow he didn't. His eyes closed and soon Ern heard the familiar snores echoing through the little house.

Ern didn't want to go to sleep. He wanted to keep awake safely and leave for Christmas Hill about one o'clock when the moon would be up and giving a little light. But it was hard to keep awake. Ern's eyes kept closing. He sat up straight. This wouldn't do. He'd be asleep in half a tick.

A thought came into his head. He remembered how Fatty had said that portry would come pouring out of you if you stood up to say it. It would be a good chance to try it now —

Uncle was asleep — there was no one to interrupt him. And it would stop him going off to sleep.

Ern got out of bed. It was cold and he shivered. He pulled on his overcoat and put a scarf round his neck. He got out his portry note-book, and his book of Clues and Suspects. He was proud of them both.

He read down his list of clues again. Then he took a pencil and wrote a few lines on the next page.

'Robbery committed January 3rd. Loot will be hidden in the old mill on Christmas Hill. Ern Goon detailed to find it on night of Jan. 4th.'

That looked good. Ern drew a line under it and thought with pleasure of what he might be able to write the next morning. 'Loot collected. Worth about ten thousand pounds.' How he hoped he would be able to write that down too !

Now for the portry. He read through his various 'poems' and decided that they were not nearly as good as the ones Fatty had made up out of his head on the spur of the moment. He didn't see the one that Fatty had written in the book about Mr. Goon. He didn't even know it was there.

Ern shut the portry note-book and put it on top of the other book. Then he stood up to begin saying portry straight out of his head like Fatty.

But somehow it wouldn't come. Ern stood there, waiting and shivering. Then suddenly a line came into his head. Ah — it was beginning !

Ern recited the line. 'The pore old man lay on the grass ...'

He stopped. Nothing else came. Now if only he were Fatty, he'd go on with another line and another and another — a whole poem, in fact, which he could remember and write proudly down.

He recited the line again, a little more loudly. 'The pore old man lay on the grass ... on the grass ... on the ...'

No, it wasn't any good. He couldn't think of another line to follow. But that was just it — Fatty didn't *have* to think. Portry just came out of him without stopping when he wanted it to! Perhaps Fatty was a genius and Ern wasn't. Ern thought sadly about this for a moment.

Then he began again, reciting loudly, 'A pore old man lay on the grass, A pore old man lay on the grass, A pore old man ...'

Mr. Goon, in the next room, woke up with a jump. What was that peculiar noise? He sat up in bed. A voice came to him from the bedroom next to his. Mr. Goon listened in amazement.

'A pore old man lay on the grass, A pore ...'

'It's *Ern*!' said Mr. Goon, really astonished. 'What's he doing, talking in the middle of the night about pore old men lying on grass? He must be out of his mind!'

Mr. Goon put on a dressing-gown much too small for him and went majestically into Ern's room. The boy stood there in the dark, still reciting his one line desperately. 'The pore old man ...'

'Now what's all this?' said Mr. Goon in a loud voice and Ern nearly jumped out of his skin. 'Waking me up with you pore old men ! What do you think you're doing, Ern ? I won't have this kind of behaviour, I tell you straight.'

'Oh, it's you, Uncle,' said Ern, weakly. Mr. Goon switched on the light. He saw Ern there in coat and scarf and he was even more astonished.

'You going somewhere ?' he inquired.

'No. I was cold so I put some things on,' said poor Ern, getting into bed. 'I was only making up portry, Uncle. It comes better when you stand up.'

Mr. Goon caught sight of the two note-books on a chair. 'I'll teach you to wake me up in the middle of the night with portry !' he snorted, and picked up the two books to take back with him.

'Uncle ! Oh Uncle, please don't touch those !' begged Ern, leaping out of bed and trying to take them from his uncle. But Mr. Goon held them all the more tightly.

'What's the matter ? What are you so upset about ? I'm not going to throw them into the fire,' said Mr. Goon.

'Uncle !' wailed Ern. 'They're private. Nobody is to read those but me.'

'Ho !' said Mr. Goon. 'That's what *you* think !' and he switched off the light and shut the door. Ern got into bed, shivering with fright. Now his uncle would read about the Loot — and the wonderful secret would be out ! Ern shed a few tears on to the sheet.

Mr. Goon read through the portry note-book first. When he came to the poem about himself he could hardly believe his eyes. How could Ern write such a rude poem ? Right down rude, it was. Talking about his uncle's eyes in that way, and his voice — and that bit about the donkey's bray ! Mr. Goon felt himself swelling up with righteous rage.

He then read the other book. He only glanced at the Clues and other Notes which he had read before. But when he came to the bit Ern had written in that very night his eyes grew rounder than ever.

'Robbery committed January 3rd. Loot will be hidden in the old mill in Christmas Hill. Ern Goon detailed to find it on night of Jan. 4th.'

Mr. Goon read this several times. What an extraordinary thing ! What robbery ? And how did anybody know where the loot was ? And who detailed Ern to get it ? That boy

Frederick, of course ! Mr. Goon gave one of his snorts. Then he sat and thought very deeply.

It was a real bit of luck that he had got Ern's note-books to-night ! Now *he* could go and find the loot instead of Ern. That would be a bit of a blow to that boy Frederick ! Aha ! He wouldn't like Mr. Goon turning up with the loot instead of Ern. And what would Inspector Jenks say to all this ? He wouldn't be pleased with anybody but Mr. Goon !

He read the bit of portry about himself again, and felt very angry indeed. Ungrateful boy Ern was ! He determined to give Ern something to remember. Where had he put that cane ?

Ern heard Mr. Goon go downstais. He heard him come up again. He heard him open his door and switch on the light — and oh, what a horrible sight, there stood his uncle at the door with a cane in his hand !

'Ern,' said Mr. Goon, in a sad voice, 'this is going to hurt me more than it hurts you. I've read that pome you wrote about me. It's wicked, downright wicked.'

Ern was astonished and alarmed. 'What pome, Uncle ? I haven't written anything about you at all.'

'Now don't you go making things worse by telling stories,' said Mr. Goon. He opened the portry note-book at the right page and to Ern's consternation he saw, written in his own handwriting, a poem addressed to 'My Dear Uncle.' He read it and quaked.

'Uncle ! I didn't write it. I couldn't. It's too good a pome for me to write !'

'What do you mean, it's "*too good!*" ' demanded his uncle. 'It's a wicked pome. And how you can sit there and tell me you didn't write it when it's in your own handwriting, well it beats me ! I suppose you'll say next it isn't your writing ?'

Ern looked at the 'Pome'. 'It *is* my writing,' he said in a faint voice. 'But I don't understand it at all, Uncle, because honestly I don't remember writing it. I don't believe I *could* make up a pome as good as that. It's — It's like a dream, all this.'

'And there's another thing, Ern,' said Mr. Goon, bending the cane to and fro in a very alarming manner, 'I've read what's in your other book too. That robbery — and the loot hidden in the old mill. You never told me nothing about that, nothing at all. You're a bad boy. And bad boys get the cane. Hold out your hand !'

Poor Ern ! He began to cry again, but there was nothing to do but hold out his hand, or else be caned on other places that might be still more painful.

Swish ! 'That's for the pome,' said Mr. Goon, 'and so is that ! And that's for not telling me about the robbery and so is that.'

Ern howled dismally and held his hand under his armpit. Mr. Goon looked at him grimly. 'And don't you think you're going loot-hunting to-night, because you're not ! I'm going to lock you in your bedroom, see ? And you can just spend the night thinking of what happens to bad boys who write rude pomes and don't tell their uncle the things they ought to know !'

And with that Mr. Goon switched off the light, shut the door — and locked it ! Ern's heart sank. Now he was Properly Done. No going up to the old mill for him to-night. A horrid thought struck his head under the pillow and he wept for his smarting hand, his locked door, and his lost hopes.

He heard Mr. Goon dress. He heard him go quietly out of the house. Ern knew he was going up to Christmas Hill. Now he'd find the loot. All Fatty's plans would come to nothing because of him, Ern Goon, and his silliness. Ern felt very small and very miserable. Then a thought struck him. He remembered the rude 'pome' about his uncle. He got out of bed and switched on the light. His portry note-book was on the chair where his uncle had tossed it. Ern picked it up and found the page with rude 'pome' on it. *To My Dear Uncle.*

Ern read it through six times. He thought it was remarkably clever. And yes, it was certainly in his own handwriting, though he couldn't for the life of him remember when he had written it.

'I must have done it in my sleep,' said Ern, at last. 'Geniuses do queer things. I must have dreamt it last night, got out of bed in my sleep, and written it down. Coo ! Fancy me writing a good pome like that. It's wonderful ! It's better than anything Fatty could have done. Perhaps I'm a genius after all !'

He got into bed again, and put his note-book under his pillow. He recited the poem several times. It was a pity it wasn't finished. He wondered why he hadn't finished it. Funny he couldn't remember doing it at all ! It showed how his brain worked hard when he was asleep.

Ern didn't mind his smarting hand now. He didn't even mind very much that his uncle was finding the loot. He was so very proud to think that he, Ern Goon, had written a first-rate pome — or so it seemed to Ern.

He fell asleep reciting the pome. He was warm and cosy in his bed. But Mr. Goon was not. He was far up on Christmas Hill, looking for loot that wasn't there !

17   UNPLEASANT NIGHT FOR MR. GOON

MR. GOON laboured up Christmas Hill in a cold wind. He kept a sharp eye for mysterious lights and noises and hoped fervently that cows and hens and cats wouldn't suddenly moo and cluck and yowl as they had done the time before.

They didn't. The night was very peaceful indeed. A little moon shone in the sky. No mysterious lights appeared. There were no noises of any kind except the little crunches made by Mr. Goon's big feet on the frosty hillside.

The old mill loomed up, faintly outlined in the darkness by the moonlight. Mr. Goon went cautiously. If the loot was there, the robbers might be about also. He felt for his truncheon. He remembered the man who had attacked him the other night, and once more thought proudly how he had sent him flying.

Everything was quiet in the old mill. A rat ran across the floor and Mr. Goon caught sight of its two eyes gleaming in the darkness. An owl moved up above, and then swept off on silent wings, almost brushing Mr. Goon's face, and making him jump.

After standing quite still for some time to make sure there was nobody there, Mr. Goon switched on his powerful torch. It showed a deserted, ruined old place, with holes in the roof and walls, and masses of old rubbish on the floor. There were holes in the floor too and Mr. Goon decided that he had better move cautiously or his feet would go through a rotten board.

His torch picked out what looked like a pile of rotten old

sacks. The loot might possibly be hidden under those ! Mr. Goon began to scrabble about in them, tossing them to one side. Clouds of dust choked him and a nasty smell rose around him.

'Pooh,' said Mr. Goon, and sneezed. His vast sneeze echoed round the old mill and would certainly have armed any robber within half a mile. Fortunately for him there was nobody about at all.

Mr. Goon then began on a pile of old boxes. He disturbed a nest of mice, and made a few rats extremely angry. One snapped at his hand and Mr. Goon hit at it with his torch. The torch missed the rat but hit the wall behind — and that was the end of the torch. It flared up once and then went out. No amount of shaking and screwing would make it light up again.

'Broken !' said Mr. Goon, and hurled the torch at the wall in anger. 'Drat that rat ! Now I can't see a thing.'

He had some matches in his pocket. He got them out and struck one. He saw some sacks in another corner. The match went out and Mr. Goon made his way across the floor to the sacks. His foot sank into a hole in the boarding and he had a hard struggle to get it out again.

By this time Mr. Goon was feeling so hot that he considered taking off his top-coat. He reached the sacks and began feeling about in them. Any cases of jewels ? Any cash-boxes ? His fingers felt something hard, and his heart leapt. Ah — this felt like a jewel-case !

He pulled the box out of the sacks. He opened it in the dark and dug his fingers in. Something sharp pricked him. Mr. Goon lighted a match to see what was in the box.

Rusty tacks and nails lay there, and Mr. Goon felt his heart sink. Only an old box of nails ! He licked his bleeding finger and thumb.

Mr. Goon worked very hard indeed for the next hour. He went through all the piles of dirty, dusty old rags and sacks and newspapers. He examined every old or broken box, and put his hand down every hole in the wall, disturbing various families of mice but nothing else. He had a most disappointing night.

He stood up and wiped his hot face, leaving smears of black all across it. His uniform was cloudy with the old fine dust of the mill. He scowled into the darkness.

'No loot here. Not a sign of it. If that boy Frederick has been pulling Ern's leg about this, I'll — I'll — I'll...'

But before Mr. Goon could make up his mind exactly what he could do to Fatty, a frightful screech sounded just above his head.

Mr. Goon's heart stood still. The hair on his head rose up straight. He swallowed hard and stood absolutely still. Whatever could that awful noise be ? Was somebody in pain or in terror ?

Something very soft brushed his cheek and another terrible screech sounded just by his ear. It was more than enough for Mr. Goon. He turned and fled out of the old mill at top speed, stumbling and almost falling as his foot caught in the rubbish lying around.

The screech owl saw him go, and considered whether to go after him and do another screech near his head. But the movement of a mouse down below on the floor caught his eye, and he flew silently down to catch it.

Mr. Goon had no idea that the frightful noise had come from the screech owl that lived in the old mill. All kinds of wild ideas went through his mind as he stumbled down the hill, but not once did he think of the right one — the harmless old owl on the rafters in the ruined roof.

His heart beat fast he panted loudly, and little drops of

perspiration ran down his face. Mr. Goon made up his mind very very firmly that never again would he go looking for loot on Christmas Hill in the dark. He'd rather let Ern go, yes, a hundred times rather !

He steadied down a little as he reached the bottom of the hill. He had wrenched his right ankle, and it made him limp. He thought of Ern safe in his warm bed and envied him.

He walked home more slowly, thinking hard. He thought of the rude 'pome' in Ern's book. He thought of all the clues and other notes he had read. He marvelled that Fatty should have let Ern go to look for the loot — if there *was* any loot. That boy Frederick was always at the bottom of everything !

Mr. Goon let himself into his house, went upstairs and switched on his bedroom light. He stared in horror at himself. What a sight he was ! Absolutely filthy. His face was criss-crossed with smears of dirt. His uniform gave out clouds of dust wherever he touched it. What a night !

Mr. Goon washed his face and hands. He took off his dirty uniform and put it outside on the little handling, because it smelt of the rubbish in the old mill. Ern found it there the next morning and was most astonished.

Mr. Goon got into bed tired out, and was soon snoring. Ern was asleep too, dreaming that he was broadcasting his poem about Mr. Goon. Lovaduck ! Fancy him, Ern Goon, at the B.B.C. !

In the morning Ern was sulky, remembering his smarting hand. He sulked too because he knew that his uncle had gone off to get the loot. Had he found it ? Would he tell him if he had ?

Mr. Goon was late down for breakfast. He was feeling very very tired. Also, in the bright light of morning, he couldn't help thinking that perhaps he had been rather foolish to rush off to Christmas Hill in the middle of the night like that. Loot in the old mill didn't seem nearly so likely now as it had seemed to him the night before.

Ern was eating his porridge when his uncle came down. They both scowled at one another. Ern didn't offer to get his uncle's porridge out of the pan for him.

'You get my porridge, and look slippy about it,' said Mr. Goon. Ern got up, holding his caned hand in a stiff kind of way as if he couldn't possibly use it. Mr. Goon saw him and snorted.

'If your hand hurts you, it's no more than you deserve, you rude, ungrateful boy.'

'I don't see what I've got to be grateful to you for,' mumbled Ern. 'Hitting me and caning me and always ticking me off. Can't do anything right for you. Serve you right if I ran away !'

'Gah !' said Mr. Goon, and began to eat his porridge even more noisily than Ern.

'Locking me in my bedroom so that I couldn't do my bit,' went on Ern, sniffling. 'And *you* went off after the loot, so you can't pretend you didn't, Uncle. It was a mean trick to play. You wait till I tell the others what you did.'

'If you so much as open your mouth about anything I'll take that cane and show you what it really *can* do !' said Mr. Goon. 'You just wait.'

Ern sniffed again. 'I'll run away ! I'll go to sea ! That'll make you sorry you treated me so crooly !'

'Gah !' said Mr. Goon again, and cut himself a thick slice of bread. 'Run away ! Stuff and nonsense. A boy like you hasn't got the courage of a mouse. Run away indeed !'

Breakfast was finished in silence. 'Now you clear away and wash up,' said Mr. Goon at the end. 'I've got to go out for the rest of the morning. You get that pot of green paint out of the shed and paint the fence nicely for me. No running round to those kids, see ?'

Ern said nothing. He just looked sulky. Mr. Goon, who had come down to breakfast in his dressing-gown, now put on his mackintosh and took his uniform into the garden to brush. Mrs. Murray next door was amazed to see the clouds of dust that came out of it.

'Been hiding in a dust-bin all night to watch for robbers ?' she inquired, popping her head over the fence.

Mr. Goon would have like to say 'Gah !' but that kind of exclamation didn't go down very well with Mrs. Murray. He just turned a dignified back and went on brushing.

Ern collected the dirty breakfast things and took them in the scullery to wash. He brooded over his wrongs. Uncle was hard and unkind and cruel. Ern had hoped to have such a wonderful time with Mr. Goon, and had actually meant to help him with his 'cases' — and all that had happened was that he was always getting into some kind of trouble with his uncle. There was no end to it.

'As soon as he's gone out of the house I'll pop round to Pip's,' thought Ern. 'The Find-Outers said they'd be there. I'll tell them about last night and how Uncle caned me. And I'll show them that wonderful pome. They'll be surprised to think I can do things like that in my sleep. I hope Fatty won't be cross because I couldn't go and look for the loot.'

Mr. Goon went off on his bicycle at last. Ern slipped out of the back door and made his way to Pip's. With him he took his portry note-book. He read the rude pome again and again and marvelled. 'I reely am a genious !' he thought, proudly. 'That's a wonderful pome even if it's rude.'

18   THINGS HAPPEN TO ERN

THERE was nobody in Pip's play-room except Bets. She had a cold and was not allowed out. The others had gone on an errand for Pip's mother.

'Hallo !' said Bets. 'How did you get on last night, Ern ? Did you find the loot ?' She giggled a little as she asked Ern. Poor Ern ! Had he gone loot-hunting all by himself ? What a simpleton he was !

Ern sat down and poured out all the happenings of the night before. Bets soon grew serious as she heard how Mr. Goon had caned poor Ern. She examined his hand and almost cried over it. Bets was very tender-hearted and could never bear any one to be hurt.

'Oh, Ern, poor Ern ! Does it hurt very much ? Shall I put something on your hand to make it better ? That horrid hateful Mr. Goon !' she said, and Ern glowed at having so much sympathy. He thought Bets was the nicest little girl he had ever met.

'You're nice' he said to Bets. 'I wish you were my sister. I bet Sid and Perce would like you too.'

Bets felt very guilty when she thought of all the tricks that the Find-Outers had played on Ern. She wished they hadn't now. Especially that poem-trick ! It was that poem, written in Ern's own handwriting by Fatty that had made Mr. Goon cane Ern. Oh dear! This was dreadful. They would have to own up to Ern and to Mr. Goon too. Fatty would hate that — but they couldn't go on deceiving Ern like that.

Ern opened his portry note-book. 'You know, Bets,' he said, ' I don't remember writing this pome at all. That's queer isn't it ? But it's a wonderful pome and I'm right-down proud of it. It was worth a caning ! Bets, do you think I can possibly be a genius, even a little one, if I can write a pome like that and not know I'd written it ? I must have done it in my sleep.'

Bets didn't know what in the world to say. She looked at Ern's serious face. Ern began to read the pome in a solemn voice, and Bets went off into giggles. She really couldn't help it.

'Don't you think it's a wonderful pome, Bets ?' said Ern, hopefully. 'Honestly, I didn't think I could write one like that. It's made me feel all hopeful, like.'

'I don't wonder it made your uncle angry,' said Bets. 'Poor Ern. I do hope your hand will feel better soon. Now wouldn't you like to go and meet the others ? They've gone to Maylins Farm for mother. You'll meet them coming back if you go now.

'Right,' said Ern, getting up. He buttoned his precious note-book into his coat pocket. 'Do you think Fatty will be annoyed about me not going to find the loot ?' he asked anxiously.

'Oh no. Not a bit, ' Bets assured him. Ern grinned at her, put on his cap and started off downstairs. He saw Mrs. Hilton crossing the hall below and hastily pulled off his cap again. He waited till she had gone and then darted out of the house.

He made his way through the village, keeping a sharp eye out for his uncle. He went up the lonely lane that led to Maylins Farm. It was a long and winding road, with few houses. Ern went along with his head down, muttering the first line of a new pome he was thinking of.

'The pore little mouse was all alone ...'

A car came down the lane. Ern looked up. A man was at the wheel, and another man at the back. Ern stood aside to let the car pass.

It went on a few yards and stopped. The man at the back leaned forward and said something to the driver. The driver opened his window and shouted back at Ern.

'Hey, boy ! Do you know the way to the post office ?'

'Yes,' said Ern. 'It's down there a little way . Turn to the left, up the hill a little way, and you'll see a ...'

'Jump in and show us, there's a good lad,' said the driver. 'Save us a lot of time. We've lost the way two or three times already. Here's half-a-crown if you'll help us.'

He held out half-a-crown and Ern's eyes brightened. He only had threepence a week pocket-money and half-a-crown seemed riches to him. He hopped in beside the driver at once. The man at the back had his face buried in a newspaper.

The car started off again — but instead of going off at the turning to the post office it swept on past it, took a left- hand turn and then a right-hand one, and then shot off at a great speed towards Marlow.

Ern was astonished. 'Here ! This isn't right !' he said. 'Where you going ?'

'You'll see,' said the man at the back, in a nasty sort of voice that sent a horrid little thrill down Ern's spine. 'We're going to show you what we do with interfering boys.'

Ern stared at the two men in alarm. 'What do you mean ? What have I interfered in ? I don't understand.'

'You soon will,' said the man at the back. 'Always poking your nose into this and that, aren't you, Frederick Trotteville ? You thought when you came along to the garage the other day you were being very clever, didn't you ?'

Ern simply couldn't make head or tail of what the sour-faced man at the back was saying. He felt very frightened.

'I'm not Frederick,' he said. 'I'm Ern Goon. My uncle is the policeman at Peterswood.'

'Don't waste your breath telling those tales to us,' said the driver, grimly. 'Trying to be so innocent ! You certainly *look* a simpleton — but you can't put it across us that you are. We know you all right.'

Ern gave it up. What with mysterious, rude pomes, canings, a furious uncle, and now two men kidnapping him, he simply didn't know what to think.

Kidnappers ! At that thought poor Ern shivered and shook. Fatty had said there were two gangs — one gang was kidnappers, the other robbers. Now he had got mixed up with the kidnappers ! This was a simply frightful thought.

He didn't know why the men thought he was Fatty. But they, of course, had only seen Fatty disguised as Ern, the day he had cycled over to Holland's garage. When they had spotted the real Ern wandering up the lane, they had had no doubt but that it was Fatty, the same boy they had seen with the dog at the garage.

Ern was taken to a garage some miles from Marlow, owned by Mr. Holland. He was driven into a big shed, and made to get out. A door led from the shed up a ladder into a small room. The men pushed Ern there.

'If you shout you'll get a hiding,' said Mr. Holland. 'You'll be here all day and if you're quiet you'll get food and drink. If you're not, you won't. We're going to take you somewhere else to-night where you can have a nice quiet time all by yourself till we decide what to do with you. It's time silly kids like you were stopped from poking your noses into other people's business.'

Ern was completely cowed. He sat down on some straw in the tiny room, and trembled till the men had gone out of the door and locked and bolted it. He looked for a window but there was none. The only light came in through a tiny

The man pushed Ern into the small room

skylight set in the roof.

Ern began to sniffle. He was no hero, poor Ern, and things were happening too fast for him. He sat there all the morning, miserable and frightened.

The door was unbolted and unlocked at half-past one, when Ern had begun to fear that he was going to be starved. A hand came in with a loaf of bread, a jar of potted meat and a jug of water. Nothing else. But Ern was so hungry that he ate the whole loaf, and the potted meat too, and drank the last drop of the water.

He was given no tea. At half-past four when it was almost dark, the door opened again and the men came in. 'Come on out,' said one of them. 'We're going.'

'Where to ?' stuttered Ern, afraid.

There was no answer. He was pushed down the ladder, into the shed, and into the back of the car. The two men got in at the front. The car backed out.

Ern was in despair. How could he let the others know anything ? He felt sure that if he were Fatty he would be able to find some way of telling the Find-Outers that something dreadful had happened to him.

He felt in his pocket. His clues were still there, all ten of them. Suppose he threw them out of the window one by one ? There *might* be a chance of one of the Find-Outers picking one of them up. They would recognize a clue immediately.

It was a very giant hope indeed, especially as Ern had no idea of where the car was going. He might be miles away from Peterswood. He peered out of the window to see if he could recognize anything at all in the darkness.

No, there was nothing to tell him where he was. But, wait a bit — wasn't that the post office in Peterswood ? Yes, it was ! They were actually going through Peterswood ! Ern wondered if he could let down the window far enough to throw out his clues one by one. He tried, but at once one of the men turned round.

'Dont't you dare to open the window ! If you think you're going to shout you can think again !'

'I'm not going to,' protested Ern. Then a really brilliant idea struck him. 'I feel sick, see ? I want air. Let me open the window a few inches. If you don't I'll be sick all over the car.'

The man gave an impatient exclamation. He leaned back and opened the window about two inches. Ern made a horrible noise as if he was on the point of being violently sick. He felt very clever indeed. The man opened the window a little more.

'If you dare to be sick in the car I'll box your ears !' he threatened.

Ern made a noise again, and at the same time threw out the button with the bit of cloth attached. Then he threw out the cigar-end. Next went the pencil-stub with E.H. on the end and then the rag.

Every now and again Ern made a horrible noise and the man glanced back anxiously. They were nearly there ! That wretched boy. Mr. Holland made up his mind to give him a fine old hiding if he spoilt the car.

Out went the next clue — the hanky with 'K' on. Then the broken shoe-lace — then the empty cigarette packet. After that the tiny bit of paper with the telephone number went fluttering into the road, and then the rusty old tin. That was the lot.

Ern leaned back, feeling pleased. Aha ! The clues he had found on Christmas Hill were going to be first-rate clues as to his whereabouts for all the Find-Outers. Ern was quite certain that people as clever as the Five Find-Outers would somehow find the clues and read them correctly.

The man looked round. 'Feel better ?' he said.

'I'm all right now,' said Ern, and grinned to himself in the darkness. He *was* clever ! He was surprised himself to think how clever he was. The man shut the window up again. The car was going slowly now, up a very narrow lane. The headlights were out. Only the side-lamps were on.

The headlights were flashed once as they came round a bend. The car slowed. Ern tried to see why but he couldn't. There came the creak and clang of gates, and the car moved on. It ran on to something smooth after a short while and stood still. Then, to Ern's terrific alarm the car suddenly shot straight downwards as if it were a lift ! Ern clutched the sides and gasped.

'Here we are,' said Mr. Holland's voice. 'Out you get, Frederick Trotteville. This is the place you were inquiring about — but you'll soon wish you had never never heard about it in your life ! Welcome to Harry's Folly !'

THE Find-Outers were very surprised when they got back to Bets, to hear that Ern had been sent to meet them.

'We never saw a sign of him,' said Fatty. 'I suppose he went home after all.'

They listened to Bets' account of what Ern had told her of the night before. Their faces became serious. It was one thing to pull Ern's leg to get a laugh out of him. It was quite another to cause him to get a caning.

'Golly ! And old Goon went loot-hunting on Christmas Hill instead of Ern. Won't he be wild when he knows it was a put-up job !' said Larry.

'We'll have to tell Ern — and Goon too — that I wrote the poem,' said Fatty. He looked uncomfortable. 'Goon will be furious. I shall get into a fine old row.'

'Yes, you will,' said Pip. 'He'll go round complaining again.'

'Ern was terribly terribly proud of the poem,' said Bets. 'He said that was the only thing that comforted him last night — the thought that he had written a wonderful poem like that, and hadn't even known he had. He thought he must have written it in his sleep. I simply couldn't bear to tell him he hadn't written it, Fatty.'

'It's a bit of a tangle, isn't it ?' said Daisy. 'In order to make Mr. Goon realize that he's caned Ern unfairly we've got to disappoint Ern by telling him the poem isn't his ! Poor old Ern ! I wish we hadn't pulled his leg so much. He's awfully silly, but he's quite harmless and sometimes very nice.'

'An awful coward though,' sid Pip. 'Look how he keeps giving everything away ! It's a good thing it wasn't a *real* mystery we set him on. He'd have given absolutely every single thing away to Goon.'

'Yes. He can't really be trusted,' said Daisy. 'But I do feel sorry about this. I wonder what's happened to him now. I suppose he went home.'

But Ern hadn't gone home, as we know. He didn't appear at dinner-time, and Mr. Goon who had got quite a nice dinner of stew and dumplings, felt most annoyed.

That pestering boy ! He hadn't painted the fence green as he had been told to. Now he was late for dinner.

'Well, I shan't wait — and if he doesn't come, I'll eat the lot !' said Mr. Goon. 'That'll learn him !'

So he ate the lot, and felt so very full afterwards that he sat down in his armchair by the kitchen fire, undid a few buttons and immediately fell sound asleep. Mr. Goon was tired after his night's hunting up on Christmas Hill. He slept and he slept. He slept the whole afternoon away. He didn't even hear the telephone ringing. He slept solidly all through the rrrr-ring, rrrr-ring, his snores almost drowning the bell.

He awoke at half-past five. He yawned, sat up, stretched, and looked at the clock. He looked again. What ! Almost half-past five ! The clock couldn't be right ! Mr. Goon took out his big watch and looked at that too. Why, that said the same !

'I've been asleep three solid hours !' said Mr. Goon quite shocked. 'Shows how tired I was. Where's Ern ? Why, he's almost let the fire out, and there's no kettle boiling for tea !'

He gave a loud yell, 'ERN ! ERN !'

No Ern came. Mr. Goon frowned. Where was that boy ? He hadn't come in to dinner ! Now he hadn't come in to tea. Gone round to those kids, he supposed, and they'd kept him for meals. Spun a wonderful tale about his crool uncle ! Ho, Mr. Goon would have something to say about that.

Mr. Goon made himself a cup of tea very quickly. He didn't stop for anything to eat. He suddenly remembered that he was supposed to go along to Miss Lacey's and hear about two of her hens being stolen. How could he have forgotten that ? If he'd gone about half-past four he could have had tea in the kitchen with Mrs. Tanner the cook. Fine gingerbread she made every week, as Mr. Goon very well knew.

Mr. Goon went off to Miss Lacey's. She was out. Mrs. Tanner the cook told Mr. Goon that Miss Lacey was annoyed because Mr. Goon hadn't come along sooner. So the policeman didn't have a chance to sit in a warm kitchen and have a piece of new gingerbread. He was most annoyed, and went pompously down he steps into the darkness of the drive.

He wondered again where Ern was. Bad boy to stay away like that. Pretending he had run away, perhaps ! Mr. Goon gave a small snort. Ern would never have the spunk to do a thing like that.

But a very small doubt crept into his mind at that moment. Suppose Ern really *had* run away ? No, no, how silly ! He must be somewhere with those kids.

Mr. Goon walked up the road that led to the post office. It was dark and he shone his torch on the ground before him. It suddenly picked up something in its beam. A button !

Mr. Goon always collected any button or pin he found. He picked this button up. It had a bit of cloth attached to it. Why — he knew that button and bit of cloth ! It was one of Ern's clues !

'So Ern's been along this way,' thought Mr. Goon. He picked it up. 'What's Ern doing, chucking his clues about like this ? At — here's a pencil-end ! I bet it's the clue he found with E.H. at the end. Yes, it is !'

He missed the rag, which had blown under the hedge. He walked on some way and saw a ragged handkerchief. He had a felling it would have 'K' on. So it had. Another of Ern's clues. How extraordinary, thought Mr. Goon. Then an idea came into his head.

'It's those kids again, playing a trick on me ! They've spotted me walking down here, and they've got Ern to chuck down his clues to lead me on ! They'll jump out at me round the corner or wet that pestering dog round my ankles. Well, I'm not going any farther ! I'm going straight round to Mr. and Mrs. Hilton to complain !'

Mr. Goon made his way to Pip's house, filled with indignation. Getting Ern to throw down clues like that to lead him up the way just for a track ! What did they take him for ?

Mr. and Mrs. Hilton were out. 'But the five children are here,' said Lorna the maid. 'If it's them you're wanting to see, sir ?'

'I'll see them,' said Mr. Goon. 'You go up the stairs first and tell Master Trotteville to keep his dog under control. Nasty snappy little beast that is.'

When Lorna appeared with her news the Find-Outers looked surprised and Bets felt alarmed. Oh dear — what had happened now ?

Mr. Goon walked in. He put down the clues on the table. 'Another of your silly tricks, I suppose ?' he said, glaring round. 'Getting Ern to chuck these about where you knew I'd find them. Ho — very childish, I must say !'

The Five Find-Outers gazed at the clues and recognized them. Fatty picked up the button. He was puzzled.

'Where is Ern ?' he asked Mr. Goon. 'We haven't seen him all day.'

Mr. Goon snorted. 'Think I believe that ? Well, *I* haven't seen him all day, either ! But I bet he's hidden in this house somewhere ! That's called aiding and abetting somebody, see ?'

Fatty thought Mr. Goon was being rather silly. 'Mr. Goon. We — have — NOT seen Ern since early this morning when he came along here for a few words with Bets. Where *is* he ?'

Mr. Goon began to feel slightly alarmed. There was the ring of truth in Fatty's voice. If these kids hadn't seen Ern all day, where *was* he then ? Surely he couldn't have run away ? No, that wouldn't be in the least like Ern.

He stared at the silent children. 'How do *I* know where that dratted boy is ?' he said, raising his voice a little. 'Worries the life out of me, he does — and you do your best to do the same. And let me tell you *I* know all about this mystery of yours ! Yes, I know more about robbers and kidnappers on Christmas Hill than *you* do !'

'I'm so glad to hear it,' said Fatty, in the very polite voice that made Mr. Goon go purple. 'Perhaps you can solve it more quickly than we can. The thing is — where is Ern ? He was very upset when he saw Bets this morning. Apparently you attacked him in the night, Mr. Goon.'

Mr. Goon could hardly speak. Then he stuttered with outraged feelings. 'Me ! *Attack* him ! I never heard of such a tale. I gave him the cane, see, for being rude.'

'Well,' said Fatty, and hesitated. Should he tell Mr. Goon now about the poem — that *he* had written it and not Ern ? No, perhaps it would be best to tell Ern first. But where *was* Ern ?

Fatty felt really puzzled. The things Mr. Goon had put on the table were certainly Ern's 'clues' — the things he had picked up on Christmas Hill. They were not all there, though.

Fatty inquired about the rest.

'Didn't you find any more clues, Mr. Goon ? Are those all you picked up ?'

'I don't know how many more you told Ern to put down for me to follow,' snorted Mr. Goon. 'But I wasn't going to go wandering over half the town to find any more !'

'Where did you find these ?' asked Larry.

'As if you didn't know !' said Mr. Goon, sarcastically. 'Where you put them, of course — or where you told Ern to put them. Up Candlemas Lane.'

'What could Ern have been doing there ?' wondered Bets.

'Don't you really know where Ern is ?' said Mr. Goon, after a pause. Another little doubt was creeping in on him. Wouldn't it be awkward if Ern *had* run away because he, Mr. Goon, had caned him ? Perhaps he had gone home to his mother. Mr. Goon decided to make inquiries when he got back, and find out. He could ring up a friend of his who knew Ern's mother, and get him to slip round quietly to Ern's home and find out if he as there.

'No. We don't know where he is,' said Fatty, impatiently. 'Haven't we kept telling you that ? I shouldn't be surprised, Mr. Goon, if poor old Ern hasn't run away to sea, or something, after your cruel attack on him last night !'

Mr. Goon for once had nothing whatever to say. Fatty's suggestion, coming on top of his own fear that Ern might have run away, made him quite tongue-tied. It was all very very awkward. He began to wish he hadn't caned Ern the night before.

He went soon after that, much to Pip's relief. He and Bets were afraid that their parents might arrive home before Mr. Goon left, and they didn't want that to happen.

'It's very queer,' said Fatty, letting Buster off the lead, where he had held him tightly for the last quarter of an hour.

'We haven't seen Ern at all to-day. Only Bets saw him this morning. And now here's this tale of clues scattered about in Candlemas Lane. Why should Ern do that?'

'Hole in his pocket,' suggested Pip.

'Not very likely,' said Fatty.

'Perhaps he got tired of his clues and just *threw* them away,' said Bets.

'Silly idea,' said Pip, scornfully.

'I'm going out with my torch to see if there are any more of Ern's clues scattered about,' said Fatty. 'I feel as if there's something wrong somewhere. I'm worried about our Ern!'

He went off by himself with Buster, his torch shining its beam in front of him. He made his way to Candlemas Lane.

He saw nothing in the way of clues at first — but farther on, at the turning out of the lane into the track that ran across the fields for a mile or two to Harry's Folly, Fatty found three or four more of the clues. He stood thoughtfully in the track, puzzling things out in his mind. Where was Ern? What in the world could have happened to him?

ERN didn't come home that night. By the time nine o'clock came Mr. Goon had worked himself into a terrible state of mind. He imagined all kinds of things happening to Ern. He had been run over. He had run off to sea and was already in a ship, being very seasick. He had gone home to his mother and Sid and Perce and told terrible tales about his uncle. All these things and many others flashed through Mr. Goon's worried mind.

He tried to find out if Ern had gone home, but no, he wasn't there. Whatever was Mr. Goon to do ! He felt terribly guilty now. He, Ern's uncle, had driven him away ! What would people think ?

'I'll stay up till eleven to see if Ern comes,' thought Mr. Goon. 'I'll put some bacon and eggs ready to cook for him when he comes — and I'll hot up some cocoa. I'll go and put a hot-water bottle in his bed.'

Mr. Goon felt quite sentimental about Ern as the night wore on, and no Ern appeared. He remembered all Ern's good points and forgot the bad ones. He felt ashamed when he remembered how he had boxed Ern's ears and caned him.

'Oh Ern, you come back and we'll get on fine,' thought Mr. Goon over and over again. Eleven o'clock struck. Mr. Goon made up the fire again. Then he loosened his clothes and settled down in the armchair. He would wait up for Ern all night.

But suppose he didn't come ? Mr. Goon considered this with a very serious face. He'd have to ring up Inspector Jenks and report his disappearance — and the first question asked would be 'Was the boy in any trouble before he disappeared ?' And what was Mr. Goon to say to that ?

He fell asleep about midnight. He slept soundly through the night, and awoke in the morning, very cold and stiff, with the fire out — and no Ern anywhere ! And now Mr. Goon really did begin to feel frightened. Something *had* happened to Ern !

The telephone bell rang, and Mr. Goon almost jumped out of his skin. He went to answer it. It was Fatty, asking if Ern had come back.

'No,' said Mr. Goon. 'He hasn't. Have you heard anything about him ?'

'Not a word,' said Fatty. 'It's pretty serious, this, Mr. Goon. Looks as if your attack on Ern has sent him off.'

Mr. Goon was too upset even to get angry over Fatty's persistence in calling the caning an attack. 'What am I to do ?' he said, in a dismal voice. 'You might not think it, Master Trotteville, but I'm very fond of Ern.'

'You hid your affection very well then,' came Fatty's smooth voice over the telephone. Mr. Goon shook his fist at the receiver. That dratted cheeky boy ! But the policeman soon forgot his anger in his worries about Ern.

'I'd better go to Inspector Jenks, I suppose,' said Mr. Goon, after a pause. 'Master Trotteville, do you think this here mystery on Christmas Hill's got anything to do with Ern's disappearance ? These kidnappers and what-nots ?'

'You never know,' said Fatty, in a serious voice. 'Er — did you find the loot the other night, Mr. Goon ?'

'That's none of your business,' said Mr. Goon, shortly. 'Well — I suppose I'd better go and see the Inspector.'

'Mr. Goon, I don't know if you'd like to wait till to-night,' said Fatty, suddenly. 'I've got an idea at the back of my mind which might just be the right one. But I can't tell you any more than that. It's *possible* I should be able to tell you where Ern is if you like to wait another day before reporting that he's vanished.'

Mr. Goon was only too glad to clutch at any straw. He was dreading having to go to the Inspector. He didn't want to say how he'd caned Ern the night before he went — nor did he want to say anything about the rude 'pome.' Why, the Inspector might even want to read it ! Mr. Goon's face burned at the very thought.

'Right,' said Mr. Goon. I'll wait another day. I'll wait up to-night till I hear from you. Poor Ern — I do hope he's all right.'

'I'll give you a ring on the phone to-night, as soon as I know anything,' said Fatty.

He rang off. He was at his own house, and the Find-Outers were due down at the shed at any moment. Fatty went with Buster down the garden, just in time to see the others coming in.

'No Ern yet,' he said. 'Goon's getting all worked up about him. And so he should ! He doesn't like the thought of having to go and tell the Inspector how he whacked him in the middle of the night !'

'What *has* happened to Ern ?' said Pip. 'I could hardly get to sleep last night for worrying about him — and thinking about those clues Old Clear-Orf found in Candlemas Lane.'

'I found some more last night,' said Fatty. 'And two of them were along the track that leads across the field to Harry's Folly ! I believe Ern's there.'

'But why ? Do you mean he went off across the fields to explore Harry's Folly, or something ?' demanded Larry. 'But he doesn't know anything about *that* mystery !'

'I know he doesn't,' said Fatty. 'All the same I think he's there. I think he must have been *taken* there, but I can't imagine why. Even if Holland came along in his car and saw Ern, why should he take him away ?'

'I expect he thought Ern was *you*,' said Bets, suddenly. 'After all, you were disguised as Ern when you went over there, weren't you — and you *might* have given the game away to him, Fatty, when you mentioned Harry's Folly. He might have been scared, thinking you knew something, and decided to capture you !'

Fatty stared at Bets, thinking hard. Then he banged the table and made them all jump. 'That's it. Bets has got it ! They've kidnapped Ern thinking he was me — and they think I know too much about Harry's Folly, because I spoke about it as I did ! Good old Bets. She's the best Find-Outer of the lot !'

Bets was thrilled at this unexpected praise. She blushed red. 'Oh — we'd all have thought of it soon !' she said.

'Yes — Bets is right. They must have mistaken Ern for me — and — and — yes, I wonder if Ern could have thrown away those clues to warn us something was up — even to show us the way to follow ?'

'That's too clever a thing for Ern to do,' said Daisy.

'Yes. It is a bit clever,' said Fatty thoughtfully. 'But in desperation Ern might be cleverer than he usually is. Tell me, Bets — what time did Ern leave you ?'

'About half-past ten,' said Bets. 'He said he was going off to meet you straightway. He should have met you coming back about three quarters of the way there.'

'I'm going out to make a few inquiries,' said Fatty. 'Stay here, all of you. I'll be back.'

Fatty went into the village, and then turned up the way to Maylins Farm. He saw a small girl swinging on a gate and called to her.

'Hallo, Margery. Did you see Ern Goon here yesterday ?

You know Ern, don't you ? The policeman's nephew.'

'Yes,' said Margery. 'I saw him going up this way yesterday morning. He didn't see me because I was hiding.'

'Did you see him come back again ?' asked Fatty. 'You saw us all walking back, didn't you, later on ? Did you see Ern again ?

'No, I didn't,' said Margery. 'There was a big car came down a little while after, and nearly knocked me over. Then you came with the others. That's all. What's Ern done ?'

'Nothing,' said Fatty. 'Here's a penny. Catch !'

He walked on up the road thinking hard. Ern had gone to meet them up there — but hadn't come back. But a car had come along soon after. Was it Holland's car, cruising round to snoop for Fatty, perhaps — and finding Ern instead, thinking *he* was Fatty.

Some way up, in a very lonely part of the road, Fatty saw where a car had suddenly put on its brakes and swerved a little to a quick stop. He looked at the marks on the road thoughtfully, his mind working. This was probably where the men in the car had met Ern, thought he was Fatty, stopped suddenly, asked Ern some question to get him into the car — and gone off with him.

The car wouldn't go to Harry's Folly in the daytime, that was certain. It was more likely it would have gone to Marlow or to the other garage Holland owned. The men would have locked Ern up somewhere for the day — and then perhaps they would have brought him back to Harry's Folly.

'And when Ern saw he was going through Peterswood he suddenly thought of chucking out all the clues he had, knowing we'd recognize them, and read them correctly !' said Fatty. 'Well ! If Ern really did do that he's cleverer than we ever thought him !'

He went back to the others, Buster trotting soberly at his

heels. Buster always knew when his master was thinking hard, and never bothered him then.

Fatty told the others what he thought. They listened in silence. 'It was Bets' sudden idea that put me on to everything else,' said Fatty. 'Well — I've got to go and rescue Ern if I can — and perhaps I can solve this mystery at the same time ! I'll go to-night.'

'Oh Fatty — don't do that !' begged Bets. 'Can't you ring up Inspector Jenks and tell him all you've said to us.'

'No,' said Fatty. 'Because I might be absolutely wrong in everything ! Ern *might* be hiding in an old barn somewhere, sulking, to give Goon a fright. And what do we really know of this other mystery ? Hardly anything ! Not as much as Old Clear-Orf knows of the imaginary one !'

'We'll come with you then, Fatty, if you're going to-night,' said Larry.

'You can't. You're forbidden,' said Fatty. 'In any case I wouldn't let the girls come.'

'But we're not going to solve a mystery — we're going to rescue Ern,' protested Pip. 'That's quite different.'

'I'm going by myself,' said Fatty. 'I shall take a rope-ladder to get over the wall — and sacks to put on those spikes at the top so that I can climb over easily. Then — aha — there'll be dark dire deeds, as Ern would say !'

'Oh *don't*,' said Bets, with a shiver. 'I wish you wouldn't go, Fatty. Please don't !'

'Well, I feel rather bad about Ern,' said Fatty, seriously. 'I feel as if he's had very bad luck all round — what with us pulling his leg — and Goon caning him for what he hadn't done — and then getting kidnapped because I once disguised myself as Ern. It's up to me to do *something*. I really *must* go, Bets, old thing.'

'I suppose you must,' said Bets, with a sigh.

They hunted for the rope-ladder, which was at last discovered on a shelf, neatly rolled up. Then they found sacks. Larry examined Fatty's torch to make sure the battery was all right. Bets slipped a bar of chocolate into his pocket. They all felt rather solemn, somehow, as if Fatty was going on a long long journey !

'I'll start about half-past eight, after I've had dinner with my mother and father,' said Fatty. 'They are going out to a bridge party afterwards, so I shall be able to slip out easily without any one knowing.'

'Half-past eight ?' said Larry and Pip together. 'Sure you'll start then ?'

'Yes. The moon won't be up. I shan't be seen at all,' said Fatty. 'I shall take the same path over the field by the stream as we did before. Sorry you can't come with me, Pip and Larry.'

They looked at him solemnly. 'Yes,' said Pip. 'Spitty ! Well — good luck, Fatty !'

21   INTO THE HEART OF THE MYSTERY

FATTY set out after dinner that night, exactly at half-past eight. He had with him the rope-ladder, and the sacks. Buster was left at home, whining and scratching at the shed-door. He was very angry that Fatty should have left him behind.

Fatty made his way to the little bridge across the Bourne. He then walked cautiously along on the frosty bank of the stream. Two shadowy figures came out from behind a tree and followed him quietly.

Fatty's sharp ears caught the soft crunch-crunch somewhere behind him. He stopped at once. He stiffened when he heard the footsteps coming quietly nearer. He saw the dim outline of a tree nearby and slipped behind it.

The footsteps drew nearer. He heard whispers. Two people then. Were they after him ? What were they doing in the fields at that time of night ?

Just as they passed, Fatty's sharp ears caught one word in the whispered conversation. 'Buster ...'

He grinned. He knew who it was following him now. It was Larry and Pip ! They were't going to be left out, whether they had been forbidden or not ! Good old Larry and Pip !

He tiptoed after them. They soon stopped, not being able to hear Fatty in front of them any more. He spoke in a mournful voice just near them.

'Beware ! Beware !'

Larry and Pip jumped violently. Then Pip stretched out his hand and touched Fatty. 'Fatty ! It's you ! Idiot ! You did make us jump !'

'We had to come, Fatty,' said Larry. 'We couldn't let you go alone. We've decided that, mystery or not, we're all in it !'

Fatty gave Larry's arm a squeeze. 'Nice of you. Glad of your company, of course. Come on.'

They went on together, the three of them. After some time they came to where the narrow cart-track to Harry's Folly ran near to the stream. They left the bank and went into the little lane. They walked on steadily and silently in the darkness till they came to the iron gates. They were shut of course. A light shone in the lodge nearby.

'We won't get over the wall here,' said Fatty. 'I don't think there *are* any dogs belonging to the lodge-keeper, but you never know. We'll walk round the wall a bit and choose a place some way off.'

They walked round the high wall. The sky was clearing now, and there was a fading starlight which helped them to see things better.

'This will do,' said Fatty. He hunted about and found a heavy stone. He tied it to the end of a rope he had, which, in its turn, was fastened to the top of the rope ladder.

'Help me chuck this stone over the wall,' said Fatty to Larry. The two boys took the stone between them. 'One, two, three, go !' said Fatty, and they heaved the stone up as hard as they could. It rose up and went neatly over the wall, dragging its short tail of rope behind it.

As the stone fell heavily to the ground on the other side, the rope-ladder was pulled up the wall by the rope attached to the falling stone. It rose up and stayed hanging on the wall. Fatty gave it a tug.

'Just right ! Part of it's over the other side — and one of the rungs has got firmly held by the spikes at the top. Pip, you're the lightest. Shin up to the top, and we'll chuck the sacks for you to put on the spikes. Then sit on them, and make the ladder fast for us. Larry and I are heavy.'

Pip was light. The ladder shifted a little as he went up, but held firmly enough. The others threw him up the sacks. Pip arranged them on the top of the wall so that they lay like a cushion over the spikes, preventing them from using their sharp points.

Pip sat on the sacks, and made the ladder as firm as he could for the others. Fatty gave it a hard tug. Yes. It was all right.

He made Pip come down again. Then he himself went up, sat on the sacks, pulled up the rope-ladder so that half hung down one side the ground and half the other — made it fast so that it could not slip, and then went down the other side, into the grounds of Harry's Folly. The others followed, clambering up one side and down the other.

'Good !' said Fatty, in a whisper. 'Now, we'll find the house !'

They made their way through thick trees. Fatty marked them with white chalk as he passed, for he was a little afraid that without some guide he might not be able to find his way back to the rope-ladder — and they *might* be in a hurry later on !

After quite a long walk the old house loomed up before them in the starlight. It looked forbidding in the dark night. Pip pressed close to the others, rather scared.

There was not a light to be seen anywhere. Fatty could dimly make out great shutters bolted across the windows. Then they came to a long flight of stone steps. The boys went up them silently. They led to a nail-studded front door, also tightly closed. The mansion seemed completely and utterly deserted.

'Do you think Ern is hidden somewhere here ?' whispered Larry, his mouth close to Fatty's ear.

'Yes', whispered back Fatty. 'There's some mystery about this place — it's used for something it shouldn't be used for, I'm sure, though I don't know what. And I'm certain Ern is here somewhere. Come on — we've still got a good way to go round the house.'

In the darkness the house seemed really enormous. The walls were endless to the boys as they walked cautiously beside them. There was no light anywhere and no noise at all.

They came to the back of the old house. A pond gleamed dully in the starlight, frozen over. Two big flights of steps led down to it.

'What an enormous place !' whispered Pip. 'I wonder what its history is.'

'Shhhhhh !' hissed Fatty, and they all stood like stone, pressing against one another. They had heard a noise — a very curious noise. It seemed to come from underground !

'What is it ? It's like some great machine at work,' whispered Larry. 'Where is it ?'

They went on round the house, and came to what must have been either stables or garages. These also were enormous. A small door stood open in one of the garages, for Fatty could hear it creaking a little as it swung in the cold night wind. He made his way to it, the others following.

'Come on. This door's open. Let's go into the garage,' whispered Fatty, and in they went. It was dark, and the boys could see nothing at all. The noise they had heard was now quite gone.

Fatty cautiously got out his torch and shone it quickly round. They saw a vast garage, with shadowy corners. In front of them was a smooth expanse of floor.

Then a most terrifying thing happened ! The floor in front of them suddenly made a noise, moved, and sank swifly down out of sight, into darkness ! Fatty was so tremendously amazed that he couldn't even switch off his torch ! He just stood there with it still shining, and in its light the boys saw the floor sink away below them. Another foot or two and they would have gone with it into blackness, goodness knows where !

Fatty snapped off his torch. Larry gripped him in fright. 'Fatty. What's happened ? Did you see the floor go ?'

'Yes. It's a movable floor, worked by machinery,' said Fatty. 'Gave me a scare to see it disappear like that, though ! It hasn't gone down for nothing. Let's hide behind these big barrels and see if the floor comes back again.'

They hid behind the barrels for some time, getting cold and chilled. Nothing happened. Fatty flicked his torch quickly on and off again. The floor was still gone ! A vast empty hole yawned below.

Fatty cautiously went to the edge, put on his torch and tried to light up the depth of blackness below him. A noise warned him to get back into hiding. He ran for his barrel.

A light, first dim and then brighter now came up from the hole where the great floor had been. Noises came up from below too. Then voices shouted. Then came a curious whining sound — and the floor came up again, fitting into place ! It really did behave like a lift that was nothing but a floor.

On the floor were three cars. None had any headlights on, only side-lamps.

Low voices spoke.

'All ready ? Five minutes between each of you. You know what to do. Go now, Kenton.'

The great garage doors now rolled silently back. The first

car rolled off the floor and went quietly out of the garage. It disappeared down the drive. When it came to the gate-keeper's lodge, it switched its headlights on and off once and waited. Peters came out, opened the gates quickly, the car slid out, and the gates closed again.

Five minutes later the three boys saw the second car go. Then after another five minutes the third one went. Then the garage doors were shut again, and the only man left in the garage whistled softly.

He went and stood on the floor, and waited. After a minute or two the floor slid downwards again, leaving the same yawning hole as before. Then there was a dead silence and complete darkness.

'Larry ! Pip ! Are you there ?' came Fatty's whisper. 'We must do something or other now. We'll have to get down underground, I think. That's apparently where everything goes on. Are you game to ?'

'Yes,' said both, in a whisper. Fatty switched on his torch in a corner and showed the others some strong coiled wire rope he had found, used for towing one car behind another.

'If we tie this to that beam, see — and let the rope drop down the hole — we can swarm down in one by one.'

It didn't take long to make the rope secure to the beam. The end was dropped into the hole by Pip. Then Fatty tested it. It held all right. He sat down on the floor and took hold of the rope.

'I'll wait for you at the rope's end,' he whispered. 'Follow me quickly.'

Down he went easily, as if he was performing on the ropes at school. Pip followed and then Larry. Soon they stood far down underground, in complete darkness. As they stood there they heard a noise of whirring and clattering some way off and a faint light came from that direction. Fatty saw the outline of a wide passage, and went down it, the others keeping close by him.

They followed the wide passage, which wound round and round rather like an enormous spiral stairway. 'We're going down into the bowels of the earth !' whispered Larry. 'Whatever's this curious winding passage, Fatty.'

'It's where cars come up to go on to that automatic floor,' said Fatty. 'Or go down ! Ah — here we are !'

From their dark corner the boys now looked out into an enormous workshop. Machines whirred and clattered. There were cars everywhere ! Two were being sprayed with blue cellulose paint. Another was being scraped. A fourth was almost in pieces. Others stood about with nobody working on them.

'What sort of place is this, Fatty ?' asked Larry in a whisper, puzzled.

'I'm not absolutely sure,' said Fatty. 'But I rather think it's a receiving place for stolen cars. They are brought here in the dark, put on the moving floor, taken down here and completely altered so that nobody would ever know them again. Then they are sent above-ground again at night — and, I imagine sold for a colossal sum with faked log-books!'

'Whew !' said Larry. 'I heard my father saying the other day that the police were completely baffled over the amount of stolen cars disappearing lately. I bet this is where they come to. My word, Fatty — what a find !'

22   A STRANGE NIGHT

'I SAY, Fatty, look — who's that coming down those stairs at the end ?' said Pip, suddenly. 'He must be the Boss. See the way the men straighten up and salute him.'

'It's Mr. Holland !' said Fatty. 'Oho, Mr. Holland, so this is your little hide-out ! You knew far more about Harry's Folly than you wanted to admit. What business he must do in stolen cars !'

'I wonder how many of the men in his garage at Marlow know about this,' said Pip.

'None of them, I should imagine,' said Fatty. 'He keeps those garages of his as a very nice cover for himself. But this is his real line. My word, Inspector Jenks would like to know about this little nest of cars !'

The men had evidently had some kind of order to knock off work for a meal or drink, for one by one they left their jobs and disappeared into a farther room. Mr. Holland went with them.

The workshop was deserted. 'Now's our chance,' whispered Fatty. 'We must scoot to those stairs over there — the ones Mr Holland came down — and go up them. It's our only chance of finding Ern.'

They ran quietly to the stairs, and were up them long before the men returned to the workshop. The stairway was spiral, like the ascending passage-way to the place where the movable floor was. But this passage-way was very narrow and much steeper. The boys panted a little as they went. At the top of the stairs was a wide landing. Doors opened off it. Another flight of steps led upwards.

'Queer place !' said Fatty. 'Must have been used in the war for something very hush-hush, as I said before. Something very secret must have been made down in that vast workshop — goodness knows what. Bombs perhaps !'

The boys looked round at all the closed doors, fearing that one might open suddenly and somebody come out and challenge them. Fatty looked up the next flight of steps. 'I suppose those lead to the ground floor of the mansion,' he said. 'Well — what shall we do ? Try these doors or go up the stairs ?'

At that very moment there came a familiar sound — a rather forlorn, hollow cough.

'Ern !' said Pip at once. 'I'd know that cough anywhere, It's so like Goon's. Ern is in one of these rooms !'

'That one, I think,' said Fatty and went quietly to a door opposite. He cautiously turned the handle — but the door would not open. Then Fatty saw that the door was bolted — and probably locked too, for the key was on his side of the door.

He unbolted the door carefully. He unlocked it. He pushed it open and looked in. Ern was lying on a bed, a pencil in his hand, his portry note-book beside him. He was muttering something to himself.

'Ern !' said Fatty.

Ern sat up so suddenly that his note-book flew to the floor. He gazed at the three boys in astonishment that changed to the utmost delight. He threw himself off the bed and ran to them. He flung his arms round Fatty.

'Fatty ! I knew you'd come ! I knew you'd follow the clues I threw out of the car. Fatty, the kidnappers got me— I—Oooh, I've had the most awful time trying to tell them I don't know anything at all. They keep saying I'm you, Fatty ! They're all potty.'

'Sh !' said Fatty. 'Are you quite all right, Ern ? They haven't hurt you, have they ?'

'No,' said Ern. 'But they don't give me much food. And they said they'd starve me to-morrow if I don't answer their questions properly. But I don't know the answers. Fatty, let's go !'

'Larry — go to the door and keep watch,' ordered Fatty. 'Tell me at once if there's any sound of somebody coming up that spiral stairway. At once, mind !'

He turned back to Ern, who was now almost in tears with excitement. 'Listen, Ern—can you do something really brave ?'

'Coo ! I don't know,' said Ern, doubtfully.

'Well, listen,' said Fatty. 'We're right in the very middle of a great big mystery here—and I want to get to the police and tell them about it before the men are warned that somebody knows their secret. Now, Ern—if we take you away with us to-night, the men will know their game is up, for they'll find you gone and know that some one has rescued you. So will you stay here, locked up, all night long, in order to let the men think everything is all right — and wait till the police come in the morning ?'

'I can't do that,' said Ern, almost crying. 'You don't know what it's like, to be a prisoner like this and not know what's going to happen to you. I can't even think of any portry.'

'Aren't you brave enough to do this one thing ?' said Fatty, sadly. 'I did want to think well of you, Ern.'

Ern stared at Fatty, who looked back at him solemnly.

'All right,' said Ern. 'I'll do it, see ! I'll do it for *you*, Fatty, because you're a wonder, you are ! But I don't feel brave about it. I feel all of a tremble.'

'When you feel afraid to do a thing and yet do it, that's *real* bravery,' said Fatty. 'You're a hero, Ern !'

Ern was so bucked at these words that he now felt he would have stayed locked up for a week if necessary ! He beamed at Fatty.

'Did Bets tell you about the wonderful pome I wrote in my sleep ?' he asked anxiously. 'You should see it. Fatty. Lovaduck, I feel so proud when I remember it. It's the best pome I ever wrote. I don't know when I've felt so pleased about anything. I feel reel proud of myself.'

Now was the time for Fatty to confess to Ern that he had played a trick on him and written out the poem in Ern's own handwriting — but Fatty, looking at Ern's proud face, simply hadn't the heart to tell him. Ern would be so bitterly disappointed ! Let him think it was his own poem, if he was so proud of it. Fatty felt so embarrassed about the whole thing that he almost blushed. Whatever had possessed him to play such an idiotic trick on Ern ?

'Ssssst !' suddenly came warningly from Larry and Pip. Fatty gave Ern a pat on the back, murmured, 'Good fellow, see you to-morrow !' melted out of the room, closed, locked and bolted the door in an amazingly deft and silent way, and then pulled Larry and Pip up the farther flight of stairs.

They had no sooner got up than Mr. Holland appeared at the top of the spiral stairway. He went into one of the rooms. The three boys did not dare to go down again.

'Better go on up to the top of these stairs and see where we are,' whispered Fatty. So up they went. They soon found themselves on the ground floor of the great mansion. Fatty flicked on his torch. The boys shivered.

Cobwebs hung everywhere. Dust rose from the floor as they trod over it. A musty, sour smell hung over everything. Fatty looked at his watch. 'Do you know it's almost one o'clock !' he said, his whisper echoing round the room mysteriously. 'Let's get out of here somehow and go and give the warning to Inspector Jenks.'

But they could not get out ! Shutters closed the windows on the outside, so even if the boys could have unfastened a window they could not have undone the shutters. Every outside door they tried was locked, but without a key ! It was just like a nightmare, wandering through the dark, dusty house, unable to get out anywhere.

'This is frightful,' said Fatty at last 'I've never felt so completely done in my life. There's nowhere we can get out at all !'

'Well — we shall have to see if we can go back the way we came,' said Larry. 'We can't go through that enormous workshop whilst the men are at work there. We'll have to wait till they go for a meal again. Come on, let's go down the stairs to Ern's landing and see if any one is there.'

They went silently down. The landing was empty. No sound came from Ern's room. He was not asleep though. He was awake, feeling very solemn and exultant. He was being a hero, being really brave for Fatty's sake. Ern felt thrilled — and hoped intensely that Mr. Holland wouldn't come and badger him again with questions he couldn't answer. Suppose he asked him if any of the others had been there that night ? Ern lost himself in dreadful thoughts of what might happen to him if Mr. Holland tried to worm a lot of things out of him, thinking Ern was hiding something from him. He felt anything but a hero then.

The boys crept down the spiral stairway. Work was in full swing again in the workshop. Mr. Holland stood with his hands in his pockets talking to another man. Nobody could see the boys because they were in such a dark corner.

For two hours the tired boys watched. Then Pip fell suddenly asleep on the stairway, his head rolling on Fatty's shoulder.

In that minute the boys slipped out of the lorry

'We'll take turns at watching,' said Fatty. 'You sleep too, Larry. I'll wake you if any one comes this way.'

So two of them slept and Fatty kept watch. At half-past three he awoke Larry, who kept watch while he slept. Still the work in the great place below them went on at full speed. Half-past five came and Pip was awakened and told to keep watch. He was fresh after his four hour's sleep and looked with interest at everything going on. Nobody came near their corner.

It seemed as if there would be no chance at all of getting out. When Fatty awoke suddenly at seven o'clock, he felt worried. Time was getting on. They couldn't stay here much longer.

A big lorry was suddenly backed almost into their corner. The boys all retired a little way up the stairway in a hurry. Then an idea came to Fatty.

'That lorry's going out ! It seems quite finished. If we get into the back, we might slip out with the lorry unseen. We've got to get out *some*how !'

The others were quite willing. When the man who had backed the lorry into their corner had got down to speak to Mr. Holland a little way off, the three boys climbed quietly into the back of the lorry. To their relief there was a partition between the driver's cabin and the back of the van, so that nobody could see them from the driver's seat. There were some old papers and sacks in the lorry. The boys covered themselves with these.

The man came back to the lorry. He started up the engine. So did two drivers of other cars. They were ready to go out. They had come in a week or two before — stolen, all of them — now they had been repainted, touched up, altered beyond even the owner's recognition — and were ready to go out and be sold again, with false log-books.

The lorry went slowly up the winding stone passage, up and up and up, following the other cars. They came to the movable floor and ran on to it. A minute's wait and the floor went upwards like a lift !

One by one, at five minute intervals, the cars ran silently out of the garage. In the last one, the lorry, lay the three hidden boys. The lorry-driver flashed his headlights on and off once, and waited for the gates to open at the end of the drive. In that minute the three boys slipped out of the lorry !

They waited in the shadow of the trees till the gates were closed and everything was quiet. Then they went to the wall. 'Have to feel our way round till we come to the ladder,' whispered Fatty. 'Fat lot of good my marking the trees as I did. Come on ! We'll soon find the ladder — and then up we'll go and away home.'

23 INSPECTOR JENKS TAKES OVER

MEANTIME Mr. Goon had been sitting up all night long, expecting and hoping the telephone bell would ring to say that Fatty had found Ern.

But it didn't ring until eight o'clock the next morning, when an anxious Mrs. Hilton telephoned to say that Pip was missing ! He hadn't been at home all night. Bets was in a dreadful state of worry and had told her mother such extraordinary things that nobody could make anything of them.

Then Larry and Daisy's father rang. Larry was missing ! They couldn't get anything out of Daisy at all except that Fatty was in charge and everything was all right.

'Daisy says that Fatty has gone out to solve a mystery, but that Larry and Pip have gone to rescue your nephew. Mr. Goon, do you know anything about this at all ?'

Well, Mr. Goon did. But what he knew was going to be very difficult to explain to angry and alarmed parents. He hummed and hawed, and then, at a banging on his door, hurriedly put down the receiver to answer the door, hoping against hope that it was Fatty with good news.

But it wasn't. It was Mr. Trotteville ! Fatty was missing — hadn't been in his bed all night ! Mr. Trotteville had tried to ring up Mr. Goon repeatedly but his telephone appeared to be engaged every time. Did Mr. Goon know anything about where Fatty had gone ?

What with Ern being gone for two days and now three more boys missing, Mr. Goon began to feel he really couldn't stand any more. He telephoned to the Inspector.

'Sir, I'm sorry to worry you so early in the morning — but there's all kinds of things happening here, sir, and I was wondering if you could come over,' said the agitated voice of Mr. Goon.

'What sort of things, Goon ?' asked the Inspector. 'Chimneys on fire or lost dogs or something ? Can't you manage them yourself ?'

'No, sir. Yes, sir. I mean, sir, it's nothing like that at all, sir,' said Mr. Goon, desperately. 'My nephew's disappeared, sir — and Master Trotteville went to find him — and now he's gone too, sir, and so have Master Larry and Master Pip. I don't know if it's the robbers or the kidnappers have taken them, sir.'

The Inspector listened to this astounding information in surprise. 'I'll be right over, Goon,' he said, and hung up the receiver. He ordered his shining black car, got in and drove over to Peterswood, wondering what Master Frederick Trotteville was up to now. Inspector Jenks had a feeling that if the could put his finger on Master Trotteville he would soon get to the bottom of everything.

He drove to Mr. Goon's house and found him in a state of collapse. 'Oh, sir, I'm so glad you've come,' stuttered Mr. Goon, leading the Inspector by mistake into the kitchen and then out again into the parlour.

'Pull yourself together, Goon,' said the Inspector, severely. 'What's happened, man ?'

'Well, it all began when my young nephew, Ern, came to stay with me,' began Mr. Goon. 'I warned the others, sir, not to lead him into no mysteries — you know what that young limb of a Frederick Trotteville is, sir, for getting into trouble — and the first thing I know is that there's a mystery up on Christmas Hill, sir — two gangs there — one robbers and one kidnappers.'

'Most extraordinary, Goon,' said the Inspector. 'Go on.'

'Well, sir, I went up to inspect one night — and sure enough there were lights flashing by the hundreds all round me — red, blue and green, sir — a most amazing sight.'

'Quite a firework show !' said the Inspector.

'Then sir, there were awful noises — like cows bellowing, sir, and hens clucking, and cats mewing and — and well, the most peculiar noises you ever heard, sir.'

The Inspector eyed Mr. Goon sharply. He had a sort of feeling that if cows suddenly mooed on deserted hills, and hens clucked and cats mewed, there might possibly be some boy there having a fine old game with Mr. Goon. And that boy's name would be Fatty.

'Then, sir,' said Mr. Goon, warming up, 'a great hefty giant of a man flung himself on me, sir — got me right down on my face, he did. He hit me and almost knocked me out. I had to fight for my life, sir. But I fought him off, and gave him a fearful trouncing. He'll bear the marks to his dying day.'

'And you caught him handcuffed him and brought him back with you,' suggested the Inspector.

'No, sir. He got away,' said Mr. Goon, sadly. 'Well, then, sir, I heard as how a robbery had been committed and the loot, sir, was to be hidden in the old mill.'

'And how did you hear that ?' asked the Inspector with interest. 'And why not inform me ?'

'I heard it from my young nephew, sir,' said Mr. Goon. 'He got it from Master Frederick.'

'I see,' said the Inspector. Beginning to understand quite a lot of things. That scamp of a Fatty ! He had led poor Mr. Goon properly astray this time. Inspector Jenks regretfully decided that he would have to give Fatty a good ticking-off.

'Then, sir, my nephew disappeared. He just went out and

never came back. Two days ago that was.'

The Inspector asked the question that Mr. Goon had been dreading.

'Was the boy in any trouble ?'

'Well — a bit,' admitted Mr. Goon. 'He — er — he wrote an extremely rude pome about me, sir — and I corrected him.'

'In what way ?' asked the Inspector.

'I just gave him one or two strokes with a cane, sir,' said Mr. Goon. 'But I'm sure that's not what made him run away, sir — if he's run away. He's very fond of me, sir, and he's my favourite nephew.'

'H'm,' sid the Inspector, doubting all this very much. 'What next ?'

'Well, sir, Master Frederick told me he thought he knew where Ern was and if I'd wait till night, he'd probably bring him back again. So I waited up all last night, sir, but Master Frederick didn't come back — and now all the parents of those kids have rung up or come to see me to complain that their boys are missing !'

'This sounds rather serious to me,' said the Inspector. 'Are you sure you've told me everything, Goon ?'

'Well — everything that's any use,' said Mr. Goon, hastily. 'I went up after the loot, sir, but I couldn't find it.'

'I wonder where in the world those four boys are !' said Inspector Jenks. 'I can't quite see where to begin looking for them. Or what to do. Where *can* they be ?'

At that very moment three of the boys were staggering home ! They had found their rope-ladder, climbed up over the wall, and dropped down the other side. They had lost their way, and wandered about for some time before they got back to the cart-track they knew. They were so tired that they hardly knew what they were doing.

By now it was getting light. Thankfully Fatty, Larry and Pip stumbled along the banks of the little stream. What miles it seemed ! At last they came to the bridge and made their way into the village.

'Better go to Goon first and tell him Ern's all right,' said Fatty. 'I'll telephone the Inspector from there. Gosh, I'm tired !'

To the Inspector's astonishment, as he stood looking out of the window, he suddenly saw Fatty, Larry and Pip walking like very tired old men up the street.

'Look, Goon !' he said. 'Here are three of them. But no Ern !'

Mr. Goon groaned dismally. The three boys walked up his front path and knocked at the door. Fatty gaped with surprise and pleasure when the Inspector opened the door to him. 'Oh sir ! This is lovely ! You're just the person I wanted to see,' he said, and shook hands warmly.

'You're not fit to stand, any of you,' said the Inspector, looking at the dirty, tired-out boys. 'Goon, put on some milk for cocoa for these three. They could do with something. Then ring up their parents and tell them they are safe. Get on with it, now !'

Goon hurried to do as he was told. No Ern ! Oh, what had happened to him ? He felt that if only Ern would come back he would never never again say a cross word to him. Never !

Fatty and the others sank into chairs. Pip's eyes began to close.

'I'll take you all back in my car,' said the Inspector. 'You can tell me your story later. I already know about this, er — rather incredible mystery on Christmas Hill, Frederick — with flashing lights, mysterious noises, and the rest.'

'Oh that !' said Fatty. 'That's nothing, sir. That wasn't a

mystery at all.'

'So I gathered,' said the Inspector. 'Ah, here is the cocoa. Thanks, Goon. Now ring up those boys' people, will you ?'

'Sir, may I ask just one question first ?' pleaded Mr. Goon. 'It's about Ern. Is he all right ?'

'Oh, Ern. Yes, he's quite all right as far as I know,' said Fatty, taking a deep drink of the cocoa. 'Gosh, I've burnt my mouth.'

'Drink up the cocoa, and then get into my car,' said Inspector Jenks, alarmed at the pale, worn-out faces of the three boys. Pip was fast asleep.

'Good gracious, sir ! I've got a story that will keep you busy for the rest of the day !' said Fatty, feeling better for the cocoa. He took another drink.

'Don't let Mr. Goon telephone to our people, sir,' he said, 'You'll want the phone yourself in another couple of minutes ! I've got a first-class mystery for you, sir ! All ready to hand you on a plate !'

MR. GOON came into the room, his eyes bulging. 'What do you mean ? A first-class mystery! Haven't you just said that mystery up on Christmas Hill wasn't one at all ? And what about those lights then, and those noises, and that giant of a fellow that nearly killed me ? What about *them* ?'

'Oh those !' said Fatty. 'Larry and Pip flashed the lights. I made the noises. And I pounced on you in the ditch, thinking you were Ern.'

Mr. Goon collapsed like a pricked balloon. 'Frederick must have been very strong if he seemed like giant to you,' said the Inspector to Mr. Goon with a laugh.

'And the gangs, of course, were all our make-up, just to play a trick on Ern,' said Fatty. 'It wasn't our fault if Mr Goon believed everything too. We didn't think he'd be as silly as Ern.'

Mr. Goon went red to the ears, but he said nothing. 'We threw down a lot of clues for Ern,' said Fatty, 'and made a story up about some loot that was hidden in the old mill. We meant Ern to go and look, but instead of that poor Ern got a caning, and was locked up in his bedroom — and Mr. Goon went to find the loot instead. But it wasn't there, of course.'

Mr. Goon wanted to sink down through the floor, but he couldn't. He sat there looking very unhappy indeed. That pestering boy !

'Well, Inspector, what began the *real* mystery was this,' said Fatty, taking another drink. 'Ern went off to Christmas Hill, as he thought — but he lost his way, and saw one or two queer things over at Bourne Wood. And that set us thinking.'

'Go on,' said the Inspector. 'So you did a bit of detecting ?'

'Yes, sir,' said Fatty, modestly. 'We soon knew there was something fishy going on at Harry's Folly, sir — the building in the middle of Bourne Wood. We went to see the caretaker — the man at the lodge called Peters — and we made a few inquiries about a man called Holland, who seemed a pretty queer customer ...'

'*Holland*?' said the Inspector, sitting up straight. 'What do you know about him ?'

'Quite a lot, now,' said Fatty, with a grin. 'Why, do you know him too, sir ?'

'We've been suspicious of him for a long time,' said the Inspector. 'But there was never anything we could put our finger on. Lived quietly with an old aunt in Peterswood, gave to the churches around — all that kind of thing — and yet his name cropped up here and there in queer circumstances. Well — go on ...'

'I disguised myself as Ern one day and went over to Holland's garage to make inquiries — and he must have recognized my name, sir — as being — er — well, a bit of a detective, sir — and so, when he saw *Ern* wandering around alone in a lonely lane, he kidnapped him — thinking he was me, sir.'

'I see,' said the Inspector. Mr. Goon sat and looked as if he really couldn't believe his ears !

'Ern was clever, sir,' said Fatty. 'He threw a whole lot of clues out of the car — pretended he was feeling sick, or something, I should think — and Mr. Goon here picked them up and gave them to me.'

Mr. Goon gulped. The Inspector looked at him. 'Very kind

of Goon. I suppose he knew you would make good use of them.'

'Yes, sir. Actually he thought we'd put the clues there ourselves to fool him. As if we'd do a thing like that, sir !'

'Well, I wouldn't put it past you,' said the Inspector. 'But go on. We're wasting time.'

'I did a bit of deduction, sir, and thought Ern must have been kidnapped and was probably taken to Harry's Folly. So I and Larry and Pip set off to rescue him last night. We got in, sir, rope-ladder and all that — and found the house deserted. But in the garage, sir — my word !'

Goon and the Inspector were listening hard now. Pip was still fast asleep in his chair.

'There was a movable floor there, sir, that sank right down. It takes cars. They go down on it like a lift and then run slowly down a winding passage deep underground. And there's a workshop there, sir — with heaps of cars being repainted and done over ...'

The Inspector whistled. 'My word ! So *that's* where it is ! We've been looking for that workshop for a long long time, Frederick. You remember, Goon, I reported it to you two years ago and asked you to keep a lookout in your district, as we had information it was somewhere here. And there it was, all the time, right under your nose ! Well done, Frederick, my boy !'

'We found Ern, sir, and he said he'd stay in his locked room all night long, so that his escape wouldn't raise the alarm. It would give us a chance to get back here and warn you, sir, so that perhaps you could catch the whole gang at work.'

'Very brave of the boy,' said the Inspector, approvingly. 'Good work ! I hope you agree with me, Goon ?'

'Yes, sir,' mumbled Goon, marvelling at the idea of Ern

appearing suddenly as a hero.

'So we left him there, and had a hard job getting out unseen,' said Fatty. 'Went out in one of their own lorries in the end ! And here we are !'

'A very fine job of work, Frederick,' said the Inspector, getting up. 'And now, as you so wisely said, I shall have to have the use of the phone for a few minutes.'

Inspector Jenks went to the telephone and dialled rapidly. Larry and Fatty listened raptly. Pip still slept peacefully on. Mr. Goon looked gloomily at his hands. Always that boy came out on top. And Ern a hero, too ! It wasn't possible that any one could have such bad luck as Mr. Goon !

Inspector Jenks spoke rapidly and to the point. Fatty listened in glee. Six police cars ! Whew, what a round-up ! He dug Larry in the ribs and they both grinned at one another.

The Inspector stopped telephoning. 'Now I'm going to take you all home,' he said. 'It will be a few minutes before the police cars come along. Wake Pip up, and we'll get cracking.'

'Look here, Inspector, I'm going with you to Harry's Folly, aren't' I ?' said Fatty, in alarm. 'You wouldn't be so mean as to leave me out of the end of it, would you ? After all, I've done all the dirty work so far, and so have Larry and Pip.'

'All right. You can come with me if you want to — in *my* car,' said the Inspector. 'But I may as well tell you that you won't be in the thick of it — only a sight-seer ! Now do wake that boy up and bring him along.'

Larry and Fatty half-carried the sleepy Pip to the Inspector's car. Then, with a roar, the engine started up and the powerful car sprang forward. Pip was deposited at his house with a few words of explanation. He sat down in a chair and again went off to sleep, in spite of Bets' frantic questions.

Then to Larry's home, where poor Larry was ordered to stay behind. Then to Fatty's own home, where a half-mad Buster hurled himself at Fatty as if he had been away for a year.

'Frederick is safe,' said the Inspector to Fatty's surprised parents. 'Bit of a marvel, as usual. Do you mind if I borrow him for a time ? All news when I see you again.'

And Fatty was whipped away again in the car, with a very happy Buster on his knee, licking the underneath of his master's chin till it dripped.

Six other police cars joined them, and went slowly along the narrow cart-track to Harry's Folly. Peters, the gate-keeper was terrified when he saw the posse of blue-coated figures at the gate. He opened without a word, and was captured immediately, pale and trembling, looking quite different from the surly, bad-tempered fellow the five children had encountered some days before.

Fatty remained behind with the Inspector in his car, shaking with excitement. What was happening ?

Plenty was happening. The raid was a complete and utter surprise. Every man down below in the workshop was rounded up — and Mr. Holland was discovered asleep in one of the bedrooms near Ern's !

Ern was not asleep. He was waiting and waiting. He didn't feel he could be a hero much longer. He was so terribly hungry, for one thing !

He was so glad to see Fatty, when he was led to the car by one of the policemen that he could hardly keep from hugging him.

'So this is Ern,' said the Inspector, and to the boy's enormous delight and surprise, he shook hands with him very warmly. 'Quite a hero, I hear — and a bit of a poet too. I must read that poem you wrote about your uncle, Ern. I'm sure it's very very good.'

Ern blushed. 'Oh, sir. Thank you, sir ! I couldn't show it to you, sir. My uncle wouldn't like me to.'

The Inspector's car moved off, with the others following in a close line. 'A very good haul, Frederick,' said Inspector Jenks. 'A neat little mystery, and a neat ending. Thanks very much, my boy. Make haste and grow up ! I want a right-hand man, you know !'

Fatty went red with pleasure, 'Right, sir, I'll do my best to grow up as soon as I can !'

They arrived at Mr. Goon's. Ern got out. He looked miserable all of a sudden.

'Come on in, Ern,' said the Inspector, pulling him indoors. 'Goon ! Here's Ern back again. Quite a hero ! And I hear he's written a very fine poem about you. Shall we hear it ?'

'Well ...' said Goon, going scarlet, 'it's, it's not very *polite*, sir ...'

'It's all right, Uncle, I won't read it,' said Ern, taking pity on his uncle. 'I'll tear it up, see ?'

'You're a good boy, Ern,' said Mr. Goon. 'I'm right-down glad to see you back. I've got some bacon and eggs ready to cook for you. Like that ?'

'Lovaduck !' sid Ern, his face beaming. 'I could eat a horse. I'm that hungry.'

'Good-bye, Ern,' said Fatty. 'See you later.'

He drove off with the Inspector, who was taking him home to report on the exciting happenings. 'That poem of Ern's,' said the Inspector, neatly turning in at Fatty's drive. 'I'm sorry I didn't have the pleasure of reading it, after all.'

'Yes, said Fatty, yawning. 'Spitty.'

'What ?' said the Inspector, in surprise.

'Spitty,' said Fatty. 'SwatIsaid.' He slumped down against the Inspector's arm, and his eyes closed. He was fast asleep !

The Inspector left him there asleep, and went in to have a talk with Fatty's parents. What he said about Fatty should have made both his ears burn ! But they didn't, because Fatty was lost in dreams that came crowding into his mind, thick and fast.

Flashing lights — movable floors — Christmas Hill — dark dire deeds — clues in plenty — spiral stairways — a dark dark house — and there was Ern, crowned with laurel leaves, a hero ! He was just going to recite a marvellous poem.

'Lovaduck !' said Fatty, and woke up.